The

N V Peacock (Nicky) lives in Northamptonshire. She has a degree in creative writing, loves True Crime, and has a darkly devious mind. In her spare time she runs a local writers' group.

Also by N V Peacock

The Brother
The 13th Girl

THE
13TH
GIRL

N V PEACOCK

hera

First published in the United Kingdom in 2024 by

Hera Books
Unit 9 (Canelo), 5th Floor
Cargo Works, 1-2 Hatfields
London SE1 9PG
United Kingdom

A CIP catalogue record for this book is available from the British Library.

Print ISBN 978 1 80436 642 4
Ebook ISBN 978 1 80436 639 4

This book is a work of fiction. Names, characters, businesses, organizations, places and events are either the product of the author's imagination or are used fictitiously. Any resemblance to actual persons, living or dead, events or locales is entirely coincidental.

Look for more great books at www.herabooks.com

Printed and bound in Great Britain by Clays Ltd, Elcograf S.p.A.

I

For those who do not feel 'normal' in this world — you are not alone, and are in good company.

Prologue

'Beautiful,' he whispers.

Her hair, soft and shiny, slips through his fingers like strands of silk.

'May I?' he asks.

Entwining their fingers, he lifts her hand to his lips and places the gentlest of kisses over her skin.

'I've waited so long. I can't believe we're finally here, together like this.' As the words fall from his mouth, he realises there is no going back. Everything he has thought about, everything he has ever wanted, is here right now for the taking. All he needs is the courage to reach out and grab it with both hands. Her. This. Now.

Cradling her head against his chest, he lifts her further into his arms. Romance isn't dead, he thinks, as he subtly manoeuvres her onto the park bench where they first met. He knows she won't appreciate this gesture. In truth, her attention is usually taken with something else. Most of their time together she has spent scrolling on her phone or taking selfies for social media, but that doesn't matter now. Today, her attention is fully on him, and for that, he will gift her the ultimate selfie – one that will be shared and liked for years to come, cementing them as a couple for the ages.

Until this day, he never thought of himself as romantic. Their relationship, although short, has transformed him from a bumbling wannabe to a dashing gentleman – the kind usually found bound in thick romance novels, and ninety-minute clichéd romcoms.

The breeze catches in her hair, making him smile. Suddenly, the thought of leaving her side, even for a minute, starts to trail tiny cracks across his heart. He has to get this right, for both of them.

'I'll make you a star,' he tells her. A promise he knows he'll keep; they are already well on the road to becoming something spectacular; the envy of the internet.

So relaxed with him, her body settles against his shoulder. Instinctively, his arm encircles her, drawing them closer. Leaning down, he kisses the top of her head, then lingers to take in her scent: citrus, with a hit of something spicy.

It is early morning, but people will be invading their private moment soon. Softy tilting her face to stare into the depths of her eyes, he watches her mouth open, just a little, with expectation.

'It's now or never,' he says.

Positioning her just right, he drops to one knee and looks up. From out of his pocket, he pulls out something shiny. Mouth dry, he asks, 'Would you do me the honour?'

Voices in the distance. Rising, he looks around. They are still alone. There's time to make this moment truly amazing – special.

'My darling, would you do me the honour of being... my first official victim?' With force, he plunges the knife in his hand through her stomach, angling it down so as to pin the corpse against the wood, allowing it to sit up unaided.

Stepping back, he says, 'Ah now, don't you look pretty?'

There's less blood than he expected, although he had already spilled quite a bit of it in the last three days. With a few minor adjustments to her pose, she appears suspended on the bench, waiting. Mistakenly alive, if it weren't for the pallor of the skin, and the two hollowed eye sockets.

'Farewell, my love,' he tells her, then strolls off into the park ready to embark on his next relationship.

When screams ring out behind him, he doesn't look back.

Chapter One

'She's so creepy.'

'Like an extra from a horror film,' Stephanie adds.

Corinne nudges her friend. 'You know, she's fresh out the nut house.'

Stephanie gasps. 'Like you said, creepy.'

I can't deny it. Like dogs and dolphins can smell cancer, people can smell creepiness on me. Every time I meet a new person, their eyes widen and nose wrinkles; I have the distinct whiff of weirdness. This doesn't make my life easy. Humans are social animals; we're programmed to instinctively seek out the acceptance of others. It's in psychologist Maslow's *Hierarchy of Human Needs*. Dr Taylor gave me it as a checklist in one of our pre-release sessions. *Tick off the ones you think you have*, she told me. I stared at it just long enough to realise I couldn't tick many boxes without lying, so put down the pen. To help with this, maintaining a job became part of my release back into the normal world; so I could be part of a team. Thanks to this condition, I now sit at the end of a long office, by a bird-poop-stained window, enduring overtly loud insults from co-workers, while trying my hardest to belong.

The people I work with may not talk to me, but I listen to them. I know their secrets. The one who steals, the ones having affairs, the bully, the eternal victim, the amateur Machiavellian, and the backstabber – it's like clichéd reality TV. Fascinating but flawed relationships played out daily to obvious conclusions. And Corinne and Stephanie are always centre stage for every drama.

'Cake?'

I look up to see Stephanie being offered the last slice of Corinne's birthday cake. It's common that I'm not offered a slice of, well, anything; I'm conveniently invisible when it comes to office treats. Not that I would accept her cake. It's homemade and I once saw Corinne go to the toilet and not wash her hands. Right now, I view this not so much as a social slight but a lucky escape from salmonella.

Corinne hands over the red velvet slice to Stephanie, then walks back to her desk. I don't even warrant a polite excuse. No matter, I'll go to the bakery at lunchtime and buy a hygiene-adherent cake; one that's uniform deliciousness is a legal requirement.

It takes less than forty minutes to finish my work. Looking at the clock, I still have an hour left to kill before lunch. To spend that time, I write a to-do list littered with small tasks like making tea, Googling TV programs, staring out the window, and of course, listening to my co-workers' gossip.

Engrossed in an article about a new true crime documentary, it takes me longer than it should to hear the girls behind me giggling. Our boss, Mr Lake, a rail-thin, sixty-year-old man with dyed black hair, is working the room. This happens at least once a week. Today, I accidently make eye contact, so he stops at my desk. Quickly, I minimise my screen.

'How're the invoices coming...' His lips silently contort in every letter of the alphabet trying to remember my name. I've been here a month now, so let him grasp a little longer before saying, 'Dinah.'

'Oh, yes. I knew it began with a D,' he laughs. 'Unusual name.'

'It's from Genesis.'

'Ah, Phil Collins' band. Am I right?'

Before I can correct him with the Bible, Mr Lake publicly murders 'Easy Lover' to a jerky display of dad dancing; a song that isn't even by Genesis. After the performance, he stares at me, as if awaiting applause. Lies aren't my thing, so I say, 'Everyone just calls me Dee.'

Mr Lake snorts, then swaggers off to flirt with Corinne. By the time I realise I should have told him I need more work, they're both laughing and sliding sly glances my way. Ignoring them, I bend down and release three A4 notebooks from my backpack. They're bulky and hard to manoeuvre, but I eventually yank them free. One book is for my sketches. Dr Taylor encouraged me to draw people; she thought that in studying those around me, I could learn to be more like them. Not sure it's working, but I do find it relaxing. The second book is for collecting ideas for filming my own documentary. When inspiration comes, it rattles about in my head until I exorcise it onto the page. My idea then sits in between the covers, rotting, until I replace it with another. Then the whole process starts over again. A few years ago, my friend Father Jacob bought me an online documentary-making course. Loving every minute of it, I learnt the steps needed to produce a world-class piece of television. Making a documentary that wins the coveted Docu-Wow Award is my dream. I'm not sure why it's so hard to get going on this goal. Perhaps I'm so focused on perfection that nothing I come up with is ever good enough. I make a note to talk this over with Dr Taylor in our next check-in session. You can't finish something you never start.

The last book is my journal. This is where I make notes of the things I see and things I don't see; the cakes that pass me by. I scribble a few words on the lack of religious understanding in today's society, and then swap to my documentaries notebook. I write, *is ignorance the new religion?* I'll never do anything with it. I should tear it out and throw it in the bin where it belongs. I don't. Ripping out pages would make my notebook ugly, and I have enough ugliness in my life.

Lunch time.

It's a twenty-minute walk to the bakery in boiling August heat. It feels as if it's been sunny forever. For the last few weeks, I've all but lived in sunglasses, ironically making the world around me appear darker.

Slightly out of breath, and with onset sunburn, I arrive at the tiny shop and join the back of the queue. Some-where in the middle is Stephanie; clearly the red velvet cake was not enough for her sweet tooth.

'Carrot cake please, doll,' she says to the man behind the counter.

Stephanie calls people things such as 'doll' and 'my lovely'. It sounds sincere when she says it, as if you've earned a badge of honour. I wish I could give out such rewards. Maybe people would like me more if I made them feel something other than weird. But I doubt I can convincingly add 'doll' to the end of my sentences without it coming out as disturbing. With my fiery ginger curls, dark brown eyes, and porcelain skin, dressed head to toe in black, Mum has hinted, not so subtly, that I look like one of those Victorian ragdolls. Although in my thirties, I barely look twenty. Being locked away does wonders for a wrinkle-free complexion.

Once served, Stephanie walks right by me and has the cheek to make eye contact. She then pushes past, as if we were strangers. I understand her reaction. It's not a good idea to be seen talking with the office weirdo.

Finally, when I reach the front of the queue, I find only a dodgy-looking egg salad sandwich left. No cakes. Stephanie, once again, got the last slice. A familiar frustration builds in me, so I close my eyes and count backwards from six, a technique used to activate a different part of my brain – a sort of short circuit, as counting backwards makes me think with my analytical hemisphere.

The man behind the counter huffs at my technique, but I don't rush. Instead, I smile sweetly and politely ask for the sandwich, which I then carefully place in the bin outside before starting the long walk back to work.

By the freshly poop-stained window, I spend the next torturous hours descending into boredom so deep it's painful.

One hour before freedom, I Google *her.*

I do this at least once a day, and I'm proud I've lasted this long before typing in her name. Louisa Black. It's a common name, so I usually have to add in the title of the documentary too, but since it's had so much recent exposure on streaming sites, today her name alone is enough. This realisation cuts me deep, as I search for bad reviews. There's a few out there, like rotten apples in an overgrown orchard. I find a new one on a particularly scathing blog. 'Crappy storytelling and sketchy subject matter' is its title. I can agree with half of that. Louisa is a lacklustre storyteller. However, as the subject matter was me, I take umbrage with the sketchy comment. As with all these articles, there's an embedded YouTube video, a two-minute snatch of the sixty-six-minute program. I don't click on it. Don't need to. I know exactly the part they've highlighted. Even after all these years, I still feel the red-tinted burn around my wrists from where I was held down. Heat from the stage lights scorching my skin. The echoes of screams still sit in my ears. My screams. By heart, I know the words they chanted over and over again. Images of crucifixes dance across my mind's eye, and the touch of a rosary being pulled over my palms itches at my skin – a stagey pseudo exorcism all under the guise of ridding me of a demon Louisa Black convinced my parents my young teen body was possessed by, and that had to be dramatically expelled for the watching cameras.

Most people try to forget the bad things that happen to them, but I make a sharp point of remembering that day, along with the other one that started it all – the accident. Although many aspects of Louisa and her story are fake, the trauma caught on screen was not.

'Tea, anyone?'

Corinne is scanning the office for cups in the air. Stephanie shoves up a twee unicorn mug. It has 'You're Special' in a fanciful font on the front. It strikes me that if you have to be told you're special on a daily basis you're probably not very special at all. Smiling, Corinne accepts Stephanie's mug. She doesn't look my way, so I oblige her by dropping my gaze and getting back to the blog post. *The whole thing is fake*, I read. It's an awful thing to say, but they don't know the full story. How could they?

At the bottom, I write an articulate and heartfelt comment that details the agonies of how I was a victim in a horrendous accident, something that mentally and physically changed me from the girl I used to be. A change so darkly pronounced that those closest to me felt the only answer was that a demon had crawled up from hell and was now living within me, controlling my violent reactions and keeping me from being the girl they knew.

I write that I'm better now. Spending all those years in St Alda's Mental Healthcare Facility helped me understand who I am, and that I'm now trying to claw back some semblance of a normal life. However, when I re-read my comment, even I think it's whiney – delete.

–

As I leave work, I hear the siren call of an ice cream van. It's coming from the direction of the park. I have about twenty minutes before the bus, so follow the plinky plinky tune like a rat stalking the Pied Piper.

Good Tree Park is a generous name to describe the slight area of green in the middle of town. It's not even big enough to obscure the urban vistas in every direction. There's not a chance in hell you'd ever forget where you were. Not a tree tall enough, not a bush dense enough, and certainly not a painted slide fun enough. It's after 5 p.m. and still the sun burns above me. Families are here, kids swarming about the park playing Frisbee and hogging the battered swing set. A wooden Wendy house sits nearby, and a group of kids are smoking in it.

The pink ice cream van has pulled up at the other end of the park, so I hike my backpack further up my shoulder and trudge across the grass to reach it before the children swarm. As I do, I notice a dad telling off his little girl. There's a strange look of fear on her face. I inch closer. Dad and daughter look nothing alike, different complex-ions, hair colour, and features. Stepdad? Tears glaze the girl's eyes and her face is contorted in an expression I know well – panic.

Chapter Two

'Everything okay?' I ask.

The man jerks upright; he's not tall, but is still taller than my five-foot-nothing frame.

'Mind your business,' he spits.

The panic on the girl's face has now morphed into terror.

'Is that your dad?' I ask her.

Suddenly, he grabs the girl's arm. As she wriggles to free herself, his grip tightens; fingers coiling her sapling arm like snakes.

Through tears, she whispers, 'Bad man.'

'Let her go,' I tell him.

He laughs at me, pulling the girl to and fro as he does. 'What are you going to do about it?'

Red flashes before my eyes. Under my breath, I start to count backwards from six.

'What the fuck are you doing?' he demands, then tries to poke me with his free hand.

Before reaching four, I swing my backpack towards him. Three hardback exercise books filled with my thoughts wallop him in the gut, knocking him backwards with the follow-through.

Holding out my hand to the girl, I watch as she quickly weighs me up, then cringes away.

'Where are your parents?' I ask.

She shakes her head. Bubbles of snot erupt then from the girl's puffy face.

'What are you doing?' I hear a shout from behind me. A woman with two ice creams is bowling across the grass. Suddenly, she drops her cold treats and the girl runs into her arms.

I look back to where the bad man landed, but he's gone.

'I'm calling the police,' the mum says.

Realising she's calling them on me, I launch my backpack over my shoulder and run from the park. Out of breath, I reach the bus stop and hide behind a group of people waiting for the Number 3.

During my torturous wait, I keep careful watch for the police; after all, I did just assault a man. Yes, he was attempting to commit a crime, but I don't think anyone but the little girl saw that part of our encounter. Am I duty-bound to report the incident? He could try to take another child. Unfortunately, as a newly released mental health patient the odds of the police believing me are slim. And the odds of being blamed for something I didn't do are high. I should keep my mouth shut.

Even though my bus is terribly late, I still have to pay the fare. I tap my phone app to pay with as much contempt as I can muster, then sit near the front.

Although I don't need to guard the neighbouring seat, I still place my backpack beside me. *I'm* the weirdo on the bus; no one in their right mind will sit next to me. Proving my point, two teenage girls race on and although I look up to offer them the spot next to me, they decide to stand, hanging off the rails like hairless monkeys smelling of perspiration and Impulse body spray.

'My dad can drive you home. It's too dangerous for you to walk alone with that nutter out there,' says one to the other.

Are they talking about me?

'Did you hear another girl is missing? Lisa something,' the other replies.

'Is that like the sixth girl?'

'Ninth.'

I lean towards them. One spots me, so I'm forced to ask, 'There are nine missing girls?'

The teen nearest snorts. 'Where have you been? Eight dead girls, one missing. All from around here. He murders them three days after he takes them.' She emphasises the word murder – as if it needed more drama.

How did this news pass me by? I know I've only been out a month, but I still go online.

'Since when?' I ask.

'Last couple of months. He calls himself the Righteous Wraith. Sends creepy letters to the press and everything.' She leans in to move my backpack to sit down. Fortunately, I manage to pull it away before she touches it. After shuffling her shopping bags to the floor, the girl slides into the seat next to me. 'You got someone to walk you home?'

'I'm good thanks,' I say, and begin sifting my memory for the last time someone said something nice to me. Am I bonding with new potential friends?

'You should be careful,' she adds.

'Are you trying to scare me?' I ask.

'Everyone *should* be scared. God only knows what he does with them for three days.'

The bus slows and the girl rises to stand by the door.

'Stay safe,' she calls out to me as they both step off the bus. Reaching down, I grab my backpack and shift it to its rightful place beside me. There's a killer on the loose. Interesting.

When I see my street, rather than pressing the bell, I rush up to loom by the door. Seeing me, the driver slows and I get off.

The house's front door is white plastic with painted pink daisies, making it appear unnatural and childish. I knock three times, trying not to squash the two-dimensional flowers beneath my sweaty fist. Although I live here with my parents, this is not my home. It smells strange, like washing powder and unknown vegetables. And it doesn't help that Mum and Dad don't trust me with a key.

Mum opens the door. 'Dee, you're late.'

Not a question, but her tone is questioning. Unsure as to how to answer, I wrack my brain for an appropriate response. It's hard. I don't really know Mum and Dad. After the documentary came out, I made it clear I didn't want to talk about my past with them; unfortunately, without the past to share, it was difficult to connect in the present, so their visits to St Alda's came less and less, in favour of postcards and letters. I never kept their correspondence; some I didn't even read. When I moved back in with them, they saw their letters weren't amongst my things. Hurt and guilt skipped across their expressions. We didn't talk about that either.

Mum gives me a tight-lipped smile, then slowly makes her way down the hall. I can tell she wants to probe as to why I'm late, but is holding in the questions. Before long, her curiosity will become a feverish gas burning through her mind; soon it will blast out. Hoping to circumvent her explosion, I say, 'Buses were bad.'

'Oh, dear. I do wish you'd let me pick you up.' She moves towards me, so I take a step back.

'I prefer the bus.'

Frowning, Mum walks into the living room, and, like a puppy, I follow.

'Was just going through some of the old photo albums,' she says, handing me an open fake-leather volume. All the pictures are of pre-accident Dee. A girl I don't remember being. These images might as well have come with the book.

'There you are in that Little Red Riding Hood outfit for the school play. Had a hell of time wrestling you out of it to wash it. You remember, right?'

Nope. Nor do I remember the Christmas after with the bike, or my birthday party with the magician. My last real memories of my parents were the weeks before the exorcism when they would assure me I'd be 'back to me again' soon. Mum claimed, 'Time heals all wounds.' It's a Bible quote. Time healed nothing; no wonder they turned away from God.

I want to ask her why she and Dad agreed to the exorcism, and let it be filmed, but I know the answer, so making her say it will only cause pain she doesn't deserve. They were desperate. Not only was I a traumatised girl on the brink of puberty, but my brain was short-circuiting on an almost hourly basis. Something as small as eating all on the peas on my plate could have me throwing crockery. Weird really; I never did much care for peas.

Without another word, she closes the album and walks into the kitchen. Unsure as to what she wants me to do, I follow her. Although large, this room feels tiny. Covered top to bottom with antique kitchen equipment. Plates and pots cram every shelf and surface. Mum collects old things because she likes that they had a life before her. Secretly, I fear the plastic spatula on the draining board has had more of a life than me.

Mum looks at the oven. 'Are you hungry?'

'Do you have any cake?'

'I think we have some left over cherry Bakewell.' She opens a few cupboards, then produces a box of Mr Kipling. 'Eat your dinner first though.'

Mum retrieves my food from the oven – the meal I'll have to wade through to reach my cherry cake reward. Placing the plate on the table, she says, 'Careful, it's hot,' then fetches my cutlery: a plastic knife and fork. I'm not sure who told Mum I can't be trusted with metal eating implements, but she's clearly stocked up, as I'm given them for every meal. I pick up the fork and prod a steaming potato.

'Eat up,' she says sitting down across from me to watch my efforts.

To make conversation, I mumble, 'Lisa-something is missing.'

Mum's hand springs towards my sunburnt shoulder, and I shift out of her reach like we're in a weird dance. 'Do you know her?'

'I don't even know her last name.'

'Well, I'm sure she'll turn up. Life can be hard at times; some people just need a break.'

'She's not taking a break. Girls on the bus said a man abducted her and will kill her in three days.'

'You misheard them. Things like that don't happen in Northamptonshire. Well, there was that one maniac who took all those young boys to make sculptures, or something equally hideous, but that was years ago.'

'Apparently, the Righteous Wraith is already on girl nine and has sent letters to the press.'

'Oh yes, I heard about him before we broke up for summer. Why ever would they call him that?'

I shrug. 'Religious thing?' The look on Mum's face makes me wince. I've offended her. 'Sorry,' I whisper.

'That's okay.' She nods, but her tone is laced with something I can't quite catch hold of – annoyance, maybe shame if she took my tone as flippant. Dr Taylor says to ask if I find someone confusing, but when I open my mouth, Mum beats me to it with, 'And you shouldn't be thinking about gruesome stuff like that. You're doing so well, let's not take a step back.'

'If I want to be a documentarian I need to be open to all sorts of topics. True crime is big right now.'

Her eyes narrow at me. 'Can't you just be happy as you are?'

I should lie, but those words don't come out. 'I'm not happy as I am.'

She grunts. 'Well, no bloody wonder; you don't have any friends. And you never will, making conversation about murderers.'

Nodding, I try to eat some peas, but the little green buggers roll off the plastic fork before I get them near my mouth. Mum's eyes widen for a second, so I smile at her.

'Good girl,' she coos. 'Oh, I almost forgot with all this blood and guts talk, I bought you a present at the antiques fair.' She hands me a paper-wrapped package. Only a few inches long, it feels light and has an odd human-like shape. Opening the present, I find a small, tarnished, silver baby doll with a stained wooden head.

'Thanks,' I mutter.

'It's a fumsup, an antique good luck charm.'

It does look like it's seen a lot of history. As I turn it over in my hand, a sharp metal edge along its tiny arm slits my finger. Blood wells up and I have to drop the doll on the table to hide my hand.

'Soldiers had them in the First World War. They carried the fumsup with them so they'd always have wood to touch for luck.'

'Dolls are not my thing.'

'But you played with them at St...' Mum's words disappear into something neither of us wants to talk about. I did used to play with dolls, but it was with my friend Cookie. We liked to pretend we were the dolls, being normal people living normal lives.

Quickly, I say, 'It's a lovely present. And I can use all the luck I can get my hands on.' I pick up the fumsup and it cuts me again. 'Damn it,' I whisper. It doesn't look particularly clean; a hundred years of germs could be hiding in its antique nooks and crannies.

Mum turns to put some dishes in the sink. I'm about to steal away upstairs with my dinner, which I can discreetly flush down the loo, when the front door opens.

'Where are my special ladies?' Dad walks into the kitchen. He hugs Mum, then turns to me. 'Good day?'

'Yep.' I quickly add, 'You?'

'Training went well, although only twenty out of the thirty teachers turned up. Some stomach bug thing.'

'I can't stand this teacher training nonsense. Mine's next week. Why can't they just leave us alone to prepare for next term?' Mum says.

'Every day's a school day, love.' Dad grins at his joke. 'Now, I'm starving.'

Smiling, Mum slips by me and, before I can stop her, she rings their antique kitchen dinner bell. 'Dinner's ready,' she sings.

The sharp sound clatters through my brain making my hands shoot to my ears. Memories of two strangers holding me down overpower my mind. Their hands too firm, their voices too harsh, and their fingernails too sharp on my bare skin. Somewhere above me a chanting man shakes a bell so loud my brain cells feel as if they'll burst like tiny balloons. Adrenaline overpowers my limbs and I spring to my feet. Red creeps into the corners of my vision.

'Oh, I'm so sorry, Dee. I didn't think.' Mum tries to put an arm around me and I almost fall over to avoid her touch. 'It was just a joke.'

'Six, five, four, three, two, one,' I whisper.

'We'll just take this down,' Dad says and, securely holding the bell in place, he removes it from the kitchen.

'Sorry,' Mum says again. 'I should have remembered.'

I open my eyes. 'It was a long time ago.' And even though it's the truth, my body hasn't been the same since I was Pavlov-Dogged to feel pain when a bell rings; doubt it ever will be.

Dad retrieves his dinner and we sit down together. Mum's already eaten and so takes the time to better assess me as I consider the oven-shrivelled pork that my plastic knife has no chance of cutting.

'Eat up, Dee. It's getting cold.' Dad motions with his shiny, metal fork.

Mr Kipling's Cherry Bakewells are waiting for me... Pushing around hard potatoes, I skewer a small piece of pork, saw off a lump, and then choke it down. I do this again and again until my plate is almost empty. Gifted with one cake and a pink pill, I'm then told to *relax* in my bedroom.

–

Nearly twenty years on, and my bedroom looks the same; stuffed with board games with pieces missing and soft toys with fur faded fur. Walls sag under the weight of boy-band posters, bands who have long since broken up, got back together, and then broken up for good. None of these things feel as if they belong to me anymore, making the room beyond claustrophobic. I don't relax here, I can't. Instead, I flick on my fan, open the window wide, then log on to my new laptop, a welcome home gift from Mum and Dad, along with a compact video camera to film my debut documentary.

Closing my eyes, I think back to the bad man in the park. What was his plan? Was he going to sell the little girl? Forcibly adopt her? Worse? I search for child abductions in Northamptonshire. A worrying number of results pop up. I promise myself that if I find a similar connected case, I'll call the police. Consequences for me be dammed. An hour later and I've found nothing compelling enough to make me dial three nines, so switch my efforts to the Wraith. I change the search to 'serial killer Northampton-shire'. As I scan the results, I finally bite into my cherry Bakewell. Soft, sweet icing gives way to tangy cherry and the unmistakeable flavour of almond. It's heavenly and I finish it before all the pages load – there are thousands. I flick the search engine onto news and find the latest posts – there he is.

Most of the reports are dripping in conjecture and rumour. The date of the first piece is over two months ago, when I wasn't around to see it. The coverage started when the killer sent a letter to a local paper claiming to have already murdered three women in their twenties. There's a screenshot of the letter, and a note that the police authenticated it. The handwriting is thin and sickly. Letters pressed together, as if in torture, it reads:

> *Hello fans!*
>
> *Three girls are dead. As a memento, I enclose a piece of Fiona's top; forgive the mess, it got a little bloody.*
>
> *With the UK being one of the most monitored countries in the world, I really thought I wouldn't get this far down my murderous rabbit hole. Surely, someone saw me pluck poor Angela off the street or visit silly Erica's home? I'm equally delighted and mystified that the police are no closer to catching me now than when I started. I guess I should stop and retire with a perfect record, a holy trinity of death. Ha, ha, ha, I won't. How could I when I now know what it's like to have such beautiful girls beneath my knives? And anyway, three is not enough, not by a long shot. I'd recommend KTK Kidnap, Torture and Kill, to any of you budding psychopaths out there. Try it at least once in your life; you can blame the whole thing on me. Follow me. Follow me. Follow me if you dare.*
>
> *Yours in blood, The Righteous Wraith XX*

A holy trinity of death? He's really playing into the religious aspect, but that's obvious. Isn't it?

An update at the bottom of the article states there have been another five murders since this letter was received.

There are three more links below to the killer's further correspondences. To be thorough, I know I have to research everything, but I'm guessing they are all of a similar nature, taunting, clichéd, sensationalised horror. And people think *I'm* crazy. This creep is not only killing, but giving free rein to any others like him. Does this mean not all the new kills belong to him? Not all the kills in the future could belong to him either. A deranged murderer. Dead and missing girls – this could make an awesome documentary. I could call it *The Rampant Wraith*. No, that sounds like porn. I'll come up with a better title later. Perhaps this Wraith is looking to become a killing guru, leading the way for amateur murderers like a cult leader or some sick social media influencer. Whichever it is, it's gold. I make some notes in my documentary book, then write a few thoughts in my journal.

Sitting back, I quickly realise how lacklustre the whole idea is. I don't have any police contacts or relationships with victims' families. Hell, I don't even have a single filmed documentary under my belt. None of that stopped Louisa when she made *Possession is Nine Tenths*; she was driven by fame and fortune. I don't want to be like her, but I do need to put my big girl pants on and grab my chance; it might be the only one I get. Every good documentary has an interesting angle, a sizzle factor, something to make the audience twist their perspective. I just need to find it with the Wraith. For inspiration, I research all the Wraith's victims. Too soon, my eyes become black holes, sucking in the gruesome details. Although most were in their twenties and thirties, the victims seem to always be referred to as 'girls' by both the killer and the press. It strikes me as a bit patronising, but what do I know?

The 1st girl was Erica Tomkins. Reported missing after a night out with friends, her corpse was found pinned by a knife to a park bench. The 2nd girl, Angela Lowestoft's body was discovered on a hiking trail in the woods, a map in her hand with a heart drawn in blood over the exact location of her body. Next was the 3rd girl, Fiona Duncan, by the A13 road, under a huge oak tree; there was a flask of sweet tea laid in her bloodied lap. Then the first letter was sent. More deaths followed: the 4th girl, Sandi Morrow, was discovered propped up by the bins next to an abandoned factory in the shade of some apple trees, a basket of which sat in a pool of her blood. After that, the 5th girl, Harmony Lee, was found on a campsite by an extinguished fire dotted with carefully cooked s'mores. The 6th girl, Mina Sharma was spotted floating in the boating lake by a dog walker; her corpse dressed in a white lace bikini that none of her family recognised. Kate Moore was the 7th girl; she was discovered hanging from a lone tree on the outskirts of the new housing estate, Cat Hall. Flowers had been woven into her hair amongst the dried blood and peeling scalp pieces. The 8th girl was Melanie Driver, the youngest so far. At just eighteen years old, she was found outside her college campus on the ground the students used to play cricket, a bat and ball playfully left by her side.

As I keep clicking, I find a grim gallery of the victims. Most photos are selfies stolen from social media; they are all big eyes and heads cocked to find the light. One has a more natural photo, the 1st girl, Erica. In it, a man in a hideous purple Hawaiian top has his arm around her shoulders, and though his shirt is the most offensive thing featured, his face is blurred out.

From when the girls were reported as last seen, it was estimated they were each kept for three days.

As horrible as the Righteous Wraith is, there's not much to set him apart from other murderers I've read about. The only unique angle for my documentary I can find is that Erica has a little sister Megan who, after the murder, became an overnight social media sensation campaigning for safer streets and female empowerment, but I'm not crass enough to take advantage of a young girl.

With a swig of warm, flat lemonade I take my pink pill. It's getting late. I should be sleeping, but I'm not tired. My thoughts wander back to the park. God put me in the right place at the right time. Thinking about saving that little girl makes me warm inside – not the kind of warmth the exhausting heat of summer brings, but a nice, just feeling. For once, my first reaction was a good one – mostly.

The bad man's face is heavy in my mind's eye, so I sketch him while I wait for sleep. That way I can keep him forever locked in my pages where I know where he is. I work on the image of the would-be abductor until his every feature is committed to paper. Then I date the page. I should tell someone. I can see in my drawing he has that look in his eye. This bad man is driven, just like Louisa. I get out my phone and take a photo of my sketch. There are two people I trust in this world: Cookie and Father Jacob. Cookie can't help me from St Alda's. Father Jacob's only limitation is that he's destined to always wear black cassocks and donate his time to the needy. Right now, I'm needy. I text him the sketch and tell him what happened in the park. He'll know what to do.

Comforted that I've now told someone, I sit by my window and gaze out into the world. Admittedly, I never thought I'd get back here. The wrong actions were like building blocks that become impossible for me, and others, to see beyond. Each rash swipe of an arm. Every harsh word. Each cultivated flash of fear on the faces as they watched me lose control over the smallest thing. It all took me further and further from the person they wanted me to be and moved me towards an uncontrollable creature masquerading as Dee. After my accident, whatever switch was flipped, it was enough of a gap for Louisa's ear worms to crawl through my parents' sanity. *A demon has settled into your only daughter, and there is only one way to get it out.* And some days I wondered if Louisa was right. But that's in the past now. I've been legally declared normal. That side of me, although neither forgotten nor fully gone, is placated by pink pills and prayers. Acutely, I'm aware that one lost moment, one slip, one sign I'm no longer toeing the normal line, and back to St Alda's I'll go. Maybe I shouldn't have hit the bad man?

My bedroom looks out over the garden, and my gaze lingers on an impressive oak tree, looming across from my window. Its leaves, dried and yellowed by the sun, crackle like fire in the breeze. Just beyond the fence is the street, so I can hear the murmur of traffic and the hushed voices of neighbours. It's still hot and although dark now, a street lamp brightly burns. Next door's dog, aptly named Lucifer, barks. To see what has upset him, I lean slightly out of the window. Below, I spot Dad's best friend Mr Davidson climbing out of his car. He lives a few doors down in a terraced house and often parks on our drive when the street is busy – something Mum brings up every time she argues with Dad.

Dropping to my knees, I put my hands together and bow my head.

'Dear Lord, I hope you're well. Could you please make the people at work like me? Dr Taylor says I need to keep a steady job, and people tend to keep around those they like. And it's been some while since I had an incident. Please look after Mum and Dad, and my friend Cookie. Amen.'

As I finish my prayer, I hear a strange noise outside my window. Mum and Dad will be in bed by now and Lucifer has stopped barking. Staying still, I listen, but there's nothing. Perhaps I imagined it and need more than one pink pill tonight. Wait, I hear it again, only this time louder, closer. What if the bad man from the park followed me home to take his revenge? With my window wide open, there's only a thin black-out blind between us.

Chapter Three

Scrambling in the dark, my hand finds the strap of my backpack, my only weapon. I heave it sack-like behind me and edge back to the window. Pulling up the blind, I'm momentarily blinded by the streetlight. I stumble backwards, forcing my eyes open.

There's no one out there. Gingerly, I peek outside the window. Looking across at my neighbour's garden, I notice Lucifer staring intently up at the tree. Probably just a cat. Funny how his temper isn't looked upon as some supernatural curse – although he might lose an essential part of his male anatomy if he's not careful.

It's too hot to close my window, so I pull down the blind and fall back into bed. Even in Trayvon Halfway House, the nights were quiet; I'm just not used to being in an estate filled with people. My imagination is twisting mundane noises into something they're not.

Body heat tiptoes up to my temples. If I'm not really better, are there more nefarious ways for doctors to remove part of me? A mind version of a ball removal – just like the exorcism was meant to extract the demon?

With my hand still grasping the handle of my backpack, I lie back against the sticky pillow and wait for sleep.

–

Three hours later, zombie-like, I shower off my night sweat, then pull on my favourite black lace dress.

Before leaving for work, I poke my head into the garden to say bye to Dad. Instead of his usual quick wave, he makes his way over, rake in hand, the prongs littered with fallen leaves.

'Did you hear a noise in the garden last night?' he asks, wiping his brow with the bottom of his t-shirt.

Is he testing me? I shouldn't admit to hearing weird noises, but denial would be a lie. 'I heard some noises last night.'

'There're quite a few branches broken up in the tree.'

'Lucifer was outside.' I then quickly add, 'Next door's dog. He was barking a lot.'

'Well, you know what they say: the heat makes everyone crazy...' He trails off after realising what he's said.

'Like the moon,' I add, hoping he sees I don't care.

Smiling, he leans the rake against the wall and cracks his neck. 'Before I forget, Father Jacob rang last night about a text you sent.'

Dad doesn't need to know about the bad man in the park, so I say, 'I'll check in with him.' I wonder why my priest called the house rather than my mobile.

As I follow Dad inside, he offers to drive me to work. Gracefully, I decline. Like Mum, he knows why I don't ride in cars, yet still he tries. As if he'll know I'm truly cured when I accept a lift in his Peugeot.

I've one foot out the door when Mum yells, 'Where's that bloody remote?' I'm not sure if she's talking to me, but I close my eyes and remember the last place I saw it.

'It's on the second shelf of the bookcase,' I yell back.

There's a kerfuffle, then Mum shouts, 'Thanks, Dee.'

I'm good at finding lost things. Being observant is my special ability. I close my eyes and get a flash of the lost object. Maybe there's a documentary in that too, although it's bad form to talk about yourself.

–

Stephanie is not in work today. I hear Corinne telling Mr Lake she called in sick. She must have a new job and is taking up her available sick days. I don't blame her. If she knew half of what people said behind her back, she'd be throwing her CV around town like sprinkles on a sundae.

After a mind-numbing hour, I've emailed out all of today's invoices, so I start to roll around ideas about the documentary.

'Tea?' Corinne calls.

I look up, but she's already disappeared into the kitchen. Closing my eyes, I imagine the day when I win the Docu-Wow, who I'll thank, and how everyone around me will admit they misjudged me…

'What are you doing?'

Corinne is hovering over me. How long has she been there?

I minimise my screen.

'You shouldn't be reading news at work,' she says pointing to the now blank screen.

'I was just looking something up.'

Her lips contort in a half smile. 'If Mr Lake sees you, you'll get in trouble.'

I want to joke, *will he sing another eighties song to punish me?* Instead, 'Okay,' slips out.

Although I click off the article, Corinne continues to stare.

'Dinah, right? That's an odd name.'

'My parents used to be religious,' I mumble back. 'I prefer Dee.'

'I wanted to… oh, never mind.'

'What?'

'Nothing.' Slowly, she turns, waiting for me to stop her.

'What's wrong?'

I can hardly believe my eyes when she rolls up her chair beside me. God has answered my prayer.

'I don't think Stephanie is ill.'

'Then why isn't she at work?'

Corinne moves closer. 'You know that big account we have with that internet company, Shiva?'

'The retailer?'

'Yeah, well, a load of invoices went out wrong and Mr Lake is going to figure that out soon. She's ducking the fallout.'

My eyes narrow. It seems ridiculous to think you can avoid owning up to a mistake by simply making yourself scarce. Once at St Alda's, Cookie ate an entire lemon drizzle that was meant for everyone's dinner. He owned up to it straight after; the guilt didn't sit right in his belly. Stephanie should just admit it, but people do silly things they don't mean; I should know. Oh, Corinne is staring at me. I've been quiet too long.

'At least she hasn't been kidnapped by a serial killer,' I joke.

'You mean that Wraith guy?'

Quickly, I add, 'I was kidding.'

She spits, 'Don't joke about stuff like that.'

'I didn't mean…'

Her nose crinkles as if the wind has changed and she's finally caught a good whiff of me. 'It could happen.'

Damn, I need to prove I wasn't serious. 'But the Righteous Wraith already has Lisa. It's not been three days yet. Stephanie is completely safe.' There, facts always make things better.

Inching closer to me, Corinne says, 'But it has. They discovered Lisa Bryan's body this morning.' She then pushes her chair back across the office.

The Wraith has killed his 9th girl. I search online for news. There are photos, something I didn't expect to see. An early morning jogger took a picture of the discarded body on their phone. It has been uploaded, then copied and pasted too many times for the internet to contain or censor. Like a digital wildfire. This poor girl's final moment of terror will be preserved forever. The photo shows she was blinded. Her eyes crossed through by a blood red marker. A slack hand rests on a book, as if she were caught mid-read. A white stained sequin gown covers her core. Just her bruised arms and legs expose her past pain. In the accompanying article it mentions the blinding is an official signature now. There's a police press conference later today. Local gruesome murders with a real signature – this story has Docu-Wow Award written all over it. I just have to work out that damn angle.

Looking around to see if anyone is watching me, I search for 'Righteous Wraith'. Oddly, the browser on this computer shows a favourite site, one detailing the killer's second letter, the one sent after the 5th girl was taken. I certainly didn't bookmark it. Someone at Lake Accounting wants to know about him too. Maybe Corinne? I think she mentioned him first? Shrugging off my thoughts, I read the Wraith's letter; maybe I'll find something I can build a documentary from?

Hello fans!

I must admit, Sandi upset me. She was a quitter. Didn't even last the night! I still kept her for the three days, though. I'd hate to not have a strict schedule, after all, you all need to know when I'll be showing up in your dark-feeds again, and, even more importantly, when I'll be on the streets seeking out my next starlet. Engagement is so essential nowadays, what with all the noise. Someone like me needs to find a way of cutting through it. Whoever will my shadow fall on next? Who's tipped for stardom? I rather like my cast as it's grown... what am I forgetting? Ah yes, Harmony. You know I took her, right? Well, she won't be in harmony with life for much longer. Ha. Ha. Ha.

I have my eyes on the next already. As soon as I saw her I knew I couldn't resist. So pretty, but I'll make her even more so. I'll make her famous. Pain is such a small price to pay when there's so many people jostling for fame. I saw this one on YouTube, trying to start a make-up tutorial channel. Bless her, only a hundred followers so far. Nothing like me. I'll lend her my influence. Maybe we'll even do a video together? Film me. Film me. Film me. If you can find me.

Yours in blood, The Righteous Wraith XX

Sandi died before he wanted her to. That was why he dumped her by those bins. She let him down. For him, her life was easy to throw away.

The 6th girl was Mina Sharma. I Google her name, and of course the first result is the story of her murder at the hands of the Wraith. Following links takes me to her YouTube channel. It now has hundreds of thousands of followers. I click on her last video, recorded months ago. There she is, smiling and happily reviewing a new foundation and explaining the difference between working with sponges and brushes. She signs off with, 'See you all next time.' All those people signed up to follow someone who will never again upload another video.

Next to the second letter is a link to an article written by a psychologist. It talks about today's quick-fix culture and how social media has turned us all into attention addicts, constantly seeking validation for our carefully curated online lives. With such ready access to platforms, it's not surprising people are clamouring for the spotlight, even if it only shines on them for a moment. But killers usually hide in the shadows? I don't understand the Wraith. Is this the angle for my documentary? The clear line he's drawing between his crimes and the state of the world today? I need to catch that police conference, watch for any mention of the letters, but I'll still be trapped in work, and I draw the line at watching TV at my desk when I should be sending out invoices. Maybe I can get a half day?

I clear the search history on my computer, then walk to my boss's office. Behind his desk, Mr Lake sits with his feet up and an outdated earpiece jammed to his head like a plastic slug. Upon seeing me lurking, he motions for me to come in.

'Um, what can I do for you?'

Forgotten my name again. Rather than risk another karaoke classic, I say, 'I've finished my work. Is there anything else you'd like me to do?'

Dropping his feet off the desk, he exclaims, 'All the invoices? No, you've not done it right. Let me get Corinne.'

'I've sent out all my client invoices for today.'

A call suddenly comes through. He slaps his earpiece and says, 'Bonjour.'

I turn to leave, but he waves me to sit down.

After ten minutes of listening to his entire one-sided conversation, Mr Lake is now staring at me. Finally, he speaks. 'You were saying?'

'If there's nothing else you need me to do, may I have a half day holiday?'

Narrowing his eyes, he leans back in his chair. 'Sure, I'll mark it down. Good to make the most of the weather, am I right?'

'Thank you,' I reply, but don't leave.

'Anything else I can help with?'

'My computer, does anyone else use it?'

'It's the company's computer, and yes, I use it from time to time when I'm watching out the window for deliveries. Why?'

'No reason,' I say, then scurry out.

Mr Lake must have bookmarked the Wraith page, but why?

-

While the bus trundles towards my stop, I text Mum and ask if she's home. Without a front door key, I need her to let me in. She comes straight back to say she's at the shops and will be home soon. Not wanting to loiter outside the house, I stop off at St Godfrey's Church. Father Jacob is always in. Nuns must do his shopping for him.

Heat slaps me as I get off the bus. It's one of those days when I'm faced with the downside of constantly wearing black. Mum keeps threatening to buy me something more colourful, something my own age and seasonally appropriate, but that has yet to happen. She probably thinks I'll be back in St Alda's soon, so a new wardrobe would go to waste. Anyway, I like my look. For far too long I wore plain cotton white tops and trousers. Now, I get to feel texture against my skin. A consistent reminder I'm normal again.

'Dee, you didn't need to come all this way.' Father Jacob always looks concerned when I'm in his eyeline, it's his default state: resting worry-face.

'I left work early and Mum's not in.'

Like a six-foot shadowy ghost, he glides through the pews, then motions for me to follow him into the church office. 'Everything all right?'

Once we sit down, he offers me a cold drink. 'Thanks,' I say, then add, 'I'm great.'

I'm about to launch into my documentary idea when he asks, 'Your text last night, do you want to talk about it?'

I like Father Jacob. He has an accepting nature, a friendly smile and a hearty laugh. There's not much more that you can ask for from a friend. Mum used to remind me that a priest in his late twenties was an odd choice for a twelve-year-old girl to have as a best friend; it's not like he could sleep over, go to the cinema with me or talk about boys, but I couldn't do those things anyway thanks to the accident. No, he was exactly what I needed, exactly when I needed it, and, in so many ways, I owe him my life. He's never let me down, but my freedom remains precarious, so I tread carefully. 'Like I said in the text, I helped a little girl in the park.'

'What about this man you drew?' From out of his cassock, he produces an iPhone; I didn't even realise cassocks had pockets. Scrolling through, he finds the text I sent last night and shows it to me.

With my eyes focused on the floor, I say, 'I hit the man in his gut with my backpack to stop him hurting the girl.'

There is a sharp intake of breath. 'You attacked him? Did you see red?'

'No, I defended the girl. He wouldn't let her go.'

'But you can't go round striking people. Remember, last time we prayed we asked God to grant you serenity in your new life. You want that, don't you?'

I nod. 'Course,' I whisper. I want to ask whether it was better for me not to get involved. Should I have stood by and let an innocent girl be abducted? Would that have been a normal reaction from a normal person? But I can't formulate the right words to ask, and I've been silent too long, as he adds, 'All that aside, it was very foolish of you to put yourself in danger.'

'You mean they'd send me back to St Alda's for that?'

'No, I was referring to physical harm.'

I shrug.

Father Jacob smiles. 'Can I show this sketch to my friend in the police? You remember me mentioning Teresa.'

Nodding, I return his smile.

'I won't tell her you gave it to me, I'll just say it's from a concerned member of my flock. And I'll leave off about the bag to the stomach.'

That's the best outcome I could have hoped for: this way, the information moves on without my reputation attached to it. 'Thank you.'

'Now, what's the reason you left work early?'

Will he think me stupid to be investigating a serial killer? Would his concern for my safety and sanity trump his loyalty to me? Damn, I hadn't thought this through.

'I just had some holiday time to take,' I say.

—

At home, Mum ignores my explanation about having the afternoon off and, assuming I caught the bug going around, flutters about me with extra pink pills and cheese sandwiches. Every now and then I'm told to hold a thermometer in my mouth. As it's only shoved into the one orifice I gratefully agree. When I settle down to watch the press conference on Sky News, Mum hands me a drink, then without a hint of embarrassment she asks, 'How many times have you pooped?'

'The usual amount,' I mutter.

'Okay. Keep hydrated. I'm going to pop down the chemist for medicine.' Grabbing her bag, she turns to stare at me for a moment. There's a glint of happiness in her eyes. She hasn't been a mum for nearly twenty years, and it's as if she's back in the saddle, never having been thrown off.

I don't have the heart to take the feeling away from her, so just say, 'Thanks.'

'Oh, I forgot. You didn't take your fumsup with you today.' Out of her bag, she pulls the grubby, wooden-headed silver doll and thrusts it at me.

'Thanks.' As I take it, it cuts into me yet again, and I have to quickly shove my finger in my mouth to stop the swell of blood. This antique little bugger is trying to kill me.

I wait to hear the door slam, before turning on the TV. Damn, the press conference has already started. There's a petite dark-headed policewoman called DCI Campbell on a podium. Her suit is too heavy for the weather and her shoulders are folded in as if already in defeat. She reads a quick statement about the murders, then holds up the killer's letters and says media outlets shouldn't have published them online. She then condemns the random photographer who uploaded the photos of Lisa's dead body and implores people to remove it whenever they see it. Her faith in the masses is sorrowfully misplaced. Something that gruesome will live on forever, passed around like a shot of pure bloody darkness. There for whenever a day is too boring or a night is lacking thrills. I've already downloaded a copy myself – for the documentary.

'This killer,' she says, staring straight into the camera, 'is taunting the police and the public with his letters, and… with what he does to his… victims.'

A man leans over to her and whispers in her ear.

She continues, 'He's not as clever as he thinks, and we are close to catching him. Questions?' she asks.

Silence morphs to mayhem.

'How many dead girls have you missed?'

'Should women of this age be worried in the Northamptonshire area?'

'Lisa Bryan's eyeballs were completely removed, were the others'? If so, what were their other injuries?'

'Why is the killer writing letters?'

Annoyingly, the DCI doesn't answer the questions. She skirts around them, doing the politician's trick of answering the question she wanted instead.

'Are you any closer to catching him?' is answered with, 'We need the public to be vigilant.'

Suddenly, it feels as if I've gone to a lot of effort to learn very little. But then a man's loud, deep voice calls out from the crowd, making DCI Campbell stop mid-sentence.

Chapter Four

The camera doesn't dramatically swing towards the voice for identification. It doesn't need to; as soon as he has the DCI's, and the rest of the room's, attention, he introduces himself.

'I'm Vlad Duncan, Fiona's husband. And I want to know what happened to the woman I love.'

The room erupts into two distinct noises. The police murmur excuses and the reporters yell and clap their support. The din is overpowering; like two voluminous seas of sound crashing together.

DCI Campbell holds up her hands. 'Please, calm down.'

But they don't. People are angry. And when people get angry, they get loud, and when there are enough of them, they become a mob.

'When will you catch the monster who tortured and killed my wife for fun?' Vlad asks.

'I'm doing everything I can. But I implore women of the county to be extra vigilant.'

'What are they looking out for?' yells out a reporter.

DCI Campbell sighs. 'Without any signs of a forced abduction, it would appear victims went willingly with the Wraith.'

'So, the public shouldn't trust anyone?' calls out another journalist.

Agitated, the DCI then disappears off camera. She used *I* at the end. Usually in things like this the royal 'we' is preferred; she personalised it. Interesting, perhaps she's my angle for the documentary, although the odds of getting an interview without credentials, or a production company behind me, are slim. Vlad was outspoken, emotional and not afraid to make a scene, perhaps I could try for him. I've never asked anyone for an interview before, so I check my course notes and follow their instructions. I find Vlad on Facebook and send a direct message asking if we could meet.

Just before Mum gets back, I flick onto the BBCiPlayer and start watching a random documentary on food waste. Her trip to the chemist bears foul-tasting fruit and she makes me drink something to replace the salts lost by the illness I don't have. It tastes as if it was mined from the bowels of hell; punishment for not speaking up and defending my truth.

Dad isn't far behind and, when he comes in, he settles onto the sofa to watch TV.

Suddenly, he says, 'How about doing a documentary on recycling? That's a big thing now.'

Mum didn't react well to our talk on the Righteous Wraith; best I keep my work secret for now. 'Good idea,' I say.

If I'm working on a documentary, I need money for travel and interview expenses. For my last year, I was given a stipend at St Alda's for working in their onsite café, but have no idea how much is in my account.

'How much money do I have, Dad?' I ask.

'I'll get a statement for you. And, since you're under the weather, I'll call you in sick tomorrow.' Dad nudges me and winks.

Lying is a sin, but is it as bad if I simply continue with an assumption someone else made? I could protest, but having a day off to start my documentary would be a godsend.

Pink pill swallowed, then I'm away to my room.

I log on to Facebook. Nothing from Vlad. It was silly to expect a reply; he doesn't know me and must be in such pain. There is, however, an update on Louisa's timeline.

She knows I'm out of St Alda's.

Chapter Five

Without thinking, I click on the latest post. It takes me straight to an interview with a national magazine. It's an odd sensation to have strangers openly discuss you; I'm still not used to it. Louisa doesn't help matters, why would she? The more insane and troubled I look, the more heroic she appears. It's like a game of Monopoly. The larger her stake of real estate, the quicker she bankrupts me as I traverse *her* board.

'*Working with such a disturbed individual was tough on my own mental health, but I believe in the power of mindfulness,*' she says.

Worked with me? That would imply consent. And mindfulness? Please! If she had truly thought I was possessed by a demon, would a bout of breathing exercises have saved her from the fires of hell?

The interviewer asks when she noticed I was in trouble.

'*Dee was always weird, but I started to notice her more evil inclinations about a month before I contacted the exorcists. Violent outbursts were becoming an everyday occurrence.*'

How can someone be *more evil*? You're either evil or you're not.

They ask her what happened after the documentary was finished.

'*The exorcism was a success, but the effects of harbouring a demon took a toll on Dee's mental and physical health. She was admitted into an asylum.*'

Asylum? St Alda's is a medium security facility. The word asylum conjures up all sorts of horrible images of insane individuals having their brains prodded and shocked. Not only has she besmirched me, but also my home.

In sickeningly sweet prose she then expresses how happy she is that I've been released and finally got a bit better; those are the words she uses – *a bit better*. Implying I'll never be fully normal ever again. After everything she did to me, she's still finding ways to shame me. Beneath the article, I type the comment, *Judas*. My finger hovers over the enter key. The word isn't a jibe or a threat, it's an accurate description, but still, I delete it. She was my first real friend, and I know how important those relationships can be. At St Alda's, there were few choices. Fate put people before you, all ages, all with varying degrees of mental health issues, and you bonded at pre-approved social times when there were enough staff to observe. My friends were Craig, and Tippy, but my best friend was Cookie. We bonded instantly. We'd both suffered major head trauma, only his caused an almost complete mental retrograde shift. At age forty-one, Cookie now, and will forever have, the mind of an eight-year-old child.

Putting my palms together, I say aloud, 'Dear Lord, how's your day been?' I pause for His answer. 'Mine's been interesting. Thank you for letting me have the afternoon off, and forgive me for not correcting Mum when she assumed I was sick. Any chance of smiting Louisa? Wait, I shouldn't ask. Sorry. On a better note, I'm looking into this Wraith business. I know you put him in my path for a reason. Docu-Wow here I come! Amen.'

The pink pill kicks in and my mind dulls. Blind drawn. Fan on.

For hours, I lie in the mid-state of sleep and awake, waiting for one or the other to take me fully. When it doesn't happen, I count sheep, a trick Cookie taught me. One fluffy white ball leaps over the fence, then another and another until their fleeces blacken and decay and their eyeballs shrink back into their dark sockets.

At 333 dead sheep, I fall asleep.

–

Mum doesn't like me to spend time alone downstairs before they get up, so I have to stay in bed until 8:30 a.m. Lying sweaty and still, waiting to hear your parents up and about, is torture. Finally, the toilet flushes and I'm free to leave my room.

'How are you feeling?' Mum asks.

'Better.'

'Your dad called you in sick, so I've made an emergency afternoon appointment with Dr Taylor for you.'

Emergency appointment doesn't sound good. 'Why would you do that? I've got my usual appointment on Friday.'

Mum rolls her eyes. 'Well, if this isn't a bug, you might need your medication changing. Sickness could be a side effect. I'd rather we get this sorted than have a relapse.'

She says *relapse*, but really that's code for *outburst*. As if I'm going to freak out like the Hulk and start tearing down the family home because the pink pills have stopped working. I take a breath, count back from six and ask, 'What time?'

'Four. Don't be late.' She rustles in her bag, finds her purse then hands me a twenty-pound note. For the taxi I won't take. 'I'd go with you, but I've got that training.' Without asking, she then makes me some toast. As I chew, I watch her gather her books and iPad.

'For the love of…' she says.

'What's wrong?'

'The blasted charger is missing again. I'm going to have to go caveman and write everything longhand.'

No other charger fits Mum's iPad; the rest of us are Android lovers. Closing my eyes, I remember the last time I saw her with it. A flash of the cable curled snake-like on the dining room floor finds me. I open my eyes, go to the dining room, and retrieve the wayward charger.

'Here it is,' I say to Mum, handing it over.

'You angel!' She winds up the wire and shoves it in her bag.

After a quick goodbye, she's out of the door and Dad is jogging down the stairs in his gardening outfit.

'Morning, love. Why don't you come and help in the garden?'

If this is the price I have to pay to get started on my documentary, so be it. I nod and follow him outside.

The oak tree by my window is shedding its leaves; it looks as if autumn is coming, even though it's pushing thirty-two again today. I gather the newly fallen leaves and shove them into a bin bag. As I do, I notice more of the tree's branches are bowed.

'What could cause that?' I ask.

'A bird; a big one. The estate is named after red kites; they're big enough to cause the damage.' Dad squints up at the tree.

'It's still odd,' I whisper.

'How's it going, Jones?'

I look over to see Mr Davidson at the fence.

'Davey Boy!' Dad yells and holds up his hand.

Taking this greeting as an invitation, Mr Davidson enters the garden through the back gate. 'That tree's seen better days,' he says.

Ignoring the comment, Dad asks, 'What have you been doing? Not seen you about in a while.'

'Got a new job. Working for your old place,' Mr Davidson replies as he walks over.

'Greaves Comprehensive?' Dad asks.

Mr Davidson's eyes swing towards me. 'No, I'm putting my copyright law to good use at St Alda's. A doctor there is patenting some new techniques soon.' He inches forward. 'Dee, you're looking well.'

At six feet tall, Dad's friend looms over me, making me cringe.

'Feel like a little gardening?' asks Dad, hope lacing his voice.

'In this heat?'

They both laugh like it's a joke.

'No, must dash. Lots to do. Good to see you up and about, Dee.'

'Later, Davey Boy.' Dad waves.

And we're alone again.

With a sigh, Dad looks around the garden. 'Nuts to this, let's have an early elevenses. I bought a cheesecake.'

After we devour a whole red berry cheesecake, he pats his belly and asks me not to tell Mum we ate it all in one sitting. He then offers to get rid of the evidence in the garden bin and we exchange conspiratorial smiles.

'Why don't you get a nap in before your appointment today,' he tells me. As I'm getting up, he adds, 'I could drive you.'

'That's okay. I'll catch the bus.'

His smile fades.

–

Upstairs, I check if Vlad replied to my interview request. Nothing. After his outburst at the press conference, he was probably inundated with offers.

I should be researching the Wraith, but instead I re-read Louisa's interview, looking for even the slightest hint that she's sorry for what she put me through. Nothing there either.

When I met Louisa, I was a teenager attending one of my many post-accident hospital stays. Her little brother was my bed neighbour, in for a minor operation. Too busy playing Nintendo, he never spoke to me, but Louisa did. In her mid-twenties, she was older and wiser. I instantly wanted to be her friend. It started with a few words each day. *How are you? What happened to you? Food's not that bad in here, eh?* Then it turned into more intimate chats about life. Even when her brother went home, Louisa continued to visit me. She painted my nails and swiped blush along my cheekbones. With painfully useless plastic cutlery, she cut up my food while telling stories about her media course at the local university. How she wanted to film documentaries and win awards.

Suddenly, I had a friend, and not just any friend, but a grown-up one who shared her hopes and dreams with me. Once I was discharged from hospital, we started having afternoon tea and lunch out at fancy places. We always ate dessert.

At home, Mum and Dad didn't think much of my ever-changing moods. I'd hit my head hard in the accident. Mum said she'd have been worried if I *hadn't* acted strangely. As I healed though, their patience wore thin. I wasn't acting like *their* Dee anymore. Of course, the more everyone around me wanted me to be normal again, the more pressure I felt. Small things began to irritate me, and a growing rage silently festered that, at the time, I didn't know what to do with. Throwing pens and plates were small fry compared to when I violently kicked the car, denting it so badly the door never opened again. Each time, guilt hit almost immediately after my actions, but that never stopped them repeating.

My parents used to have faith. They attended church twice a week and never missed an important mass. Louisa used that to her advantage when she suggested I was possessed. Omens were divined and the more I tried to control my feelings, the worse it got. Next thing I knew I was pinned to the floor being exorcised. My anguish filtered through Louisa's camera lens. Now and forever, I will always be both the protagonist and antagonist of *Possession is Nine Tenths.*

At first, I tried not to watch Louisa's documentary, even though I went on to watch it thirty-three times. It, of course, never changes. I'm always the tarnished star. The ugly creature held down by the heroes and expelled back into hell. Tortured for hours with bells smashed about my head and sage smoke gagging my senses. At the end, the have-a-go exorcists declared me cured. Traumatised, my episodes turned even more violent and my thinking clouded. Three days later, I was admitted into St Alda's on Father Jacobs's recommendation. My 'exorcism' had not been authorised by the Catholic Church, so he didn't have an official invitation to the documentary. It didn't stop him from publicly declaring Louisa an 'unscrupulous cad' for using my pain to further her career. Or from alerting the authorities to her actions – not that there was much they could do. The one thing Louisa never gambles with is paperwork. Everything about *Possession is Nine Tenths* was signed off by Mum and Dad. They were there, the whole time. Her people telling them that it wasn't me going through the pain and torment, but the demon within me who needed to suffer. Like I'd contracted unholy food poisoning and had to purge the evil to recover. And all that was better to believe than the truth.

Years later, I found out the people who 'saved my soul' were only self-proclaimed spiritualists. Louisa hadn't even researched those she paid to attack me that day. One was wanted by the police and the other had previously been charged with beating his wife up in a fit of rage – none of which made it into the documentary.

With my own documentary stagnant in my mind, and not wanting to subject myself to more gardening, I catch the midday bus ready for my 4 p.m. with Dr Taylor.

St Alda's sits on a massive expanse of greenery, its many buildings making it larger than some villages, and yet with its security minimal it still manages to exist right next to a street of domestic homes. Dr Taylor lives in that street. When I visit her home office, I sit on an IKEA armchair and tell her about the thoughts I feel appropriate to share. I have a standing appointment with her after work on Fridays; it was part of the conditions of my release, so this impromptu visit needs to be dealt with carefully. I loved St Alda's, but I've already lost so much of my life there. I can't go back, not when I have a chance to be normal again.

As I'm too early for the appointment, I visit Cookie first. The entrance to the hospital is made of bright red bricks and serves as a sort of St Peter's waiting area. You show your ID to the carers, tell them who you are visiting, and they decide your fate. Today I don't have to show my ID. Brenda is on duty and remembers me. I receive a warm smile and the doors open.

I check my stuff at reception and a nurse called Coal walks me towards the hospital café to wait for Cookie. Coal knew me when I lived here; he tries to make small talk about the weather, but in the end settles for comfortable silence.

The café has no name. It's small with dark, oddly sized tables and chairs of different styles and hues; a collection of the eclectic. There are no mass-produced paintings or positivity-inducing posters here. It's a dim and unpredictable room that belongs in a mental health facility.

Being an unscheduled visit, it takes a while for Cookie to appear. As an ex-patient, our meetings are supposed to be pre-sanctioned. Fortunately, Dr Taylor feels our relationship is beneficial to both of us, so we avoid a lot of the usual red tape.

I hear Cookie first; a wheezy laugh reminiscent of Mutley from *Wacky Races*. When our eyes meet, confusion crosses my friend's face, which is quickly enveloped by a grin.

'Hello, Dee.'

Touching another patient is frowned upon; even so, Cookie takes the seat beside me, just a thin barrier of air separating our bare skin. His face is marked with acne scars and what remaining hair he has is a deep chestnut brown. No stubble. Always smells like pine trees. Missing teeth due to excessive sugary drinks and snacks, and a backbone in a consistent state of spasm due to sitting on the floor most of the day; all has taken its toll on his middle-aged body.

I only realise how much I've missed him now I'm this close. For a moment, I wish we were meeting together on the outside. No one watching, no time limit, and a massive slice of cake to share. But this wish will never be granted. In all the time Cookie has been at St Alda's, his adult brain has never recovered, and his family prefer him here – out of sight.

'Have you come to play?'

'No, I just got the day off.'

'No work?' He cocks his head to the side.

'Dad called me in sick. But I'm not sick.'

'You're skiving!' He points at me and giggles.

He's right. I am. But I didn't do it on purpose, so that has to count for something.

'It's all good though. Can we play for a bit? Pleeeease?' He claps his hands.

Now I'm closer, I see bruises discolouring his exposed skin. What game has done this?

'How did you get…?'

Cookie's lips contort; without teeth, it looks like gurning. 'I've missed you.'

'Missed you too,' I admit.

Cookie falls silent.

'What's wrong?'

'I'm all alone.' It's an odd thing to say for someone who lives with hundreds of other people, but as most rarely have the mental energy to socialise, it does make loneliness sharper – always within reach of a friend, just never close enough.

'I'm still here,' I say. 'And I'll try to visit you more often.'

'That's what Craig and Tippy said when they got let out.' Cookie's lips purse.

'Tippy died,' I remind my friend.

'Yeah, well, that witch still broke her promise.'

I change the subject. 'Guess what? I'm going to do a documentary on a serial killer called the Righteous Wraith. I've approached one of the victims' husbands, Vlad Duncan, for an interview.'

Cookie chuckles. 'Vlad? He's not a vampire is he?'

'Vampires don't exist.'

'But we read stories about them.'

I lean forward. 'They were all make-believe. Monsters don't exist.'

'Demons do,' Cookie says, then blushes and quickly looks down at our feet. 'Sorry.'

'That's okay. But just in case, I'll eat garlicky pizza before I interview him.' With Cookie smiling, I continue with my news. 'I've done a lot of research. I think I'll call my documentary *Northamptonshire's Nightmare*. Wait, that's too generic...'

'I had a nightmare last night.'

Cautiously, I ask, 'Was it one of the usual ones?'

'No. A new one. I was hurting someone. I heard her screams when I woke up.' Cookie looks away and shifts in the seat.

Screams in a place like this are not out of the ordinary, but this kind of dream is very different from the replays of the brutal fall that twisted the normal, fit, adrenaline-junkie Graham Cookson into an eight-year-old who plays with dolls.

'You were hurting a woman?'

'Lisa.'

Lisa? 'Have you been watching the news?'

My friend's shoulders straighten. 'No, I only watch the soaps.' He leans in. I can smell tea on his breath. 'I do visit outside, though.'

With supervision, patients are taken on limited trips, but with staffing issues, they have dwindled over the past few years. What's my friend talking about?

'Do you mean outside in your dreams?' I ask.

Cookie inches closer, then drops his voice to a whisper, 'Promise you won't tell?'

I nod.

'Cross your heart?'

I mimic the gesture.

'There's a hole in the fence behind the big red berry bush, big enough to crawl through. At night, I walk to Good Tree Park and play on the swings. Only at night though, after bed check.'

This has to be a fantasy; Cookie can't get out of the building, let alone escape the grounds.

As if reading my mind, he adds, 'I got moved to a downstairs room a few months ago. They must think I'm ready to go outside on my own again now.'

'Who are *they*?'

Cookie whispers, 'I didn't mean to, but a few nights ago I made Lisa scream.'

'You couldn't hurt anyone. It was just a nightmare.' My hand reaches out to touch my friend but, coming to my senses, I quickly snap it back.

He stares at me. The café doesn't have its usual bustling soundtrack, so the silence between two people can creep up and out into it, like dark food colouring on white icing. It's not uncomfortable, but still feels like a waste; after all, we don't have long with one another. Every second is precious.

Loudly, he asks, 'Hey, you remember the arts and crafts building?'

Although it's a jarring change of subject, the memory makes me smile. 'Yes, Father Jacob was allowed to visit us there. Lots of nooks and crannies to hide in, and remember when we slid down the laundry chute?'

'Yes! Father J never even told on us.'

'Didn't you say it closed down when I was at Trayvon?'

'It's all boarded up. But, it's been left unlocked… We should so do the chute again. Or we could play dolls there?'

It's then I remember the fumsup. I take it out of my pocket and dance it across the table to my friend. Eyes alight, Cookie takes the grotty old thing and cradles it like a tiny baby.

'Careful, it's got a sharp edge,' I say. 'It's meant to be lucky. Doesn't seem to be bringing me any luck, though.'

'Perhaps you have to take better care of him to attract luck,' he says. After he kisses the top of the fumsup's hideous head, I'm reluctantly given it back. Pushing the grotesque thing at Cookie, I say, 'You keep it.'

'No, he belongs to you, Dee.' He moves to put the charm into my bag. As I jerk my backpack away, my friend frowns, then lays the old doll on the table in front of me, like a sacrificial offering.

While stroking the fumsup's head, Cookie asks, 'Do you still feel the demon? See red?'

'Sometimes, but I can handle it now.'

'So, you're *really* normal,' Cookie mumbles.

I nod.

My friend leans towards me. 'Sometimes I wonder what would happen if old Graham came back. Where would I go? I don't want to die, Dee.'

I hate that Cookie's eyes are glazing with tears. Although diagnosed with the same affliction of a severe head injury, our symptoms are very different. Cookie's personality changed completely into a child. After his fall, it was like another soul had slipped into Graham's body.

'You're too much fun to die,' I tell him with a giggle.

Cookie hiccups a laugh.

'Look, I have to go soon. I'm due at Dr Taylor's.'

'You promised you'd play dolls with me.'

'Course, I'll go after we play dolls.'

Grinning, Cookie disappears, then remerges with a small toy chest.

We spend twenty minutes dressing the dolls and pretending to shop for clothes together. Gossiping at a coffee shop made out of a shoebox. We talk about boyfriends and families we don't have, and never will. It's strange how much fun playing at normal can be.

–

Dr Taylor is an impressive-looking woman, easily as tall as Father Jacob. With short dark spiky hair and porcelain skin, she strikes an imposing figure.

'Dee! Great to see you,' she says, motioning for me to follow her into the waiting room. 'I'm just finishing up with another client, give me five minutes.'

Not wanting to sit down, I linger by her office door. As she opens it, I hear her say, 'That was good work today, Andy.'

I shouldn't, but I steal a glance. A well-built man is sitting in her office, his dimpled cheeks ruddy and his eyes bloodshot. He looks like he could use a fumsup. Mumbling, he rises from the chair. As she moves to let him out, I see he's just as tall as her. After shaking her hand, he heads out the door. Quickly, I scurry back out of his path.

As Andy strides into the waiting room, he stops and checks his phone. Not wanting to make eye contact, I slowly step towards the office door, to start my appointment, but Dr Taylor waves at me.

'Give me a few minutes to put away my notes, Dee.' She closes the door.

'Dr Taylor's great, isn't she?' Andy suddenly says. The unprompted remark makes me jump. Not noticing, he continues, 'Employs some unique methods in her therapy. Have you been a patient for long?'

I nod.

'I started a couple of months ago. My life's a mess right now, so a friend recommended I come.' He rambles on while I stare at the office door. It's not until I hear *wraith* that I look back at him.

'Pardon?'

'Sorry, I shouldn't be verbally vomiting my problems all over you. I'm Andy, by the way.' He extends his hand. I haven't touched another human being for years; I'm not starting with this random. I smile instead.

'Dinah.'

'Nice.' He sniffles. 'You some sort of goth?' He points at my black lace sundress.

'You some sort of fashion police?' I reply.

'Sorry, takes all types to make the world go round.' He smiles and I can see his teeth are too white. In fact, Andy looks like he just stepped out of a posh menswear catalogue; what sort of problems could he have? Wait, I'm sure he said wraith.

'What about the Wraith?' I ask.

'I shouldn't talk about it.' He purses his lips, deepening his cheek dimples.

True documentarians can pry out the deepest, darkest secrets from subjects, like gritty pearls from slimy oysters. 'Talking helps,' I offer.

'I just spent an hour discussing it.'

'Discussing what?'

Andy motions for me to sit on a nearby couch. I do, and he drops down next to me. 'Some assholes online think I'm this Wraith guy. Fucking armchair investigators are ruining my life.'

My eyebrow rises involuntarily. 'People think you're a serial killer?'

Andy's hands spring up, almost in surrender. 'I'm not the killer. The police cleared me. I've got alibis.'

'Then why do these people think you are?'

Shrugging he says, 'Beats me. They call themselves Wraith Finders,' he says.

With a chuckling snort, I say, 'Surely, Wraith Wranglers would sound better.'

'Yeah, 'cause alliteration is always the best literary device when you're ruining someone's life.'

'Sorry.'

Suddenly Dr Taylor swings open her door. Concern crosses her features as she sees her last patient sitting with her next. 'Did you forget something, Andy?'

'No,' Andy snaps, getting up.

Wait, this is a big, fat documentary angle that can't get away. This could be the next *Making a Murderer*.

Rising, I state, 'I'm working on a documentary about the Wraith; I'd love to interview you.'

Through a half smile, he replies, 'I'll think about it,' then hands me his mobile. 'Put your number in.'

'You could use it to get your side across,' I add, then tap in my digits. He calls me. My ringtone is *The Addams Family* theme. Blushing, I discard the call.

Chuckling, he says, 'You've got my number now.'

'Thanks,' I look down at my phone. He's the first person outside of Mum and Dad and Father Jacob to call me.

Andy opens his mouth to say something else, but stops. After getting a look from Dr Taylor, he leaves.

From the door, my doctor stares at me. I think she's going to tell me off for talking with Andy, but she says, 'I'm proud of you socialising. It's the kind of progress I like to see. Come in.'

Once inside her office, I perch on the edge of a seat across from her desk and place my backpack between my feet. The leather of the chair is still warm from Andy, making me squirm.

'How are you? Your mum said you've not been feeling well.' She pulls out a notebook and pen. 'Shall we look at your medication? I think you are on right dose, but we can experiment a little,' she says, cocking her head to the side.

I clear my throat. I didn't drink anything at the café and documentary angle-finding is thirsty work. My eyes wander to an oversized vase on her desk brimming with fresh lavender in clear water. It dazzles in the only window's sunlight.

'May I have a glass of water, please?' I ask.

She writes something down, then clicks off her pen to fetch water from the cooler in the waiting room. Tilting my head, I try to make out what she wrote, but her handwriting is like ancient hieroglyphics, a dead language only she knows.

After handing me a glass, she sits back down, folding her long, thick legs over one another. I look down. The glass is only half full. Is this some kind of optimism test? Am I supposed to be grateful for having just two gulps of water? I should be; there are people who don't get any gulps at all. I take a sip, then place the glass on the floor by my bag.

'The pink pills are good,' I say. I want to add that Mum's worries are unfounded, but it would feel like I'm calling her a liar.

'Okay. So...' Dr Taylor says, clicking her pen back on. 'How's the job going?'

I think through what I *can* tell her; I certainly don't want to mention how quickly I finish my daily work, then spend my time Googling Louisa. I can't look as if I'm endangering my job, it's crucial to my continued release. My thought-editing makes me silent too long, so Dr Taylor fills the gap with, 'Are you still controlling it, the red?'

From our very first session we referred to my condition as *red;* we didn't anthropomorphise it, just gave it the colour, as that's what happens to my vision. Red. A cloud, a mist, a flood, no matter the weather analogy, it always has the same effect. I lash out. The technical name is amygdala hijack, when your brain assigns the most extreme reaction to stimuli – fight or flight. And ever since the accident, my fight has always outweighed my flight. Seeing red is a cliché, but clichés exist for a reason, and calling it anything else felt wrong.

'Yes. Whenever I need to, I count. And I take my pills and pray.' I know the last precautionary measure doesn't mean much to her scientific mind, but I won't lie and say I don't.

Taking my words at face value, she smiles, then changes the subject. 'You saw Cookie today. You know you should give us more notice.'

Bending, I scoop up my glass and take another sip of water. Coal must have told on me.

'Are you very thirsty?'

'It's just hot,' I whisper, then finish off the last drop of water.

'You're quiet,' she says. 'Are you sleeping? I know these long days are playing havoc with my equilibrium. Is the blackout blind helping? You could buy ear plugs to really block everything out. Cutting off the senses can be relaxing. In Buddhism it's referred to as a dark retreat.'

'Dark retreat?' I like the sound of that; creepy and relaxing is an intriguing combination.

'Yes, it's all about quieting the mind and listening to your inner thoughts. After researching the technique, I've begun to advise it as an exercise to all my patients; what with the modern world today being so invasive.'

She's referring to the internet and social media. We've had many a discussion about its impact on mental health, especially my mental health. It's not hard to find Louisa's documentary online – I should know.

'Are you finding your digital feet?' she asks.

'I'm on Facebook, but I'm not being invaded enough to need a retreat.' If anything, it would be nice to have more contact.

As if answering my thought, she adds, 'These things take time. Just remember, you didn't choose your fame. *Possession* thrust it upon you.'

Bending, I retrieve my notebook, and write that down.

She scrawls something down herself, making us appear mirror image scribblers.

I finish first, so say, 'I think I've decided on a topic for my documentary.'

'That's wonderful, Dee. Tell me about it.'

This is the part of our sessions I love the most, where, for around ten minutes, Dr Taylor deliberately lets me chunter on, uninterrupted and without internal editing. She hasn't realised that I know this is one of her therapeutic techniques. An invitation to let loose a freeing diatribe to a person who listens without judgement or butting in with a 'one-upmanship' story to prove they are better than you. I open my mouth to reveal my Wraith idea, but then wonder if her reaction will be the same as Mum's. Once again, I'm quiet for too long and she narrows her eyes.

'You know, Dee. You can tell me anything. Just like with my other patients, we have doctor-patient confidentiality. Our relationship can't work any other way.'

Better to ask. 'Are there any exceptions to that?'

Taking a deep breath, my doctor uncrosses then re-crosses her legs. 'If you were to talk about hurting someone, then I would be obligated to report it.'

As I'm not hurting anyone, I say, 'I'm doing a documentary on the Righteous Wraith.' Odd: blurting just those few words makes me feel as if I was an over-inflated balloon that's now only carrying a comfortable amount of air.

Dr Taylor cocks her head. 'Is that wise?'

'Lots of people have put together documentaries on serial killers.'

'This one is…' She looks away and shakes her head.

'What? The Wraith is no more dangerous than any other killer.' Remembering my research, I add, 'or any different.'

'He's courting the media. He's bold and clearly enjoying his time in the spotlight. Those people are highly dangerous. What if he were to…'

She's worried about my safety. I need to show her I can handle danger. 'I saved a little girl in the park the other day,' I tell her.

'What?'

Grabbing my book, I find the drawing of the bad man. 'He tried to abduct her, and I stopped him. Here.' I angle the sketch towards her.

Dr Taylor glances down, then back up with concern. 'That was a very silly thing to do.'

I shrug. 'I'm tougher than I look.'

Nodding, she gently pushes aside my sketch. 'Okay, Dee, but let's not revel in violence. That's not good for you, or your situation. Understand? So I didn't just hear what you said. And you shouldn't tell anyone else.'

She's still protecting me. I nod my agreement, then ask, 'What do you know about serial killers?'

For a moment, she shakes her head, but then a smile flashes over her face. 'A mentor of mine had a theory about them.' Rising, she retrieves an olde worlde white ceramic bust of a skull. On it are marked sections of the brain. Together, we've stared at it many times. She used it years ago to explain amygdala hijacks and how my accident affected my brain. But today, she highlights the whole limbic system. 'Many killers have taken a bump to the head, here. As you know, a traumatic brain injury to this area could alter one's reactions to even minor stimulus.'

'You think the Wraith was in an accident? Like me?'

'Hard to say. I've found profiling to be, at best, a waste of time, and at worst, dangerous as it can cause bias.'

'Fascinating,' I whisper.

'You know,' she says, 'you took some pretty hefty bumps to the skull during your accident. Then I wager several more in that pathetic side-show exorcism. If you like, we can scan your brain again now you've got things under control; see what's what in there?'

The thought of people seeing inside my head jars me. There'd be no hiding what they find. What if I'm not as healed as people think? 'That's okay, I've had a lifetime's worth of hospitals.'

'I understand. When I first diagnosed you with amygdala hijacking, I admit I wondered whether we'd ever get to this point in your treatment.'

I have to ask. 'You didn't have faith I'd ever be normal?'

'No, I'm just saying I'm proud of you. Most head injury patients don't get better. They are trapped by it forever.' She means Cookie. 'You're quite special.'

Putting the skull back on the shelf, Dr Taylor smiles at me, then neatly rips the used pages from her notebook, places them in an A4 white envelope, then locks them in the massive cabinet that sits behind her desk. When I first came to Dr Taylor, I thought it odd that she should own such a piece of furniture. It's huge and wooden with ornate cherubs draped over its edges. It looms behind her like a towering structure poised to fall. Most doctors have metal filing cabinets that sit below their desk, discreetly out of the way. Not Dr Taylor, she boasts something that belongs in a C.S. Lewis novel. I think it's why I liked her from that first session. She doesn't fit the mould either.

'So, let's wrap up today with words of wisdom.' Reaching into a drawer, she pulls out a book entitled just that, *Words of Wisdom*. It's the type you could buy in any high street shop, but she holds it as if it were a Bible signed by God himself. I imagine His curly scripture on the inside front cover, *To Dr Taylor, Keep the faith, lots of love, God*.

She flicks through the book, then stops at a page. 'It's not who we are, but who we do that is important.'

Raising an eyebrow, I'm about to tell her she hasn't read that right, but she beats me to it.

'Oh, my. That doesn't sound good.' Laughing, she puts the book aside. 'But we have found some lovely sayings in here before so let's not judge it on this one hiccup.'

'Everyone's journey is different,' I say echoing one of my personal favourites.

'Indeed. And let's not forget, you are what you eat. How many cakes have you snaffled up today, Dee?'

'Not as many as I'd like,' I mutter.

She laughs, but I wasn't joking.

'Looking forward to our next session already,' Dr Taylor sings after me as I scurry from her office and out into the blazing sunlight.

–

Knocking three times on the front door summons Mum.

'Dr Taylor okay?' she asks as if it were a social visit.

'Seems so.'

Mum waits a full minute for me to elaborate, and when I don't she wanders off. Damn, I should have asked her how her training went, maybe later.

After dinner, a dry steak pie and chips, I retreat to my bedroom. Although I've not heard from Andy about my idea for a documentary, I want to check out the Wraith Finders site. Theories and finger-pointing is one thing, but I need to know what they are claiming.

'Need a lift tonight?' Dad is at my door.

'Tonight?'

'That writing thing?'

He means Inspiration Cometh, the uninspiring name of a writers' group that meets at a pub down the road. It's meant to be for all manner of creative people, but the majority are amateur filmmakers. I've only managed to attend one meeting, and hadn't intended to return, but the hopeful look on Dad's face makes me change my mind.

'Yes, but I can walk.'

After gathering all my stuff, I make my way there. The pub is a little grimy, and the bar staff rude, but the building is old and has a dark feel to it that I like. When I walk in, I spot the group's usual table and move to sit at it. Weird, the meeting should be starting in a minute, but no one else is here. If no one turns up I can just go home and work on the documentary… no, there they are. Members have already gathered at a different table. Heaving my backpack over my shoulder I walk across to join them. As I slip into the chair nearest the door, no one acknowledges my arrival.

'Welcome, all,' says our organiser Janet, a middle-aged housewife with too much time on her hands. 'First off, I hear Trudy has finished her short film for Halloween. A little bird told me it'll be premiered at the film festival Frightening Fest.'

Trudy flushes red and nods. For someone who writes the most disturbing horror I've ever read, she gets embarrassed easily.

'Okay, so let's start with Donald. You have an idea for a short screenplay?'

The pub is dead on a Wednesday night, so it's mostly just the group here. Donald doesn't need to stand up to read aloud his work, yet he does. As a man, he worries me. Short yet wide. Shaved head, and sporting a long black beard that could rival any pirate. His small–rimmed gold glasses perch on the end of his nose, making him appear mole-like. If the eyes are the window to the soul, his windows have black–out blinds.

'This came to me last night.' He rustles some papers, then coughs to clear his throat before reading aloud.

I zone out. I need to do more research, look deeper into Andy; friend him on Facebook and devise a list of questions for our interview for when he comes back to me – if he comes back to me. My phone is still annoyingly quiet. I'll need to thoroughly examine the Wraith Finders website and make contact with them. Cover both sides. That's what all the good documentaries do; they expand their information nets – give the audience the whole catch of the day, then let them decide what to believe. Louisa had a clear objective. A narrative to sell her work to a gullible audience, telling everyone I was possessed by a demon. I won't be like that with Andy. I'll make sure…

'Her footsteps quicken as I track D down the street…'

What? Did Donald just use my name? Infringement!

'Voice-over: D is tall and, even in the dark-lit street-lights I can see her blonde hair is shiny and long and curly.

Her eyes a deep, vivid blue that will soon reflect back my eager face.'

Not me then. And dark-lit doesn't make any sense; how can something be lit by the dark? 'Um, can I stop you there?' I say.

Donald narrows his tiny eyes at me. 'What is it?'

'Why use an initial?'

'I don't want the victim to be identified. Using D adds an air of mystery. As if the victim could be anyone.'

Anyone tall and blonde with the initial D, is what I want to say, but don't.

'Are you submitting this to Frightening Fest?' Janet asks.

'Well, I'm not sure. It's still a foetus of a film.'

'Oh, it sounds like it'd be perfect. You should enter,' Janet adds.

The rest of the group murmur their agreement.

Ignoring them, Donald continues his bland stalking film. It finally ends with his character, who I suspect strongly is him, abducting D and hinting of the 'fun he'll have with her baby-blue eyeballs.' It's beyond boring, clichéd, and in especially bad taste with a serial killer currently abducting girls and taking their... wait.

'Can you read that last bit back, Donald?' I ask.

The group groan, but Donald smiles. 'Did you like it?'

I want to say that it is the literary equivalent of fast food – tasteless, unfulfilling and available everywhere, but I don't. Instead, I say, 'It's very now.'

'Whatever do you mean?' Trudy asks.

Damn, I can't mention the Righteous Wraith, I'll be showing my hand that I'm researching him. 'Stalking is very in right now.' Lame answer.

'Oh, I thought you were bringing up the Righteous Wraith,' Trudy says, damning any chance I had of putting the documentary worms back in the can.

'Yes, well. My killer is different. You'll see when I write the next scene.' Donald then fumbles with his pages, his cheeks growing red.

Janet takes a big swig of wine. 'I saw something on Facebook about that killer before I left the house,' she says. 'The Righteous Wraith has been caught.'

Chapter Six

Too late. I won't need to produce a documentary on Andy being accused of the killings if they already have the real killer in custody. It could become more of an *I-told-you-so* piece, but they never do very well with viewers.

Springing up, I say, 'I have to go.' Then make a run for the door. No one says goodbye, but I hear the usual sighs of relief behind me.

Back home, to avoid a social debrief, I make excuses to Mum and Dad that I'm exhausted and need to get to bed. I then search for the story online, but don't find a word about the killer being caught. After three hours my frustration starts to bubble and, rather than face the red, I just accept I've been a fool. I could never have written, filmed and edited a whole documentary alone before this violent idiot was caught; he clearly wanted to be – you can't become pen pals with the media and expect to continue your murdering undisturbed.

-

Knock, knock, knock jolts me awake.

With the blind down, I'm not sure of the time, so lean across to check my phone: 3:33 a.m. I wait to hear the sound again, but there's nothing. Must have imagined it. Turning over, I close my eyes, then hear a familiar tune.

It takes a few seconds for me to realise it's my mobile. Clumsily, I swipe to answer.

'Hello?' I say.

'I just got fired over this shit.'

'What?' I ask, rubbing my eyes.

There's a shuffling on the other end of the phone.

'Andy?' I check the caller ID to confirm.

'I just can't take it anymore.'

'Why were you fired?'

'I'm being group stalked! There were people outside my work. Then they moved to my flat. Everywhere I look, there they are – watching me.'

'What people?'

'Wraith Finders. Camped outside. Waiting to catch me *wraithing*.' Andy's voice is cracked and distorted, like a broken mirror.

'Are you safe?'

'I'm not there anymore. I moved out of town a few weeks back. I had to get away. They don't know that though, so are still waiting to accost me there.'

'How do you know?'

'Doorbell camera.'

A fact pinpricks my thoughts. The killer has been caught, why are they still harassing him?

'But the Wraith's been caught.'

'They'll never catch him.'

Odd response. 'If people are on your property, you should call the police. That's your home. They're breaking the law.'

'I've had enough of the police.'

With my sleep-addled brain, the only help I can give is to offer hope. 'How about we film an interview tomorrow? Something we can upload to YouTube right

71

away. It'll give you a chance to talk about how this has affected you.'

I hear heavy breathing. 'Andy?'

Without confirmation, or a goodbye, he hangs up.

Did he consent to film the documentary? I don't remember. To ensure we're both on the same page, I write a text to confirm just that, but as I go to press send, my finger stiffens. This is serious. Andy has a lot of trauma to work through. Who am I to offer help? Maybe I should ease into making documentaries, start with one on recycling and work up to people falsely accused of murder. But then, I might miss my chance to do something amazing. *Possession* was Louisa's first documentary. Nothing stopped her from rushing in and making my story her own.

I press send.

–

In the morning, I find Dad has called me in sick for another day. After a valiant attempt to eat rubbery eggs and leather-like bacon with plastic utensils, I take a packet of cakes and a thermos of tea up to my room. While waiting for Andy to text back, I devour all the cakes and finally check out the Wraith Finders website. It's crude and cumbersome with a seemingly never-ending labyrinth of links. Venturing down each, I try to find an article on the Wraith's arrest, but there's none. You'd think Wraith Finders would have reported his capture – that he was *found*. I scan their list of members. Most are handles, rather than real names; all apart from the organisers, Mr and Mrs Watson.

As he said, Andy is all over the site, along with wild theories about his movements at the times of the abductions. One member calling themselves Rabbits Foot, not the correct grammar, has uploaded photos of Andy at all the body dump sites. In each picture he is stood minding his own business, oblivious the Wraith is behind him, heaving a dead body. As evidence goes, it's pretty compelling how he was there at every dump site, but other people are in those photos too; after all, the wraith chooses public places. Although, maybe I'm just giving Andy excuses since, for my documentary to work, he needs to be innocent. No. The police cleared him of the murders, and they know what they're doing. He had alibis, and there are no time stamps on these images. We only have the photographer's word when each was taken. It's not real evidence. Mum and Dad had more evidence that I was possessed by a demon than these guys have about Andy being a killer.

As armchair investigations go, it's childishly finger-pointy without much evidence to back it up, kind of like a digital torch-wielding mob. And, as I Google further, I find similar online incidents. Many of which had disastrous ends where the accused was not the monster who deserved a pitchfork thrown into his life.

Even more disturbing, I find another site dedicated to the killings, but, unlike Wraith Finders, this one is a fan site. Post after post with anonymous handles spilling their fantasies about the torture and murder of women. Do any of them suspect Andy? Should I contact them? Reading some of their sick thoughts makes me wonder how these people are allowed to exist in the normal world. They could be anywhere. Sitting across from you on the bus. Handing you a sandwich in the bakery. Even right now, sitting opposite you, eating the dinner you made. The third Wraith letter has really got them riled up. It talks about the 7th girl, Kate Moore. A petite, dark-haired, personal trainer whose social media was littered with photos of fun times with family and friends. She even had a little boy.

> *Hello fans!*
> *I see the police found Mina. Good for them. Although, always being late to the party must get old. Have no worries though, I've captured my next pet. Caged and waiting, she has spirit! All teeth and claws this one. Funny how we use knives and drugs to settle down animals, but when the person next to you misbehaves you give them excuses. Those online are giving me excuses for my ill behaviour. Curiosity and boredom are the fuel to my dark fires. Now, must dash, there's work to be done. I want to put some real effort into my next offering. Love me. Love me. Love me if you'll admit it.*
> *Yours in blood, The Righteous Wraith XX*

As much as it'll change the angle of my documentary, I'm glad they've caught him. This killer needs to pay for what he's done. The pain he's caused.

I'm so lost in research, I completely forget about lunch until a strong meaty odour hits my nose. Our neighbours, the Bronsons, are having a BBQ. I imagine an array of smoky delights lined up that I can easily tear into with my fingers, no plastic knife needed.

Mum tells me our families used to be friends. I babysat their youngest daughter Hayley. She's twenty-seven years old now. As I settle by my window, I spot her by their house. Almost a foot taller than me. Long dark auburn hair, perfect curves and a light tan liberally sprinkled with freckles. Catwalk bound. What strange friends we'd be. She, gorgeous, radiant and funny with an effortless smile. Me, looking like an overzealous extra from *The Dawn of the Dead*.

Grabbing something from her car, she must feel me watching her as she turns around. From this distance, I can't tell if she's smiling, but she does lift her hand to wave. Do people wave their hands up and down or side to side? I must hesitate too long, as she flips her hair across her shoulders, then disappears inside her house.

The Bronsons stopped talking to us after *Possession is Nine Tenths* came out. They'd heard rumours about my condition, but seeing it exposed on screen had truly hammered the final nail into the coffin. When I was released from St Alda's, I'd expected to come 'home' to a different house, that Mum and Dad would have run themselves out of town. They didn't. I thought they were brave and stubborn. Later, I found out that the house was in negative equity. I once heard Dad tell Mum they were *fiscally fucked*. It had made her laugh, but only for a moment.

Stomach rumbling, I plod downstairs. In the kitchen, Mum is dusting her antique crockery. She chunters to me about the neighbours and how annoying it is when Mr Davidson parks in our drive. I nod where appropriate. After an agonisingly long time she finally says, 'It's chicken nuggets for lunch.' As if to prove it, she opens the oven door to show me an array of reformed, bread-encrusted chicken bits sizzling on the shelf. Wait; did that nugget on the far-right look like Jesus? Is God sending me a sign?

'We're doing *The Crucible* for the first term back. I'm covering the witch trials that happened all over the world.' She sits at the table and I follow her.

Mum's trying hard to include me in things. I even once saw her referring to a list of 'approved topics' to talk with me about. Today though, she forgets the invisible boundaries of our dialogues and starts a rant about the Pendle Witch Trials.

'Do you know how many innocent women died?' she asks.

I want to answer, no one does, but the words don't come out quick enough as she answers her own question, 'Too many. What's worse is that they attacked herbalists, scientists, and girls with mental illness...'

At the words *mental illness*, she blushes and looks away.

I want to tell her I don't mind. I'm better now, as long as I keep up with my schedule of medication, appointments with Dr Taylor, and nightly prayers, I'm reasonably normal again: no seeing red, no violent thoughts, and certainly no unhinged demonic-style behaviour. However, I don't. It would open a doorway to discuss the past. I'm not ready for that yet, and I'm not sure she is either. Instead, I nod and take the tray out of the oven. On closer inspection, the nugget looks more like Elvis than Jesus – a sign from The King rather than God. As I manoeuvre six nuggets from the baking tray, I burn myself right where the damn fumsup cut me. Mum sees the red mark appearing on my hand. She takes two steps back and observes me from a safe distance, as if I were about to fit. I'm not going to lie and say that being hurt is pleasant – pain will always tingle the primitive side of my brain, just like anyone else – but before St Alda's, I would have let that feeling gather its red clouds and shroud my actions. Not today, though.

'I'm fine,' I say, sucking my finger. 'I should probably go back to work tomorrow.'

Breathing a sigh of relief, Mum sits down. 'How are you getting on there? Made any friends?'

'Not really,' I admit.

'People can take a while to warm up. You're new, remember?' she says.

'Two more people have joined after me and they get invited out.'

Sighing again, she says, 'Well, how about you do something nice for the office. You told me once they like cake. We could bake one together.'

The thought of spending hours in a hot kitchen making idle chit-chat with Mum makes me shudder. 'I don't want to put you out. I'll buy some cakes at the bakery.'

'Okay, I'll give you your bank card tomorrow.'

I chase nuggets around the plate with my plastic fork, dipping them in and out of tomato sauce until they are saturated red, and easier to hide amongst the tomatoes in my salad. Then, quickly, I slink upstairs before Mum can protest.

Back in my bedroom, I sit at my desk. There's still no message from Andy, and half my day off has already slipped away. I text him.

How are you? Do you want to meet today?

No reply.

Hours tick by while I refresh news sites for a story on the Wraith being in custody. Wait, Janet said she saw it on Facebook. I log on and find an anonymous post in the local chat group about the Wraith being caught. There are over a hundred comments already. Most are simply glad it's all over, others are angry and asking where the poster got their information from. The author hasn't replied to anyone, and when I click on their profile it's marked as private.

Knowing there are cakes downstairs, I sneak down and grab a fondant fancy – a lemon one. Dad is too busy drinking in the garden with Mr Davidson to notice and Mum is watching TV. Upstairs, I eat the cream top first, savouring the feel of it against my teeth. Cookie and I always ate cakes at St Alda's like this, making them last.

Still nothing from Andy, so I send a second text. Perhaps he's ignoring me because he doesn't need me now? After all, I was only useful when he was being accused, and if the killer is caught, he's de-facto innocent. No creepy, wet behind the ears documentarian needed to exonerate him.

I pop the rest of the Fancy into my mouth in one go; soft sponge with just a hint of tangy lemon. Mouth full, I lean over and check my phone for the fiftieth time today. Finally, I have a message from Andy.

Something has happened!

Chapter Seven

'My wife has left me!'

'I'm so sorry,' I say. His house, his job and now his wife is gone, it's like he's living a country and western song.

'She'd just had enough.' Andy's voice is low, like a kitten's purr. 'My boss was one thing, but this.'

His own wife thinks he's the Wraith? 'But she has to know you were telling the truth now the Wraith is in custody.'

Silence. Has he hung up? There's no dial tone, or is that not a thing anymore? 'Andy?'

'That was fake news,' he sighs.

'How do you know?'

'Because it was me who posted about it on Facebook. Happy now?'

Kind of. As awful as it sounds, if the Wraith is still at large, I still have a killer documentary on my hands proving Andy's innocence. But why would he do something so silly? 'Why?' I ask.

Andy huffs on the receiver. 'I didn't do it to be malicious; I was just tired of all the shit-slinging. In fact, you actually gave me the idea at Dr Taylor's.'

I did? Thinking back, I reply, 'Not sure I said to tell everyone he'd been caught.'

Ignoring me, he continues, 'Thought I'd at least get a few days of respite if everyone thought he was in prison.'

Even I think it was a dumb plan. Then again, I've never been accused of being a serial killer. 'We should do that interview. I can even speak to the police – get that you were interviewed then released on record.' I grab a pen and my notebook. 'Who was your contact?'

'Don't remember.'

'What? Surely you've got their details. Was it DCI Campbell?'

'Look, I need to go for a walk, clear my head. I'll text you an address and time for the interview. Keep it weird.' He then hangs up.

Keep it weird? What does that mean? I replay our conversation over in my mind. Surely, he knows the names of the officers running the case, or at least has the name of the one who waved their truncheon over him like a fairy godmother and declared him innocent of all charges.

And his wife left him, the woman who knows him better than anyone. Who stood in front of God and took vows to honour and cherish him forever. If she doesn't believe in his innocence, could Andy really be the Wraith?

–

Being in my bedroom for most of the day, the heat has built, so much so I feel like a chicken nugget in an oven. After a cold shower I check my phone: nothing further from Andy.

Pink pill swallowed. Blinds pulled. Fan on.

Kneeling, I say, 'Dear Lord, I hope being omnipotent isn't too taxing, but I really need to ask, is Andy the Wraith? You'd tell me, right? I mean, you wouldn't set me on this path to try to exonerate a guilty man. I'd end up the laughingstock of the documentary community. Perhaps you can give me a sign he's innocent, and that I'm doing the right thing; something more than a chicken nugget Elvis. Do remember to help keep me normal. I might not be considered eligible to live out here in the real world if I falter. Not sure why I'm explaining this to you, after all, you see and hear everything. God bless Cookie, Father Jacob, Mum and Dad. Amen.'

With the taste of the pink pill still in my mouth, I lie down on my bed.

Lucifer is barking. The neighbours have left him alone in the garden, again.

Hours pass. My brain wriggles and writhes in my skull, twisted with dark thoughts stickier than my skin. Getting up, I pull the blind back up, letting in both the light from the streetlamps and the summer heat. Being alone and feeling alone are two very different things. Behind a wall sleep Mum and Dad. Father Jacob is a call away, but reaching out shows weakness and I need to be strong to be free. I wish I could call Craig, but his brother whisked him away so quickly, we didn't have time to say goodbye, let alone exchange contact details.

Back in bed, I spot the faint outline of my camera on the desk mocking me. Could Andy be lying to me? Dr Taylor once told me I was smart, just not street-smart because of my time in the home. Necessary life lessons passed me by. Can I really trust my own judgement?

–

Three more prayers, two barking performances by Lucifer, and one hour of sleep later it's morning and I'm haunting the breakfast table. I can't stand cornflakes. Using my plastic spoon, I push the slop around in the bowl until it becomes soup-like, then I place the dish in the sink.

'Feeling better?' Dad asks.

'A little sleepy.'

'These hot nights are making us all cranky. Could have sworn I heard someone outside in the garden last night. You didn't get up, did you?'

'No,' I say.

Shaking his head, Dad downs his coffee.

'You'll be late for work, get a wriggle on.' Mum hands Dad a lunch box.

'Are you at school today?' I ask.

'Yeah, got roped into a summer catch-up class. See you later.' They kiss and he disappears out the front door.

'Well, I think I might ride the bus with you today,' Mum says to me.

God no. 'Why?'

'Well, you're going to find out anyway.'

'Find out what?'

'That killer struck again last night.'

'Who'd he take?'

'I don't remember, it was on the local radio.'

I rip my laptop from my bag and log on. I search 'Righteous Wraith' and up pops the latest story... Dara O'Connor was last seen at one in the morning on the street outside her home. There's a photo. She's a pre-school teacher who ran marathons for animal charities; long blonde curly hair, just like a princess. Only a little younger than me, but her eyes are not as dark as mine; instead they are vivid blue, full of life.

'I'm safe to ride the bus alone. The Wraith only takes one girl at a time. It's his MO.' I smile at Mum.

'I'm not sure how I feel about you knowing such horrible things.' Mum closes my laptop lid. 'Your dad says you're working on a documentary. It's not on this killer, is it?'

Technically, it's on Andy now. 'I'm just interested in local news.'

'All right then.' She leans across me to put my lunch into my backpack. My hand shoots out and intercepts it before she can interfere with the private innards of my bag. The sandwich baggie is heavy; I dread to think what congealed filling is lurking between those two slices of bread.

–

The Number 3 is buzzing with gossip and worry. You can hear and feel it, like a swarm of wasps. Eavesdropping is impolite, but sometimes it's the only social interaction I get in a day that doesn't come from doctors or my parents, so I close my eyes and listen. Girls talk about their horror at being potential victims. Men discuss the incompetence of the police. Some, with small voices, talk about how they can relax until Dara turns up, sans eyes.

Poor Dara. Before I can stop myself, my mind conjures the dark image of her abduction. The way the shadows of her street, somewhere she should have been safe, twist into a sinister figure. A hideous creature that stalked her and… wait. Dara begins with D and her abduction sounds a lot like Donald's clichéd screenplay, written days before she was taken. Could it… no. As evidence goes it's flaky; worse than the absurd theories Wraith Finders put forward about Andy. And nowhere near enough for the police to take seriously. However, Donald did have the initial of her name right, and her description spot on. Could it simply be coincidence? His script was lacklustre, but in hindsight oddly prophetic; the Wraith must stalk victims. Get their routines down. Figure out the right time and place when they fall off the social radar long enough to be spirited away. Could Donald be the Wraith?

We pull up to the stop before the office and I reluctantly get out. I walk to the bakery and buy two large cakes, a virtuously creamy Victoria sponge and a heavenly lemon drizzle. They're heavy and awkward, but somehow the scent of sugar spurs me on to walk faster. By the grace of God I reach the office without dropping or sweating on them.

No one is here yet, so for the moment, I'm alone.

Placing the cakes on a spare desk, I grab two knives and some plates. Before I realise what I'm doing, one of the knives is in my hand hovering over the Victoria sponge. I shouldn't take a slice before everyone sees them in their glorious wholeness, it would be uncouth, but I can't seem to drop the knife. Marvelling at the cool heft of the steel in my palm I stare at my reflection in the blade. Is this what killers feel when they have their victim splayed out before them? An undeniable sensation of desire mixed with the forbidden? Before I can stop it, the tip of the knife dances towards the powdered sugar top... The office door opens. Quickly, I place the weapon down and scuttle to my desk. I watch as my co-workers come in and spot the sugary treats. As they creep up to the table, I hear whispers. They need an invitation. I decide to send an email to all staff. I look back through my own and find one Corinne sent out for her birthday. I copy and paste it, substituting birthday for 'because it's Friday'. Unlike the flurry of witty messages *replied all* to Corinne, no one responds to my email. Gratitude must come after they eat.

There's an oddly sombre feeling at work. Stephanie flutters about the office like a starved hummingbird, and Corinne keeps looking over at me. Perhaps she is waiting for the perfect time to have a slice of cake?

Thirty invoices processed and my work is done. It's half eleven and I have the rest of the day to look busy.

'Tea?'

Corinne is doing a round. Her eyes land on everyone but me. I watch as she gathers the mugs and takes them into the kitchen.

Thirsty, I get up and follow her. She jumps when I suddenly appear in the doorway. Am I that frightening?

'What are you doing in here?' Corinne asks.

Since I am in the kitchen, the question is redundant. Is she trying to make conversation? 'Just want a cuppa with my cake,' I say and wink. We're bonding, this is good. Mum was right about the cakes.

'Um, don't you have work to do?'

She's concerned about my workload. That's sweet. 'I've done the invoices for today.'

Stopping mid-pour of the kettle, Corinne stares at me. 'You've what?'

Wait, I shouldn't have admitted how quick I am. I don't want to appear big-headed. 'I can help you with yours, if you like?' There, everyone likes it when people offer help... but Corinne's face looks as if I slapped it. I didn't, did I? No, there wasn't even a spot of red in my vision.

'I've been here for six years, I don't need *your* help, weirdo.' And with that she grabs the tea tray and barges past me.

After sitting back at my desk, I watch as Corinne pulls her swivel chair across to sit with Stephanie. They whisper and side-glance my way. After a few minutes, both disappear and I'm left wondering what I said that was so wrong.

Thirty minutes later, I receive an all-office email. A huge batch of important invoices went out wrong. I bet that was what Stephanie did that got her calling in sick. She must feel awful. Her unicorn mug is now sitting with a cold cup of tea on her desk. I should make her a new one, so she can have it with a slice of cake. It might make her feel better. Everyone makes mistakes. But, as I rise to fetch the mug, I notice another email sitting top of my inbox, just addressed to me. It's from Mr Lake.

Come to my office now!

Chapter Eight

'I'm disappointed, Dee,' he says. 'It seems I trusted you before you'd earned it.'

Corinne and Stephanie are in his office too, both looking squarely at me.

He's found out I've been Googling on work time. I try to say sorry, but he pulls out a stack of papers first.

'A few days ago, our top client, Shiva Retail, had all their month's invoices marked as zero, so their clients think there's nothing to pay that month. They have potentially lost thousands of pounds. Now, when Dr Taylor asked us to take you on, I waivered at how well you would cope with the pressures of accountancy work, but this is unacceptable. If we lose Shiva, we could go under.'

Peering at the invoices, I can see they're not mine. 'I didn't do these,' I say.

Corinne huffs. 'We thought you'd try to blame the Other Dee.'

'What Other Dee?' I ask. What the hell are they talking about?

'The demon,' Stephanie spits. 'We all know about you. How do you think it makes us feel to be working with a crazy person?'

'But I'm normal, now,' I say.

'I'll have none of your lip. HR has said you need to go on gardening leave while we sort out this mess.' Mr

Lake pulls out a piece of paper from beneath the incorrect invoices. 'Sign this.'

Red creeps into my vision. Losing my temper is the worst thing I can do. But I am innocent, and this job was part of my release conditions. 'Mr Lake, I sent out all *my* invoices correctly. I didn't touch Shiva's file.' I look over at Stephanie, waiting for her to admit her mistake.

'Corinne?' asks Mr Lake.

'I saw Dee working on them before she took those days off.' She turns to me, 'You should have just said something sooner so we could have corrected it.'

'But you can see who logged into which account,' I say.

'Me and Corinne both trained you when you got here. You saw both our log-in details,' Stephanie counters, then looks to Corinne for confirmation.

'That's right. I know we should have been more secure with our details, Mr Lake, but...'

'This is not your fault. We're like a family here. We trust one another,' he says.

'Why would I even do it?' I all but wail.

'It's obvious you're not happy here.' Corinne says off hand.

Stephanie shrugs. 'Yeah, it's not like you really fit in.'

There's no logic in their argument, but the more I try to explain it wasn't my mistake, the madder Mr Lake becomes. Eventually, to stop the rising tension in my bones, I sign his paper work saying I'll go on gardening leave. I hate gardening. Dad has been making me do it since I moved back in. But at least I'm not fired. One last time, I part my lips to protest, but the words cling to my teeth like toffee.

Mr Lake, along with two teen male apprentices, then escorts me off the premises.

I didn't even get a slice of my cake.

–

Waiting for the Number 3, I roll around today's events in my mind as if they were cotton candy on a stick. Each layer more twisted and peppered with sour air than the last. It shouldn't surprise me that I've been accused of something I didn't do. Look at what happened with the little girl in Good Tree Park. I probably saved her life. Did I get any thanks? No. Her mum acted as if I was a monster who crawled up from the sewers intent on snatching the fruit of her loins.

Deciding not to go home and explain the day's events to Mum and Dad, I abandon the Number 3 bus route and walk into the outskirts of town for the Number 5. It's late, but eventually trundles up. Its windows do not open, so the heat is oven-like in its intensity. I imagine my internal organs spitting, growing grey, and shrivelling as they cook. Passengers complain loudly about the weather, but I bet these are the same people who complain about the cold in winter. No one is ever happy. My seat is worn with holes, and large parts are threadbare. I can see sponge padding poking through. It's as if the seat's porous yellow soul is showing. Manoeuvring my finger into the gap, I touch the padding: it is yielding, soft, and strangely moist.

'What are you doing?' asks a quadruple-chinned woman in a sweaty sundress.

I want to tell her to mind her own business, but instead admit, 'Wondered what it felt like.'

'Weirdo,' she whispers, then turns away. She asked the question, I just told the truth; so who's the real weirdo?

There's a lovely little farm with a quiet café on the road out of town. It's a fair walk from the bus stop, but I need to figure out what to do with my documentary, and this place has free Wi-Fi.

Fortunately, I still have my bank card, so I sit down and order a strawberry milkshake, then settle in with my laptop. For a moment, I stare at the screen, my thoughts locked in battle. Could Donald be the Wraith? No, I'm just jumping to conclusions, like Mr Lake did to me today. I didn't send out those Shiva invoices, I know I didn't.

Making decisions is hard; for so long, they were taken out of my hands. St Alda's decided when and what I ate. What time I went to bed. What I wore and who I could see. It's done deliberately, of course. Freeing your mind from making small decisions allows for more mental bandwidth to deal with bigger issues. Problem is, once those decisions become yours again, it's like being given a hoard of pets you neither understand nor want but still need to look after. Andy, for all his randomness, needs help. If we'd have met at St Alda's, I would have offered my friendship. Out here, in the normal world, you offer help first, and a documentary would be good for us both. That is, if he's not the Wraith.

Has God given me a sign about Andy's innocence? Not that I saw, but maybe I wasn't looking in the right place. I text Father Jacob asking about what signs can look like – not every godly communication can be a burning bush or a heavenly herald. He comes back quoting a few vague Bible passages. As I go to thank him, I receive a text. Andy. He apologises for his odd telephone call; his wife leaving was just the last straw. Does he want me to say something? Text? Call? He's not asking about the interview. Confused, I check Wraith Finders and find a discussion about Dara. Where Andy was when he took her, how he did it without anyone seeing and how he's been getting away with being the Wraith and tricking the police. There's even a photo from Rabbits Foot showing Andy loitering on Dara's street dated a few days before her abduction; lots of conjecture and not much evidence. Andy must feel terrible. I should call him. After the first ring rips through my ear, I push my mobile into the middle of the table and watch for the screen to show when he answers. It takes seven rings.

'Are you okay?' I ask.

He huffs. 'No, this is a nightmare. I can't even get my things from the flat. I'm left wearing stuff from storage.'

'Where are you living?'

'I moved back into my parents' old house on the outskirts of town. The only reason I wasn't living here before was for my job. Course, that's not a problem now.'

I know all about having to move back home. 'I'm sorry.'

'Sorry doesn't help me.'

'I *do* want to help. Let's get started on the documentary and conduct the interview today.'

'I'm not in the mood.'

Not in the mood to give his side of events? How can I help Andy when he doesn't want to help himself? 'I understand, but you should get your story out there.'

'Okay, we'll sort it out later. I'm too busy now, I have to get back to torturing Dara.' He hangs up.

Did I hear him right? I don't have much of a sense of humour, but that must have been a joke; a joke in bad taste, but a joke none the less.

As I nurse the last of the milkshake, my thoughts drift to the Wraith's newest girl. Can she be saved?

–

My standing appointment with Dr Taylor is today. I get there early and stop off at St Alda's to see Cookie, but Coal tells me my friend isn't allowed any visitors today. Asking why gets me nowhere. And as I'm my friend's only visitor, it feels a little personal.

Trudging back outside, and with time on my hands, I check if Cookie told me the truth about the hole. I follow the fence around the back of the estate, looking for the escape hatch. After twenty minutes of lifting branches and manhandling foliage, I find it hidden by a bush that I distinctively remember birthing red berries in winter. Without knowing it was there, I'd have never spotted it, so neither would the hospital staff. I crawl through and find myself, once again, on St Alda's estate.

Change happens whether you want it to or not, and when I scan the grounds and spot the old arts building, I feel a cold twinge. Cookie said they'll tear it down soon. Another piece of my past is being eradicated, and for what? It wasn't its fault builders cut corners and filled it with asbestos. It didn't choose to have poison running through its bricks.

Not knowing when I'll get another chance to say goodbye, I head over.

Part of me assumes it'll be locked. But it's not. There is tape over the doors declaring health warnings, but the doors open. Although the sun is still beating on the world outside, it's dark inside the building. All the windows are covered with newspapers; it has a thousand stories blocking out the sunlight. I flick the light switch and nothing happens. It has been disconnected from the grid, not surprisingly. I turn my phone into a torch. Calling it creepy does not do the place justice. Shadows seem to dart about, avoiding my light. This isn't at all what I remembered.

To the left of the main corridor is the crafts room. I walk inside. There's a smell of piss and damp. With deadly asbestos in the walls and ceiling, it's the very definition of a death-trap. Goosebumps prickle my skin, and for the first time since the start of this heatwave, I feel cold. How could this building have become like this in such a short amount of time? Before, I made Christmas cards in this space with glitter. Now it's an expanse of dirty floors, chairs with broken limbs, and abandoned metal beds, seemingly contorted by force rather than time.

There's a bed turned over in the corner, its leather restraints dripping down its twisted limbs. I step closer. A mattress is attached to it, covered in plastic. It smells damp and artificial. I pull the bed upright and it sits before me like a great grey dog, waiting. It's been years since I sat on a bed like this. The staff only used restraints in the beginning, and only at night for my own good. Violent nightmares of my so-called exorcism would often throw me to the floor as I slept. My wrists are thinner than the average woman's, so they had to make extra holes in the straps to secure me, saving me from broken bones. This bed has no extra holes. I'd easily be able to slip from this one, if I didn't want to be controlled. Before I know what I'm doing, I'm climbing onto the mattress, closing my eyes and willing myself back to when I lived here, neighbours with Craig, Tippy, and Cookie. We'd chat for hours. Play board games, each game three times to appease

Craig's love of the number. We would then eat a lovely three-course dinner; Tippy would always give me her dessert. Friends who have mental health afflictions tend to understand one another. Empathy grows with personal experience and in truth, all we had were each other. How easy it would be to give in and be committed back… No. Swinging my legs around, I shimmy off the bed with a little jump and continue my walk down crooked memory lane. Only a few steps over I spot a dark stain on the floor in the corner. Above it, a rusted pipe sticks out like a jutting bone. I can't remember when I had my last tetanus shot, so I walk by giving it a wide berth.

Across from the craft space are the meditation room and a small office. I try the office door. Locked. I wander into the meditation room. I used to love this space. It had soft purple walls and seemingly hundreds of beanbags and cushions. There was an oil heater in the corner that was used in the winter and all the cupboards were crammed with soft blankets. The mindfulness lady would burn lavender oil, which gave off a sleepy, peaceful vibe. It's not like that now. The heater is gone and the cupboards are bare. In near darkness, the room is oppressive and stifling, like when you're made to close your eyes, but don't want to. All the soft furnishings are gone, but there are still speakers set up in the top of each corner of the room. Before, we had guided meditations through woods, the seaside, and the rainforest. Places I'd never been before; it was a pink pill sort of calm. But today the speakers are silent and I'm not anywhere lovely; instead I'm here, knowing a perfect part of my past can never be recaptured.

There's a big metal staircase that sits across from the entrance. Cookie told me once that by jumping on certain steps in a particular order you could reach a parallel world.

It used to worry my friend when I did it, as if one wrong move and I'd be lost.

Upstairs, to my right is the large art studio. It holds even more beds and, when I look in the cupboards, I discover all the paints and brushes are gone. To the left of the corridor is the supply room with more empty cupboards, but these still hold a secret: you can pull the backs aside and sneak through them into the kitchen's storage cupboards. Craig and I used to do this so we could watch the staff make scones. We were always noisy, so it was no secret we were there. Gifts of freshly-baked goodies were then deliberately left by the door for us. Together, we would devour some, then take the rest back to our friends. Even now, I can feel the warm raisins on my tongue.

I move one of the boards aside and step into the kitchen; this is where the laundry chute sits. Peering down the yawning hole I remember how brave I was when we found it. I slid down first.

There's a noise. Gruff voices of builders, probably surveying the place ready to tear it down. Not wanting to be caught, I quickly say goodbye to my past, and I scamper back outside. Once there, I've never been so grateful for the sun. It smoothes out my goose bumps, warming me like a blanket.

Dr Taylor's street backs onto the grounds – I can even see her house from where I stand now. Yet annoyingly, as the hole is further down, I have to walk up and around the gate to reach it. There never seems to be a straight path to where you want to go.

Fully meaning to tell Dr Taylor about the fence, I march up to her door. As I raise my hand to knock, I hesitate. The hole alone is not proof that Cookie is escaping for nightly jaunts. My friend would have to get out of the building first and, with the airlock doors, he'd need a staff member to allow him access, something I highly doubt would happen. Bringing it up now seems pointless, and would maybe even get me into trouble for visiting the arts building one final time. Best not to say anything.

Before going into the office, I down a few cups of water from the cooler. The milkshake isn't sitting well. I imagine it curdling in my stomach, churned into stinky pink lumps by the heat…

'Are you feeling better?' she asks.

I turn at her voice, then nod. Not being able to speak with Cookie is still worrying me, so I ask, 'Is Cookie okay?'

Dr Taylor shifts in her chair. 'No. He's not.'

Chapter Nine

'What's happened?'

'Calm down, Dee.' Dr Taylor puts her hands up. 'He said some disturbing things to a nurse.'

'What things?'

'I can't discuss another patient with you. You know this.'

Thinking back to my last visit, I say, 'My friend is lonely without me.'

'Saying goodbye to someone is hard in any situation, but when they get better and leave, it's even harder. Remember what it was like when Craig left?'

Craig didn't want to go. Suffering from obsessive compulsive disorder, leaving somewhere he knew and felt safe was painful for him. Regardless of how much 'better' his brother claimed he was.

'Out of curiosity, what would you have spoken to him about today?' she asks.

I wanted to talk to him about the invoices at work, and how I feel lost and out of my depth with Andy, trying to help someone who doesn't seem to want my help and maybe doesn't even deserve it, but I can't say any of this to her. Confidentiality or not, you only get to live free if you're doing it right. 'Just wanted to talk about the documentary.'

'Lovely. What have you got so far?'

I open my mouth, but nothing comes out. In truth, I've no clue what I have. A vague idea, a man accused who could be guilty, an eerily written hack screenplay; it all adds up to a mess of diddly squat. Most of which my doctor can't even discuss with me as her confidentiality would extend to Andy, too. I close my mouth.

Dr Taylor smiles. 'Perhaps we can talk about it in another session? How are you sleeping?'

'It's hard in this weather. And St Alda's has air conditioning. I only have a fan at home.'

After writing a note, she nods. 'Understandable. But this heat won't last forever, nothing does.'

What does that mean? Squirming in my seat, I feel the need to pee, so nod along to make the session end as quickly as possible. Conversations blend. Minutes last for hours. I wonder what Cookie said? If I should still interview Andy? And how long can I maintain bladder control before I pee myself?

'That's great. I'll book an appointment.'

Did I just agree to something? 'Pardon?'

'The floatation tank. I'll book it for you, and email over the details.'

I should ask her what a floatation tank is, but that would prove I hadn't been listening. It sounds pleasant enough, so the agreement sinks to the bottom of my thoughts.

As Dr Taylor rustles in her drawer for the wisdom book, I notice her vase of lavender now displays red roses nestled amongst the purple stems. Catching me staring, she blushes. In all the years I've known my doctor, I've never seen this reaction. Did a loved one give her those flowers? It's weird to think of my doctor like that. That she has a life beyond these walls.

'Just as an aside,' she says, 'how's your social life coming along, Dee?'

'I'm trying to make friends,' I say. 'I go to that writers' group. I saw my neighbour, Hayley.'

'The girl you used to babysit for?'

I nod.

'It's good to be part of the world.' Her gaze drifts to the flowers on her desk, and a soft look of longing flashes over her features. 'Have you thought about dating, now you have things under control?'

Blushing, I shake my head. The key years I should have been looking out for 'the one' that everyone talks about were spent living a half-life in St Alda's.

'You should consider it. When you find someone who makes your heart skip a beat, someone you'll do anything for, well, that's what life's all about.'

Romance isn't something we've ever talked about, and quite frankly having my heart skip a beat sounds painful. I must look confused as she says, 'Just think on it. We can always discuss it again.'

–

The Number 3 is late, but there are the usual faces on it; it relaxes me to see them. I'd like nothing more than to talk to one of them about what happened today at work, to ask why Corinne and Stephanie singled me out to take the blame for something I didn't do, but that would be weird, weirder than being caught touching seat innards. People on the bus don't know me. I don't know them. Sudden regret at not texting Mum about work simmers in my stomach. Would she march into Lake Accounting and demand they apologise to me? Or would she take their side, assuming I'm not good at my job, or even competent enough with maths to know the difference between a number and zero? Best not take the chance. Surely the truth will come out – it always does, right?

At dinner, Mum and Dad are quiet, so I excuse myself early to secretly work on *Creating a Wraith*; no, that's another awful title.

Taking my pink pill, I listen to Lucifer bark while I stand in front of the fan. Before climbing into bed, I pull down the blind. Slipping to the floor, I say, 'Dear Lord, me again. I hope you're doing well. Can I ask you something? Could you please clear this whole thing up at work? Not to be a bother, but I'm also still waiting on that sign about my documentary. Andy's not being particularly useful. There's something else too.' I lift my hands to whisper behind them. 'I can't help but think Donald could be' – I gulp – 'inspiring himself? Is he the Wraith? And let's not forget another girl has been taken. Can you help Dara? Sorry, you would tell me if I were asking too much of you?'

Silence.

'Bless Mum, Dad, Craig wherever he is, and especially Cookie. Amen.'

–

In the morning, I find a mass of new blogs, websites, and social media groups about Dara's disappearance have sprung up like daisies from a grave. Megan – the 1st girl Erica's little sister – not wanting to miss a chance to be noticed, is quoted on most of them. There's even a link to a new vlog. I click on it and see her childish face, slightly grotesque with its adult mask of make-up, filling up the screen.

'Hey there, lambs. It's me Megan here. Holla!' She whoops a few times like a primate. 'Serious note, guys.' Looking into the camera, still at the right angle to look pretty, she continues. 'A new, close friend advised me to put out a plea directly to the Righteous Wraith, so here goes. Let Dara go. Stop being a bully and rethink your choices…'

Holy crap! What is she doing? Even I know it's dumb to publicly address a serial killer – he's not some classroom bully, he's a full-blown torture killer of the most dangerous kind, and she's… what? Calling him out for bad behaviour? Why are her parents letting her do this? Who the hell is this 'close friend'? There are already a hundred comments on the video, most from kids with generic words of encouragement and some weirdos with various RIP messages for Erica, the other girls, Dara and… Megan herself. Unable to look at it any longer, I click off. Her parents should be ashamed for letting their naïve daughter do this. The Wraith is all about publicity and clearly goes online for his letters… How could they… how… Red dances before my eyes.

'Six, five, four, three, two, one,' I count.

Reaction averted, I take a deep breath, then turn my attention back to my documentary. The course said you need a storyboard before you start filming. You can't go off willy-nilly pointing a camera in everyone's faces. After learning this, I hated Louisa even more – she'd planned everything before turning up at our door that day. I wonder what that scared teenage girl looked like in her storyboard picture; a frail creature held down on a stained mat. Even though time was of the essence to *save my soul*, everyone waited for her to set up the perfect scene in the family front room; after all, she had to get her angles, rather than her angels, right. In reality, it took three hours of incense, chanting, bells and being prodded with a cross before I started screaming. Most was edited out for dramatic effect. To this day, I don't know why *Possession is Nine Tenths* gained such notoriety. The truth was barely a garnish to Louisa's hideous meal of lies.

Before starting my storyboard, I log on to Facebook. Louisa has added an update.

> Hey, Tenthers, I've just been told I've won the prestigious Docu-Wow Award for my newest work Superstition, Society's Secret Power. I'm so excited and feel so loved!!!xoxo

Scrolling down the comments, I see sycophantic words vomited all over her timeline by her celebrity friends. God damn her! How is she living such a wonderfully charmed life after what she did to me? How in hell can that be fair? I take out my fumsup and roll it around in my fingers. 'Touch wood, Louisa Black will move away, far away to somewhere with no broadband.' Catching my finger on its stupid head, blood blooms across my fingertip, seeping into the lucky charm. I'll probably get tetanus. I throw the annoying thing across my bed and it falls with a slight thud against my wardrobe.

'You alright, Dee?' Dad calls from downstairs.

I thunder to the landing and yell, 'Why can't you all just leave me alone?'

Footsteps. Dad appears. 'Fancy going to the swimming pool this afternoon. Cool off?'

'It's not the weather.'

'What's happened?'

'Louisa won a Docu-Wow!' Under my breath I whisper, 'Six, five, four, three, two, one.'

Wrinkling his nose, he draws his mouth into a thin line across his face. 'In a way, you won it too, Dee. Without you, she'd have no career.'

'Rub it in, why don't you!' I stomp back into my room, slamming the door behind me.

Dropping to my knees, I grip my hands together. 'Dear Lord. What the hell? Louisa has won a Docu-Wow. How did you let this happen? I thought we were friends. Is she better at praying than me? Does no good deed go unpunished, and no bad deed go unrewarded? I'm trying to be better, I really am. Father Jacob tells me you're busy, but I deserve some divine intervention. Amen.'

The day creeps by. I start my documentary storyboard three times; each time, the whole thing looks tired and defeated, so I give up and instead reach out to subjects related to the case. I find family and friends of the victims online and pop them an email. It's still raw for them at the moment, and I understand I'm prying open an emotional wound, but this is how great documentaries get made. I make another plea to Vlad, telling him about my documentary with Andy and the Wraith Finders. I even email the DCI in charge of the case. Deep down, I know it's futile. I had people contact me through the years about *Possession*, and I never replied to any; maybe I should have.

Andy is my last message:

Ready when you are for the interview.

Later, more to check on me than feed me, Dad brings up a plate of cucumber and cream cheese sandwiches. I soldier through two quarters before I throw the remaining mess of moist white bread out of the window towards Lucifer's garden; it'll be a treat for him when he comes out for his barking session later.

I could really go for some cake – a sharp carrot cake singing with cinnamon and dripping in cream cheese icing, but I'd have to go downstairs to see if Mum bought any today, and I don't feel like doing that right now.

An hour drags by and my inbox remains hauntingly empty. It was silly to think anyone would get back to me. Who am I really? And they're probably all very busy right now.

After a cold shower, I feel better. Dad was right: I needed to cool down.

I take my pink pill and pull down my blackout blind. Maybe Dr Taylor is right too; I should buy some ear plugs and go on a dark retreat. Would God mind if I take a leaf off the Buddha's tree of knowledge?

Finally, as night draws in, I search online for news on Dara. Although she has not been found yet, the police assure Northants residents they are doing everything in their power to bring her home safe.

In my head, the Wraith is an evil shadow lurking on the edges of society, ready to pounce on stray innocents, but it's more realistic to think of him as a terrible person pretending to be something he's not to get close to his victims. DCI Campbell said, *for some reason, the victims went willingly*. I stare at a photo of Dara. Happy smile, mischievous eye-twinkle, and beautiful. What did she do that was so wrong?

My knees ache, so I climb into bed to say my prayers. 'Dear Lord, I'll keep this short. If you won't help me, can you at least help Dara? Bless Mum and Dad and Cookie. Amen.'

With my mind whirring, I curl into my black cotton sheets, which smell of last night's sweat, and close my eyes… Three knocks draw me from a dream. I squint at my mobile: 3.33 a.m.

'Yes?' I yell out.

No answer.

–

St Godfrey's is a large, old church that attracts Catholics from four estates. Canon Matthew is the new priest in charge. He's a tall, middle-aged man who rarely smiles. This Sunday morning, he stands robed and ready at the altar. An iPad sits before him, steadied on an ornate plinth. Throughout his preparation for the sermon, his glare systematically rests on each of the arriving congregation. When those eyes land on me, his nose wrinkles. He may be new to the region, but he still has my creepy number.

When the sermon begins, I feel as if people are watching me, so I move to stand beside Father Jacob. Being my friend, he accepts that I'm not technically a practising Catholic. When Louisa convinced Mum and Dad their daughter was possessed, he baptised me, but hasn't forced any further religious ceremonies. He's one of the few truly good people I've ever met. He helps others – whatever their religion, whatever their inclinations, whether they are possessed by a demon or not.

'And smite!' Canon Matthew shouts out dramatically, pointing to the sky, then to everyone in the pews, his finger lingering on me. 'The righteous will rise…' On closer inspection, our new canon looks a little worse for wear. There are marks on his arms, and a bandage wrapped mummy-style over his thumb. In comparison,

Father Jacob looks the same as he did the first day we met. Either he has the best face cream in the known universe, or God truly has blessed him. Today though, I notice lines drawn through his complexion. His worry for me is leaving its mark. Worry that started on the day we met outside this very church. The day *it* happened.

Dr Taylor told me I distance myself from my trauma. Every time I remember the accident it feels as if it happened to someone else; like I'm watching it on a screen... The girl, no more than twelve, looked both ways before crossing the road, just as she was taught. She had been to the local shops and was carrying chocolate ice cream in a thick plastic bag. Even though she had walked that same road all her life with a parent or friend, alone the world looked new and exciting. The bushes a brighter shade of green. The pavement more solid beneath her feet. The car heading towards her, shinier... faster. Suddenly, she was airborne, the full force only hitting her when she slammed back down to earth, broken, torn, and covered in blood. Pain settled into her flesh and bone, like a squatter. An engine revved and the car pulled away through an angry cloud of fumes, never to be seen again.

My ice cream is going to melt, she thought. A scream. Eyelids heavy, she looked up and saw a freestanding crucifix planted in front of the church. Jesus, in his own pain, stared down at her with pity. Victims together.

A hand took hers. 'Help is coming, just hold on.'

Tasting blood, she couldn't answer.

'I'm Father Jacob. Squeeze my hand if you can hear me.'

She tried to stand, but her limbs refused to do as they were told, as if they now belonged to someone else.

'Hold on, the ambulance is almost here.' Father Jacob bowed his head and prayed. Jesus heard him, he couldn't help it, he was right there watching. Whooping sirens arrived and strangers flooded in.

'A car hit her. I saw the whole thing.' Father Jacob let go of her hand and stood aside so, like Jesus, he could watch over her.

Strangers touched her. Bones ground together. Light birthed dancing red dots in her eyes, until her vision folded into darkness...

When I awoke, it took less than a day for my parents to pull aside the doctors and claim I wasn't acting like Dee anymore. My voice had changed, the words I used, the flashes of temper that before their cool-headed child would have shied away from, began to explode forth. *That's not our little girl*, they complained and perhaps it was easier to believe it the fault of a determined demon that had crawled into my soul rather than an avoidable crack in my skull. I was never given the luxury of making the decision myself.

Breaking my thoughts, Father Jacob nudges me. 'Let's sing today, eh?'

I nod and mouth lyrics of a hymn I don't understand. The church is brimming with good Catholics today – my voice, or lack thereof, will be concealed by the din.

Afterwards, Canon Matthew freely offers the blood and flesh of Christ to a line of ravenous people. The whole thing reeks of cannibalism.

Father Jacob asks, 'Will you take Communion?'

'No thanks,' I say, looking around, expecting all eyes to be on me.

Father Jacob rises, receives his sacrament, and then walks to the back of the church to sit with me again. I try to smile, but it's not a happy smile, it's a smile to tell him I'm grateful he asked. People haven't asked me to participate in anything for a while now. Maybe I should have let Canon Matthew feed me a dry, tasteless morsel and then swallowed the sticky port that makes me light-headed. Appearing normal might help. Dr Taylor says, 'fake it till you make it', which, now I think about it, seems neither right nor fair.

Canon Matthew is wrapping it up. Looking at the crowds of inadequately fed and watered people, he gives his final thought, 'Seek first his kingdom and his right-eousness, and all these things will be given to you as well,' he claims, with a forceful hand gesture.

Father Jacob raises an eyebrow, then turns to me. 'Has something happened you want to talk about?'

Does he know about work? No, that's silly. Why would Mr Lake contact my priest about incorrect invoices? I want to brush his question off, but I can't. 'What have you heard?'

'Nothing. I can just sense something's wrong. Is it the man from the park? I told Teresa about it; she says there haven't been any recent reports of stranger child abduc-tions, or attempted ones.'

'That's good,' I mutter.

Offhand, he adds, 'Are you settling into *things* okay? Keeping a lid on that…'

'Demon?'

'…temper, cheeky.' He laughs.

'Things are going to be different now I'm not so confined. And life for normal people can still be taxing, right?' I look around me as I say it. Those in the church must all have issues too. Some might feel low, like Tippy. Some might even get a little obsessive over aspects of their life, like Craig… but of course, none of them have had a complete change of personality after a blow to the head. 'Doesn't everyone have problems?'

My answer doesn't come, as Canon Matthew beckons Father Jacob away.

I linger for a moment. Should I have told Father Jacob about work? Maybe talked about my Wraith documentary? I could call it *Wraith Wars*! No, that's far too dramatic and there would need to be more than one wraith for them to declare war against one another.

Dara.

Although a stranger, she slips into my thoughts again and I wonder if she's still alive. She hasn't got long left, if any time at all. I'm in the right place to make a difference. My palms come together and I close my eyes. 'Dear Lord, sorry to bother you at home on a Sunday, but I need your help. Like I mentioned before, Dara is in a horrible situation. Can you please save her? Amen.'

Turning to leave, I wave at Father Jacob, who is now flanked by an elderly couple. He waves back, then unsuccessfully tries to extricate himself from the pensioner huddle. Quickly, I escape before he can.

In the oppressive heat, I walk towards the bus stop. Waiting are two old women in their Sunday best. Sun hats, pearls and wearing pastel colours reminiscent of day-old vomit. They chatter about the weather. Hottest month they've ever known, apparently. Then they slip into the conversation they really want to have – about the Righteous Wraith. I edge closer to listen.

'Well, I think that Dara's had her chips. It's been three days,' says Yellow Pastel.

'He'll be onto number eleven soon enough,' Pink Pastel adds.

'Did you read in the paper about how he left that poor Lisa Bryan?'

Pink Pastel sighs and scratches her lower back, her wrinkled fingers raking towards her bum. 'Yes, poor thing.'

'I wonder what he's done with Dara.' Yellow Pastel adjusts her hat. 'Left her like spoiled meat out in the sun?'

'Where though?'

'Based on all the others, I reckon it'll be somewhere with trees, somewhere public, not too busy, but where it's bound to be discovered quickly!' She finishes her sentence with an excited shrug.

The bus comes and, for some unfathomable reason, I don't climb on. I watch as Pink and Yellow Pastels, framed by the streaky bus window, get comfortable in their seats ready to continue their morbid discussion.

Has it been three days? Damn, they're right, it has. And if the Wraith is on schedule, then my prayers were wasted. Dara is already dead. Her body is out there somewhere waiting to be found. Finding things is my speciality, but I'm not sure TV remotes and chargers are in the same league as corpses. Dr Taylor says experimenting can lead to gaining insight. If I were to find Dara, it would be good for my documentary. It might also prompt Andy to get back to me; maybe even some of the other people I contacted, too. I can do this.

I text Mum that I'm meeting a friend after church, then catch the Number 6 bus. It's the one that feels right. As we enter Maple Industrial Estate, I rise and make my way to the front of the bus.

'Your stop?' asks the driver, his eyes on the button for the bell, rather than me.

'Yes please.' I cover the bell with my palm, but don't push it.

As the bus slows, I lose my footing and my backpack flies out, almost striking a man on the seat behind me. 'Sorry,' I say, but he still gives me a dirty look.

I'm the only one to get off at this stop, which makes me even more confident about my hunch.

I'm going to find Dara's body.

Chapter Ten

I'm always right about where lost objects hide. It's that righteous feeling that still has me wandering around an industrial estate four hours later. If the killer holds true to his MO, then Dara's body has been discarded. And I'm sure it's somewhere here. Office buildings and factories surround the Maple Industrial Estate; it's a rabbit warren of companies, warehouses, and odd patches of withered nature. It's beneath a particularly sickly tree that I think I'll find Dara's corpse – waiting just for me.

While I'm here, I start filming scenery shots for the documentary; the kind I can narrate over when I'm not interviewing a subject. My new camera is heavier than I thought it would be. I pan around the estate, catching glimpses of weekend factory workers on late shifts smoking pot on their breaks.

Technically it's early evening, but the sun still beats down like a bully. There's little shade here, so it's hard for me to capture the right mood for the shots. When tackling subject matter as dark as serial killers and dead women, the ambience needs to be sombre grey, not cheery yellow. Although bright, it's dusty and the air smells like a cock-tail of chip-shop fat, chocolate biscuits and petrol fumes. Then there's the noise. Men shouting, trucks screeching, music escaping the rolled-down windows of idling cars, rippling metal shutters, and the oddly consistent sound of traffic coming from the main road, all add up to a cacophony of chaos. The fourth girl, Sandi Morrow, was found by a factory, though not in this estate. She was tall and muscular from playing semi-professional netball, and it was those long limbs that got her spotted behind an abandoned car, its metal body carved up by sordid graffiti.

Giving up on filming, I stow my camera and explore the estate. I make a mental note of the business names as I lumber past: Johnson's Builders, Lester Logistics, Crater Chemicals, Dollop Foods, and Industrial Gas Ltd. There's a boarded-up factory at the far end, a casualty of the last recession. As I walk towards it, I see its gates are locked with a thick chain and padlock. Chicken wire wraps around it, making it appear as a dangerous metal present. It would be the perfect place to dump a body. The signage outside says it was once a cake factory called Doolittle's Treats. I imagine beautiful slices of all my favourite sugary wonderfulness trundling down a conveyor belt. It must have smelt divine. If only it were still open, I could have worked here. I'm sure they would have let their workers eat as much cake as they liked.

Suddenly a shape moves behind the metal fence. Dark and fast. I position myself so I can spy through the chicken wire. As I do, the metal violently vibrates, making me stagger backwards.

My eyes focus. A Dobermann is pressing itself against the fence to reach me. It's not barking; instead, its tail is wagging.

'Who are you?' I ask the dog.

Through the fence, I lift its ID tag. 'Daegon. That's a pretty name.' As I go to move my hand, he quickly turns his head to lick my fingers. He must be so lonely. No one to look after him, play with him, or even acknowledge he exists. Daegon's only job is to protect a boarded-up factory that no one in their right mind would break into. And how torturous for him to smell the ghosts of all those tasty cakes. Guard dogs probably have a very basic diet, poor thing. Looking along the fence, I spot a bigger gap further down; reminding me of Cookie's hole in the fence. I think every fence should have a hidden gap. Whether it's keeping something out or keeping something in, it's not fair to cage all hope. I head towards it and find I can reach both arms through. The dog follows me and soon I'm tickling his ears and getting slobber up my wrists.

'Well, you're a lovely boy. I don't suppose you've seen anything suspicious?'

Daegon snuffles my hand, oblivious that I'm leaning so far through the hole I'm actually trespassing on his territory.

After another hour hanging around Maple Industrial Estate, I realise the only suspicious thing here is me. Perhaps the killer was going to dump the body, then saw how busy it was and changed his mind. Annoying – I've never been wrong before about the location of a lost object. Craig used to joke I could find the Holy Grail if I set my mind to it. Damn it, I wanted to get a shot of me finding the body, then call the police. It would be the selling point for *The Northants' Wraith*; Jesus, that's a boring title.

As I turn to go, I take one last look around – in films, this is usually when the protagonist finds something. Nope, this place is just as annoyingly empty of corpses as when I arrived.

'Hey, what are you doing?'

I look over to see a man in blue overalls, his sleeves and trousers rolled up to expose hairy, reddening limbs.

'I was just leaving.' I yell, then weave between the factory buildings, heading for the main road.

Maple Industrial Estate is larger than I thought it was and, as I trudge towards the bus stop, I notice another cluster of small warehouses. Flies are everywhere. I hear them buzzing around my ears, their spindly legs trying to touch my skin. Batting them away, I catch a whiff of something sweet.

Something here is very wrong.

Chapter Eleven

She *is* here. The 10th girl Dara. Behind a corner of a building, I spot a wisp of blonde hair trailing through the grass. Simultaneously, I want to look, but also don't want the image of what I see to be forever in my brain; there's enough horror in there already. I take out my mobile and call the non-emergency police number. The operator notes the details with all the enthusiasm of a depressed teenager. His voice so monotone, I wonder if he's heard me, so repeat the location of the body, then hang up without giving my details. Clearly, discarded corpses are not as special as they once used to be in Northampton-shire.

As I wait for the police, I play with my camera. And before I know what my feet are doing, I'm edging toward the flies, then slowly around the corner of the building. Scanning the grass, I catch sight of a bare leg, pale with burgundy bruises and slits dissecting the skin – a map of pain etched over her flesh. Online, I saw the photos of Lisa. I know what's here, but the memory of a jpeg on the screen is very different to reality... I scan up to her face. No eyes, only hollow caves. There's dried blood on her ears and nose too. Brownish trails trickle down her naked breasts. Lisa's dignity was covered, but Dara only has the luxury of a towel draped across her groin. I suddenly get the urge to cover her body, but I have no jacket, and the police will be here soon. Her mouth is slack and the lips that once curved into an easy smile now droop to one side exposing more blood, and… I step closer. The tongue is missing. A ragged stump of flesh sits in its place. More disturbing, if that's possible, is a small hole where her hairline meets her forehead.

What else did he do to her? Leaning over, I notice her hands. All her fingers are missing. Does he keep them as trophies? Worse, does he eat them?

Juxtaposed against the horror of Dara's body is the quaint plaid blanket beneath her. As if she was simply sunbathing topless. Were all the others positioned in such a way? On my phone, I find the image of Lisa. It's hard to tell due to the angle of the photo, but… I expand the image, training my focus to the right of the poor girl's hand. Yes, there's a book beside her. *A Stargazer's Guide to the Sky*. A dead body of a girl positioned as if she's on a romantic date? Twisting the normal notion of romance around like this, it has to mean something sinister and cruel? Although, perhaps everything is topsy-turvy in this man's mind.

Now, Dara doesn't look loved at all. In life, she had a rosy hue, her hair dusted with highlights that reflected the sun; she smiled and had joy in her eyes. After he was finished with her, only the broken shell remains.

Is this the sign from God I've been asking for? The celestial thumbs-up that I'm on the right path with my documentary? Andy couldn't have done this to Dara. I've been inches away from him and anyone who could cause this amount of pain would have sent my hackles up. My so-called demon would have sensed it — although I've never been good at trusting the right people.

Stepping back, I check up the road. No police cars yet. Did the dispatcher even report it?

I shouldn't look again, but I do. People need to remember her as she was, a vibrant young girl with an easy smile; only the police will have the evidence of how he left her. No one else should stand witness to her death. What that jogger did to Lisa by uploading her photo was awful, yet another degradation. However, someone should acknowledge what happened here. I take one photo of Dara. I'll keep it secret, to honour her pain.

As I bend down for the right angle, I tell her, 'I'm sorry this happened to you.' I want to take her hand to seal the apology with a touch, but fear I'll leave DNA evidence if I do. She'll understand; she's probably with the nine other girls in heaven, waiting for their chance to take vengeance on their killer. An eye for an eye.

Suddenly, two police cars pull up, so I quickly hide my mobile. Wait... if they take my details, they'll check my history. An ex-mental patient is a great suspect; they'll pin every murder on me. I was in the halfway house on the edge of the hospital for the past year. The carers only help you into a routine to aid your transition back into society, they don't watch your every move; I could have easily slipped away and committed umpteen crimes. Damn, I need to run. Ducking down, I creep along the side of a factory until I'm out of sight. I then sprint towards town, my bag bouncing against my back as I run. There'll be a bruise there in the morning, but it'll be nothing compared to what happened to the Wraith's 10th girl.

–

Back at home, Mum insists on me eating a limp salad with a cold cut of pork from their Sunday lunch. Every time

I look at the meat, I see Dara's leg. It pokes out from beneath the lettuce, mocking me. It's hard to cut with a plastic knife; the fork won't even skewer the meat. As I chew what I can, I find that I'm glad it was me who found Dara, not some crazed internet troll who would have splattered her death photo across the internet like the jogger who found Lisa.

The news of the latest body dump is already online. I'm even mentioned as an anonymous tipster. I take my pink pill later than usual so I can do more research. If finding Dara's body is a sign, is it for Andy's innocence or his guilt? After reaching for my journal, I write, *is Andy the Wraith?* Being a prick isn't mutually exclusive to being a murderer. But those Wraith Finders are convinced it's him. I check out the website again. There's a new discussion, but this time it's behind a member wall. I request to join the group.

Satisfied with my progress, I pull the blind down and turn on the fan. Lucifer is already in the garden tonight, snuffling around and randomly growling.

Damn, almost forgot my prayer. 'Dear Lord, I get it. I didn't pray early enough, so your help was not in time to save Dara. Thank you for sending the sign, though it would have been nice if it had been a little more conclusive about what you want me to do. Could Andy have done that awful thing? I can only conclude that, in trying to help him prove his innocence, his guilt, if it's there, will become evident. You can't prove a negative... although that doesn't sound right. Anyway, I do hope you're taking good care of all the girls in heaven.'

There's a scuffle outside my window, then more barking.

'Amen.'

Lucifer's yaps descend into another growl. In the silent darkness of my room, I curl up and fall into an uneasy sleep.

At some point in the night, I hear a whisper, 'Dinah.'

Half asleep I turn over to answer, but the reply sticks in my throat.

—

I hate pretending I'm going to work, but I'm still unsure what gardening leave is and as no one has said anything else, I just carry on with my morning routine. Mum hands me a pack-up and I flash the fumsup to show I still have it. After leaving the house, I ride the bus as usual, but plan on travelling two stops further to sit in a diner. But when I check my phone, I see an email from Mr Lake asking me to come in and talk. For a moment I think it's because I found Dara and am finally getting some recognition for doing a good deed, but of course it's about the invoices and how much money I've potentially lost the company. It's getting serious: what if they ask me to pay it back? I'm going to have to tell Mum and Dad. If I'm not careful, I'll end up Cookie's neighbour again, and although playing with dolls can be soothing, it's not the life I want anymore. I have stories to tell. I want to record my documentary, figure out what's going on with Andy. Maybe even save an 11th girl from the Wraith's clutches.

No, I have to get ahead of this. I email back that I'm not responsible for sending out the wrong invoices. I say they should check if Stephanie accidently did them and is blaming me because I'm new.

I have time. I should speak with Dr Taylor. She knows I wouldn't lie about making a mistake. What's the point?

Eventually you get found out. I also really want to talk to her about *Keeping up with the Wraith*; no, that sounds like a bad reality show. I write in my journal – *think of a better title!*

I catch another bus to Dr Taylor's and knock on the door.

'We don't have an appointment today, Dee,' she says by way of greeting.

I want to blurt out everything on her doorstep, but instead ask, 'Can we talk?'

She steps aside and I walk into her home.

'I'm just finishing with another patient. Can you wait here?'

Nodding, I sit on her leather couch.

Mid-step, she turns back to me. 'I'm worried, Dee. This isn't like you. You were just here on Friday. Do you remember?'

'I remember. I just really need to tell you something.' I try not to look at her when I say this. Unsure as to when the whole doctor-patient confidentiality kicks in.

'Okay. I've got twenty minutes between clients. We'll talk then.' With that she turns from me and opens the therapy room door. A waft of lavender fills the waiting room. As she closes the door behind her, I catch a glimpse of her current patient – Andy. He doesn't see me, and for a moment I think about leaving. He didn't reply to my 'ready when you are' text for the interview, and bumping into one another could be awkward. Before I know what I'm doing, the fumsup is in my hand. Its dirty wooden head nestled in my palm. If it went to war with a soldier, I wonder what horrors it saw. If any of its many stains are tears or blood. My finger finds the lucky charm's sharp edge and I gently stroke it, daring it to cut through my flesh.

'Things will get better, Andy,' I hear Dr Taylor say as she opens the door. 'Get back to what makes you happy. Start your nature walks again.'

Striding into the waiting room, Andy lifts his eyes and spots me. 'Are you following me?'

'What? No. I'm one of Dr Taylor's clients too. We met here, remember?'

'That's right. Yeah. Just odd we have similar appointment times.'

What's he getting at? Quickly, I say, 'So when would you like to do the interview? We don't have to do anything live, we can just record it. I'm keen to get the documentary going.'

'Me too, I'll text you.' And with that he leaves.

Before I can dissect what's happened, Dr Taylor waves me in. 'You're going to interview Andy?' she asks.

'Yes, but I'm not sure he's telling me—'

Raising her hand, she says, 'Please, I can't discuss patients. You wouldn't want me telling other people about our talks.'

Everyone knows about me anyway thanks to Louisa, is what I want to say, but I stay silent.

Smiling, she motions for me to sit on the plush leather chair opposite hers. I do, expecting her to take the seat behind the desk, but she doesn't. Leaning back, she instead balances against it, so close to me I can smell her last cup of coffee. It's horrible and I lightly recoil to avoid her breath.

'Tell me, what brings you here?'

I open my mouth.

'Hang fire, I can't find my pen.' Dr Taylor turns to shuffle the stuff around on her desk.

Narrowing my eyes, I point to the floor. 'It's under the desk, not on it.'

She bends down and emerges, pen in her hand. 'That's one hell of a skill you have, Dee.'

'Finding stuff is my thing,' I say offhand as I retrieve my phone from my bag.

'It's also a sign of possession. I looked it up last time you magically found my purse for me.'

'What did you say about possession?'

She shakes her head. 'Apologies, we've known each other for so long now, and discussed so much about super-stition and faith together, I forget myself at times. I should be more professional. Now tell me, what brings you here today?'

I should tell her about work. Mr Lake's email is making my phone itch my hand.

'Dee?'

Quickly, I try to think through what will happen if I tell her.

'Dee, are you okay? Perhaps we should call your parents?' Leaning over, she lifts the receiver on her desk phone. 'Shouldn't you be at work now?'

No! I put my hands up to stop her. This was a mistake. Without thinking, I kneejerk, 'They gave me the day off. Can I interview you about the Wraith?' I then swap my phone for the camera in my bag.

'No,' Dr Taylor snaps.

'It's for my documentary. You said you'd help.'

Huffing, she turns back to looming over me. 'I never actually said that.'

'I just want an expert opinion. You don't have to talk about Andy.'

'You know I can't discuss any aspect of my patients. Although, I once thought of myself as a student of criminology…' She moves to one of her enormous bookcases and pulls out a textbook. 'You can borrow this.'

I take the book. It's a criminal psychology textbook by a Dr Hawk. 'Thank you.'

'I worked on that book with her.'

'Wow, and you didn't want to pursue it? Not that I'm not grateful you went into therapy.'

An odd look crosses her face, one I've not seen my doctor wear before. 'It was a while ago now. We disagreed on a number of important things.'

Interesting. 'Like what?'

'Oh.' She waves her hand as if to dismiss the question, but then answers, 'She thought people could never change, and I've always felt that, with the right doctor and treatment, they can. I mean, look at you. When we first met all those years ago, you were volatile and isolated. Now you're practically like the rest of us. You have dreams and a job. I'm so proud of you.'

I can't tell her about Mr Lake now. Not when she thinks I've come so far. 'Thank you,' I say.

Dr Taylor then stands up and walks to the door. 'I have another patient soon. Read the book, and perhaps we can discuss it more at our regular appointment on Friday.'

Nodding, I get up. As I do, my camera slips through my fingers. Dr Taylor lunges forward, catching it before it hits the floor. 'Can I make a suggestion about your documentary?'

'Of course.'

'Find someone to help you. You'll feel more obligated to finish it with someone else involved. Also, the Wraith is still on the loose. It would be safer to work with a partner.'

Catching sight of the flowers still on her desk, I ask, 'Are you happy?'

'A partner of any kind can be scary, but when it works, it can make your life better.'

I roll the idea around in my mind. Where would I even find one?

Recognising the look on my face, she smiles. 'Contact the university media department. Students are always looking for work experience.'

'Okay.'

'I'll find you the email address.' She makes her way around the desk, then taps on her laptop. Quickly, she then writes something down for me. 'Here.'

Surprisingly, the idea of having someone working with me lifts my hopes. 'Thanks, Dr Taylor.'

'One last thing,' she says, reaching into her drawer. She pulls out *Words of Wisdom* and randomly selects a page. Reading it to herself first, she then flicks to another page. 'Ah, this is more apt. *If you move in shadows, you become shadows.*'

I try to look thoughtful, but fear it's coming across gassy.

'Oh and, Dee, I found a spa with a floatation tank. It's in town, so easy for you to get to.'

'Thanks again, Dr Taylor.'

After safely stowing the paper and my camera, I march out of Dr Taylor's office. My stride is stronger, and my head held higher. Mr Lake can kiss my arse; I won't need his job when my documentary about Andy comes out. It'll be the next *Don't F**k with Cats*, it'll surpass *Possession is Nine Tenths* in every way and Louisa will come crawling back, wanting to be my friend again. Not that I'd accept her back. Yes, Jesus forgave Judas, but secretly I bet he wanted to cave in that traitor's mug with his dusty sandal. Everyone has dark thoughts now and then, it's just people brave enough to express them who are labelled as bad or defective. They've never bothered me – at least they're honest. It's people who hide their real feelings who are the ones to watch out for.

—

While I'm by St Alda's, I stop in and ask to talk to Cookie. Dr Taylor wouldn't tell me what he said that got him in trouble, so I decide to go directly to the source.

I shouldn't be allowed in my friend's room, but Brenda is the nurse on duty today. She slips me through the airlock doors into the main building and then down the familiar corridor of the mixed ward on the ground floor.

'Just keep the door open, okay? No hanky panky,' she says, smiling, and nudges me.

The thought makes me cringe. I love Cookie, but not in that way.

Bedrooms at St Alda's are small, but stylish. For a lifer like Cookie, there's individual design touches. He has a toy box, board games, picture books lining the shelves and drawings of stick figures holding hands beneath a smiling sun.

The hole in the fence might be there, but for Cookie to secretly be going out into the real world, he would have to escape this room first. Although St Alda's is not a maximum-security hospital, I can't see how that would happen without help. Debating this, I fold a few items of clothing left on the floor, then perch in the corner on a thin wicker chair, like a creepy doll from a horror film, and wait for him to wake up.

Yawning, Cookie stirs. Noticing me, he grins. I don't scare my friend as I do everyone else.

'You okay?' I ask.

'Yup.'

'What did you say that got you in trouble?'

'Noooooothing. I'm tired of it now.'

The annoyed look on his face makes me drop my questioning, for now. 'I have news.' I slip off the chair onto the floor. Cookie follows suit and we sit cross-legged opposite one another.

'I've thought of an angle for the documentary. I'm interviewing a man who is being accused of the Wraith killings.'

Cookie raises an eyebrow. 'That sounds bad.'

'What?'

'What if he's a monster?'

It's been a thought in my head too. But even if Andy is the Wraith, he wouldn't target me. Weirdos possessed by demons are not ideal victims. 'I don't think he is.' I say the words, but not even I'm convinced.

'Perhaps you can find out whether he's innocent or guilty? You don't have to believe him. Everyone tells stories.'

'That's a great idea. I don't have to make a decision about it for the documentary, just go where the evidence leads.'

'Do you want to play dolls?'

'Sure,' I say, 'let's do that.'

Once the dolls are freed from their chest, I see they're damaged. Eyes blacked out with felt pen, limbs broken at painful angles or pulled off all together. Hair matted with what smells like rancid strawberry jam.

'What happened?' I ask, picking one up.

'Shall I tell you a story? Are you sitting comfortably?' He points at the doll I'm holding. 'Her name was Dara.'

Chapter Twelve

Making up stories about people was a way to pass the time in St Alda's. I can't even count the number of horror scenarios Louisa starred in. But it's disturbing that my friend has concocted a story about the 10th girl, Dara, whose dead body lay before my eyes only hours ago. Patients can watch TV, but not the news. Last we spoke, Cookie mentioned having a nightmare about Lisa, but that's a common name; Dara isn't. How does he know it?

'Her ankles hurt,' he says. 'As she lies in the dark, it's hard to see what's pinching her skin and bone. Jerking, Dara reaches towards her leg. Her hand makes it just past her neck before she jolts to a stop. Swearing, she pulls at all her limbs. Movement is painfully impossible.'

This is oddly specific, and doesn't sound like my friend.

'Shall I continue?' he asks in a teacher's tone.

'Yes.'

'"Help!" The surrounding darkness gulps down her cry.' Cookie takes a deep breath. 'She doesn't know where she is. What's the last thing she remembers? Catching the bus? No, getting home. She fed her cat, Marshmallow. Texted her boyfriend to come over a little later, *Love Island* was on and she wanted to watch it without his droll commentary. Pink pyjamas, a glass of red wine on the couch, and she's turning on the TV when there's a knock at the door. Annoyed her boyfriend hadn't read her text, she opens it, then nothing.'

The floor feels cold beneath me. 'What happened next?'

'Dara waits for her eyes to become accustomed to the dark. They don't. There's only black. "Help me, please," she cries, wriggling her arms and legs. Her movement becomes frantic the louder she whines.'

'Where is she, Cookie?'

'Wait, you'll ruin it… "*Shhhh*," comes a voice. "*Why am I here?*" Dara asks.' Cookie has changed tone to give Dara a distinct high-pitched timbre.

'"*Shhhh*," the voice soothes, as the lights flick on. Tangled in a spider web of manacles, Dara realises the mattress below her is slippery and plastic. "*Why am I here?*" she asks.

'"*Shhhh*," says the voice. "*You're here because I have taken you.*"

'"*No, please. Why can't I move?*" Dara exclaims.

'"*Shhhh*," says the voice. "*You can't move because I've tied you to the bed.*"

'"*Stop it, no. Please, turn the lights on,*" Dara begs.

'The voice laughs. "*It wouldn't help, I've taken your eyeballs.*"

'Dara screams!' Cookie suddenly lets out a scream, making me jump.

'Everything all right in here?' asks Brenda, appearing at the door.

I open my mouth to answer, but nothing comes out.

'Just telling stories like we used to.' Cookie puts a finger up and shushes her.

'Oh good, I hope they're scary ones. They were always the best,' Brenda says, then leaves.

'Where did you hear that from, Cookie?'

'Was it scary?'

'Yes, but not in a good way.'

Cookie's head cocks to the side. 'Scary is scary.'

'You didn't answer my question.'

My friend begins to rock back and forth. Gaze everywhere but on me.

'Where did you hear that story?' I push.

'Let's play dolls.'

'No. Where did you hear that about Dara?'

Cookie looks down at the disfigured toys. 'Oh, I played dolls with someone else.'

'Who?'

'Someone,' he sings.

'Are you going outside?'

'I get to be free.'

Is my friend meeting up with the Wraith? It would explain the dream and story. But Cookie couldn't hurt girls. Even spiders are carefully placed outside under his watch.

'I have to go. I'll see you soon.' I get up and make my way to the nurses' station.

'Bye, bye,' Cookie calls after me. 'Bye, bye.'

Storming up to the nearest nurse I see, I say, 'Can I ask something?'

Vaguely recognising me, her nose twitches. 'Should you be out of your room?'

'I don't live here.' I should end the sentence with *anymore*, but don't.

'Oh, sorry.'

'Has Cookie had any other visitors?' I ask.

'Graham Cookson? Not that I know of. Well, I apart from you.'

'Have you seen his dolls?'

'Yes, he got them a little messy. Are you complaining? We tried to fix them, but he said his friend wouldn't like that. I assumed he was referring to you.'

Not me. 'Is someone letting my friend out of here at night?'

'What's this all about?' Her fingers edge towards the phone.

I need to get out of here. 'Okay, thanks.' I say and quickly leave. God forbid they were to grab me and look at my exercise books – filled with Wraith facts. Oh, and there's also the photo of a very dead Dara on my phone.

On the bus home, I think through Cookie's story. It was detailed, more so than any other story I'd heard from my friend. I wonder if I can check out Dara and see if the *Love Island* thing, the cat, and the boyfriend are facts. Maybe on Facebook? If they are there, it'll be even more of a worry, Cookie should have no access to social media either.

The ping of a phone message disturbs my thoughts. Vlad has come back to me. He wants to meet ASAP and gives me his mobile number. I message him that I'm free whenever. I see the little dots appear as he replies: *Tonight at the Hare and Hound pub 7 p.m.*

–

The Hare and Hound is an old coaching inn a twenty-three-minute walk from the house. As soon as I reach the doors, I feel the building has an edge of something cold. Looking around, I don't see Vlad, so almost leave, then remember there's a beer garden. It's a nice night, so I'm betting he's outside. Picking my way through friends and couples dining together, I push open the door and am slapped in the face by the heat.

'Dee?'

I follow the voice to Vlad. He's sitting under a tree smothered in fairy lights rendered pointless by the bright sun. An empty pint glass haunts the table before him.

'Hi,' I say back, then make my way over. 'Can I buy you a drink?'

'We won't be here that long,' he snaps.

Gently, I perch on a bench opposite. I've already upset him and don't know how.

'What gives you the right?' he asks, jabbing a finger at me.

'You agreed to this interview.'

'This isn't an interview. I want to know why you think you can make money off my wife's murder.' His eyes are glazed with anger and alcohol.

'I don't.' I almost add about finding Dara to prove I'm part of this Wraith business too, but stop myself.

'You're on *his* side.'

'Whose?'

'Fucking Andy Fryer. Everyone knows it's him.'

'But the police didn't charge him.' I so wish I had a name for an official confirmation on that.

'The police are fools.'

'What makes you say that?'

Vlad scoops up his pint glass, then drains the last dribble of beer.

'Look,' I say. 'I'm a documentarian. I don't come down on any one side. But, if it were you accused of committing a crime you didn't do, you'd want someone to help you.'

Snorting, he stares down at his sandal-clad feet. 'You've no idea what you're getting into.'

133

'Wraith Finders? Are you a member?'

His glare snaps back up at me.

Rolling my lips together, I try to think about what I'd want someone to tell me if I'd lost someone I loved. 'What if everyone is focused on Andy, but it's not him? The real Wraith could escape justice.'

Vlad's face softens. 'You can't be this naïve,' he mutters.

'I'm sorry about Fiona,' I say. 'But help me find out who the Wraith really is.'

'You already know who he is.' Tears threaten to fall from the corners of his angry eyes.

'Will you go on record with your thoughts?' I reach into my bag for my camera.

Suddenly, he stands up. 'You have no right to do what you're doing. None!' He then storms off through the garden towards the car park.

This is how I've felt towards Louisa. She had no right to film me, to interfere, to hurt me. But I'm trying to do some good. As Cookie said, my documentary can either finally prove Andy innocent or guilty.

–

Back in my room, I text Vlad I'm sorry he feels the way he does, and that I hope he's okay. He replies with a middle finger emoji.

Pink pill swallowed.

Andy still hasn't messaged back, making my defence of him sting. Is he playing me?

I check Dara's Facebook page. It's only partly public, so I flick through past posts and photos where she forgot to turn the privacy settings on. She did have a boyfriend, and a cat, but there are no mentions of names. There are comments about *Love Island*, but there are also posts on other TV shows too. In one photo she has a glass of red wine in the air. An hour of scrolling and I can neither confirm nor deny Cookie's story. It's infuriating. Part of me thinks I should mention it to Dr Taylor, but no doubt she would ask for evidence it was real and not just in his head. After all, it was pretty outrageous, and I don't want to get my friend into more trouble for nothing.

My legs hurt from walking, so I don't kneel to pray; instead, I perch on the edge of the bed.

'Dear Lord, please look after Cookie. I understand you two aren't on the best of terms with what happened to him and all, but I think you'll get on better when you accept him for who he is now.' I pause. 'I have to admit, I'm worried, but what are the odds of Cookie knowing the Wraith?' I wait for a response from God, but all I hear is Lucifer yapping. 'Please stop Mr Lake from firing me – after all, you know I'm innocent. Look after Vlad, I feel he needs you now too. Amen.'

Big yawn. Fan on. Blind down. I drift into sleep.

Knock. Knock. Knock.

Opening my eyes, I stare into the darkness. Was this what the girls saw before they died? Blackness unfolding on and on into the middle distance. Squinting, I try to make out the shapes of furniture in my room; where my desk is, where the window sits, but all I see are dancing dots of red and blue light taunting me. I lean across and check the time on my mobile: only three and a half hours before the normal time I get up.

Rather than sleep, I turn on a light and pick up the textbook Dr Taylor lent me. I flick to the chapter on serial killers. Dr Hawk claims these disturbed individuals always have a reason behind what they do. Killers are all the same, it's just those reasons that will vary. What possible motive could be behind the Wraith's murders? He named himself 'righteous' in his letters, so he thinks he's justified in his actions, assuming he knows what the word actually means.

I scroll to Dara's photo on my phone. Eyeless, finger-less, blood caking every inch of skin. A fly, caught in mid-flight, aiming at her lips. A surge of guilt makes me switch it off, but my curiosity quickly takes me back. What reason could ever be just enough to do this?

–

Mum and Dad know about work. In the morning, they sit me down and ask if I sent the wrong invoices out on purpose, if, in a fit of temper, I wanted to make the company pay for some imagined slight. I tell them the truth, that I never touched those invoices and I wasn't mad at anyone. The problem is, in my defence, my voice climbs from steady to a shriek. While trying to sound innocent, my tone creeps up to guilty panic.

'Okay, love. Make sure you talk it over with Dr Taylor. Maybe she can get you a new job, eh?' Dad presses his lips into a tiny smile, then leaves the room. Mum stays a little longer, silent as her fingers play with the tassels on the sofa. I need to get on with my day, and this talk has already sucked up too many precious minutes.

Getting up to leave, I watch Mum throw a cushion across the sofa. Do they want me to confess to something I didn't do? Perhaps they think I've relapsed, or worse still, think I am really possessed and can't handle living a normal life. They're wrong. I've not had a serious episode for years. I've got everything under control.

Instead of going to my room, I grab my mobile phone, camera, purse and books. Then, in an act I've never even considered before, I steal my bankcard from where it's kept in Dad's bedside drawer. I can't spend the day without money.

Like a bulky shadow, I scurry out the back door. I'm across the road before I remember I don't have any data left on my phone to check my emails. How close to the house do you have to be to piggyback on the Wi-Fi?

'You okay?'

I look up to see Hayley Bronson, a good foot taller than me in high heel sandals and denim shorts.

'Um, I'm fine. How are you?'

'I'm great, but *you* don't look fine.' She narrows her eyes, then glances behind me at the house. 'Are you running away from home, or something?'

'No, just had to get some space. The parental units are hovering.' Do grown-ups even say 'parental units'?

'I get it. I had to move back home too. Split up with my boyfriend. You know, when I'm feeling claustrophobic, I go down to the coffee place in town.'

Is she inviting me to coffee? 'The one with the blue sign?' I ask, getting a phantom whiff of cake.

'Yeah, that's it.'

The cake smell is coming from Hayley. Her perfume has strong vanilla top notes. 'Do you want to come with me?'

'Sorry, I'm off to work in a mo. But it's always really busy, you'll love it.'

'Does it have Wi-Fi?'

'Yeah, everywhere has Wi-Fi.' She lifts an eyebrow, then steps back from me. 'Later, gator,' she says.

'Later, gator,' I echo, trying to smile and not look weird. Is my eye twitching? I put my finger up and hold the eyelid still. Hayley walks towards her car. As she does,

I notice her shorts have two silver stars sewn onto the back of them, one on each cheek. Quickly, I look away. Although Hayley clearly wants people looking at her bum, I don't want to be one of them.

The Blue Sky Coffee Room is, well, blue. Everything is blue. The chairs, the tables, the mugs, the walls and even the ceramic plate and knife that come with the scone I order. Blue. It's not my favourite colour, but it's somewhat calming. I curl into a big navy leather sofa, like a witch's cat, and log on to their public Wi-Fi. While I'm waiting for Andy's reply, and access to Wraith Finders, I conduct more research and find a copy of a new letter the killer sent to the media. I take a screen shot, then read it several times. The Zodiac Killer put clues and ciphers in his letters, maybe there's something in it?

> *Hello fans!*
>
> *Believe me... I'm most concerned over the apparent lack of care over the ladies of Northamptonshire. I've taken 10 now. 10! Double digits! And it seems the police are no closer to catching me than when I took my 1st girl; sweet Erica. This is all their fault. Every drop of spilt blood, every scream of pain, every lost eyeball. Why can't they catch me? I leave my empty dolls for them to find. I never hide my light under a bushel. And this is not the largest county on the map. I'm a homebody; I don't play anywhere else. Perhaps this is all a conspiracy? Clickbait for you, my loyal fans, to keep your eyeballs glued to screen and page?*
>
> *If they refuse to catch me, I'll continue my rampage. All those lost lives will be due to their ineptitude. Stop me. Stop me. Stop me if you dare.*
>
> *Yours in blood, The Righteous Wraith XX*

I can't see any clues. He's local, but there are thousands of men in Northamptonshire. He's arrogant, but that too is an unfortunately common trait. He's clearly taunting the police and acting as if he's some sort of internet celebrity, although sending handwritten letters is a bit old school – perhaps the only way they can't be truly traced? But why send them in the first place?

The letters don't sound like Andy, although I'm yet to spend any real time with him to fully conclude that. What am I missing? I'm so annoyed, I buy another coffee and a brownie. As I ram the cake into my mouth and taste its heavenly dense chocolate goodness, my phone beeps with a new email.

Ashley Frampton. This is who the university has put forward to assist me with the documentary. Attached to the email is an alarming amount of paperwork, none of which I can comprehend, let alone provide. Fortunately, they copied him into the email too, so I contact him direct. I keep it short, saying I need a camera operator for a true crime documentary. He comes straight back, and although his words are misspelt and the grammar is bordering on unreadable, he says he'd love to work with me, as long as I have a camera, as he can't access the university's equipment during the summer break. I arrange to meet him this afternoon. No annoying paperwork needed.

People are like buses: once I arrange everything with Ashley, I receive a text from Andy telling me he will meet me tomorrow morning for our first official interview. He gives me the address of his parents' house. It's a short message without pleasantries and ends with two emojis: a knife and an eyeball. His finger didn't slip, he sent them on purpose. Callous, just like his joke about torturing Dara.

Maybe he has a warped sense of humour? Or maybe he's not-so-subtly admitting something? The police said they cleared him, but then they could have got the alibis wrong – they're only human. No, it can't be him. Dr Taylor treats us both, and she knows I'm working with him; surely she'd have warned me. Although she has mentioned doctor-patient confidentiality a number of times now, is that her beneath-the-radar version of a warning?

I agree to the meet-up. I don't recognise the address, but I'm sure I can work out the nearest bus stop and Google Maps can take me from there.

I've a little time before Ashley arrives, so I do a deep-dive into Andy's social media, ready for the interview. A few months ago, he appeared incredibly dull. Few friends, just a wife and the odd work colleague. Now, his timeline is polluted by random people unmasking him as the Righteous Wraith. Insults, threats and more. Trolls bullying him to a degree that shocks me. As I scroll through an outrageous array of swearing and angry emojis, I'm surprised Andy hasn't deleted them, or made his profile private. Weird.

The blue-apron-wearing baristas are looking at me funny, so I order another drink and a slice of blueberry crumble cake. Quietly, I then move tables nearer the door; that way Ashley will be able to spot me as he walks in.

Just as I sit down, someone taps me on the shoulder. 'Are you following me?'

Chapter Thirteen

It's Stephanie. She's pale, but wearing bright red lipstick, a colour that makes it difficult to concentrate on the words slipping from her bloody lips.

'Um,' is the only reply I can muster.

'I was nice to you, I...' She trails off, realising she was never nice to me, so has no proof to back up her statement. 'You tried...' she whimpers, '...to blame me?'

Oh, I kind of did. 'I didn't mean to... I just know *I* didn't do anything wrong.'

'But you did! I've worked there for years and those invoices were the biggest fuck-up possible. Massive client, and if we lose them, everyone loses their jobs. Why would you do that?'

I try to rise to face her, but she is standing too close to me. 'I didn't. And if you didn't then that only leaves Corinne who has access to the invoices.'

'Corinne trained me! Oh. That's rich. Why won't you just say sorry and admit it?'

Red dots crowd the edges of my vision, like onlookers to a disaster. 'Six, five, four, three, two, one,' I say beneath my breath.

'What the fuck?' Hands up, Stephanie edges back from me, then adds, 'Check your emails, mental case.' Then turning, all but sprints to the back of the coffee shop.

I handled that all wrong.

Annoyed at myself, I check my emails. There's one from Mr Lake. He says they almost lost Shiva Retail thanks to my error, but Corinne smoothed everything out. She saved the company. Typing out a long reply, I go into detail about my innocence, offering proof that Shiva was not my client, and telling them to check the log in details to the system, then asking Mr Lake how he can be so stupid to believe Stephanie and so closed-minded to not believe me. Red words spill out of me, but then I stop and delete everything, and decide to let it sit for a bit. As long as Mum and Dad don't know the depth of this mess, I can continue beavering away at my *Wrong Wraith* documentary – no, for all I know Andy could be the right Wraith.

Ping! At last, good news. It's a welcome email telling me Wraith Finders have let me join, giving me access to all group pages. The organisers, David and Paula Watson, now have semi-professional headshots and contact details in pride of place on most pages. I email, short and sweet, asking to interview them for a documentary on the Wraith. I don't say it's anything directly to do with Andy as that didn't go down very well with Vlad, so I'll spring that on them when they're in front of the camera. That's what Louisa did, and it certainly worked on Mum and Dad.

A few minutes later, I receive a reply from the Watsons. They're overjoyed I want to interview them and ask if I can meet Friday lunchtime at a greasy spoon café called the Hungry Piglet. Suddenly, my work feels as if it's coming together. I can do this. Beat Louisa at her own game, become a word-class documentarian, win the Docu-Wow. This will be my new job. I'll show Cookie and the others at St Alda's that you can lead a good, normal life; it's never too late. I won't end up like Tippy.

Another hour races by as I write an outline for the documentary. I pull together a timeline of all the troll comments using Andy's Facebook, noting when they started, what fuelled them, and the 'evidence' they claim is behind their accusations. I compare the timeline with what I know about the Wraith case. When and where the girls went missing, then where their bodies were found. Some of what the Wraith Finders say makes sense, but there are gaps in their logic you could drive the Number 3 bus through.

I'm too busy to notice Ashley Frampton at first. But when I clock him standing at the door, I see he's a little like me: awkward and weird. I know it's him because he's wearing a Quentin Tarantino T-shirt and a thin, beige granddad cardigan. His look screams film student. I wave at him and he hurries over to my table.

'Good to meet you,' he says and sits.

Bending down, I retrieve my camera. When I look up again, I find he's now queuing for coffee. Patiently, I wait for him to be served, all the while wondering if I've made a horrible mistake in asking for help. Dr Taylor isn't always right. And I seem to be doing well on my own now.

Eventually, Ashley is back, an iced coffee to go in his hands. As he sits down, he asks, 'Did you want another drink?'

Rather than have him queue up again, prolonging this encounter more than necessary, I shake my head.

Eyeing my camera, he says, 'So, you're looking for a cameraman?'

'Yes, I'm filming a documentary and need someone experienced. What experience have you had?'

He sneers, redundantly blows on his iced coffee, then takes a slurp. 'I'm a third year.'

'One moment,' I say and then check my phone to see if the university has recommended any other candidates. It hasn't.

Ashley reaches over and takes the camera. 'Not my preferred model. But I can make it work. You need help editing?'

That's a good point. Editing software can be expensive. 'That would be great.'

'The university has an editing suite. As a third year, I can access it any time.'

'Excellent. I need some interviews covering. If you're free tonight we can run over—'

'I'm busy tonight.'

'That's okay, the interviews are tomorrow morning and Friday lunchtime. We can then do some connecting shots—'

'Oh, no, I can't make tomorrow either.'

This isn't going well. There's no point in having a partner if they're not there for you. I'm about to air this concern when Ashley adds, 'But Friday is great – will lunch be on you?'

I'm not paying for his services, so the least I can do is treat him to something at the Hungry Piglet. 'Sure.'

'What's your documentary about?'

If Ashley is filming everything, I can't exactly keep my subject matter secret. 'The Righteous Wraith. There's a group online pointing fingers at this man I know.'

'Why?'

'They believe he's the Wraith.'

Ashley takes a deep breath. 'And you believe he isn't?'

'I'm not sure,' I admit.

'Cool. Guess we'll go down the rabbit hole together. Email me the details of this group, and the subject, and I'll see you at the café.'

–

At home, Mum and Dad bring up the invoices again.

'I really think we should speak to a union rep. What do you think?' she asks Dad.

He shakes his head. 'Dee isn't in a union. Maybe Dr Taylor can wade in?'

'I didn't do it,' I say.

'Well, this is to be expected, acting out like this,' Mum says, ignoring me.

'I'm not surprised that job didn't work out. Dee needs something more creative.'

'I'm right here.' I glare at both of them.

'We can't all do what we want in life though, eh?' Mum says. 'But we should seek legal advice.'

'How about Davey Boy?' Dad says. 'He's a solicitor.'

'I know he's your friend, but he gives off a creepy vibe. And doesn't he do patents rather than employment law?'

'My best mate's not creepy.'

'We'll talk about it later.' Mum nods at her own statement, then leaves the room.

Before going to bed, I check my to-do list and feel content I'm making progress. I'm supposed to see Dr Taylor on Friday, I'll explain everything about work to her then. After all, I am innocent. You can't prove an innocent person guilty. Maybe this all happened for a reason. I'm innocent, I know that to be one hundred percent true, so perhaps Andy is too. Wait! God has a plan for me; he's showing me what Andy is feeling. Only armed with this empathy can I go forth and put right the wrong. That's it! The invoices are the sign from God! Andy is innocent. My shoulders slump at this thought. I hadn't even realised how tense I was over it. Finally, I have all my documentary ducks in a row.

The pink pill feels different tonight, and my fingers are clumsy on the laptop. Putting everything away, I slap my hands together. 'Dear Lord, don't worry, I got your sign about work and Andy. Although, you could have just told me. Teaching me a lesson like that is a bit dangerous – I've seen people put away again for a lot less than losing a job. Nevertheless, I trust you'll see me vindicated. And I promise I'll help Andy. Knowing he's innocent now makes me feel…' I yawn, '…much better. After all, it would have been awkward if I tried to prove his innocence and he turned out to really be the Wraith. Bless Mum, Dad and Cookie, amen.'

I close my eyes and begin to drop into a deep sleep…

Lucifer is barking. The shrill sound invades my dreams. I wake up and fumble with my phone. 3:33 a.m. Damn, I forgot to pull down my blind; the dim view of the street looms before me. Suddenly, there's a flash of light. Narrowing my eyes, I edge towards the window. What was that? A camera? Another flash comes; a wave lights up the world. It's lightening. I count to ten before I hear the thunder. I've never seen a storm like this. Bright green sparks dissect the sky. What's going on? I look it up online. My exhaling breath mists my phone screen as I see green lightening is rare, but natural. Sometimes the earth's atmosphere causes the colours in the light. The knowledge doesn't stop me feeling like this is another, more concrete, sign from God.

My documentary is blessed. Andy is definitely innocent.

–

By morning, I feel as if I have a definitive path. God is
letting me know everything will be okay. My innocence at
work will come out. In the meantime, I've been given the
gift of time to work on proving Andy's innocence. This is
the feeling I've been missing all these years – purpose.

Downstairs, I see Mum and Dad sitting silently at
the kitchen table. Both are red-eyed with shiny cheeks.
They've been crying.

Something awful has happened.

Chapter Fourteen

'Come on, love, sit down. There's something you need to know.' Dad motions to a chair.

Slipping down, I place my backpack between my feet and I rack my brain as to what could have them in this state.

'You remember Hayley Bronson? You used to babysit her.' Mum moves her hand towards mine.

'What about her?' I ask, inching back.

'She was abducted last night.' Mum whispers the last part, but I still hear it.

'What? I only spoke to her yesterday morning.' I look to Dad who covers his mouth with his hand.

'Someone snatched her after her shift at work. She's a waitress at that Italian restaurant near the town centre,' Mum says through tears, big, fat ones that dribble down her chin.

'The police were canvassing the neighbours late last night. You're such a heavy sleeper after your pill, we thought it best not to wake you,' Dad says.

Before I realise what I'm doing, the fumsup is between my fingers, its sharp edge caressing me with a gentle nip. 'It was the Wraith, wasn't it?'

Both nod.

Mum looks out of the window into the street. 'It's so terrible, especially after what happened with Hayley earlier this year.'

'What happened?' I ask.

'Let's not get into that right now,' Dad says.

'No, tell me,' I press.

Mum sighs. 'Hayley broke up with her boyfriend and tried to commit suicide.'

'What? How?' I can't imagine someone as perfect-looking as Hayley Bronson feeling so low she would try to end her life.

'It was a cry for help, really. She didn't take enough paracetamol to kill herself. But the doctors were concerned about her mental health. They moved her back home from Oxford to keep an eye on her.'

Her parents put Hayley into the path of the Wraith. He doesn't hunt further than Northants. Their love for their daughter might be the very thing that gets get her killed.

'Just because she felt she wanted to die, it doesn't give a sicko the right to hurt her,' I say.

'I know, love.' Dad tears up.

Mum suddenly jerks her hand towards my cheek. I dodge her, making her eyes sadder. I don't need her motherly touch. It would feel like a lie if I accepted it.

Andy's interview is today. Finally getting him to this point, I don't want to miss it, so I say, 'I want to work on my documentary, is that okay?'

Dad smiles. 'Of course, love. You go off and solve the riddles of recycling.'

I leave them crying together, theorising about what if the Wraith had chosen me instead. It's one thing to be sad something bad happened, but another to be sad about

149

something that hasn't happened; an event that sits in your imagination, yet to break free into the real world. What they're forgetting is that I am safe. The Wraith, whoever he is, wouldn't touch me. Weirdos have a sixth sense about one another. You don't catch lions hunting and eating other lions. It's just not done.

Before catching the bus to Andy's house, I stop in at St Godfrey's. I didn't pray soon enough to save Dara, but I should try for Hayley. It's early, so the only people there are nuns, who give me evil looks, and a few pensioners who mumble when I sit too near them. Putting my hands together, I silently ask God to save Hayley. During my prayer, I begin to whisper the scenario of the police finding an extra clue in the letters and caving the murderer's door in just before he blinds her. Red-tinged anger wriggles free from the thought and I'm suddenly demanding God strike the killer down with a green lightning bolt –

'Dee?'

I open my eyes to see Father Jacob.

'You all right?' he asks.

'I came to pray for my friend.'

'Cookie?'

'No.' Even though I say it, I realise that, while I'm here, I probably should do that too. 'My neighbour Hayley was taken by the Wraith. She could be the 11th girl.'

'Dear Lord, from your street?'

'From town, near where she works.'

Gathering up his cassock, he sits beside me. 'I'm very sorry. I didn't know she was your friend.'

Friend might be a stretch, but there was potential.

'I'm sure the police will do everything they can,' he tells me.

'But they haven't saved any of the girls yet.'

'I'll pray for her.' Father Jacob then clasps his palms together and closes his eyes. Watching him, a thought hits me; praying is pretty useless in this situation. How many people managed to get a prayer in before Dara was killed, and nothing changed? God's eye is no longer on the Wraith ball. Should I even believe Him about Andy? But the signs, when they did finally start appearing, were quite dramatic. Who would go to all that trouble about something they weren't sure of? No, I have to trust God. Canon Matthew has said in his sermons that He knows all, He sees all; who am I to doubt that?

–

The bus ride to Andy's house takes forever. The driver pauses at each stop to pick up passengers. It's as if everyone and their dog want to travel this route to nowhere. Without the bus gaining speed, the open window by my seat does nothing but allow the sun better access to me.

I still can't get my head around Hayley, and that she tried to commit suicide. Tippy's demon had been body dysmorphia that in turn led to depression, but she had got better, so much so they let her out. Craig had warned us that he thought she'd be better off staying, but his judgement couldn't be trusted. After all, he had mental health issues too. The next day, he was proved right. Tippy threw herself in front of a rush-hour train. It took longer for her to be cleaned off the tracks than she'd spent free on the outside. Father Jacob had spoken with me before the funeral. He told me what happened to Tippy had been a tragedy, but that we are only the custodians of life, not the owners; to steal it is a sin. I wanted to ask why God would let Tippy do such a thing – trains are unreliable at best, it would have been easy for Him to delay one long enough for someone to see my friend and help her – but in the end I said nothing. If the Wraith has his way with Hayley, her death won't be as peaceful as paracetamol.

Finally arriving, I find Andy's house sits on the side of a dual carriageway. It's both remote and busy at the same time. The building is all stone and thatch. There's no zebra crossing here, so to reach it I have to walk a quarter mile out of the way to use an underpass.

Halfway there and out of breath, I stop and check my phone. Using my bank card I top up the credit, so I can now access every app without Wi-Fi. I check on Hayley online, but there's no news.

Should I be doing this? My judgement isn't exactly tip-top, but I believe in God, and that He has a plan for me. Andy is innocent, isn't he? It's times like these a normal person would call a friend to talk through their doubts and seek advice. Fake it till you make it.

I can't call Dr Taylor about Andy, and Father Jacob might tell Mum and Dad what I'm doing, so I call Cookie. Coal answers the phone and after a little scuffling, I hear my friend's voice.

'Hello!'

'I'm glad you're there,' I say.

'Where else would I be, silly?'

'You remember we spoke about Andy?'

Cookie exhales. 'Right.'

'I'm about to meet him alone, at a house in the middle of nowhere.'

'No one will hear his screams!' The joke ends in a raucous giggle and snort.

'So, you think I'll be safe?'

The question is ridiculous. My friend has no concept of mistrust or background information to make a decision about my safety, yet, when I'm told, 'Of course. I've never known anyone quite like you, Dee,' I feel warmth spreading through my stomach, like a gulp of hot tea.

'Thanks, Cookie.'

'You're welcome. And remember, you're never truly alone, you've got your demon.'

After saying goodbye, I hang up.

With renewed vigour, I shuffle up to Andy's house. He doesn't answer when I knock. Do I have the wrong time or worse the wrong address? Have I walked all this way and psyched myself up for nothing. There's no car in the drive and it is deadly quiet. I knock again. No one comes. Not wanting to leave, I text *I'm here*. No reply.

Annoyed, I wander around the side of the building. It's a much bigger house than it appears from the road; it seems to stretch on forever. Towards the back, I find a dark wooden gate sectioning off a garden. Standing on a nearby rock, I peer over. Amongst an expanse of land is the shape of someone bending over a hole in the earth, a spade raised over their head, ready to strike.

Chapter Fifteen

'Andy?' I call out.

The shape turns.

'What are you doing?' I ask.

'Dinah! There you are.' His tone is cheerful as he waves with his free hand. 'Just a spot of gardening.'

No *sorry* for keeping me waiting or not answering his phone, which he clearly has tucked in the back pocket of his jeans. Andy might not be a killer, but he is rude.

'Didn't think you were here,' I reply. He's a documentary subject, not my new best friend, so I add, 'Thought I'd made the trek for nothing.'

'I didn't hear you knock.' He beckons me to follow him into the house. 'This is my mum and dad's old place. It's much quieter here than the flat in town and at least the Wraith Finders don't know about it.'

'Sure,' I mutter, wondering how long Rabbits Foot will take to find out and upload a photo of this house.

The latch on the gate is old and rusty; it takes me three attempts to undo it. All the while, Andy doesn't offer to help and is oblivious to his ungentlemanly manner. Finally, the gate swings open and I walk into the garden. There's upturned turf everywhere. Mound after mound of earth, each more suspicious than the last. Beside them are holes just big enough to bury a part of a body, or several small parts.

'What sort of gardening are you doing?' I ask.

He rubs his head, then carelessly throws the shovel to the ground. 'I'm putting down new grass. This heat wave killed my last batch.'

As I nod, I wonder why grass seeds need holes that big.

'I know what you're thinking.'

He does?

'You're thinking, *why is he doing gardening in this heat?*' He shrugs. 'I just want a patch of green I can escape to any time I need it. My own little nature retreat.'

Without another word, Andy then walks off. Am I supposed to follow? Hoisting my backpack higher on my shoulder I scurry after him.

'Have your family always lived here?' I ask, jogging to keep up with his long strides.

Ignoring my question, he leads me into a kitchen where he retrieves a can of pop from a fridge big enough to fit me in whole. He doesn't offer me a drink. His cold behaviour is leading me to think he's changed his mind about working with me; either that or he's a sociopath. I saw plenty of them at St Alda's, I know the signs, but it doesn't justify people accusing him of killing girls.

The kitchen is huge, and is floor-to-ceiling mahogany wood, giving it a dark, reddish vibe. There are paintings of herbs lining the walls and several antique crosses. Some with a pained Jesus strapped to them, some more Celtic in appearance. A sizzle of a spitting memory jars my thoughts. He catches me staring.

'We collect them,' he explains.

'Crosses?' I whisper.

'This place used to be an old rectory. Dad bought it and turned it into a house.'

An odd sense of injustice sweeps across me. This building had a purpose, and Andy's family stripped it away, brick by brick. They moulded it into something it was never meant to be. My mouth opens to question their actions, but I snap it back shut.

'Let's start.' Andy says.

The dining table and chairs are made from thick wood, perhaps even carved from old pews. Struggling with its weight, I pull out a chair and sit down. After freeing my camera, I begin setting up.

'The light is good in here, let's conduct your interview in the kitchen,' I say.

After draining his drink, Andy cocks his head at me. 'You're filming it?'

'Of course, it wouldn't be much of a documentary if I just took notes,' I say, training the lens on the chair opposite me.

Andy sits down and straightens himself up. He has dirt smeared across his forehead, but I don't point it out; it'll look better on film, make him appear more human.

'How long is this going to take?'

'About an hour, maybe less if we get everything in a few takes.' I reach into my bag and pull out the legal waiver I printed from my course. 'Can you sign this? It just says that I can use what we film.'

'Just what we film? What about other things we talk about, off camera?'

I consider this. 'Well, it's not usually covered, but if you want it to be, you can write a note on the waiver to say you're good with it.'

Andy picks up a pen, then only signs his name. When he hands the paper back to me, I put it safely in a compartment of my backpack. 'Ready?'

'An hour is longer than I thought it'd take,' Andy says running a dirty hand through his hair.

'I'm going to go out on a limb and say an hour of your time to get across your side of things will be worth it.'

'Yeah, yeah. Let's start.'

I flip through my notebook and find my research from earlier. 'I'm going to ask you questions, but my voice will be edited out, so I need you to state the question in your answer, can you do that?'

'Sure.'

'When did you first become aware that you were being accused of the Wraith murders?'

Andy shifts in his seat. 'I first became aware of the accusations last month. A group online had investigated the first five girls' abductions and had tied me to the locations they were taken from. It wasn't fair of them to—'

'Andy. Please only answer one question at a time. You can go into more detail later. Also, you don't want to come across as ranty.'

'Ranty? These arseholes ruined my life!'

'I know, that's why I'm here.' I stare at him as he rolls his lips into an ugly line. 'Andy, what tangible evidence did the group use to accuse you?'

'Photos I'd taken around Northamptonshire and uploaded to Facebook. Silly things, like selfies. The police had released statements about where the victims were when they were abducted, their homes, train station, places like that.'

'And you were at these locations?'

'Yes, I was at, or near, these locations, along with hundreds of other people. But then a member of the group began to follow me, taking more photos.'

'Rabbits Foot,' I say. 'Do you have any idea who that is?'

'Wish I did.' Andy cracks his knuckles.

'How about girls nine and ten, Lisa and Dara – where were you then?'

'When Lisa was abducted, I was at work. We have to clock in and out, so there's evidence I was there when it happened.'

'Can you show me the timecard?'

Andy shakes his head. 'I was fired. I can't exactly ask for my timecards.'

'You can ask the police – it's your alibi.'

'I told you, the police don't think it's me.'

'What about Dara?' He'd have already been fired when she was taken. 'Do you have an alibi for when she was abducted?'

'I was arguing with my wife.'

A pissed-off spouse isn't much of an alibi. 'Would she say as much?'

'Probably.'

'To the police?'

'They have enough on their plate without me adding to it. It's better they spend their energies finding this creep before my life is ruined any more than it already is.'

Turning off the camera, I ask, 'Off the record. Are you the Righteous Wraith?'

Laughing, Andy sits back in his chair. 'Wouldn't that be a kicker, eh? Do I really need to tell you people can be cruel? That they can lash out and make assumptions.'

'You didn't answer the question.' I stare at him, my full weirdness concentrated through my eyes.

'I'm not the Wraith.'

'Good,' I say, then turn the camera back on. 'Talk to me about Wraith Finders' impact on your life.'

At this, Andy's eyes narrow and nostrils flare. 'They've ruined my life. Wraith Finders have turned everyone against me. They have no evidence. They have no reason. They have no...' he trails off into a panic attack. Sharp breaths pound at his chest and for a moment I look around for a nurse to administer a sedative, before remembering I'm no longer at St Alda's.

'It's okay, calm down,' I say. 'Take a deep breath. And another.'

After he does as I ask, his expression shifts from anxious to pissed off.

'See what they've done to me,' he says.

'I get it. It's why we're doing this documentary. Are you okay to continue?'

He nods. 'Are you interviewing the Wraith Finders?'

'Yes. I've taken on a film student called Ashley who's going with me to meet them.'

'Can I hear what they say?'

Narrowing my eyes, I try to think through whether it's ethical to show him other people's interviews. 'No, you shouldn't. It might affect your views and opinions going forward. To make a good documentary, we have to be as unbiased as possible.'

'Unbiased? Don't you believe me?' Andy edges his arms across the table. Although the distance is too great for him to touch me, I still feel the heat of his skin against my hands.

'I think it's a good story, and if what you're saying is true, we need to tell it. I know what it's like to be accused of something you haven't done.' I want to tell him about the Shiva invoices, come across as a kindred spirit, but I don't. My business isn't his; his business is mine.

'Okay. Have you done any documentaries in the past?' he asks.

The answer is obvious, and it makes me wonder if he knows about *Possession is Nine Tenths*. 'Yes,' I say.

'I watched one the other night about a guy in America who went to prison for killing his girlfriend. People think he's innocent now. These things happen a lot, eh?'

'Thousands of actual criminals are convicted too, though. The system isn't quite right, but it's not that broken either. And anyway, that's the US. Britain isn't as dramatic.'

Andy stares at me. I'm really thirsty now and the thought of asking for a drink crosses my mind, even if it's just water from the tap. 'Andy, may I...'

'You should go.' He puts the lid down on my laptop and pushes it across the table.

I look at my notes. 'I've still got some questions.'

'I'm tired. We can finish up another day.'

There are at least ten more questions I need on film. Remembering how hard he was to pin down this time, I ask, 'Can we get something in the diary now?'

'Not yet,' he replies, staring past me.

'Okay. I'll be in touch to sort out another time.'

He doesn't see me out; instead, I have to leap awkwardly through his reseeded garden of little open graves. I'm not sure I got everything I needed in such a short interview. I kick myself for not refreshing my documentarian skills beforehand. I asked the right questions, but I didn't probe. I just skimmed the scum off the surface, so scum was the only thing caught in my net.

Back at home, I take a bath to relax my weary muscles. Whilst soaking, I put on my favourite 90s bands. It's been years since I've had such luxury. I feel almost human again.

Mum coaxes me from the bathroom with a real cream éclair. She doesn't mention the business with Mr Lake, which makes me think it's alright now. God knows I learnt the lesson He meant for me, so is sorting everything out.

While devouring my cake, I review the footage of Andy. He stares straight at the camera, no fear, no quick glances away, but his look is familiar. I flip through my sketchbook and find my portrait of the bad man in the park. I captured the look in his eye perfectly; it was calculated and hard, just like Andy's.

Listing all the points he gave me about the accusations, I note down his timeline, checking it against his Facebook profile and the Wraith Finders' site. For every explanation Andy gives, Wraith Finders debunks it with evidence they unearthed. Google Map locations and times of Rabbits Foot's photos; the date he was 'let go' from his work doesn't match. Yes, some of what Andy told me is hard to prove, but it's just as hard to disprove, and the Wraith Finders seem hell-bent on cornering Andy. I can't find a single thread on their forums that discusses any other suspects. There is, however, a thread about Hayley. Police have publicly linked her abduction to the Wraith. Dear Lord, please help her.

–

Being off work, I arrive early for the Inspiration Cometh meeting. I choose the seat in the far corner and free my notebook from my bag. As I start to reread my notes from Andy's interview, Donald turns up. He puts down his laptop and heads to the bar. Not even an acknowledgement – what did I do to piss him off? Did I say out loud that his work is clichéd? Or perhaps he found out somehow I suspected him of being the Wraith?

With a drink in his hand, Donald sits two seats away from me.

'Hi,' I say.

He takes a long slurp of his flat-looking beer. Perhaps he's just in a bad mood. Not everything is about me. I'm just convenient to ignore. I'm not a friend or even an established member of the group. Maybe I should ask him about his screenplay. Mum says people enjoy talking about themselves, and Donald has proven this true week after week.

'How's the—'

'Evening, fellow creatives!' Janet sweeps in, sunburn tattooed across her arms and nose.

'Have you been in the wars?' Donald asks her, nodding to the red patches.

'Awful weather, isn't it? You forget to put on sunscreen when you're at home. Got these wounds pottering about the garden.' Sighing, she sits across from me.

'Janet, can I ask a question?' I say.

'Course, yes, um...'

'Dee,' I add, ending her mental grasp for my name. 'When you reseed grass in your garden, do you have to dig holes?'

Nodding she replies, 'You have to bury the seeds, or else the birds will peck them up.'

'Big holes?'

'Not especially.'

'So, a hole the size of say, a hand, would be too big?'

Her eyes widen. 'Yes, much too big.'

'Unless it's not seeds being sown, and it's lumps of turf,' Donald pipes up.

'Oh, thank you.' That could explain Andy's weird gardening technique – hopefully.

When Trudy arrives, Donald and Janet move their chairs away from me to talk about her work. With our short conversation over, I drop my gaze to my notebook. As I do, I notice the massive sweat stains spreading blob-like under the arms of Donald's t shirt. They're so big, at first I mistook them as part of the material's pattern. He smells too, although faintly – there's a musty, familiar odour about him. Scanning more carefully, I spot something strange clinging to his huge beard. One long, dark, auburn hair.

'Are you giving us more of your script tonight?' Trudy asks him, as she settles down with a giant glass of white wine.

'Yes, if no one else has anything to read.'

Is the hair the same length as Hayley's? It definitely looks the same shade.

More people file in around us. I don't remember their names, but I do remember their work. There's Fantasy-Girl who writes indulgent fan fiction, Horror-Boy who is usually too ashamed of his dark thoughts to share much. Ethereal-Woman who dresses in floaty, flower-coloured sun dresses yet writes the grittiest crime I've ever read, and finally I'm-Just-Starting-Out-And-Have-No-Idea-What-I'm-Doing-Woman, who has yet to produce any work and seems content to just come along to chat about her family.

'I think this is everyone,' Janet says. 'There's a lot of members on holiday.'

Without introduction, Donald pipes up to talk about the next scene in his clichéd stalker film. Intently, I listen, all the while trying to look only slightly interested.

It begins with his protagonist abducting another girl, this time a redhead who served him dinner at a restaurant that night. He waits for her in the street, and then, just as she is within safe distance of her car door, he approaches and asks if she has jump leads as his van won't start. It descends from there in both taste and quality. The Wraith took Hayley from outside the restaurant she worked at, although Mum and Dad both knew this, so that must be public knowledge. DCI Campbell mentioned all the girls were abducted without a fight, so his 'I need help' scenario is intriguing, but not proof of anything. Then there's the long red hair still clinging to his wiry beard. Either he's stealing ideas off the news, which wouldn't surprise me, or he could be the Wraith. I'm terrible at reading people, so at this point I can't discount anything.

After Donald finishes, there's a bout of undeserved compliments, then the meeting descends into a social. Usually this is when I gather my stuff and, unnoticed, slip out the door, but this time, I linger – watching and listening. As flimsy as my evidence is, I owe it to Hayley to at least check Donald out.

He's the first to leave, saying his cat has run away and that he wants to get home while it's still light to look for her. Apparently, she's something special, a ghost tabby. Sweat is now dripping off Donald's nose and into his empty beer glass. He's acting so suspiciously; it's setting my teeth on edge. If you'd lost your cat, why would you wait until the evening to find her? If I'd lost something I loved, I'd be searching the streets, not drinking down the pub. As he gets up and leaves, I say goodbye to everyone, then follow him into the street. I know from previous group conversations he lives nearby; I just don't know where.

I try to keep my distance, but he's a painfully slow walker and, all too soon, I'm directly behind him. The street smells of his BO, so much so it's like swimming too long underwater. I stop and pretend to tie my shoelaces just to get a gulp of fresh air.

Being just steps behind the man you're following is not exactly covert, but it's the only way I'll discover where he lives. Be able to snoop around. Find out if he's really the Wraith or, more likely, some hack writer. Although it's not as if he'll have a sign on his house saying 'Righteous Cottage' or something. I'll have to figure out a better plan.

Stopping mid-step, he turns his head. He's on to me. I scurry into a nearby front garden to hide. Through the dying leaves of a bush, I watch him twist back around, then walk up a little path to a mid-sized house flanked by families playing in their front gardens. Can you success-fully keep kidnapped young women in a housing estate?

After checking no one is watching, I leap over his neighbour's scattered junk, and sneak between the houses. Although both probably claim to be detached, I have trouble squishing my small frame down the alley separ-ating them; I have to pull my backpack off my shoulders and hold it in front of me as I move. As I creep around the building, I come to a large fence that divides his and the neighbour's garden. Pulling a big terracotta pot over, I step on it and peer in. It's just a garden. A bit of yellowing grass, some drooping flowers. It looks like every other garden you'd see this summer. Andy's random lawn holes were more suspicious than Donald's yard. I'm so disappointed I lose my balance and fall off the pot. Landing awkwardly on my foot, I cry out. Keeping as still as I can, I wait for Donald to discover me spying on him. He doesn't.

I should go home. This whole thing is downright silly.

Decision made, I skulk out of the garden. With the sun still blindingly bright, there are no shadows to hide in, so when my phone goes off, I feel as if a giant spotlight has landed on me. Grabbing my phone, I go to turn it off as quickly as possible, but see it's St Alda's. Cookie. I answer with a quiet, 'Hello?'

'Dee! You're alive. I was just checking up on you after your call…'

'Hey, Cookie. Can I ring you back?' I whisper.

'Why, what you doing?' he sings the last part.

'I'm just outside at the moment.'

'Okay. Ummm, yeah. Can you do me a favour?'

I look around, but don't see anyone. Not even Donald has spotted me, so I slip behind a fence and crouch down onto the flaky earth. 'Shoot,' I say.

'Can you interview me for your documentary?'

'The Wraith documentary? Why?' My mind's eye takes me back to the doll box, and the story.

'I… just… ummm…'

'Why would you want to be interviewed?' I push.

'I have to go, they're calling me.'

There's a scuffle on the line, and I hear a familiar voice. Dr Taylor.

'Who is this?' she asks down the line.

'It's Dee. Is Cookie okay?'

'Yes, he's fine. He wasn't supposed to use the phone.'

'Oh, sorry.'

'Don't worry, I'll speak with him. I'll see you at our next appointment.' She hesitates, then says, 'I'm proud of you, Dee. You're being very brave making this documentary.'

As I hang up, I wonder how brave I actually am. What if Hayley is in that house? What if I could have not just saved her, but all the Wraith's would-be victims, if I'd kept pushing on? Damn, I need to see inside. Dr Taylor all but told me to. Time is running out for Hayley. If Donald is the Wraith, I only have two days before she's... I should call the police, but what evidence do I have? A shitty screenplay and one stray auburn hair? They'd send me back to St Alda's lickety-split; I guess at least Cookie wouldn't be lonely anymore.

The sun is going down. A cool breeze plays across my face. It's like divine intervention as, when I close my eyes, I suddenly feel something rubbing against my ankle. I look down to see a petite black cat. I bend to tickle its ear. As it rests its head into my hand, I'm surprised to see a white undercoat hiding beneath its dark fur. Could this be Donald's lost ghost tabby? It would make his cat comments less incriminating. And if he has lost it, then returning it could get me inside. I scoop the feline up and walk to his door. Before I can over-think it, I knock three times.

Donald answers the door. He's shirtless and his pudgy chest is sprinkled with grey wire-like hair.

'Dee?' His eyes fall onto the cat in my arms.

'Midnight! You found her.' Lunging forward, he swoops up the cat for a cuddle. He's gentle and she purrs at his touch.

'I saw her at the top of the road. Thought I'd check if she was yours.'

'She is!' Looking down at the cat he coos, 'Where have you been?'

'Are you alone in there?' I ask.

'What?' He goes to close the door on me, but I step forward.

'I'm covered in fur. Do you have a brush or some Sellotape?' I ask.

'Sure, wait here.' Donald turns and gently places Midnight on his hall carpet. She meows, then saunters off into the house. He then partially closes the door and disappears.

Is this usual? Do people whose beloved pet you just saved make you stand on doorsteps rather than invite you in? Or is it just me?

Damn it. My hand shoots out and I push the door open. This could be a huge mistake, entering someone's home uninvited. But I might also save my friend. Be brave. I step inside, and head towards the furthest door. Opening it, I see a modest living room with a massive plasma TV and a wall-long bookcase full of DVDs. Apart from him banning books from their own bookcase, he's not committed any crime so far.

The house is surprisingly small and I quickly open every door downstairs and check each room. I can hear Donald in the kitchen. He's talking to Midnight, softly and gently as if the feline is a child. The stairs loom before me. I shouldn't be doing this; it's trespassing, but I have to know for sure, for Hayley's sake. I leap up the steps and find only three doors on the landing. One door is to a slim bathroom, the other a bedroom and the third a study; this must be where Donald writes his screenplays. Quickly, I shoot back downstairs.

There's a rustling in the kitchen. My host has just remembered I'm still waiting on his doorstep. I sneak back outside. Just as I get there, he emerges with a big, bristled brush.

'Try this,' Donald says, handing it to me.

I take it but, when I look down, see more fur on it than on me, so hand it back. 'Don't worry. Thanks anyway.'

'You never talk much at group. What are you working on?'

Hesitating, I try to come up with a decent lie. Instead, I blurt, 'A documentary on the Righteous Wraith.'

'Sounds exciting. Perhaps we can discuss it next time?'

'Sure. And I'd like to hear more about your screenplay.' As I say this, I hear shuffling behind me. I turn to see a short, round woman waddling her way up the path; her long auburn hair gathered in a floppy bun on top of her head.

'Who's this?' she screeches at me.

'Oh, this is Dee from the writers' group. She helped find Midnight.' In the blink of an eye, Donald's face morphs from potential psycho killer to hen-pecked husband.

'That's an odd name, Dee? Couldn't you afford any more letters?' The woman laughs. Moving forward, she shoves me out of the way with her hip so she can get in the house. 'I've told you before to stop writing that shit. More things to do round here than you can shake a stick at.' Mrs Donald wrinkles her nose at me, then toddles towards their kitchen.

Now I know why Donald writes stories about killing women. And with a wife like that knocking around the house, the odds of him getting enough time alone to abduct, torture and kill young women, are slim to say the least. Her red hair explains my only other evidence on Donald. I've been a fool.

He smiles. It's the first smile I've seen him wear while looking at me, and it drips with a request: *don't tell*. At group, he acts like the big man; at home, he's the anaemic shadow to a bigger woman.

'Fuck sake, Donald. Get on will ya? That bloody cat needs feeding.'

His stare drops to the floor. 'Coming.'

'How long have you been married?' I ask.

'Twenty years.'

'You'd have got less for murder.' I chuckle so he knows it's a joke.

'Donald!' she screeches again.

'See you next week,' I say, then begin the long walk home.

–

Tonight, the pink pill is hard to swallow. I feel as if I should leave it off the menu, so I can keep my senses sharp for Hayley. The problem is, I only have one potential suspect and, on God's orders, I'm filming a documentary to prove his innocence.

Before pulling down the blind, I check online for any news. Another letter has found its way to the media. Before reading it, I take a quick, deep breath.

> *Hello fans!*
>
> *Here we are again. I've taken 11 girls now. Hayley is so lovely, but I'm afraid she won't be for long, unless you get your act together. I know there have been budget cuts in the police, but I'm making it easy for them. I've left clues everywhere. Why has their forensic team not tracked my DNA down? Well, I must admit, I'm enjoying the public's attention. I feel like a one-man show, a magician who deliberately saws his beautiful*

assistant in half. I might try that on Hayley. See how many strokes before she expires. After all, even serial killers get bored.

Find me. Find me. Find me… before I disappear!

Yours in blood, The Righteous Wraith XX

Poor Hayley is as good as dead. I kneel and put my hands together.

'Dear Lord. Me again. Please help Hayley Bronson. She's a nice person and doesn't deserve to be tortured and you know what else. If you're too busy, please send me a sign as to where she is so I can help her. As much as I don't want to go back to St Alda's, I won't mind getting in trouble if it helps Hayley. You're trusting me to help Andy, so you know I'm capable. What do you think?' Silence. 'Bless Mum and Dad and Cookie. Amen.'

Blind down. Sleep steals in and rips the day's thoughts from my mind.

Knock, knock, knock…

I look over at my mobile to see it's 3:33 a.m. Lucifer is barking, but that wasn't what woke me; I heard three distinct raps.

Mum or Dad is at my door.

'Come in,' I say.

But the door doesn't open. I get up and peer outside to find an empty hall. Strange, perhaps I dreamt it. Back in bed, I can't sleep. I'm good at finding lost things. I found Dara's body – what would stop me from finding Hayley alive? Getting up, I shove on a robe, more for modesty than warmth, then switch on my laptop.

Online, the police and press are oddly quiet about Hayley's abduction. They do, however, mention she was last seen at the restaurant where she worked. The thing is, I don't know which restaurant that was exactly. There's at least five Italians in the town centre alone. People say that to find something you lost you need to look in the last place you saw it. There might be a clue there.

A light is on in Hayley's house. Someone is awake. I shouldn't go over. It's just, by the time I think about this, I seem to already be knocking on their front door.

Mr Bronson opens it. Red-eyed, clothes rumpled and smelling stale. 'Yes?'

'Sorry to come over so late. But I saw your light on. I spoke to Hayley the day she was… Is there any news?' I try to look sympathetic, yet fear I just look creepy, especially as I'm on his doorstep in an oversized T-shirt and robe, asking about his abducted daughter.

He stares at me. Perhaps he didn't hear the question. I open my mouth to repeat it, but he slams the door in my face. What the hell? I wasn't asking for the documentary, but in an effort to find Hayley before it's too late. Sure, it would be a great piece to include in the *Wraith's Wrong Doing's* – urgh, another terrible title – but ultimately, I'd like to help before there's no one left *to* help. Hayley is nice, and her safety was once in my care as her babysitter.

I steal across the Bronsons' drive and am about to sneak back home when I see Hayley's car. The police must have towed it back from the restaurant. I shouldn't, but I try the door handle. It opens. A waft of Hayley's vanilla perfume hits me. It would be easy to get in the car to search, but I can't do that. Instead, I lean across, keeping my feet firmly on the gravel drive. There's CDs scattered everywhere, and wads of old parking tickets shoved into every crevice. In the back, there's a pile of clothes. I grab the nearest thing. It's an apron from Donamache's Italian Wonders.

This must be where she worked. I put everything back where I found it, then run towards the house.

The front door is closed. It locked behind me, and I don't have a key.

Damn it. If I wake up Mum and Dad I'll be in trouble, and I'm already in far too much of that as it is. Wait, the back door. Dad usually forgets to lock that. Silently, I move between the fence and Mr Davidson's car, which is once again parked on our drive – Mum won't be happy. I twist my hand through the gap in the back gate and unlock it. Tiptoeing, I make my way into the garden. Lucifer barks, announcing my presence. As I turn to quieten him, I notice there's a shape in the big oak tree above me. It's a bulky, black lump perched in the top branches, obscured by dying foliage. What the hell is that?

Chapter Sixteen

Can birds grow that big? I jump up and catch hold of a low branch, which I use to swing upwards into the tree. Upon my approach, the shape quickly climbs higher, more monkey-like than bird. I raise my hand and poke at it. The shape unfurls and I see it's a thin man. Dressed in a shiny black leotard, a Lycra mask covering his face, with only slits for eyes and a mouth.

'Hey!' I yell at him.

There's no reply, and although his face is covered, I'm sure he's smiling.

Grabbing hold of the next branch, I swing further upwards and catch his foot. As I do, he opens his arms wide, then topples off the tree and falls into our garden. Lucifer growls through the fence. I see a streak of glistening black sprint across the lawn, then use our wheelie bin to pole-vault the fence. Dad was right: the heat really does bring out the crazies. What was he even doing up there? Will he come back? I know I should tell someone, but who would believe me?

I make my way to the back door. I need to be quiet; Mum and Dad's bedroom window is just above. The door handle is metal, cool to the touch. I press it down. There's a click... It opens. It's the first genuine smile I've felt on my face for years. I slip inside and close the door behind me. I shouldn't lock it – everything needs to be just as

Dad left it – but that weirdo in the tree is bothering me, so I lock the door. Once upstairs, I turn on my laptop and check the address of Donamache's. It's outside of town, but not far from the bus stop. I can walk it. Time is running out for Hayley. If the Wraith keeps to his schedule, he'll dump her corpse soon. She could already be dead. The police haven't released much about the kills; the only information I know comes from illicit photos and seeing Dara. I'm not a forensic scientist, but more happened to her than the public know.

I set my alarm for 6 a.m.

-

Did I really see a man in a black Lycra jumpsuit in the tree? No, even to me, that sounds like some sort of episode. Just to be safe, I sketch him into my book. He now sits with the park's bad man; captured forever. I date the page and scrawl beneath, *Real?*

Before Mum and Dad get up, I write them a note, a tiny lie about wanting to get some shots for the recycling documentary. I catch the first bus of the day to Donamache's. It's a small, redbrick building crammed between shops on the side of a busy road. There's no car park, just spaces on the street. I step up to the front door and read the opening times. It only serves lunch and dinner, so the Wraith took Hayley after one of those shifts. It closes at 2 p.m. and 11 p.m., giving an hour window for cleaning up. That means she was either taken in broad daylight on a busy road or on a dark and almost deserted street at night. I'm no criminal mastermind, but I'd put money on the latter.

I spend time loitering around the building, but I don't feel or find anything useful. Perhaps you shouldn't act on ideas you have eye-wateringly early in the morning. As I turn to walk back to the bus stop, I spot a car indicating to drive down a narrow road to the far left of the restaurant. I didn't even think it was a road. I follow it to a small car park, dimly lit, and so close to Donamache's you can smell the ghosts of last night's garlic. There's a pay station for parking tickets hiding in a far, dark corner. I go up to it and feed it some coins. The ticket pops out and I instantly recognise it as the same as the ones Hayley stashed in her car.

I hang around the car park with my camera, taking a few shots, recording background noise. Watching. No visions, no immediate realisations like I've had with remote controls or other unimportant junk. No, when there's a life on the line, my strange ability is annoyingly useless.

Eventually, boredom creeps in and I catch the bus home.

I knock three times on the front door before Mum finally lets me in. As she does, she says, 'Dee, you have a visitor.'

In the living room, Father Jacob is making small talk with Dad.

'What are you doing here?' I ask.

'I came to talk to the Bronsons across the road, so thought I'd pop in and see how you're doing.'

'Good,' I quickly reply.

Father Jacob narrows his eyes. 'Well, perhaps we can go for brunch and talk about it. My treat.'

He knows I'm hiding something. Has God ratted me out?

Father Jacob escorts me to the pub where the writing group meet. I've never eaten here and the menu is disturbingly basic. I decide on a salad and Father Jacob orders an all-day breakfast.

'Dee, look, I had an email from Louisa Black's agent. She'd like to get together with you. I'm thinking she wants to apologise.'

Shrugging, I say, 'I guess the Lord does work in mysterious ways.'

'So you'll meet with her?'

Red. I feel the colour tickle at my senses. 'Six, five, four, three, two, one.' I haven't been in the same room as Louisa since the so-called exorcism. Would seeing her, breathing the same air, be enough to propel my anger over my careful counting? Making me stagger backwards on my mental health journey? Maybe even propel me back to St Alda's? 'No, I can't do that.'

'Please forgive her, Dee. You will feel so much better if you do,' Father Jacob says. 'Turn the other cheek. An eye for an eye leaves the world blind.'

I should say yes, use it as a learning experience, but I can't, so shake my head.

'I understand, but trust in God,' Father Jacob adds. 'He will always steer you in the right direction.'

I think about the signs I've received about Andy's innocence. 'Does God often test people?'

'Sometimes. Do you think you're being tested?'

'It feels that way.'

Father Jacob stabs at the bacon on his plate. 'Canon Matthew was telling me the other day that we are all constantly tested. That wickedness in the world is often wrapped in pretty paper to tempt us from God's path.'

I'm not great at reading people, but at this I see frustration flash in his eyes. 'Do you like Canon Matthew?'

Shaking his head, he replies, 'He's very good at his job. Got the church's website working and has us on social media now. He even does TikTok videos. And the congregation has grown since he took over.'

Weird, all positive things, but he shook his head *no*, he doesn't like him.

'Although, I do suspect the killings might have a lot to do with the higher numbers. Lapsed Catholics usually circle back in times of worry.'

'That's a good thing, then.'

He sighs, 'The devil has many tricks.'

At this, I ask a question I should have asked years ago. 'Do you really think I am possessed by a demon, Father?'

An odd expression falls over his features. Not his worry face, but a relative of it. He says, 'No, Dee.' Yet a 'but' starts to form on his lips, before he swallows it back down.

–

Late afternoon and it's too hot to stay in the house, so I leave with the intention of working at my new favourite coffee shop. I pack my notebooks and camera, then string my fumsup onto my backpack, so he can come with me. Cookie might be right: if I take better care of him, perhaps I'll be luckier. As I step out onto the street, I look over at the Bronsons' home. It's quiet. I want to speak with Hayley's mum, tell her how sorry I am. However, my presence might make matters worse.

Hoisting my backpack onto my shoulder, I cross the road. As I do, I look back again at the Bronsons'. Sitting on their garage roof are three tiny sparrows. All in a row. Maybe that's a good omen. Just as I think this, a massive black crow flies down onto the roof and sits next to the little brown birds. Two sparrows quickly fly off, abandoning their friend. I reach into my bag for my camera. I'm not sure why, but I have a weird feeling. As I lift the camera and turn it on, I see the crow peck at the last sparrow. It's odd; I thought crows were carrion birds? I'm guessing the sparrow thinks the same, as it holds its ground. A loud cackle sounds from the big black bird as it raises its beak. In one, almost slow-motion movement, it grabs the sparrow by the head and pulls it forward. The little bird squeals and writhes, but to no avail. The crow bangs it against the garage roof, and then skewers its beak through the brown feathered body. I've never seen anything like it. And I've got it all on film. Bird-on-bird violence. Perhaps it's the heat? The relentless sun has affected the crow's tiny brain. Or maybe it's just a cannibal taking advantage of a sparrow's ignorance. I keep filming as the crow pulls out small intestines and other tasty soft bits for its lunch. I can use the footage in the documentary, something shocking and unexpected. A metaphor for the Wraith, the big black shadow who steals the lives of innocent, pretty things. Like the crow, the Wraith will look normal, up until the point he raises his knife to strike.

The bus is late. People waiting are tutting, puffing, and muttering. I tut and puff with them, it's nice to feel part of a crowd. I get into the act so deeply that it takes a while for me to notice I have a text. When I look, I find a number I don't recognise. I open it:

> Hi Dee, I'm Betsy, Andy's wife. He told me what you are doing and thought I should get in touch too. I'm around now if you'd like to talk somewhere. Betsy xx

I hate strangers who put kisses on text messages. I don't want them and haven't earned them. Also, I feel obligated to echo the sentiment back, and I'm not a kisses kind of person. I text that I'm getting the bus into town, then ask if she'd like to meet at the Blue Sky Coffee Room in an hour. She texts straight back with *yes*, accompanied by even more kisses.

Early to Blue Sky, I order a large iced coffee and brownie, and sit away from the window seats; the thought of strangers spying on me as they walk by is leaving me colder than the iced drink – which turns out to be much less tasty than it looked on the picture behind the counter. The whipped cream has sunk, forming a grey, watery film. As I chase an ice cube with my straw, I shudder. Someone is watching me. It could be Stephanie – we crossed paths here once before – yet when I scan the seats I don't see anyone I know. Funny. I expect the sensation to die down, but it only gets worse, so much so I consider texting Betsy to meet at another venue.

Only on my third scan of the room do I see him.

Chapter Seventeen

Ashley Frampton is covering most of his face with a copy of *Lord of the Flies*. He lounges in a corner on a leather sofa. Every now and then, he looks over at me, then quickly looks away. Is he too scared to talk to me? I should say something to him. Perhaps he can work the camera for the interview with Betsy? If she agrees to one. As I get up to speak with him, he's suddenly on his feet and out of the door. There's half a muffin and a full cup of warm coffee left on his table. In his haste, he's also forgotten his book. Strange. I pick up the novel, intending to give it back to him when we meet the Watsons.

'You must be Dinah.'

Betsy is suddenly standing in front of me. Prettier than I expected, and her hand already outstretched to shake mine. Deftly avoiding the manicured digits, I motion for her to sit.

'Nice to meet you. Call me Dee. Can I interview you for the documentary? *The Wraith's Revenge?*' Quickly I add, 'That's a working title.'

'Of course, that's why I'm here. I'm glad you're helping Andy.'

I pull out the camera and use my notebooks and Ashley's abandoned book to elevate it to train on her. I then slide across a waiver. She signs it and pushes it back.

'How do I look?' she says, puckering her lips.

'Fine. Andy said you left him. Are you back together now?'

Betsy flips her long blonde hair over her shoulder. 'No, not while all this craziness is going on.'

In marriage, don't you promise in front of God that you'll love one another for better or for worse? And surely the 'worse' is when you need that partner the most. It's then I remember my notes on Andy are in the book holding up the camera, but the angle is too perfect to lose, so I make the decision to have the interview more conversational.

Turns out, Betsy is a good interview subject. She indulges in her feelings often, and doesn't do the politician move of answering her own question, rather than mine. She tells me her job is in PR and she's had clients threaten to leave her firm over Andy's issues. She claims even her brother has got in trouble at work over it.

'I admit,' she says with a coy look to the camera, 'I doubted Andy at first. Especially when The Power of Three told me to leave him or leave them.'

'Power of Three?'

'That's my PR firm. The power of three is a common technique in sales and marketing. We use it to emphasis a point. Saying something three times in a row makes it more memorable.'

I must look confused as she clarifies, 'Like when you're looking for a house, they say, location, location, location.'

'Oh, I get it.'

Betsy is wearing a low-cut summer halter dress and her shoulders are beautifully tanned, reminding me of Hayley. Her lipstick is almost the same shade as Hayley's too. Every now and then, she laughs or puts her hands up in shock and bends down low enough for the camera to catch a glimpse of her bra. I'll have to edit the hell out of this interview.

'I mean, we have way more techniques than just that so our clients make the most of the spotlight when it swings their way, but you get the idea.'

I nod.

'So, what made you want to film a documentary?'

It's jarring to be asked a question when it's my job to do the asking, so I counter with, 'So, where did you meet Andy?'

Betsy grins. 'You know, if you want to be in the spotlight yourself, you need to learn to answer questions too.' Without warning, she jerks forward and grabs my camera, then trains it on me. 'Tell me, Dee. What made you want to film this documentary?'

It's hot in the coffee shop, but staring into the camera lens sends a cold sweat dribbling down my back. I hear a phantom bell and smell incense. The people talking and laughing around us suddenly sound as if they're chanting. 'Six…' I say, but I can't think of the next number. 'Three?'

'Dee?'

I shut my eyes tightly. 'Four, I missed out four.'

'Dee? Are you okay?'

Opening my eyes, I find Betsy has placed the camera back on herself, almost as if she'd never turned it around on me at all.

'I'm sorry, what did you want to ask me?' she says, a kind smile on her face.

'Um, yeah. Um.' I try to remember my notes, then just ask, 'So, what's Andy like?'

Still smiling she replies, 'Andy's a gem, but has always had a dark side.'

'Dark side?'

'To be precise,' she leans forward, her cleavage poking out of her top. 'He has a fascination with serial killers. Although don't we all?' she laughs.

I think about this statement. Yes, most people are drawn to learn why these sickos do what they do, it's why true crime is so popular, but revealing this certainly doesn't help Andy look innocent.

'Did you discuss this much with him?' I ask.

She shrugs. 'Not really, I mean, he showed me letters he got from that nineties killer. What's his name?' As she cocks her head, Betsy's blonde hair shimmers slightly in the sunlight streaming through a nearby window.

Not having any name to offer, I patiently wait.

'Oh,' she says, 'William something. Anyhoo, any other questions you'd like to ask?'

Might as well ask the burning question. 'Do you think Andy is the Righteous Wraith?'

She half smiles. 'No. He's neither righteous nor wraithful.' I know she means wrathful. 'Is that everything, Dee?'

I quickly check the recording, then nod at her.

'Thank you again for helping Andy. He doesn't have many friends, well, apart from my family. He's a bit of a loner really. We've had issues, but what married couple doesn't these days. He doesn't deserve all this nonsense. Those Wraith Finders need a new hobby.'

'Crowd-sourced investigations seem more likely to cause a crime than solve it.' I don't look up as I speak, just keep rewinding and randomly spot-checking the recording.

'Yes, I do hope people stop taking it seriously. Just because something is said online, doesn't mean it's true.'

An odd statement from someone in PR. 'But you must know the power of the media?' I ask.

She nods, making her hair dance on the tips of her bare shoulders. 'Of course, but regardless of IRL or online, people should watch what they say.'

'IRL?'

'In real life. We tell our clients never to put something online that they wouldn't say to someone's face.'

I stop faffing about with the camera to think about all the people through the years who attacked me and my 'performance' in *Possession* online.

Betsy continues, 'And the police have already ruled out Andy.'

Looking back up at her, I ask, 'Who was the police contact?'

Her hand springs to her chest. 'Oh, I don't know a specific name. All of them? Well, must dash. I need to buy a cake for a birthday.'

I open my mouth to quiz her on the type of cake she's picking up, but she's escaped before I can get the word *icing* out.

Once I'm home, I tell Mum I've already eaten to be spared her odd salad creation. She calls it the 'what came first' salad, as drooping lettuce camouflages both cooked chicken and boiled eggs. Gently I'm quizzed as to what I ate today, and whether it was more than just pieces of cake.

'Well, a growing body needs vitamins,' Mum says.

As I've already done all the growing I'm ever going to do, a puzzled expression falls across my face.

'At least take some fruit juice.' She pours orange juice into a plastic cup and hands it to me.

'Thanks,' I say.

Her eyes linger on me, so, before going upstairs, I take a few gulps. It's the kind with bits in that are intent on invading every nook and cranny of my mouth. I'll be picking pulp out of my teeth for days.

I save Betsy's interview on the laptop, then review my footage from the car park by Hayley's restaurant. I don't see anything new or useful; just that it's an obvious place for a serial killer to grab a victim. I'm surprised the council didn't name it *Abduction Point Pay and Display*.

To relax, I sketch Betsy. She's pretty, so I use more colour than usual. After finishing, I compare it to a still from the recording and give myself a pat on the back for my artistry. Finishing up, I date the page and hide the book back in my backpack.

With the Watsons my next interview, I check Wraith Finders again. By far, the most fruitful parts of the site are the message boards and forums. Hundreds of have-a-go investigators all popping their two-pence worth into the piggybank of accusations against Andy. If all the comments were to be believed, Andy is a bogeyman of Creepypasta proportions. Appearing everywhere there is a hint of murder. There is even a list of cold cases that they link to the Righteous Wraith that he hasn't admitted to in his letters. All of it is clearly crap. The victims are children or elderly people and so don't match his MO at all. I make a note of all the members on the site and begin to work back from their user profiles to find out real identities. Most lead to dead ends; after all, it's easier to point digital fingers from behind the anonymous safety of a screen. One name does grab my attention though, a man calling himself Coolsalot. He doesn't start any discussions on the site, but always has a comment. Scanning down the newest discussion about Hayley, I notice he's put: *Andy targeted another beauty, am I right?*

All the other comments are dripping in accusations, laughable evidence of Andy's whereabouts, and even theories on where he's keeping the girls for three days. Being a surveyor, he has access to all sorts of properties. Hell, if they knew he was now living at his parents' old house, with its remote location partnered with a holey back garden, they'd have a field day.

My hands ache for some reason; maybe it's stress. Putting my palms together to pray stings, so I make this one quick. 'Dear Lord, hope you're well. I'm happy everything is moving along and people are asking to be interviewed. Not the victims' families though, they're not replying to my emails.' Quickly, I make a note in my journal to contact them again. 'Lord, okay, I'm not sure why you let the Wraith hurt and kill, but you need to help Hayley.'

Hayley's face pops into my mind. I want to rescue her. But my odd ability to find lost things ironically feels lost to me now. Time is running out. I close my eyes and remember the last time I saw her. Hair shining in the sun, those sparkly stars on her shorts. The smell of vanilla.

'Lord, this gift you gave me isn't working… can you step in, please? Amen.'

It takes a while to fall asleep, and when I do, my mind sinks into a terrible dream. There's a room. Bright and white. Not the usual setting for a nightmare, but that makes it worse. I can't get out. No door. No window. As I fumble around the walls, there's suddenly someone in front of me. Cookie. Bending over a lump in the middle of the room, he doesn't notice me. It's then I see what he is looming over: Hayley. A long thin knife is nestled in my friend's hand. I try to shout, but no words come. Cookie falls forward and plunges the blade into Hayley. Her body judders and suddenly the white room is bathed in black.

'Want to play dolls with me?' he sings.

Adrenaline jerks me awake.

—

My breakfast cereal is gritty and tasteless. But that's okay, I have a café lunch to come with the Watsons. I check my emails to ensure no cancellations and find a quick confirmation email from Mrs Watson, saying that she's looking forward to meeting me today. Lovely manners for someone ruining an innocent man's life.

The shrill cry of the house phone kills my thoughts. Mum gets up to answer it. I put my dish and plastic spoon in the sink and hear Mum stifle a little cry. They've found Hayley. I'm too late. I should have tried harder, done more, asked for help.

She comes back into the kitchen with her eyes on me. 'Dee, I need to tell you something.'

Dad puts down his paper. 'What's wrong?' he asks.

She turns to me. 'Cookie is dead.'

Chapter Eighteen

'He can't be dead,' I say.

'You have your appointment today with Dr Taylor. You should talk to her,' Mum says.

'I'm so sorry. I know you were close.' Dad awkwardly moves to pat my arm, but I rise from the chair before our skin collides.

'Cookie's not dead,' I mumble.

'Love, why don't you stay home today?'

I can't. Grabbing my backpack, I rush through the door, away from their sympathy and demands.

At the bus stop, I bend over and puke up the cereal. Cookie is dead. How could this happen? I just spoke to him, he was fine. Damn! The gap in the fence; did that have something to do with it? I should have told Dr Taylor about the nightly jaunts. I'm far from normal, but I had a responsibility to look out for my friend. Instead, I acted like a fellow inmate, gleeful at breaking the rules, rather than upholding them for safety. But, in truth, I'm not sure I believed his stories; after all, someone would've had to let my friend out of the main building first.

More people gather at the bus stop. They complain about the smell of vomit, but I don't care. I'll never see Cookie again. Someone I've known for decades, who accepted me for who I really am, is gone forever. As if to punctuate my point, across the road, I spot a family.

Mother and father hand in hand; a child each clinging to the other side. The mother is pretty but older than me. Closer now, I spot the lines on her face are not from age but laughter. A familiar thought rips across my mind like pulling off an old plaster: *I'll never have that.* Never be wanted by a partner. Never be called *Mummy.* Never be happy. My skin will remain line free, until age weathers it. At St Alda's, these thoughts were fleeting; after all, no one around me had a normal life either. But on the outside, I'm noticing it more. Hell, even Dr Taylor has found someone to make her smile. If my doctor were here, she would point out that normal doesn't necessarily mean happy. There's a sad and complicated truth there.

The bus comes and I slip onto it like a ghost. As much as I know I should stay on the route and circle back to the house, pull down my bedroom blind and sleep away the hollow feeling in my chest, Cookie would want me to carry on with my normal life.

–

The Hungry Piglet Café is all red gingham and kitsch; it has cartoon pigs grinning at you while you eat their bacon and ham. After I tell the owner that being in the documentary is free advertising, he greedily signs a waiver for us to film here. He even offers to feed us all, which although lovely, makes me suspect he recognises me from *Possession is Nine Tenths.*

Ashley arrives with a huge camera and tripod and starts to set up in a dark corner of the café. Where did he get that from?

I should tell him to move, that this project is mine, and we need to occupy a table near the window for natural light, but I don't. All the energy I had inside me today has withered. I wonder if they'll have a funeral for Cookie at St Alda's? Will his family finally visit him, this one last time?

Ashley doesn't acknowledge me as I approach, so I set down my bag and pull out my own camera.

'We don't need two,' he says. 'Managed to borrow this from work.'

'Work? I thought you were student?'

'I am. I've got a part-time job at a sales and marketing place. Just increased my hours for the summer.' He turns on his camera.

Ashley thinks he knows better than me because he has a job. And he probably does, but this is my documentary. 'Two cameras are better. I want more than one angle.' I use a nearby wooden utensil box from another table to elevate my shot.

'Sure, teamwork makes the dream work,' he says, but his eyes don't meet mine.

'Why didn't you say hello yesterday in the coffee shop?' I ask.

With a huff, he plonks down onto a nearby chair. 'I wasn't at a coffee shop yesterday.'

'Yes, you were. You left your drink and half a muffin.' I almost add the *Lord of the Flies* book to the list of his abandoned items, but don't.

'Not me.'

I should drop it, but I'm not in the mood to be trodden on today.

'Perhaps I should contact the university and ask for someone else's help with this?'

'I've blagged the equipment now. Let's just crack on.' He says it as if he's *my* boss.

Counting be damned, I'm about to unleash the red I know lives deep down in the pit of my soul, when a couple bustles through the door. They point at the cameras and head straight over. Next thing I know the woman is coming at me for a hug. She's skinny and has brown straw scarecrow hair; her bones jut out towards my body like weapons. Side-stepping her, I wave my greeting instead.

'So glad to meet you,' she says.

'You too, Mrs Watson. Thank you for agreeing to this.'

As she sits down, her husband, who looks the exact opposite of his wife, ninety pounds overweight and so tall he has to stoop when he comes in, tries to hug me too. Ready for it, I step backwards, almost falling into a nearby table.

Instead of looking hurt, he laughs. 'Don't want to make the boyfriend jealous,' he says and nods to Ashley.

'He's not my boyfriend.'

Mrs Watson smiles, then leans in and whispers, 'Good, you're a pretty little thing and can do much better, Dinah.'

'This is my cameraman, Ashley. And you can both call me Dee.'

They wave at Ashley, who seems oddly oblivious to everything.

It takes more time than I would have hoped for us to set everything up. All the while, the café staff hovers, delivering drinks and trying to photobomb shots.

Finally, we are ready to begin. After the Watsons both sign waivers, Mrs Watson scoots forward, her husband looming behind her like a mountain. At first, I ask easy questions, nothing too intrusive, about the group's origins and how they run it. I don't mention my connection with Andy.

Mrs Watson does most of the talking. She tells me of their shared love of true crime, and how the two bonded over famous unsolved cases when they first met. She says Northamptonshire has a history of attracting the kind of men who prey upon the innocent. I sit quietly, the smell of bacon in my nostrils, and listen to her draw unsubstantiated conclusions about police conspiracies and hints about cults lurking in a local woods. I find it difficult not to butt in with questions and contradictions, so make a habit of taking a sip of coffee every time I want to correct her on something. It's like a bizarre drinking game and sees me four coffees down too quickly, my slender hands shaking with the caffeine.

My mind wanders from the interview too many times. I'll hear a voice and look up to catch a glimpse of Cookie, staring at me, waving, smiling, and beckoning me to join him.

'…And that's when we thought we should do something about it,' Mrs Watson finishes.

Blinking, I check my camera. Did we really just go full circle?

'Were there any other questions?' she asks, then takes a bite of her bacon sandwich, which I don't remember her ordering, let alone the waitress bringing.

Ashley asks, 'Do you still think Andy Fryer is guilty?'

I throw him the stink-eye; I was keeping that question until last. Cameramen should stay behind the equipment – neither seen nor heard.

'Yes.' Mrs Watson looks over to her husband, who nods.

'Can you repeat that in a sentence please?' I ask. 'It's just the question won't be heard.'

'We think Andy Fryer is guilty. Guilty as sin,' she says.

'But what about his alibis?' I adjust my camera to frame only her in my shot.

'Flimsy. And…' She leans further forward. 'What if he's not working alone?'

'Serial killers always work alone,' Ashley says with an eye roll.

'Not always, what about Fred and Rose West? Or the Moors Murderers? They worked together.' Mrs Watson looks over at her husband, who purses his lips and nods.

I can't believe his wife Betsy could have anything to do with the murders. She seems too nice and normal.

'Yeah, but there are more solos than duos.' Ashley steps out from behind the camera and I resist the urge to throw the salt pot at his head.

'What's your point?' Mrs Watson begins to lift herself from the chair. They're going to leave.

'We should take a break,' I say. 'Get some dessert.'

I watch as Ashley turns off his camera, but I leave mine running.

'We've never done anything like this before, have we?' Mrs Watson says to her husband who nods. 'We'll have to update the group when we get in.'

The waitress steps over and asks us if we want anything else. I order a Victoria sponge for the table along with more coffees.

We make idle small talk for a while. I want them to relax, really open up. The idea of two Wraiths is intriguing, but it would blow up my documentary; it could mean Andy is guilty after all. But who would he be working with if not Betsy? Who could he trust that much? No, that's silly, and I can't forget that God wants me to help him, and the Lord isn't in the business of supporting serial killers.

When we start filming again, I throw Ashley a look that hopefully warns him to stay quiet this time.

'Crowd-sourced investigations have recently come under scrutiny. How do you justify running Wraith Finders?' I train my camera on Mr Watson. He needs to speak up soon or be demoted to a scenery prop.

'Well, I think that—' Mrs Watson says.

'Can Mr Watson answer thisone, please?'

'Sure.' She sits back to let her husband speak.

'Yes, things can get out of hand, but crowd-sourced investigations have been around much longer than the internet. The TV show *Crime Watch* is a version of crime-solving crowd-sourcing, appealing for witnesses on a large scale. Then there's the old-fashioned posters to jog people's memories. It's solved more than it's harmed, just look at…' and he carries on, and on, and on. I realise after five minutes that this is the real reason Mrs Watson kept her husband silent – once he gets going, he never shuts up.

As the lunch crowd flood out of the café, I wrap up the interview.

'If you need more interviewees, I can ask other members?' Mrs Watson offers.

'That would be great. I'd especially love to connect with Rabbits Foot, as they are providing the photos.'

'I'll ask him.' The Watsons then leave the same way as they entered, with a flurry of inappropriate comments and hugging attempts.

They're not even fully out of the door when Ashley says, 'Christ, that was slow. You should have asked more about Andy. Is this your first time behind the camera?'

Not wanting to admit it, I snap, 'I was waiting until they were relaxed, *then* I was going to throw Andy at them. But you shot that to hell. Is this *your* first documentary?'

He has the decency to blush. 'Fine. What's next?'

'Pack up. I thought we could get shots at some of the body dump sites.' I pull out my exercise book and show him the list. He reaches to grab the pages. Feeling as if he's trying to seize a piece of me, I yank it back. 'Let's work back from the 10th girl, Dara; Maple Industrial Estate on the edge of town.'

'Okay. I'm parked just outside.'

Damn. I didn't realise he'd have a car.

'What's wrong?' Ashley narrows his eyes at me.

'I'd rather use the bus and meet you there.'

'You don't trust my driving?'

'It's not that.'

'Oh, the accident. I get it, although the car hit you — perhaps you should be more fearful of being a pedestrian.'

'What? How did you know?'

'*Possession is Nine Tenths*. They show it on the media course at the university.' He throws out this fact as if it's not incendiary and bound to burn me alive.

'You knew who I was this whole time?'

'Yeah, Louisa Black is due to give a talk at the university next week. You should say hello. You probably haven't caught up in years.'

Red. My mouth opens...

'Whoa, no need for that language.' Ashley is backing away from me.

Did my head spin round? I can't see green vomit anywhere. 'Sorry. I don't much like Louisa Black,' I say.

'Yeah, I gathered. Fuck.'

Hell, I don't even remember swearing. Am I that stressed? No, I'm only just making headway. Hayley needs me to find her. Andy needs me to exonerate him. I'll take another pink pill tonight. Doubling the dose should settle me back down.

'Should I call your doctor or something?' he asks.

I shake my head, but he keeps staring at me, as if any minute I'm going to levitate or climb the walls like Spider-Man. To break our uncomfortable eye contact, I pull out my mobile and check it. There's a text from Andy. He wants to know how the Watsons' meeting went and wondered if I could come around now to finish his interview. Not wanting to lose the invitation, I text yes, and that Ashley and I will be there soon.

'What's your angle with all this Wraith stuff?' Ashley asks, gesturing to the equipment. 'It would make more sense if you covered something you knew about. Like mental homes or demons?'

My mouth puckers up and I have to look away.

'I didn't mean to be rude. Can I ask you something?'

Could I stop him?

'Were you really possessed?' He moves closer to me. 'What did it feel like?'

'I'm tackling this story because Andy asked me to expose what's happening to him.' I take a step back and hit a chair with my foot. I want to add that God seems to be telling me to as well, but that sounds weird even in my head.

Ashley huffs. 'You answered the wrong question.'

'Maybe you asked the wrong question. Now let's get on. Change of plan. Andy is at home, so let's finish up some more of his interview.'

'Anything you say.' Ashley writes down the address. 'Hey, want me to at least take your stuff there?' He reaches for my backpack.

'No!' I jerk my shoulder back.

'Whatever. I was just trying to be nice.' With that, he leaves.

I have a mile trek with a heavy backpack in the devil's heat. Maybe I should have let Ashley take my bag, but the thought of it being out of my sight makes my skin itch. All my books and footage, everything that matters to me, is in there, even the ridiculous fumsup that refuses to be lucky.

In an attempt to lighten my load, I dig out Ashley's book, *Lord of the Flies*. If he claims it's not his, then I'm not going to lug it around with me anymore. As I go to place it on the table, I notice something odd about the pages. Black spots stain the edges. I flip through the book and discover another reason not to be in alone in a car with Ashley. Drawn over the text are sketches of droopy-limbed, gutted, eyeless girls. All of whom I recognise as Wraith victims.

Chapter Nineteen

He's waiting for me.

Ashley's car is a small, dirty, dark-blue Fiat with three big scratches down the passenger side, a dented bonnet, and four mismatched tyres. He's sitting in the driver's seat playing on his phone.

His book is weighing down my bag. Have I just brought the real Wraith to Andy's door? No, lots of people draw dead girls, yet don't kill any.

I knock on the window. 'Hey.'

Ashley stows his phone and gets out. He frees his camera bag from the backseat, then locks his car. 'I know it's a piece of shit, but it gets me from A to B a lot quicker than a bus. If you'd like, I can drive you round on short trips, get you used to cars again? It could make your life easier.'

Ashley's round face is already reddening in the sun, so I simply nod at him. Not a commitment to accept his help, but an acknowledgement that at least it was offered – and also confirmation that his car is indeed a piece of shit.

Smiling, he moves towards the house. 'Spooky place this, an old house in the middle of nowhere. With us walking towards it, it's kind of like the start of a horror film.'

'Worse still, it used to be an old rectory.' I laugh, but it's strained and escapes as more of a worried gasp. I then remember the busy main road on the other side of the property and feel a little easier, but only a little.

We walk to the door. I knock. No answer. *Damn you, Andy, you better be here.* I knock again.

'You sure he's home?' Ashley asks.

'I'll check around the back,' I say, scampering off to where I found Andy last time. He's not there either. I scan the garden with its giant molehill lumps and dying plants. Worried thoughts begin to dance as I remember Ashley's book. I shouldn't be alone here with him.

'Dee?' Andy appears behind me.

'Thank God.'

'Why?'

I almost hug him. 'Doesn't matter.'

'Well, your cameraman is already inside. Where'd you get him from? The Big and Creepy store?'

'Well, I came from the Little and Creepy store.'

Andy laughs. 'Guess you did. Come on.'

In the kitchen, I pass my laptop over to Ashley, so he can record straight onto it, whilst uploading his copy of the Watsons' interview.

We both set up our cameras and Andy encourages us to look around the house. He's more talkative today and tells us a little history about the place. How the Fryers used to be butchers and made their money in meat. The house renovation was his parents' dream, not his, but it did give him a taste for buildings. After his mum and dad died, he sold the butchery business and funded a career in surveying. For sentimental reasons, he couldn't sell the house. When he married Betsy, they moved into the city centre and only came out here at bank holiday weekends. The Fryers tried to keep most of the old rectory intact, so the building is stone and even though it's still hot as hell outside, the irregular grey bricks give off a cool vibe that feels good against my skin.

With my camera, I wander alone further into the house. It's almost magical, exploring a place from another time. The battery light beside my finger starts to blink. I kick myself for not recharging it last night. A rookie mistake, one I doubt the world-famous Louisa would have made. I can't believe she's talking at the university. I must tell Cookie… The urge to put my hands together is too great. I join my palms. 'Dear Lord, please tell me if Cookie is with you. I need to know he's safe, and—'

Bang. Bang. Bang.

What the hell was that?

Andy didn't mention that someone else was in the house. The sound is coming from one of the rooms. I edge towards the door. 'Hello?'

Bang. Bang. Bang.

Gripping the handle, I pull open the door. Inside is a small room filled with cardboard boxes. Stuff piled so high, sunlight from the window barely sheds a shred of light. Quickly, I turn on my camera torch.

I know I shouldn't, but I really want to open the boxes. They're not mine and I have no business being in this room, let alone going through Andy's personal stuff, but I can't help it. Setting down my camera, I peek into a nearby box… Weird, it's a cheap-looking black velvet top hat, the kind magicians wear. I dig deeper. Just women's clothes. Probably belonging to Betsy. He must have been so miserable when she left that he boxed up all her stuff and shoved it out of sight. The top garment is a red dress. It's sparkly with sequins, and although the colour isn't my thing, I lift it up and hold it against myself. As I do, a piece of denim drops out. Bending, I pick it up. Opening it out, I see a pair of shorts. I turn them around and find two silver stars sewn onto the back pockets. Just like the ones Hayley was wearing the day the Wraith abducted her.

No. There has to be more than one pair of these shorts in the world. I check the label: It's My Look. Yes, there are several It's My Look shops around Northamptonshire. Betsy and Hayley probably just have the same taste in clothes. Still, it's a big coincidence. I shouldn't, but I roll up the small denim shorts and hide them in my bag. I'm about to dig further into the box, when I hear Andy calling my name.

'Coming,' I yell back.

Bang. Bang. Bang.

Weird, it now sounds as if it's coming from below this room.

'Dinah?' Andy yells, closer.

Bang. Bang. Bang.

It's probably in my head. I've heard the same thing at home. Three distinct knocks. Crouching down, I bang on the floor three times.

'Where are you? Ashley has set everything up.' Andy appears in the doorway.

'Just getting some background noise in this room. It has great acoustics.' I get up.

'You shouldn't be in here.'

'Sorry. Shall we crack on?'

Andy watches me leave the room. As we walk together, he asks, 'What were the Wraith Finders like?'

'I shouldn't talk about them with you.'

Bang. Bang. Bang.

Instinctively, I turn at the knocking sound behind me.

'Pipes,' Andy says. 'They're old. The house creaks and knocks constantly. That won't ruin your recordings, will it? Did you pick up anything last time?'

'No, I don't think so.'

'We can always go somewhere else.'

'That's okay.'

'Let me just go and check the boiler. I'll turn the heating down, so there's no more banging.' He then jogs back to the boxes room.

It's thirty-three degrees outside, why would he have the heating on? Maybe it's for hot water?

I find my way back to the kitchen. Ashley is in there fiddling with the sound equipment.

'Can you crank up the microphone?' I ask.

'Why?'

'Just record a little in the hall for me.'

Sour-faced, he picks up the microphone and slinks out of the kitchen. I watch my laptop as he records the house. There are spikes in the sound waves, like little hills on a skyline. It's a powerful mic, so it could be just a curious mouse squeaking or indeed the boiler knocking.

When Andy returns, I watch him interact with Ashley. I have a lot of weird evidence mounting in my back-pack. Ashley's book of random murder drawings. Denim shorts that could have belonged to my abducted neighbour. Could they be working together? No, they've never met before. They shook hands when we walked in. As they move around the kitchen, it's obvious they're not comfortable with one another. And you could only murder girls with someone you know well. And how would Ashley know I was going to contact the university for help? Random thoughts are creeping into my logic and corrupting it. My faith is wavering. One more thing to talk to Dr Taylor about. Damn, my appointment – I'm going to be late if I don't leave now.

'Let's come back another day for a second interview,' I say, grabbing my laptop.

'But we're all set up?' Ashley whines.

'I forgot I have an appointment. Sorry.'

Ashley shakes his head. 'I can take the helm on this one?'

'No, let's just come again another day.'

Turning with a huff, he begins to pack up. 'You're the boss,' he mumbles.

'Need a lift back to your house?' Andy asks, huffing. Did I annoy him by not even shooting one frame today? Or maybe it's because I wouldn't talk about the Watsons.

'No, no. I'm good thanks.'

'She prefers public transport,' Ashley says, then gives me a weird knowing look.

'Oh, that's good, I guess. Saving the environment one exhaust at a time.' Andy smiles at me. 'Betsy was like that.'

Was like that? I stow my stuff and look up at him. 'Is there any chance you and Betsy could get back together? She does believe you're innocent.'

'But she didn't at first. That kind of mistrust is hard to get past.'

'Yeah, I know all about mistrust.' I look over to Ashley. 'Are you good to come back here another day with me?'

'Just tell me when.'

I leave them together. No doubt, Ashley will tell Andy about *Possession is Nine Tenths* now. My demonic worms will be well and truly out of the can and crawling everywhere.

Luck is on my side. The bus arrives on time and it takes me to Dr Taylor's office with minutes to spare. St Alda's looms in the background. Without Cookie, I have no reason to visit it now. All the other patients I knew either got better or died. Sometimes both.

Dr Taylor is wearing a vivid pink blouse, which shows off her massive boobs and matching sweat stains. I'm the last patient she sees on a Friday, and I can tell her heart isn't in it today. Her week must have been as hard as mine, her hair is greasy and dripping from her usual tight bun, and her eyes appear dull and disinterested. She greets me with a forced smile and leads me into her office. I sit down.

Sighing, she says, 'So, what would you like to talk about today?'

'Cookie.'

'I'm sorry he died.'

'What happened?' I ask.

She sits back in her chair, arms crossed over her enormous bosom. 'I shouldn't talk about it with you.'

'Can you at least tell me how he died?'

'Cookie was sneaking out of the grounds. Did you know that, Dee?'

Lies or truth, both have consequences. Fortunately, Dr Taylor continues without waiting for my answer. 'Your friend was leaving St Alda's at night without permission.'

I look away. I should have said something about the gap in the fence, but...'To get out, Cookie would need to be let out of the main building first,' I say, then realise my friend's death really is someone's fault.

'Would you have done that, Dee?'

This time she waits for my answer. 'Left the building and grounds at night? No. And like I said, someone in St Alda's would have had to let my friend out.'

'We are looking into that. But, as you remember, St Alda's isn't a prison. Do you often go out at night now?'

'I don't live at St Alda's anymore,' I mumble.

'But you've lost your job, which was a condition of your release. That's why you barged in here the other day, Dee, wasn't it? Let's talk about that.'

I'm doing too well to go back to St Alda's. My documentary needs to come out. I still have time to find Hayley.

'It was a misunderstanding. They thought I sent out some invoices wrong, but it wasn't me.'

'Who was it, then?'

I think back over my encounters with my work colleague. 'It might have been Corinne. She tried to blame Stephanie at first, then turned it on me. I'm thorough, you know I am. I wouldn't do half a job and I know the difference between zero and a number.'

Dr Taylor shrugs. 'I can't disagree with any of that. I believe you, Dee. There are some unscrupulous people in the world, and most of them are still out there, doing what they want unhindered by rules; rules that you must live by.' She sighs. 'I know Louisa is coming back to the county for a talk. That alone is bound to unsettle your mind. Why don't we look into changing your medication?'

'No. The pink pills work, I just need...'

'What?'

'Help. My best friend died. And you still haven't told me how.'

'It won't help to know the details.'

'Shouldn't I be the judge of that?' I say.

She takes a breath. 'He was run over by a car.'

'What?' Damn, damn, damn. Just like me. My head falls into my sweaty hands.

'I'm sorry, Dee.'

I hear Dr Taylor moving, and look up in case she's heading over to me to give comfort. She doesn't, she's simply shifting in her chair. She knows me too well to make that gesture.

'Death is a natural part of life,' she offers.

Natural? Red, just for a second. 'Colliding with a car isn't very natural!'

'Count back, Dee.'

I do, but only inside my head, so it doesn't stop her from continuing. 'Now do you see why I was shielding you from it? And why Louisa might also trigger an episode?'

'Louisa was…'

'Cruel and did something slightly illegal and incredibly immoral, but she wasn't the root cause of your condition. That was the hit and run in front of the church.'

I had a list of things I wanted to talk about with Dr Taylor. However, none of it seems important now.

'Shall we find a time to talk more about Cookie? Perhaps you can help with the funeral arrangements? Make sure he gets the send-off he wanted.'

I should ask about his family. But they considered him dead the moment they left him at St Alda's. His death is just paperwork to them.

'I'll help,' I whisper. Then louder add, 'I have a lot to do. Can I go?'

'We need to talk about this work situation some more.' She leans forward, tenting her fingers.

'It wasn't my fault, I told you.' A hint of red tickles the sides of my vision again.

'I said I believe you.' The words are calming, but her pen violently assaults a page in her notebook. 'But perhaps it would be best for you to move back to St Alda's, just for a little while. Get your bearings again?'

'I won't voluntarily commit myself. You'd have to force me. I've done nothing wrong. I'm trying to help with Andy and the Wraith. I even found Dara's body...' Oh damn, I shouldn't have said that.

'What? You found a dead body? Dee, this is most disturbing. How did you find it? Did you know it was already there? Did you call the police? How do you feel?'

Closing my mouth, I silently count back again, just in case.

Dr Taylor presses on, 'I'm not accusing you of anything. I'm your doctor, what you say to me is in the strictest confidence.' She gets up to stand behind me, blocking my exit.

'I'm good at finding things, remember? And you know I'm doing a documentary on the Wraith.' I can't see the expression on her face, or what she's doing. Feeling her looming behind me is so uncomfortable I rise to face her. 'Believe me, don't believe me. I'm done with being accused of stuff I didn't do.'

She takes a deep breath. 'Do you remember all those times we spoke about the brain?'

Is this a test? 'Of course: pterion, amygdala, limbic system.'

'Nothing wrong with your hippocampus and cerebellum then.' She laughs.

'Guessing they deal with memory.'

'I've checked your medical history many times. In the accident, you hit your head hard. Classic traumatic brain injury that started your amygdala hijacks along with PTSD from the accident, which in turn presented to—' she hesitates – 'the less educated, as being possessed by a demon.'

What is she getting at? 'But I'm fine now, or you wouldn't have let me out,' I say.

Dr Taylor smiles at me; it's the kind of smile I see on the faces of mothers with small children. 'Everyone, regardless of their mental state, can make mistakes now and then. But you should own up to them.'

She does think I sent out those invoices, and that I'm lying about Corinne because I don't want to get in trouble.

'Dee, you need to remember that just because someone does one thing wrong, it doesn't mean they are doing everything wrong.'

'I'm not doing everything wrong,' I whine. 'Don't you believe me?'

'Enough to let you go today. Don't make me regret it.'

Quickly, I leave the office. I sprint to the bus stop and then have an anxious ten-minute wait while I watch for men in white coats sporting human-sized butterfly nets to swarm across the road. They don't appear.

–

Mum is waiting by the front door. Clearly, not everything I say to Dr Taylor is in confidence as she knows more than she should. She forces me to eat a hot dinner of fish fingers and mash with acidic red cabbage fresh from the jar, and then orders me to my room.

Emptying my bag, I find the denim shorts I stole from Andy. With time on my hands, I search the It's My Look website, but don't find a pair with stars on the back pockets. They don't look too worn, but maybe they're last season's stock? There's an It's My Look shop in town. I'll go there in the morning and ask the staff.

Spending all day trying not to think about Cookie, yet still having to talk about his death, has exhausted me, but my mind won't stop racing. Cookie wanted to tell me something about the Wraith. My friend had information about Dara, and to a degree, Lisa… I think. But, in truth, all I have are snippets of childish thoughts, imaginings and discussions that I never had the chance to straighten out into a cohesive story: the ultimate unintentional, unreliable narrative. As much as I don't want to dwell, there is one person I should tell about Cookie's death. I call him.

'Father Jacob?'

'Yes, Dee. Will I see you at church on Sunday?'

'Cookie died.' The two words cut my throat as I let them loose.

'I'm so sorry. We will say a prayer for Cookie together.'

Placing the mobile on speakerphone, I kneel and lay it before me. Father Jacob takes me through a lovely prayer, using beautiful scripture and messages of hope and love. By the end, I feel Cookie is at peace. Both the man he used to be and the child his injury left him as. After amen, we hang up.

I should take two pink pills tonight, but my to-do list demands I have my wits about me. Dr Hawk's book states that victimology is often the key to unravelling the killer's psyche.

Before I worked back from the latest victims, but today I start my research with the 1st girl, Erica Tomkins. Her

Facebook profile is still live, albeit quiet from the date the Wraith took her. It's also public, crammed with fish-face selfies and bland memes. I scan down her timeline and see she was annoyingly normal, vapid in some posts, misspelling words and ignoring careless typos, but she was pretty with bright blue eyes and strawberry blonde hair, and so all was forgiven by her many friends. I'm about to give up when I see a long-forgotten post about a boyfriend. She has included one photo with him partially in view, wearing a familiar hideous Hawaiian shirt. Even with so few of his features to go on, I instantly recognise him. Andy.

Chapter Twenty

Andy was Erica's boyfriend! He cheated on Betsy. Although, maybe they split up, then got back together? But Erica was the 1st girl. Killers tend to target someone they know for their first victim. Is this evidence? I haven't seen this photo on Wraith Finders. Should I show them? No. Andy is innocent. I'm unsure as to the circumstances, but it's wrong to jump to conclusions. I take a screenshot of the photo. I'll ask him about this at our next meeting. Having an affair with the first victim is suspicious, but, as Dr Taylor said, just because you do one thing wrong, doesn't mean you're doing *everything* wrong. Still, do the police know about it?

After pulling down my blind, I go to bed.

-

In the morning, I sneak out before Mum and Dad are up, then catch the bus into town. After buying a breakfast muffin from the bakery, I head towards the high street.

Our local It's My Look is huge. Colour is everywhere, along with sharp-looking racks and massive sale signs. Clothes as far as the eye can see. There's a huge staircase, which I'm presuming leads to even more clothes. Struggling to see any assistants, I push further into the shop. There's a pay desk, although unmanned. I head to it. As I wait to be spotted, I retrieve the shorts from my bag.

'Do you have the receipt for your return?'

I look up to see a girl has appeared. She's taller than me but looks much younger.

'No, I'm not returning anything. Can you help me?'

'I'll try.' She leans over the counter.

'These shorts have your label in, but I can't find them on your website. Do you know anything about them?' I hand her the stolen shorts.

Taking them, she lays them flat. 'They are this year's stock.' She heads off into the shop and returns with another pair of identical-looking shorts, only this pair have no stars on the pockets.

'But what about the design on the back?' I ask.

'Someone has added them on. They didn't buy them like this. It looks good.'

A chill grips my body. They *are* Hayley's shorts. What are the odds that Betsy bought the same pair and then added the same stars in the same place?

'Are you okay?'

I stare at the girl. 'Not really. I think they belong to my friend Hayley,' I mutter.

'Did you want me to see if we have a pair in your size?'

'No, no. Thank you.' I stuff the denim back into my bag, then get the hell out of the shop.

The Wraith keeps girls for three days, but there's no telling when he kills them. It might not be until just before he dumps the body; Hayley could still be alive, and if she is, she doesn't have long.

If I ever needed my weird lost object finding trick, it's now. I stand at the bus station. Without looking at the buses, I get on one that feels right. Once sitting down, I close my eyes. Passengers ring the bell a few times, making me wince, but I shake it off. I can do this. That's not the same bell as those people used on me. I am in no danger here. A twinge tickles across my brain. I smell vanilla. Excited, I rush off the bus without looking where I am, only to find I'm in front of St Alda's. My senses are telling me I need to be locked up again.

-

Back home, I knock, knock and knock again at the front door. No answer. Mum and Dad must have already left for the day. Without a key, I'm homeless until they return, so walk to the pub and hide in the corner where Inspiration Cometh usually haunt.

Too many thoughts crowd my mind… Hayley's shorts were at Andy's house. He used to date Erica. Is that enough to prove he really is the Wraith? Can I trust my own judgement? After all, I trusted Louisa once. But God was telling me to help Andy; He can't be wrong, can He?

I check my emails. The Watsons have messaged. Mr Watson's rambling habit doesn't translate to the written word. Their email is curt and straight to the point, listing further evidence of Andy's guilt – personal things they hadn't published on the website, probably due to their intrusive nature. If I didn't know better, I'd think this email came from entirely different people.

The evidence attached is more photos. Andy caught in places, dated and marked with exact locations, some that weren't included on the site. There are eleven attachments in total. I open them in order and it's like an eerie déjà-vu of the photos of the Wraith's victims. From the 1st girl Erica, all the way up to the 11th girl, Hayley. There's even one showing Andy in a place I recognise, Maple Industrial Estate; and it's not just the location of Dara's body, as the file name reads: *Maple, where Fiona was last seen alive*. I Google her online obituary. *Survived by her husband Vlad*, it says, *missed by her colleagues at Crater Chemicals*. I remember that name; its office is in Maple. In the final photo, Andy is having dinner alone at Donamache's Italian Wonders; his server's face can't be seen, it's obscured by her long auburn hair.

Although damning, it begs the question, if they were watching him this closely, why didn't they then catch him in the act?

I have a quick look at the Wraith Finders web page; there are no updates, and no new conversations in the forums. No new photos from Rabbits Foot either. I text Mum and ask when she'll be back at the house and get the answer that she's shopping and will text when she's finished.

While I have the time, I log on and find another new article on *Possession is Nine Tenths*. Why won't this go away? Louisa has, of course, pimped out this wonderful review of her torturing me, but as I click onto her page, I see she has updated her status. It says *RIP Hayley Bronson*. What the hell? Has Hayley been found? I search for her online. An article barely three minutes old pops up. Hayley was discovered in Good Tree Park. The same park I walk through to get the bus to and from work. The same park where I stopped a child abduction. This morning, she was spotted stuffed inside a wooden Wendy house by the swings. No eyes, bruises decorating her cold flesh. Never to smell like vanilla again. A toy tea set at her feet.

If I was the type of person to cry, I would. I tried to save her. But I'm not a police officer. I'm not a detective; I'm not even a fully functioning normal person. *I'm so sorry, Hayley*.

There's more beneath Louisa's post. Never to waste a promotional opportunity, she talks about her visit to the local university, then hints about the new project she's started work on. As I stare at these words, her status once again updates.

> Hey there Tenthers, it's a difficult time for my home county of Northamptonshire, and I'd like to help. My next documentary will be on... the Righteous Wraith.

Chapter Twenty-One

Damn!

She's already started her Wraith documentary, which is simply entitled *Search for the Righteous Wraith*. There's links to exclusive trailers that parade publicly released photos of the victims, and a press release from a streaming service saying how much they paid for the documentary – too much. She's moving too fast for me to catch up, even with the footage I already have. She has quotes from DCI Campbell, Vlad, and the media outlets who received the letters. Of course, she's further along. She has a name; a name earned from my blood.

Front and centre of this announcement, there's a video link to a live stream. I click it to find Louisa grinning at me. A second or two ticks by as she cocks her head to find the best angle for her traitorous mug – all the time she's still recording.

'Hey there, Tenthers. Got a treat for you today. Let me introduce you to... Megan.' Standing aside, she shows the twelve-year-old sister of the first victim, her face slapped with the same sarcastic smile as Louisa's.

'Hey there, lambs,' she echoes.

'So, Megan, you've been pretty vocal about what happened to Erica. Tell me, why do you think the killer refers to himself as righteous?'

'Because he's a—' There's a loud beep that blocks out her rude noun. 'He murdered my only sister, and other girls. He's a—' Beeps again.

I know what it's like to lose control of your words. To let that red demon speak for you, but this is online, public. The Wraith could be watching – *is* probably watching. Megan is young, she doesn't know any better. But from the smirk on Louisa's face, she clearly does. Taking advantage of a young girl worked for her in the past, so in her eyes, I guess, why not do it again? Let little, clueless Megan bait a serial killer live online. She was obviously the 'friend' Megan spoke about in her first attempt to catch the killer's eye. Louisa is truly awful, and has clearly already written her storyboard for her documentary, but for all her research and filming she doesn't have what I have. Hayley's fleeting friendship, the experience of finding Dara's body, Andy's words, and the Watsons' accusations. That's all mine. My idea. My work. My burden.

I jump when my phone beeps in my hand. Mum's back and needs a hand with the shopping.

-

An orange juice carton has exploded in the car boot. Mum's angry and, as I'm the one who drinks the juice and is present at the peak of her annoyance, I bear the brunt. Matters are not helped by the fact that Mr Davidson has not only parked in our drive, but is blocking it. Swearing loudly, and cursing Dad's best friend, Mum storms into the house with the shopping. As I help, I try to tell her about Hayley, but can't get a word in. She switches from tirades on crappy packaging, to Dad not manning up to

Davey Boy, to my new knack for losing jobs, so swiftly that a lull in her words never appears.

Kitchen towels in hand, I decide to set about cleaning the boot of congealing juice. She bought the one with the bits in again.

'Whatcha doing?'

I look up to see Mr Davidson.

'Juice exploded,' I reply.

'Oh dear, you're not going postal, are you?'

He has a grin with a hint of expectation – I think.

'No, are you?' I mutter.

'Well, it's good of you to clean it up. Bet you didn't have to do stuff like that in the loony bin, eh?'

Unsure what he means, I nod. I cleaned up a lot of things in St Alda's café. It's not something that bothers me, why should it bother him?

'Mum doesn't want you parking in the drive anymore,' I tell him, hoping he'll take the hint and leave.

'Oh, your dad didn't say anything. He's scared of her too, eh? Probably where you get your temper from, eh?' Mr Davidson is growing a whisper of a moustache across his lip. The hairs jiggle when he talks. 'Want some help?'

I'm so entranced with his dancing facial hair that I don't decline in time, so he reaches for the kitchen towels. Pulling off too many, he then dabs at some orange.

'Thank you,' I mutter.

'Don't mention it. Hey, Dee. How'd you like being back in the world?'

What does he expect me to say? Tentatively, I push out two words, 'It's good.'

'Bet it is. Nothing like being free.' He takes in a deep breath.

Wanting to end this interaction as quickly as possible, I take the kitchen towel from him.

'Well, I best move my car. Catch you, catch you, catch you later,' he says with a laugh. Good Lord, is he adopting a catchphrase?

—

After unpacking the heavy shopping bags, I spy a box of cakes and sneak it out before Mum notices. I then take the kidnapped baked goods to my room: jam sponges, all yellow and yummy. If I keep them somewhere cool and dark, they should last me the next three days.

With Louisa working on a rival Wraith documentary, I'll need to move fast on mine. Figure out what's going on. I have Hayley's shorts in my bag. Stolen from a box in Andy's room. I heard knocking, but I've heard a lot of knocking recently, always three knocks. I can't talk to Dr Taylor; she's on the brink of signing me back into St Alda's now, thanks to the debacle at work. Hayley was wearing those shorts when she went missing; I saw them. They are in my bag. Ashley could be a killer; he seems to have a worrying habit of drawing murder victims on the pages of classic literature, a hobby that even the patients at St Alda's would have recoiled from. Do Ashley and Andy know one another? Could they be the two sides of the Wraith coin?

I have pages upon pages of research on the murders. All the evidence I have right now points to either Andy, Ashley, or me – the newly released mental patient. God has to be testing me, but why? I need to speak with Father Jacob. I can tell him anything, he never judges.

I look down at the fumsup hitching a ride on my backpack, its blank wooden face devoid of emotion or answers. Leaning across, I squeeze its head between my fingers.

'Touch wood, I'm wrong about Andy and I don't get accused of anything else.'

I text Father Jacob saying I need to talk, and ask if I can come down to the church today. His text back says, *of course*, and suggests I pop down in an hour.

An hour is a long time to sit with your thoughts. I grab my laptop and begin looking through some of the footage of… I can't even think of another crappy name for my documentary now… *Wraith Invaders*?

Ashley's camerawork is oddly good. He's a virtuoso with natural light. The angles are great, the sound perfect. I watch a bit of the Watsons' interview, then the background shots of Andy's house. There's a sound file there, sitting in the same folder. It's the one I asked Ashley to record by the boxes room to capture the knocking. I turn up the volume and play it. Crackles and echoed bumps – white noise. I'm about to turn it off when I hear the three bangs. With each bang there seems to be a small voice.

'Help. Help. Help.'

Chapter Twenty-Two

One simple word spoken, ever so quietly, three times. What if it was Hayley and I just ignored her? I could have helped. Saved her. Or what if it was Betsy? What if Andy kidnapped her and is holding her until she believes in his innocence, and I could have freed her? What kind of normal person would miss a chance to help someone in danger? Suddenly, my vision clouds as if I'm looking at my room through a peephole. Pinkish shadows dance across the walls. Eating three cakes helps to settle me. When was the last time I had a pink pill? I take one, then lie on my bed counting my breaths. I must drift off, as I'm suddenly jolting awake.

Shaking off the feeling, I yell to Mum that I'm going out and I hear her ask about the cakes she bought. I don't answer; I'll tell her how lovely they were when I get back.

In a daze, I catch the wrong bus and instead of reaching the church, I end up in town again. I text Father Jacob I'm on my way, then catch a second bus. It's hot. Both buses feel and smell the same, like ovens swimming in strangers' sweat. I have to hold my breath on the second one to keep from vomiting. When I get off, I gasp in hot air too quickly and choke myself enough to have to bend over. Suddenly, bile rushes up my throat and I puke. Nestled beneath pieces of jam sponge is the half-digested pink pill. I don't have any others on me to take. Without it, I could slip, lose my temper at the wrong time. No amount of counting backwards would help. Reaching out, I pluck the pill out of the foul goo, and slowly edge it towards my mouth…

'Dee?'

Father Jacob is striding up the street towards me. Dressed in a black cassock, he wears his usual worry-face.

Dropping the pill, I hold up my hand, cough and stand up straight. 'I need your help.'

'Should I call an ambulance?'

Do I look that bad? 'No.'

'Okay, come inside the church where it's cool.'

As we sit together on a pew, I notice Cannon Matthew lurking by the altar, so have to whisper for fear of my secrets echoing across the nave. 'I need to talk.'

'About what?' he asks.

Confession time. I blurt, 'I'm doing a documentary about this guy, Andy, who is being accused online of being the Wraith, and I'm now thinking they might be right.'

Silence.

I continue, 'I found these at his house.' I reach into my bag and pull out the shorts.

'Just because he likes to cross-dress, it doesn't mean he's a serial killer.'

'No, Hayley was wearing these the day she went missing. I saw her go to work in them. I checked with the shop they're from – Hayley added the stars, they're *her* shorts.'

Father Jacob takes them from me. 'And you found these at this man's house?'

'Yes. I also recorded this.' I pull out the laptop and play him the recording. 'Listen, it's a girl's voice asking for help three times.'

'Oh my,' he says, then crosses himself.

'I heard knocking too but discounted it. I've been woken up in the night by knocking before, I thought it was just in my mind. Always around 3 a.m.'

'Three knocks?'

'Yes.'

Father Jacob takes a breath. He neatly folds the shorts up and puts them back in my bag.

'It's known as the devil's call. Three knocks at 3:33 a.m. mocks the Father, the Son and the Holy Ghost.'

'I'm not possessed!' My raised voice draws the attention of Canon Matthew, who throws me an evil look.

'It could be psychosomatic. Have you spoken with Dr Taylor?'

'I can't. She's on the verge of getting me committed, again.'

'Please stop working on this documentary.'

'I can't. God wants me to do it.'

'He's spoken to you?'

'He sent signs. There were the invoices at work, and the green lightning.' Excitedly, I remember the footage I recorded of the birds. 'And there was this crow on the roof.' Saying these things to anyone else would sound mad, but Father Jacob understands.

'Are you sure you're interpreting His signs correctly?'

'Mostly,' I admit. Thinking back, perhaps I used them to keep me on the path I wanted to walk. Maybe God was warning me not to trust Andy?

Shifting on the wooden pew, Father Jacob looks over at Canon Matthew. Less than three seconds slip by before he makes his way over.

'Everything okay, Father Jacob?' he asks.

224

At over six feet tall, Canon Matthew looms over me, his black cassock and matching shawl making him shadowy and sweaty in the heat.

'Of course, just speaking with one of the flock.'

'We were talking about signs from God,' I add. Maybe Canon Matthew can shed some unbiased light.

'Oh, I see. Have you seen many, young lady?'

As he's barely older than me, I baulk at this address, enough to spit out, 'Yes.'

'Well, that's good. God is speaking with you. Are you listening?'

I don't answer quickly enough, as he leans down towards me. 'Girls these days can be lost so easily. I'd hate to lose you… again.' With that, he turns away and waves at a loitering nun.

Lose me again? I turn to Father Jacob. 'Does he know about…?'

'*Possession is Nine Tenths*, I'm afraid so. I didn't tell him, just confirmed his beliefs when asked.' My friend's cheeks redden. 'I hope you don't feel I betrayed you?'

'Course not.' And I mean it; I couldn't blame Father Jacob for anything other than being a great friend, the only real one I have left. And Canon Matthew is right; I have to listen to God. It's just, who am I to interpret Divine Will? I need to enlist professional help. With as much determination as I can edge into my voice, I say, 'I'm going to the police to give them all the evidence. Let them decide.'

'Good idea. Would you like me to go with you?'

Turning up with a priest would appear as if I'm being escorted. 'No, that's okay.'

After saying goodbye to Father Jacob, I check the bus schedule. There's just one bus that stops near the town's new high-tech police station, although there's a good mile-long hike between where I'll be dropped off and where I can hand in the evidence.

I catch the bus, which is oddly low on passengers. The limited body heat coupled with the ability to open this bus's windows gives me a cool space to think. The police seem desperate to make some progress on this case, what if they arrest me? Although weedy, I'm a good suspect. I have no alibis. I'm home every night and can easily sneak out of the house; I could have used the hole in the fence at St Alda's when I was at the halfway house. I've been contacting victim's families and have a ton of Wraith facts on my computer, not to mention the search history I always forget to clear. Turning up with evidence and trying to insert myself into their investigation would be the icing on the perfect suspect cake! The only question left would be where I kept the girls, but I'm sure they'd find a way around that.

Damn! I need to get the hell off this bus. If I produce this evidence, I'm as good as arrested. They'll judge me just like Mr Lake did, guilty by reason of weirdness. If a whole online community can turn on Andy, who isn't nearly as odd as me, then it wouldn't take much for people to start looking my way. Maybe I can drop it all off and give an anonymous statement, like I did with Dara's body? Wait, it's only anonymous if they don't see you, and the police station is bound to have CCTV. But I told Father Jacob I'd do it. More importantly, being brave now could save the 12th girl.

The building is brand new. It smells of plastic, paint and freshly cut wood. The walls are made of darkened glass, giving it an open yet unfriendly vibe. Blessedly, it is rocking air conditioning. I take a long, deep inhale that chills my lungs, and freshens my skin.

The reception desk is large and has three police officers manning it. There are people before me, lining up to complain and report crimes. Every time I look around, I see something new in the room. A man with dirty blonde dreadlocks hiding something in his pocket. A bruised woman clinging to her chair. Three young boys with worry betraying their cocky exteriors. A teen girl is gripping a pink fluffy bag to her chest. A slim man helping an old lady up from a chair. More police flood in and out like the waves of a dark, determined sea. As I move further up the queue, I watch the boys laugh and step back and forth on the spot, the nervous dance of amateur criminals.

'Can I help?'

I turn back to see a smiling policeman.

'Can I speak to DCI Campbell, please?'

'She's out at the moment. Can anyone else help?' He leans over and presses a button behind the desk.

This is a massive mistake! I should leave right now, but I can't seem to move my feet.

'You okay?' he asks.

'Is there another senior officer here?'

'I'd need to know what it's about.'

Father Jacob's friend; she's in the police. 'What about Teresa?'

'Do you know a surname? Rank?'

I think about this. Father Jacob did mention it, but I can't remember, so shake my head.

'No bother,' he says. 'Let me check for you.' He types something into a nearby computer. I expect the windows to suddenly become barred, and a hundred stun guns to be aimed at my heart...

'I don't seem to have any Teresa listed.'

'That's okay, don't worry. I'm just being weird.'

He raises an eyebrow. 'Weird or not, we want to hear what you have to say.'

Just as he tells me this, the young boys bark with laughter and start pushing one another. The old lady yelps and the policeman I've been speaking to steps out to caution the boys.

What am I doing here? Telling the police felt like a good idea before, but now I'm here, I'm sweating, even in the air conditioning.

Taking the opportunity to slip through the chaos, I turn on my heels and run out of the station.

I miss the bus by seconds. I watch it pull away, spitting back dusty fumes in its wake. Couldn't God have helped me out? Or perhaps this is my punishment for not handing in the evidence I'm hoarding.

My feet hurt, but I still trudge off on foot; in the time I'd have to wait in the sun for the next bus, I can make it into the town bus station's shade.

Past the bakery, past Lake Accounting, and suddenly I'm standing on the edge of Good Tree Park. Here, I hesitate. There's police tape still sectioning off the Wendy house. A group of random people are taking photos with their phones; morbid selfies that'll haunt social media forever with *#bodydumpselfie*. Poor Hayley, I didn't find her in time. Now she'll be just another name to sit beside so many others. Only her murder will define her, not that she had a kind yet broken heart, or smelt like vanilla. No, she'll be *the 11th girl, who was dumped in the Wendy house.* Red threatens my vision. My fist jumps out and catches part of the tape, bringing it down with my jab. I could have saved her. I should have saved her. I feel my heart bang against my ribcage, 'Six, five, four, three, two, one.' The feeling is still there. Closing my eyes, I try again. 'Six, five, four, three, two, one.' With each number I take a deeper breath, feeling the boiled air fill my belly.

Exhausted, I buy a 99 Flake and settle onto a bench with wooden splinters that unceremoniously poke my bum. I concentrate on the taste and feel of the ice cream. Cool and creamy, and, although the cone becomes soggy too quick, it's a welcome break. Halfway through my treat, I hear a loud caw. A huge crow is resting on a bin beside me. Without fear, it stares at my ice cream, then flicks its black eyes to me and back. Craig once told me crows can recognise and remember human faces. That if you're mean to them, they tell other birds who you are. Cookie took this story to heart and began hoarding food to feed the birds around St Alda's. My friend was always kind. I break off the end of my cone and throw it to the bird as an offering. It flaps its wings and grabs the morsel in mid-air.

'Impressive,' I say and, once it's finished the first piece, I throw another. This one drops to the ground and the bird swoops down to retrieve it.

'Not so clever this time,' I whisper.

Finishing my ice cream, I debate whether to buy another. As I do, I see a familiar figure striding across the park. Andy. What's he doing here?

Regardless of my new worries, it seems rude not to at least say hello. As I wave, I see he's meeting someone. Edging closer, I recognise Andy's companion. It's the bad man.

Chapter Twenty-Three

Andy and the would-be child abductor loudly greet one another, then hug.

In horror, I watch as they buy blood-red ice lollies and lay down together on the grass. Edging out from the bench, I sit behind them with my exercise book, close enough to eavesdrop.

Andy says, 'It's been way too long. Thought you were keeping your distance.'

Child-snatcher replies, 'Soz, I just wanted to get an update. You're having way too much fun.'

They laugh.

'Not as much as you'd think. I'm being watched like a hawk. That damn website has everyone and their dog on me.'

Is Andy shamelessly talking about having fun being the Wraith? Is the bad man his partner in blood?

He adds, 'You know work fired me.'

'Really? You were their best surveyor.'

'They said the rumours were killing their business. They used that word, *killing*.'

'Ironic, much?'

They laugh. Friends together.

'I'll stop by the house later, eh?' asks Child-snatcher. 'I left some equipment in your basement.'

'Sure, but you can't stay the night. I want to get that documentary-demon there again tomorrow. She's better at her job than I thought. She might have something.'

'Do you need help? I mean, she's kind of weird.'

'She's like sixty pounds soaking wet.'

They both laugh about my thin frame.

'Okay, say *hi* to Betsy for me.'

'Will do,' Andy replies.

Child-snatcher gets up.

'See ya, Warren.' Andy waves.

As Warren turns to wave back, our eyes lock.

The park is too open to run and hide. Damn it. I should tell them I've gone to the police, but instead I stand up, hoist my backpack over my shoulder and yell, 'See ya, Warren. You too, Andy.' Then stride over to where a crowd has gathered by the ice cream van. Might as well show him that this documentary demon is going to be one hell of a satanic thorn in his killer side.

For a moment, they both watch me. Warren then whispers something to Andy. Both laugh, then turn to leave the park together.

I heard nothing of use between Andy and Warren. Neither of them specifically mentioned being the Wraith, sending letters to the press, or even abducting and killing girls, but I can read between the lines. It does make sense if there are two Wraiths working together, just like the Watsons theorised. Andy has solid alibis for when Warren is out on the prowl. God was wrong! Although, more likely, I interpreted His omens all wrong. They weren't signs of encouragement, they were warnings. Andy. Is. The. Wraith!

After buying another ice cream, I slump onto the grass and think. Seeing Warren with Andy has helped. At least

I know now that Ashley is innocent. God has a plan, and it wasn't my strange ability to find lost things that led me to Good Tree Park at the right time, but my sweet tooth.

Once I'm home and safely eating a bland salad, I pull out my laptop. I find the police email address and fire one off for the attention of DCI Campbell. I should have done this before; I was just so intent on getting the cursed items out of my possession that I lost sight of technology. I suppose, for Ashley's sake, it was good I didn't send an email sooner. With that damning book, he'd have been the real innocent man on the Wraith Finders website. I tell the DCI everything: the documentary, the shorts, the voice on the recording, and even me stopping Warren taking a child from the park. Vomiting everything I know onto the screen feels great, it's like a... well, a self-imposed exorcism.

Before I pull down my blind for the night, my mobile pings and I see a text from Father Jacob asking how it went at the police station. I text an emoji with a shush finger. It's vague and hopefully conveys I don't really want to talk right now. He texts back an emoji of his own – a worry face.

-

Knock, knock, knock.

My eyes are sticky and hard to open.

'Dee? You okay?' Mum is yelling through my door.

'Yeah.'

'It's past ten. You need to get up.'

I hear her move away, then come back. 'Dee!'

'Yeah?'

'Did you take the cakes I bought?'

'Sorry. I thought they were for me.'

Mum sighs. 'I was going to ice them and take them across to the Bronsons.'

'I'll buy some more.'

'Okay. Today, though. I want to go over with our condolences this afternoon.'

She's going to ask me to come with her. I'm not sure I can. Not after Mr Bronson saw me creeping around their house in my nightie. Especially not after I didn't find their daughter in time. Or after I heard Hayley's final cries for help and ignored them, believing Andy's lie that it was the pipes. The pipes! I'm such a naïve idiot. Not even Cookie would have fallen for that one.

Dragging myself out of bed is hard. Even though the sheets feel sticky and the heat in my bedroom is stifling. I forgot to put the fan on last night. I put it on now and dry my moist skin in front of it. I pull on some black leggings and a big grey T-shirt, then slowly make my way downstairs.

Mum is in the kitchen, eating breakfast alone.

'Where's Dad?'

'It's Sunday, he went swimming.'

'I wanted to go to early Mass today, why didn't you wake me earlier?' I sit down at the table and watch her eat.

'Dad thought it best to let you sleep. You don't have to go every week. Father Jacob will understand.'

My parents tolerate Father Jacob, but as they rarely, if ever, visited St Alda's, they never saw how dedicated my priest truly was to my recovery. How often he would visit. They only found out about the online documentary course when I came out last month. I'm not great at reading people, but I think Mum might be trying to sever

233

my ties to the church… or maybe not. I wish I could just come out and ask. 'Mum…'

'I need those cakes, Dee. Remember to replace the ones you stole yesterday.'

'Sure,' I say and grab my backpack. It's heavy with my laptop, exercise books and damning evidence inside.

Suddenly, her hand shoots out as if to grab mine, but instead she seizes the fumsup attached to my bag. 'He's not really brought you much luck, has he?'

I move forward so the charm slips through her fingers. 'We don't know what could have happened without him.'

While Mum tries to fake a smile, I quickly exit.

The bus into town is late and everyone is staring at me. I'm usually in church by now. Sitting with Father Jacob, pretending to sing and pay attention to Canon Matthew. It feels weird to be out in the world on a Sunday morning. When the Number 3 finally pulls up and opens its doors, I'm so sweaty and tired, I barely make it up the steps to scan my card.

'Out of the way.'

I look behind me to see a round woman, with an even rounder child, pushing onto the bus.

'Wait your Goddamn turn,' jumps past my usual thought process.

Shocked, she pulls her child away from me.

Slowly and deliberately, I move down the bus to sit at the back. With a mechanical sigh, we drive off. The rude woman is glaring at me. I should look away, but I don't. Instead, I stare at her until her face is hazed with red and she twists her gaze to the window.

Once I reach town, I go straight to the supermarket and buy some plain cupcakes and a big chocolate cake for me. As I wait for my bus home, I open my cake and begin to eat it. It's difficult to bite into, being round with no edges, but I still manage it. No one stands near me at the bus stop. A bedraggled, aging, gothic doll shovelling chocolate cake into her mouth at the speed of light can't be very attractive, but I'm hungry and need the sugar.

Sitting on the ground, I pull out my journal and place what's left of the cake to my side. I write about how it feels to misread obvious signs that a normal person would understand instantly, then make a note to tell Cookie about it later… Cookie is dead. Why can't I remember that? To me, my friend is still waiting for our next chat. Why hasn't Dr Taylor emailed about his funeral?

I remember the day of Tippy's funeral at St Alda's. Closed casket. Dark clothes. Short service. From opening prayers to final farewell, my anger boiled. She was considered normal enough to leave. Why had she done something so stupid? Tippy could have spoken to any of us about her blue feelings. Mixed with my red ones, we made purple together. Purple is a good colour. Cookie cried throughout the ceremony and Craig lurked at the back of the room. I could hear him counting the ceiling tiles, 'One, two, three,' he said over and over, then multiplied the amount in his head to tell me the exact number after the coffin was taken away.

Maybe Craig will come to Cookie's funeral. It would be good to see him now we're both considered normal.

After Mass, Father Jacob texts again about my trip to the police station. There is no emoji that could successfully answer his question, so I type the truth. The DCI in charge of the Wraith case wasn't there, so I emailed. He texts back, I'm proud of you for trying. He shouldn't be. I chickened out. Put my own selfish needs before society's. I don't finish the chocolate cake; with renewed faith, I walk off towards the police station once more. I need to tell them everything about Andy and Warren in person; it doesn't matter who I tell, as long as it's someone who can stop the Wraiths.

It's not as busy at the station today. I walk straight up to the counter and ask for DCI Campbell, telling the policeman on reception that I emailed her and have news on the Wraith case. He picks up a phone and calls her down. Real life and TV are very different beasts. On screen, DCI Campbell looked imposing against the podium in her grey power suit. In the flesh, she is almost as small as me and is wearing white linen trousers and a thin strappy vest that exposes two whole armfuls of tattoos. With the sun hitting the station's windows at every angle, she looks like an angel.

'Can I help you, madam?' She extends a hand.

'Jones, Dee Jones.' That came out more James Bond than I intended.

I would shake hands but I have stray pieces of chocolate cake decorating my fingers, so fear leaving a stain on her.

'The desk says you have something on the Righteous Wraith case? That you emailed me?' She moves me across the station into a small room.

I hesitate by the door. Did she not read the email?

'Can I get you a cold drink?' she asks.

'Yes, thank you.' I step inside the room. She closes the door behind me, then disappears. I sit down at the table. It feels good to drop my backpack from my shoulder.

'I hope diet is okay?' she says, coming back and placing a cold can of pop in front of me.

'Thank you.'

'You're welcome.'

'As I said in my email, I've been working on a documentary about the Wraith, and I've uncovered some evidence.' I pull out my laptop. 'I recorded this at Andy Fryer's house the other day.'

I play the file and watch her face as she listens.

After, she smiles at me. 'Andy Fryer? The man Wraith Finders have been harassing?'

'Yes,' I say.

'Are you a member of Wraith Finders?'

Technically, I am. 'Yes, but I did it for my documentary.'

'And what channel are you with? BBC? Netflix? Channel 4?'

'I'm independent.'

'As evidence goes, I'm afraid that noise could be anything. It's human nature to find words in random noises, just like when we see shapes in clouds. Do you have anything else, Ms Jones?'

'Let me play it again for you.'

The DCI holds up her hands.

My chocolatey fingers hover above the keyboard. I should show her the shorts, but they don't really prove anything either, and I don't know for sure Warren's thwarted crime in the park was reported. Still, I have to keep trying. 'There are two of them.' I shuffle out my sketchbook and show her my drawing. 'His name is Warren and he's friends with Andy.'

Without looking, she pushes aside my book. 'Ms Jones, there's not enough evidence that Andy, or anyone else he knows, is connected to the case. Now, I can't go into detail here, but trust me when I say that we are no longer looking at Mr Fryer for these crimes.'

'I know, he has alibis, but can't you see the evidence you need for an arrest is split between two men?'

She motions to my drawing. 'We have interviewed Warren Roland, he's Andy's brother-in-law.'

'Betsy's brother?'

'You know Betsy?'

'I interviewed her. She even has some doubts about her husband.'

Taking a deep breath, DCI Campbell throws me a sympathetic smile. 'To make an arrest, the law requires us to have enough evidence, and in this case we don't.'

Lurching forward, I try to press play again on the laptop, but she stops me.

'I'm sorry, that's not evidence either.' She looks at me like I'm an injured puppy on the road. 'Are you okay? Can I call someone for you?'

'No, you can arrest Andy and Warren before they take the 12th girl. I heard them talking in the park, they all but admitted to…' My voice is now screechy and wild as I try to remember the exact words I heard. '…they said…'

DCI Campbell takes a big swig of her drink. 'I'm sorry, but we can't arrest people on hearsay. But, if you would like to make a statement, we can do that now.'

Statements are signed, they are used as evidence in court cases. I can't do that, with my history of mental illness they'll… Oh, I should have given a different name. What was I thinking! This was a mistake. But if I say no, it'll look even more suspicious. 'Okay.'

She leaves and I quickly pack away my laptop. Cracking the door open, I peer out. The DCI is talking with another officer; he's reminding her that the Wraith's handwriting didn't match either Andy's or Warren's. While their backs are to me, I slip out. I'm about to make a run for it when I hear the officer raise his voice. He says something about charging for wasting police time.

Quickly, I make my way to the front door. Fortunately, more people are here now, so I escape the police station without anyone spotting me. Sometimes it helps to be small.

I run towards the bus stop, my backpack jumping up and down on my spine like a tantrum-wielding toddler. DCI Campbell might try to find me, she has my name and one of my email addresses, but she didn't believe me anyway. I need help, and clearly the police are in the dark. But there are some people I can reach out to with this new evidence – the Watsons. They started this whole thing with Andy; they'll believe me.

–

Mum says I bought the wrong cakes, but they'll do. Hating the thought of the Bronsons getting something subpar, I spend time helping her ice and decorate the wrong cakes, but decline the offer to go with her to take them over; I can't have Mr Bronson reminded of my visit the other night. Once alone in the house, I email the Watsons, telling them I found evidence that Andy *is* guilty and that he's not working alone. I ask them to contact me ASAP.

Andy and Warren will take another girl soon. She'll be plucked out of her life like a flower by the side of the road. She'll be tortured, blinded and murdered, then left exposed for the world to see. Her name will be famous, but it'll be a lot to go through for fame.

My phone beeps, telling me I have an email. It's the Watsons. Finally, I'll have some backup. I open it to see a short answer.

Checking Wraith Finders, I find a thread. Short and sharp, like a dagger. It tells members that they are in the midst of a legal battle regarding the allegations. Then it goes on to point out members are still free to act accordingly – they're not saying give up, just that they have given in, albeit temporarily.

The Watsons are the only members of the group I know. And if being part of Inspiration Cometh has taught me anything, it's that you need personal connections; just turning up isn't enough for you to truly belong. I need to talk to these people.

I search the site for the most active thread. There's one from Rabbits Foot talking about Andy's past. Remembering Betsy's words on Andy's dark side, I post about him sending letters to a serial killer. Expecting it to take a while before I get a reply, I go to log off, but suddenly there are three messages dropping down the screen.

That's so dodge, says one.

Which killer? The Starseller Slasher? asks another.

I bet he's asking for pointers, claims the newest avatar to the group.

It was that guy who murdered those harlots up North, states another.

Before I can react, there's ten handles on the thread, all of which add to my statement. Suddenly, Andy didn't just write to a killer, he was helping him kill women. And now he's plotting to get him out of prison, along with several other killers and various lowlife criminals. It feels as if I've lit a match in a firework factory. Boom! There's another accusation about helping other killers. Boom! Up pops a theory about yet another murder spree. Boom! Old photos of Andy as a child are uploaded, each with a more terrifying story attached than the last. I have to believe Betsy told me the truth, and therefore I told the truth about his letters, but how come so many people online think it's okay to take a grain of truth and plant it in a field of lies?

> Why won't anyone stop Andy?
>
> Letters to killers? Just like the letters the Wraith has been sending?
>
> Who here has had enough of words?
>
> Someone needs to watch him twenty-four seven, am I right?
>
> Where is he now?

As Dad, the maths teacher, would say, right answers, wrong equations. I might be considered defective, but even I can see a dark snowball rolling down a steep hill. I can't trust these people to help me uncover the truth.

I'm alone.

The urge to kick and punch something rises in me, but I fear I'll break a bone. Also, nothing in Mum and Dad's house deserves to be broken. Well, nothing else.

Falling onto the living room sofa, I click on the TV. Mindless weekend afternoon repeats assault my senses. I close my eyes and clamp my hands over my ears. It's not the dark retreat Dr Taylor suggested, but the isolation helps me focus. The Wraith has to be Andy and Warren together. How did the police clear both of them? Warren tried to abduct a little girl in broad daylight, that's not the crime of a newbie. What am I missing?

'Dee?' The sound is muffled, but I still hear Mum's voice.

Taking my hands from my ears, I open my eyes. 'Yes?'

'You okay? You've been outside a lot this week; do you have sun stroke?'

'Don't think so.'

Mum tries to place her palm against my forehead, but I dodge her attack. 'Perhaps it's all the sugar. You need to lay off the cakes.'

Over my dead body, I want to say, but nod instead, then ask, 'How are the Bronsons?'

'As you'd expect. I think it's worse because the killer is still on the loose.'

Should I tell Mum what I know? But then I'd have to admit I was working on the Wraith documentary behind her back. 'I'm sure he'll be caught soon.'

'I hope so,' Mum says, then walks away into the kitchen, probably to boil some eggs for another What Came First salad. What did come first? Is a question still a question even though it has no answer?

Chapter Twenty-Four

Later, I force my sweaty palms together and whisper, 'Dear Lord. How's it going up there?' I pause. 'Okay, scratch my request for you to help Andy. I have a sneaking suspicion he might well be guilty. I guess your signs were warnings after all. Not sure how Andy managed to be ruled out by the police so quickly, but he's obviously very clever. I could do with some help with this whole situation. Those girls did not deserve what happened to them. If you could perhaps throw me a more obvious and specific holy bone that would be great. And…' I hesitate. Saying the words aloud makes them real, but I feel it's worth mentioning. 'Could you keep that red part of me in check? I kind of like living in the real world. Serial killers and sociopathic work colleagues aside. Bless Mum and Dad and yes even Ashley; sorry for thinking the worst of him, but you saw what he drew in that book. Come on, what was I meant to think? Amen.'

I'm still awake at 3:33 a.m. when I hear three knocks. This time it sounds as if it's coming from the window. It's all in my head. None of this is real. Perhaps I'm wrong about everything. St Alda's was quiet and my mind was never troubled there. I picture Cookie's fluffy white sheep jumping over a fence, each with a pleasant baa, only the animals quickly turn black and their bleating morphs into screams.

'Did you go out last night?' Dad asks me over breakfast.

As I push scrambled eggs around my plate with a plastic fork, I reply, 'No.'

Mum appears beside me. 'Did you take your pill?'

Dad looks at my plate. 'You're not eating properly.'

'I'm not a fan of eggs,' I say, shoving my breakfast plate away.

'Well, you like them in cakes,' Mum says.

'They're different there.' I get up and put the kettle on for another cup of tea. 'They work as part of a team with sugar and butter. On their own they're nothing, but together they're amazing.'

Dad considers this. 'Never thought about that before.'

'Let's not get sidetracked,' Mum tells him, then looks over at me. 'I spoke with Dr Taylor. She's worried about you, but reckons your work thing is just a misunderstanding. She thinks you're under a lot of stress.' Her arms snake towards me, but I inch away. 'I can't imagine how hard it is for you having to adjust to normal life after... so long.'

'You know,' Dad says, 'you can talk to us.'

I should tell them both everything, but don't. I suspect proving the identity of the Wraiths is something I need to do alone. If it wasn't, God wouldn't have taken Cookie from me.

'Dr Taylor also mentioned she's booked you in for the floatation tank experience. I wrote down the details.' Mum produces a yellow Post-it note. I really hoped this weird experiment of Dr Taylor's was going to be forgotten, although she did tell Mum she believes in me; I owe it to her to at least try it.

After zoning out during a lecture about being all I can be, one I'm sure the kids in their classes hear daily, I escape back to my room and review my notes. My documentary is once again dead in the water. You can't say someone is innocent whilst knowing they're guilty. I debate this fact for too long, only snapping out of it when an email arrives from Ashley. He asks me to come to the talk at the university to face Louisa in person. Says he has a lot of people who have taken advantage of him in the past and he knows it'll help. I email back I'll meet him there. I've waited long enough to battle this particular demon.

And just like with Louisa, I'm going to have to deal with Andy and Warren. Find irrefutable evidence of their guilt, something that no one can deny. I check the news for Wraith updates. There's another letter. Handwritten and scanned onto the news site as an easily downloadable jpeg.

Hello fans!

I'm most disappointed in Northants police.

11 girls. 11 girls. 11 GIRLS! I should have started years ago. The ineptitude of the boys in blue is staggering! Teamwork does not make the dream work in this constabulary. Perhaps the investigation needs someone else at the helm? I guess you want to know about the 12th girl? I already have my eye on her. It'll be spectacular. I must admit, secretly, I don't want you to find me till after I get my hands around her throat. Her death will cause such a stir that maybe number 13 won't be needed. Perhaps there will be an outrage so big, the people will rise up to defeat me, rather than relish me? Probably not. The sick thrill of death is all too addictive for the British public. Why catch me when I'm entertaining you all so. What's a few dead girls in comparison to the show I'm putting on? Maybe I'm selling too many news-papers, getting too many clicks, gaining too high page views to reveal me just yet. Their deaths are payment: blood and body parts as currency.

Well, my five minutes of fame could be running out soon. Punish me. Punish me. Punish me, if you dare.

Yours in blood, The Righteous Wraith XX

Who is this 12th girl Andy and Warren are referring to? Me? My death wouldn't cause uproar; if anything, it might be considered a public service.

'Dee?' Mum yells from downstairs.

I cross the landing and shout back, 'Yes?'

'Come down.'

Mum and Dad are wearing their idiotic sun hats. Floppy brown straw hats that make them look like gorm-less scarecrows.

'Why aren't you ready?'

'Ready for what?'

'Really! This morning, you agreed to come to Lake Accounting with us. Settle this invoicing business once and for all. Don't you remember?'

Did I agree? Wait, when was the last time I had a pink pill? Will my red kick in when unfounded accusations start flying? I should take one now. 'I need to go back upstairs to do something,' I say.

'No, we're going now,' Mum says, stopping me mid-step.

'Love?' Dad is looking at me as if I'm a wounded animal poised to strike. I'd never hurt Mum and Dad.

Without replying, I quickly collect my backpack, then manoeuvre past them. 'Okay, I'll meet you there.'

'That's ridiculous. Just drive in with us.' Mum reaches out to grab the top of my arm. Turning on my heels to avoid her, I lose my balance and fall against the door frame.

Dad lurches forward, but stops himself before his hand touches me. 'You okay?' When I don't answer, he and Mum step outside.

'Perhaps she should get the bus.' Dad unlocks the car.

Mum's eyes are wild. 'No, I've had enough of this! She wasn't in a car when she was hit. This fear is irrational, she can't spend her life on buses.'

Their car is a huge red six-seater metal monster. Dad opens the passenger door for me, and its grey plastic interior is revealed like stained teeth. Mum lunges to grip my arm. Stumbling away, I fall within touching distance of the car's gaping mouth. The ground doesn't cushion my body, but attacks it as we collide. My backpack takes the brunt of the crash. Quickly, I scramble up to ensure my laptop and camera are still in one piece. They are.

With daggers in her eyes, Mum says, 'You better think long and hard about this.'

The car looms before me. I can't. 'No!' I scream.

'For God's sake. No more of this shit!'

'That's enough!' Dad yells at her. Turning to me, he says calmly, 'Just get the bus, Dee. We'll meet you there.'

I hear him, but I'm looking at Mum. Face flushed and hands trembling, she glares back. This happens now and then. People only have so much patience, and where it wears thin dark anger can poke through. Funny, I bet no one wants to randomly exorcise her.

Leaving them to argue, I run towards the bus stop. After an outburst like this, Mum usually buys me a cake to make up for it. I need to focus on the sweet treat, rather than the inevitable bruises where I hit the ground.

Fortunately, the bus is on time. I'd hate to think how much angrier Mum would be if I made her wait longer than necessary. Rushing up to the offices, I spot them lingering outside.

'Don't look so worried, Dee,' Dad says as I approach. 'No matter what happens, we'll keep you out of that place.' He means St Alda's. His tone implies it's bad, and although it isn't, I still don't want to go back, not when there's so much I have to do.

'Thanks,' I mutter.

Dad holds out a hand to me, as if I'm a little girl. I ignore it and stroll in, leaving them to trail behind. Mr Lake greets us by his office door.

'Glad you made it,' he says.

Everyone sits down and I choose the chair closest to the door.

Mr Lake looks at Mum and Dad, not me. 'You know why we're here today.'

'I'm afraid so,' Mum says.

'Well, we've talked it over internally, and feel that, due to the severity of what happened, Dee can no longer work here.' He sighs. 'And she needs to apologise to both Stephanie and Corinne regarding her accusations. Not good to make up lies about co-workers, am I right?'

'That's a shame. Is there no way we can work this out?' Dad asks.

'Nope. Can't employ people who endanger top client relationships. We were lucky they didn't fire us for incompetence.'

I say, 'But...'

'Okay, Dee.' Mum stands, and I stay seated. 'Time to pay the piper.'

'Corinne and Stephanie are in the conference room.' Mr Lake gets up, too.

I'm innocent. The only crime I committed was being a convenient stooge to pin everything on, which is exactly what could happen with the Wraith. This blew up in my face – will that too? Only a hunt for a serial killer is going to explode more spectacularly than an office spat. Damn, but I can't let them take the 12th girl. And what if she's younger than the others, more the age of the little girl in the park Warren targeted? Like Megan, a twelve-year-old who's now publicly called them out twice, thanks to Louisa. The Wraiths love attention; it's why they keep sending those letters. Holy crap! Megan *is* going to be the 12th girl.

'Dee!' Mum yells at me. 'For goodness' sake, let's get this over with.'

Jumping out of my chair, I lead them all to the conference room. Inside, seated around a table too big for the space, is a solemn Stephanie and a smiling Corinne.

I open my mouth, but nothing comes out.

'Dee is sorry for trying to blame you for her mistake. She's a lovely girl when you get to know her,' Dad says.

'I want the apology from *her*.' Corinne points at me. 'After all, she besmirched my name.'

'Go on then,' Mum tells me.

I should say, *sorry I got involved*. Sorry that Corinne screwed up and then couldn't admit it like a good person.

'Sorry.' I have to say it. Being locked up back at St Alda's while Andy and Warren are hunting Megan is the worse of two evils. A child's life is in my hands. I say it again, 'Sorry.'

'There now, hope you all can forgive her,' Dad says and then follows Mum and Mr Lake out of the door.

Stephanie, fear and anger in her eyes, leaves too.

It's just me and Corinne remaining, the two of us who know the truth.

She grins at me. 'It's good you took responsibility.'

Glancing at the door, I tell her, 'They can't hear us. You can drop the charade.'

'Charade?'

'We both know it was you who zeroed those invoices. Was it a mistake, or did you do it on purpose?'

'I'm not stupid.'

I shake my head. 'Then why?'

'In a few months, I'll be leaving and I plan to work direct for Shiva Retail. They lost a lot of money because of those bad invoices. All the interest on delayed payments, not to mention those cheeky companies who just took the first invoice they got. It was a big fuck-up, they're not staying here, so they'll need someone they can trust to run their accounts in-house.'

I open my mouth to ask another question but stop when I hear the door open behind me. Stephanie is back.

'Come on, Corinne. You shouldn't be alone with her,' she says, staring straight at her friend and ignoring me.

'Good point.' Corinne rises. 'Who knows what lies she'll make up next?' She then pushes past me out of the door.

As Stephanie is about to follow her, I reach out to catch her arm, but my grip stops at the sleeve of her blouse. A look of pure horror spreads across her face.

'Shiva is leaving here,' I whisper. 'You'll lose your job.'

The horror on her face multiplies. She stumbles backwards, leaving her sleeve to slip through my fingers.

Turning tail, she all but runs away. No doubt she'll tell everyone how creepy I was – that won't be breaking news – but maybe she'll now question what is happening and can do something about it before Corinne's plan is fully executed. It's a small sacrifice to my reputation for a greater good.

After double-strapping my backpack, I emerge to find Mr Lake standing with Mum and Dad by the front door. As I approach, he says to me, 'I bet you feel like a weight has been lifted, am I right?'

Stopping in my tracks, I reply, 'Pardon?'

My ex-boss narrows his eyes. 'I bet you feel like a weight has been lifted,' he repeats.

But that wasn't the part of the sentence that rang out to me. *Am I right*. He's used that phrase before, and one of the members of Wraith Finders says it too.

'Mr Lake, are you Coolsalot?'

He hesitates for a second. 'Um, well, I'm not cool at the moment. This heat is awful.'

Mum lets out a nervous laugh.

Looking from Mum to Dad, I ask, 'Can I speak with Mr Lake alone?'

Puzzled, they both step into the kitchen.

'It's not illegal you know,' Mr Lake whispers.

'That's a yes, then. You're part of Wraith Finders. It's why my computer history had Wraith sites on. I'm a member too. I've found the Wraith – both of them.'

'Whatever are you talking about?'

'Andy Fryer *is* the Wraith. He and his brother-in-law are in it together.'

I expect a hearty slap on the back, maybe even my job back for ingenuity. I get neither.

Stooping down so we're face to face, Mr Lake says, 'I'm not involved in the Fryer lawsuit.'

'But, I think they are going to go after that kid online, Megan, the 1st girl's little sister. She's twelve. Get it? Their 12th girl!' I all but shout the last part.

Mr Lake stares, then says, 'That's the most tenuous theory I've ever heard.' He looks around us. 'You're worse than I thought.'

'If you don't want to help, why were you part of Wraith Finders?'

'I was only in the group to meet women.'

'Women?'

Shuffling his feet, he admits, 'It's hard to find someone these days. Got to keep on the lookout.'

On the lookout? Wait, Mr Lake is wiry and could probably climb a tree. 'Are you the man in black from my garden?' I whisper.

His eyes narrow. 'Mr and Mrs Jones, can I have a word?'

Only Mum stays with Mr Lake. Dad walks me through the office and out onto the sweaty street.

'Go to the bus station before your mum comes out and we start the car dance all over again, eh?'

Nodding, I turn and head towards the bus stop. I didn't want to go back to that boring job anyway. I'd never have had the time, not now I'm trying to save a girl's life.

I walk through Good Tree Park, keeping an eye out for the Wraiths. Think of the devil and he will appear: my phone beeps. It's a text from Andy. I open it to see a novel of a message. I skim it to find him explaining away Warren, and what he thought I overheard. It even covers when I first 'met' his brother-in-law, saying that it was *his* little girl he was talking to that day. He's estranged from his wife and she is denying him access. Andy gushes that I'm a good documentarian and that he really thinks I'm onto something with his story. It's a long and overly complicated yarn that ends with another invitation to his death-trap old rectory. Delete. No way was that Warren's daughter in the park; they looked nothing alike, and she referred to him as a *bad man*. How naïve does Andy think I am?

Sitting beneath a dry and dying tree, I check online for Megan. In photos uploaded yesterday, she appears older than when I first saw her. She's now wearing a small silver crucifix. If people thought I was possessed by a demon, then an angel possesses this girl. No one will believe me that she's in danger. It's down to me to save her. And not just from the Wraiths but from Louisa too.

–

Back at home, I eat a day-old doughnut Dad left out, then go to my room. Mum is ignoring me. She does this every now and then. It's my punishment for not travelling in the car, not apologising straight away, and for being different, defective and deranged. Her glare slices through me and Dad is too tired to stop her. I wish I could tell them about the Wraiths and what they plan to do, but if the police don't believe me, what could Mum and Dad do?

I don't take a pink pill. I know I'm in danger of my amygdala being hijacked, but the pills dull me, and I'll need all my faculties for what's ahead.

Megan's contact details are far too easy to find online. I email and ask if I can come over tomorrow for an interview. I don't have much time to worm my way into Megan's life. I might have to do some light stalking to ensure she's safe. Fortunately, her mother comes back to me. She says they would love to do an interview. She gives me their address and says how much she enjoyed *Possession is Nine Tenths*. She thinks I'm working with Louisa. I don't correct the error, instead I message back, we're looking forward to meeting you. A necessary deception for the greater good.

Guilt and responsibility are odd feelings to have together. They're a cocktail whose flavours cancel each other out. I can only feel one at a time and suddenly guilt grabs me by the brain. What if I can't save Megan? I should contact DCI Campbell, warn her about the Wraith's intended 12th girl. Even if she thinks it's me making threats, it might give the police the impetus to watch over her. I open an email and begin typing up my theory. I have no real evidence to back any of it up, but I send it anyway. She must be on her emails as I get a reply straight back.

> Dee, please come into the station to make your statement. DCI Campbell.

The tone is dismissive. She still doesn't believe me. Now I know how Cassandra felt in her Greek tragedy. The gift of prophecy is a curse. The Wraiths will go after Megan. I'm not sure why the police have not thought about this themselves. They must have seen the last letter too.

Hours slip by. Darkness drips across my window. It's so quiet. No barking. Maybe Lucifer has finally given up on his nightly serenades. Still, he should be making some noise. I poke my head out of the window to look over into next door's garden. No Lucifer. No one in black Lycra straddling tree branches, either. Mr Davidson's car is gone too. Mum has at least got her way about that.

Louisa's talk is in the morning. I need to get some rest, but my mind is still rolling around the lost opportunity of my documentary. It would have been epic to prove Andy innocent and expose the Wraith Finders as online bullies, but the truth doesn't fit that narrative. The wrong Wraith now looks like the right Wraith, but perhaps I can do something with the documentary footage already recorded? For a moment, I stare at my photo of Dara's empty shell. Then, slowly pull out Hayley's shorts. How dare Andy and Warren take girls out of this world for their own pleasure? Who the hell do they think they are? What makes them special? How many lives have they ruined? I think back to how angry Vlad was with me, and I hadn't even done anything to him. If God can't step in, then I'll have to be His instrument. Energised, I rewrite my storyboard.

My documentary will now be *Hunting the Wraiths*.

Chapter Twenty-Five

Lucifer is missing. I find this out over breakfast.

'Bet you're glad. You said he kept you awake at night,' Mum spits. She hasn't forgiven me for yesterday, but at least she's talking to me now. 'Haven't seen the poor little thing for ages.'

'What's his owner said?' I ask, trying not to look too interested.

'Daren't ask Mrs Grant directly, but the Larkins, over the other side, told me he disappeared one night. They've not seen or heard him since.'

Why would Mum not talk to Mrs Grant? I'm about to ask when it hits me... I'm the reason. It's not just Mum who suspects I'm somehow to blame. She thinks Mrs Grant will have the same theory; the mental from next-door killed her dog.

Dad rolls his eyes. There are no silly jokes or laughter today. I hate that I'm the cause – or more precisely, that Mr Lake's biased view of me is. He believed Corinne over me. He sided with the guilty party. And even when he found out we were Wraith Finders together, he didn't change his mind.

'What are you doing today?' Dad sips his tea and stares at me with a mixture of interest and worry, reminding me of Father Jacob.

'I'm going to the university to look over my documentary footage.' A lie close enough to the truth. If I were to mention confronting Louisa, I'd be locked up in my room within nanoseconds.

'The recycling documentary?' Dad says.

'How much does this region recycle?' Mum asks, not looking at me.

'Not as much as they should.'

'No one ever does,' Mum whispers.

'I have to catch the early bus.' Rising, I grab my backpack and escape before I have to reel off any fictional recycling statistics.

–

The university has three campuses, something I wasn't expecting. I first go to the wrong one and have to email Ashley to give me the full address. Finally, after one more bus journey, I make it to Lecture Theatre Three.

I hoped no one would turn up to see Louisa talk about something she knows nothing about, but it's heaving with people. Today, I deliberately wore black skinny jeans and a large plain T-shirt with my hair in a ponytail; it's my attempt to look young and blend in with other students. The only issue is the heat. I'm already sweaty and slightly light-headed from the sun.

'Dee!' Ashley waves at me.

Everyone is looking. Damn.

As I slowly make my way towards him, I notice the smile plastered across his face, smugger than any grin I've seen on Louisa. He'd told people I'd be here, and they didn't believe him. My presence has vindicated him.

As people take their seats, they point and whisper at a massive photo hanging at the back of the stage. It's of me. Younger, thinner if you can believe it, hair drenched in sweat, my body held down by sideshow exorcists who took time out from their torturing duties to smile for the camera. Below, it says in big red letters, *Welcome Tenthers*. If I had a gun, I'd shoot it. Stand up, aim at the picture of that poor, ill girl and plug it until the bullets ripped the features, tearing it asunder into ribbons of red. But I don't have a gun. Someone like me can't even use metal spoons.

Ashley squirms in his seat next to me. He smells musty, like he hasn't showered for days. He's still wearing the same T-shirt he wore when we last met.

'You should take your book back,' I say, trying to hand him *Lord of the Flies*.

He looks at it and shakes his head. 'Told you, not my book.'

'You were reading it at the coffee place. I saw you. You don't need to lie. I know you're not the Wraith.'

Suddenly, Ashley snaps his head around to stare at me. His pin prick eyes punctuating his flaring nostrils. 'You thought *I* was a killer!'

There are so many people in the lecture hall that his accusation, although loud, is fortunately lost amongst scuffling and murmurs.

'Well, your drawings are pretty dark. Anyway, I don't think that anymore. In fact, I know who it—'

'Welcome!' A man's voice rings out, silencing the hall – and stopping me from revealing my secret. 'I'm Professor Gregory of the media department.' As he starts to introduce Louisa, Ashley stands, snatches the book from me, and walks away to lurk by the door, as if it's him who may need a swift exit. 'She needs no introduction. Winner of this year's Docu-Wow Award. Her first documentary, *Possession is Nine Tenths*, is one of the most controversial pieces to possess our screens. She has gone on to produce further documentaries on mental health in the UK and religious extremists. And she's not going to mind me telling you that she just signed a three-book deal with a major publisher.'

What. The. Hell.

'Here she is, Louisa Black!'

Is one of her books about me? Are all of them? It was a mistake to come here.

The professor moves aside and motions like a game show host. From the right of the hall, *she* walks onto the stage. Applause. Too much of it. I have to put my hands over my ears. I watch as she waves at everyone, then grabs the microphone. The errant professor tries to kiss her cheek and stay on stage, but she pushes him away. No one shares the spotlight with Judas.

'It's so good to see you all,' she says and looks out into the crowd. Cringing, I watch her eyes dart about the room. Scooting down in my chair, I hide behind the student in front.

'Thank you so much. I really appreciate your support,' she says, her eyes still scanning the room. Could Ashley have told her I'd be here?

'So, let me start by telling you about *Possession is Nine Tenths...*'

I try to block it out, as she educates a room full of strangers on how desperate I was. How my parents were struggling with my red-tempered demon. How the church wouldn't help and so she, the hero, stepped in with a camera and a couple of snake-oil salesmen who claimed to be able to exorcise out the devil himself.

I've heard, and read, this version of events many times, although it seems like every time she tells it, she adds in a little something else to make herself more virtuous, more loveable, more heroic – just more. This time, the new piece of the story is that she got involved off camera too, that she looked in on me when I went away. She never set foot in St Alda's: Dr Taylor knew how I felt about her and wouldn't have allowed it. I almost put my hand up to call her out, but I don't. I'm not sure why I came here, what did I think would happen? That I would be able to tell Louisa what she did to me, the pain she caused, and gain some sort of peace? That, once bathed in karmic release, Ashley would become my friend and help me take down the Wraiths? I'm an idiot.

'It has been such a wild ride,' she says. Suddenly, in my mind, I see her dressed as Toad of Toad Hall driving a racing car and tooting her way through my life. The image is so clear I get out my sketchbook and begin to draw.

I'm so engrossed with my toad picture that I don't notice them at first – people looking at me.

'Six, five, four, three, two, one,' I breathe, then feel my heartbeat. I'm okay. I can do this.

'I'm so glad she's here today. Come on up, Dee, say hello to everyone.' On stage, Louisa beckons me with the crook of her finger like a witch inviting me into her gingerbread house.

My seat is so wet and hot, I fear I've peed myself. Truthfully, I did it so many times during my 'exorcism' that it wouldn't surprise anyone. Still, as I get up, I run a hand down the back of my leggings to make sure it's sweat and nothing worse.

'Come on, Dee!'

She sounds happy, as if she planned this.

With my backpack on my shoulder, I slowly inch past all the clapping people, as if I'm a performing monkey seeking their applause, not a scared woman shying away from strangers who chose to see her in one of the worst moments of her life.

Slowly, I step up on the stage.

'Six, five, four, three, two, one.'

Louisa beams a smile; did she hear me counting? Without warning, her arms open wide to hug me. I step back and almost fall over.

Laughter.

'I just wanted to publicly credit Dee for all her help with *Possession is Nine Tenths*.'

Did she just acknowledge me? I'm so shocked, my hand springs to my mouth.

'Look how well she's doing. Although still in black. And in this heat.' Comically, she wipes her brow.

More laughter.

As I edge towards her, my fingers dance by my side. The professor is staring at his phone; he's the nearest potential saviour, and he's not even paying attention to my painful humiliation.

Louisa looks me up and down. Smirking, she asks, 'Now, what do you think about my new documentary on the Righteous Wraith?'

My legs buckle and I almost topple over. It would be so easy to give up. Lock myself away again in a place I felt safe. But what about Megan? The Wraiths will claim her, then a 13th girl, and a 14th girl... No; I need to keep my head, so Megan can keep her eyes.

'Dee, surely you've seen my Facebook posts?'

Why is she doing this? What could she gain? I have to stand up for myself. Courage is next to godliness, or is that cleanliness? I step towards Louisa, invading her personal space.

'I think you're very brave,' I say. 'To put yourself in the crosshairs of a sick individual.'

It pleases me that she pales at this statement; whether she thinks I'm referring to myself, or the Wraiths, is up for debate.

The silence stretches out too far. A murmur spreads across the hall. Coughs and sniffs ring out. I grin at Louisa.

Leaning in further, I then add, 'And you put a twelve-year-old girl in those crosshairs too, all for your next grubby grab at fame.'

She stares at me. Did she not realise she was repeating the past? Taking advantage of a child, putting her in danger for her own means?

The slight worry on her face doesn't last. Instead, she returns my grin – a 300-watt light bulb compared to my flickering candle, outshining me as always. Leaning in, she whispers, 'Have I pissed you off? Where's that demon temper of yours?'

My hand itches to push her back. I can feel her breath on my skin.

'Why don't you stop fighting it and just take a swing at me?'

I step back, but she moves with me. Looking down, I see I'm almost to the edge of the stage. The audience is deadly silent. A few years ago, I would have felt this pressure so keenly, I'd have done anything to rid myself of it. Flail. Scream. Attack. My amygdala, engorged with adrenaline, would have felt fit to burst. Now, though, I've come so far. I know I can take this feeling; I don't have to act. I won't give Louisa the satisfaction.

'Careful, Dee, you'll fall off the stage,' she jokes loudly to the audience, offering her hand for me to take. Then she whispers, 'What are you waiting for, you mental?'

Six, five, four, three, two, one, I say in my head. People are depending on me. More girls will die if I don't stop the Wraiths.

Louisa's hand edges closer to my skin.

'Don't touch me,' I seethe, then sidestep away from her. Once there's more than an arm's reach between us, I can breathe again.

'This is such a treat to have both documentarian and subject together after so many years. Are there any questions?' the professor asks, stepping between us.

Hands go up and I quickly decide not to answer anything. I won't help this Judas any more than my pain already has.

'Over there,' the professor says pointing.

A skinny emo girl rises and looks at me. 'I just wanted to ask Dee whether *Possession is Nine Tenths* changed your life?'

Damn it. Not answering shows complicity. 'For the worse. It changed my already damaged life for the worse,' I say, staring at Louisa. What the hell did she expect? That I would forgive her all her sins and open my arms? That we'd hug in front of the masses and play nice? I know Father Jacob will be disappointed in me, but lying is a sin too.

Another girl gets up. 'Louisa, you made a lot of money out of *Possession*, did you share it with Dee? Help her afterwards?'

I like these students.

Louisa clears her throat, not once but twice. The professor hands her a bottle of water and she takes a swig, then says, 'It doesn't work that way. And Dee got the help she needed. How else could she be here now?'

'My family were publicly ruined, and none of us saw a penny. This woman is a fraud who—'

'You, there, do you have a question?' cuts in the professor.

A man rises. It takes me a moment to recognise him. Dressed in a loud Hawaiian shirt, it's Andy.

Chapter Twenty-Six

'Do you think you really were possessed by a demon?' He looks dead at me, no smile, just a blank face awaiting my reaction, poised to go whichever way the situation demands.

'Of course, she was. That's why the exorcism worked,' Louisa says and takes another swig of water.

Sitting next to Andy is Warren and on his other side is Betsy. Now I see her with them, I can see through Betsy's well-manicured mask. She's not a pretty publicist who hugs strangers; *she's* one of them. There are three Wraiths. There must be. It would explain why the girls were abducted without a fight. It's less scary when another woman approaches you.

Then it hits me. The notes to the press were Betsy. That's why the police couldn't match the handwriting. She's been drafting their dark press statements! Curating their infamy. Making the most of the bloody spotlight drawn upon them.

Have they followed me, or are they here because Louisa is touting them as her next project? I glance around the room. There are three exits, one at the back, and one at each side of the stage.

Warren gets up and, smirking, asks, 'Which demon was inside you?'

Believing it to be a valid question rather than a smutty taunt, Louisa pipes up, 'The demon never named itself. But the people I brought in were strong enough to expel it anyway.'

'We have a clip, if everyone would like to see?' The professor steps forward, and in full-on game show host mode gets the crowd chanting *yes*.

Warren and Andy sit down, their eyes never leaving me. Damn.

The video plays and suddenly the room is filled with my screams.

Slick red warms my vision and I shake it off just in time to focus on the exit sign. I run. My backpack bounces against my spine in a familiar rhythm. The voices of the swindler exorcists, who tortured me for hours, fade behind me. Now I *can* run. I couldn't then, but I can now. I shoot through the lecture hall and make it outside. Without slowing, I turn into the quad. The bus stop ahead is too close to the university, I need to make it to the next one, where I won't be spotted by jeering film students or murderous Wraiths.

'Slow down!'

Looking behind, I see Ashley lumbering after me. I stop. 'What are you doing?'

Out of breath, he jogs up, then bends over to put his hands on his knees. 'I was…' he pushes out, '…checking on you.'

'I thought you hated me now.'

'Nah, I was just annoyed.' He catches his breath. 'You're not the first person who suspected I was violent or something, when I'm not.'

'I won't be the last if you keep drawing like that.'

He smiles. 'Yeah. Sorry. I shouldn't have lied.'

'Why did you?'

Ashley blushes. 'It was embarrassing. Those were my private drawings. And sorry, I didn't mean for that all to happen back there. The girls were right. You should have been paid for *Possession*. That woman took advantage of you at a terrible time in your life just to get her five minutes of fame. I don't believe in demons.'

'The devil will hear you if you say that too loud.' I smile.

'You know,' he moves closer to me. 'Your disorder isn't your fault. We can't control our brains.'

Ashley has such an earnest smile that I nod my agreement.

'And hey, Dee. You stood up for yourself.'

'Not like I wanted,' I reply, my feet still aching from running away.

'I thought you did great. It was her who came across as callous and inept.' Out of the blue, he asks, 'Do you like Marvel?'

'I watched the films at St Alda's.' Memories of me, Tippy, Craig and Cookie with little bags of popcorn, excited for our weekly movie night, fill my mind.

My face must betray my sadness at never having those nights again, as Ashley quickly adds, 'Marvel had heroes with mental health problems. Legion, Typhoid Mary, Moon Knight. I always envied them.'

'Envied their powers?'

'No, their courage to do what's right regardless.'

Strange, I'd never considered my red thoughts and actions as courageous before, let alone a power. Can anger ever be a good thing? Ashley seems to think so. 'Thanks,' I say.

'But you could use a sidekick still, eh? We are still working on *your* Wraith documentary, right? Even after what she just said in there?'

'Hell, yes. More so because of what she said in there.'

'Okay. You texted that we are interviewing the Tomkins family. How'd you swing that?'

I turn and start to walk towards the next bus stop. 'They think we're working for Louisa.'

Ashley bursts into laughter. 'Oh, Dee, that's priceless.'

'Yeah, I'll meet you there.'

'Are you sure you don't want a lift? My car's a bit of a mess with crumbs and cookies all over it, but I can soon sort that out.'

'That's okay. If I had a car, it'd be covered in cakes too. Nothing personal. Public transport is fine.'

'Okay, text me the address.'

Ashley wanders off towards the university car park and I continue on to catch the bus.

Interesting morning. I stood up to Louisa. I learnt that there are people who feel the same way as me about *Possession is Nine Tenths*. And I discovered Wraiths are currently on a three-for-two offer. Fortunately, I have sketches of all of them, which I'll show to Megan and her parents to ensure she doesn't trust or go anywhere with them.

The bus is busy so I have to stand the entire journey. While trying to remain upright as I'm jiggled about, I think through what I should say to Mrs Tomkins. How do I tell her that the only daughter she has left is in danger? And will she believe me?

–

Ashley has beaten me to the Tomkins' house. Standing by his car, camera in hand, he watches as I approach.

With a jerky movement, he then waves as if we're old friends. Maybe he is my friend. Friends argue, they fall out. God knows Cookie wasn't always nice; he'd have random childish bouts of sarcasm just as my anger could trigger him into moody silence.

'Bus was late then, eh?' Ashley says.

'That's public transport for you.'

'Yeah, buses are crap, but I know why you use them.'

I raise an eyebrow.

'You don't like cars because one hit you.' He smiles. 'That's okay. I get it. I don't like cars either. This one is a real money pit.' He nods at several small dents on his bonnet. 'Ready to rock and roll?'

'Yep, let's see how this thing plays out.'

As we walk up the path to the Tomkins' front door, Ashley nudges my shoulder. 'Sorry again about that bitch back there. I do get why you hate her.'

'Thanks, but I don't *hate* her. I just don't want to spend any more time with her.'

It's then I decide that I will tell him my theory about Andy and Warren, and now Betsy. If Ashley truly is my friend, he'll believe me. I need an ally. With the police not listening, my parents looking at me like I'm a monster, and Dr Taylor probably already printing off my section papers, Ashley could be all I have. Father Jacob says he believes me, but if it comes down to it, he'll keep me safe above anything else, and it's not me I'm worried about now.

The Tomkins' house is huge. It's a new-build with three storeys. Megan's mum opens the door and rushes us inside. It must be so quiet in their home now with just one daughter.

As Ashley follows me in with the camera, she looks behind him. 'Louisa coming later?'

'Her talk at the university ran late,' I say. Not a lie; she's probably still there soaking up the admiration.

'Oh, okay then. Come through.' She motions for us to walk up the stairs. At the first landing is a door that opens up into a living room. Megan is there. Spotting us, she rushes over. She's wearing a Panic at the Disco T-shirt and now has green stripes through her blonde hair.

'I'm so happy we're doing this,' she all but sings.

'Is here all right to film?' Mrs Tomkins asks.

Ashley opens their curtains to let in some natural light. 'Should be fine,' he says. Suddenly, I'm reminded that Ashley drew death pictures of Erica. It would have taken a long time to finish such an intricate sketch; time he spent birthing a grotesque image of this woman's murdered daughter. Rolling around this thought, Ashley's smile now appears more disturbing than friendly.

'Are you going to show me the questions first?' Megan asks. 'Like Louisa did?'

'It's best if we can get an honest reaction,' I tell her.

Her bottom lip juts out, wobbling. 'But I want to practise.'

'In documentaries, you have to tell the truth, and when you practise a reaction, it's not truthful anymore.' As I say this, her mum puts an arm about Megan's shoulders, which is quickly shrugged off; reminding me of how I am with my parents.

The whole interview is stunted by Megan's obvious acting ambitions. Reactions are forced, even though they shouldn't be; after all, her sister was brutally murdered. During the takes, Megan plugs her new blog, and Instagram account, with shameless abandon. Even Ashley rolls his eyes a few times. If I'd had an older sister who was murdered, I'd be out for revenge, not using the tragedy to make myself a social media darling. By the end, the footage is almost useless. Especially as Mrs Tomkins continually listens out for Louisa's arrival, which of course is never going to come.

When we pack up to leave, Megan asks if she can get final approval of the footage we use. Ignoring her arrogance, I instead beckon her mother to a private corner of the room. I'm going to have to lie again, but it's a whitish lie, one that will hopefully stop something terrible happening.

'Was that what you needed?' she asks me.

'Yes, thank you. Look, the police won't admit this, but there are suspects in the Wraith case. Between you and me, there are three.'

'Why wouldn't they say?'

'They're afraid of the information being leaked. If the suspects find out they're close to being arrested, they could flee.'

She looks thoughtful. 'But *you* know who they are?'

'I have sketches.' I pull out my sketchbook and flick to the pages of Warren, Andy and then Betsy.

Mrs Tomkins studies them with a narrow-eyed stare. 'That's Erica's old boyfriend.'

'You knew about that?'

'She didn't know I knew, but Megan showed me her sister's diary.'

Erica kept a diary. Few do these days. At St Alda's it was encouraged, but the discipline to write daily was both taxing and depressing – what life events could patients with such basic routines write about?

Suddenly Mrs Tomkins snatches my sketchbook from my hand. 'One's a woman,' she says.

'Yes, and they're saying in the latest letter that the 12th girl will be dramatic.' I look over at Megan who is now dancing for an uncomfortable-looking Ashley.

Her mum takes a sharp intake of breath, then looks at all three sketches again.

'And… you shouldn't trust Louisa. She doesn't have Megan's best interests at heart, only her own. I should know.'

Mrs Tomkins nods that she understands, then says, 'I'll keep her home and off-camera until they're caught. You said that's soon, right?'

'Sooner than they think.'

'Thank you.'

I'm so taken aback by her gratitude I almost topple over. No one has said those words to me in a long time. With a vigilant mum, Megan should be safe for now.

–

Ashley and I meet back at the coffee shop to go over the footage.

'We can use hardly any of the Megan interview,' Ashley says.

'I know, she comes across like a tween sociopath. We can't accidently vilify a child social media influencer.' I shove half a chocolate muffin in my mouth and let the sugar and fat tickle my tongue.

'Perhaps we can play around with her reactions. Edit in a soul?' Ashley downloads the footage onto my laptop.

I have to tell him who the Wraiths are. They've not killed men yet, but they might if Ashley accidently swerves into their path.

'There's something I need to tell you. Something you may find hard to believe,' I say, the taste of chocolate lacing my words.

'Okay.' He looks sceptical. Damn, if he doesn't believe me, I could lose his help. But I can't let the Wraiths keep killing.

'Andy *is* the Wraith.'

'What? No? Him being victimised by that online group is what this whole documentary is about!'

'And he's not working alone. There are three Wraiths: Andy, his wife Betsy and her brother Warren. They were all at Louisa's talk today.'

'That doesn't prove anything. Half the town was at that talk.'

'There's also what we picked up at Andy's house. Listen.' I press play on the recording. The coffee shop is quiet and the noise attracts the attention of people sitting at the other table; they throw me evil looks that I volley back.

Ashley hears the sound. He then rewinds it to listen again. 'What do you think it is?'

'Can't you hear it? It's Hayley calling for help.'

'It could be anything. A cat or a bird. Or even the house settling. It was an old building, Dee. Practically stone age.'

'You don't believe me?'

Sighing, he takes a swig of coffee. 'I'm not saying that. It's just, as evidence goes, it's flimsy. What did Andy say when you confronted him with the recording?'

My nose wrinkles. 'I haven't confronted him.'

'Shouldn't you give him a chance to explain? Isn't jumping to conclusions how this whole thing got started in the first place?' Ashley sits back in his chair.

'He knows I know. He tried to explain everything away in this long rambling text. And I overheard him and Warren talking about it all in the park – oh, and I stopped Warren abducting a little girl in Good Tree Park. There's actually a lot of evidence—'

'What? You never mentioned a little girl in the park. When was this?'

'A while ago.'

'Can I see Andy's text?'

'I was angry, so I deleted it.'

'That wasn't smart.' Ashley leans forward and sips his coffee.

Wait, the shorts. 'I also found a pair of denim shorts in that box room at Andy's house. I saw Hayley in them the day she was abducted.'

'Did you talk to the police? Hand them in for DNA?'

'They didn't believe me. And I doubt there's much useful DNA on them after I manhandled them.'

Ashley looks around, then puts the lid down on my laptop. 'Look, you don't have a very stable history, and this whole Wraith business must be stressful. Perhaps we should both go to Andy's house to confront him together. Ask some questions for the documentary.'

'That's a great idea.'

'Okay, we'll go there tomorrow. Text me when you're free, I'll meet you there.'

I watch my new friend leave, then begin to gather my things.

'Dee?'

Half expecting Stephanie, I look up, but instead find Betsy.

'What are you doing here?' I snap.

'Wanted to see if you were okay, after what happened at the university.' Gathering her long skirt, she perches on the seat opposite.

'Why would you care?' Then another thought hits me. 'And how did you know I was here?'

'We met here before, remember? And I can read people pretty well. I guessed you were a creature of habit.' Laughing, she then flips her hair to one shoulder. 'I also called and asked the baristas to let me know when you were here.'

'How very stalkerish of you,' I spit, putting my camera away.

'Don't you want another interview?'

I cock my head. 'An interview with a Wraith?'

Her eyes widen. She's shocked I've figured it out. 'Why would you say that?'

'You're working with your husband and brother. I know it's the three of you.' Damn, I shouldn't have tipped my hand.

Getting up. Betsy shakes her head. 'I'm not the Wraith, and neither is Andy or my brother. I'm shocked you even think it.' She sniffs. 'Hurt, really.' In a waft of sickly perfume, she stomps away, leaving me to wonder what her plan was. My best guess: making me doubt myself.

-

I don't remember getting home or going to bed, but I wake up at 3:33 a.m. again. There's tapping on my window. The noise is light, not the usual three random knocks I'm used to hearing.

Wondering if there is a black-clad man in the tree again, I get up and open the blind. It's raining. This is a good sign. The heat wave has been mercilessly murdering plant life. There was even talk of a food shortage in winter if things didn't get better. God is telling me everything will work out. With Ashley by my side, I'll be able to confront Andy and his other Wraiths. The Watsons will be redeemed, and the needless gory deaths of Northamptonshire's girls will stop.

Moving my laptop from the open window, I notice the rain has already wormed its way inside. My fingers are wet. Wiping them down my night shirt, I leave a scarlet stain. Mouth slack with horror, I hold my hand out of the window to cup fresh rainfall. Bringing it in, I turn my light on and gasp. It's raining blood.

Chapter Twenty-Seven

Frantically, I wipe my hands again and again and then pull off my nightie. Naked, I spring onto my bed and cower as far away from the window as I can. This is in my head. The red from my mind has spilled into reality. When was the last time I took a pink pill? I don't even remember my last prayer. Damn. I slip off the bed and clasp my hands together.

'Dear Lord, your signs are really confusing. Did you know that? Does this' – I thrust out my stained hands – 'represent the blood of innocent people? Or is it the Wraith's blood? I wish you'd be more specific. No wonder your followers keep getting stuff wrong. Or is it not a sign at all, and it's all in my head? I've never had symptoms like this before, but then again, I've never gone so long before... you know. Can you let me know what's going on? Amen.'

–

The moment I wake, I shoot across the room and look out the window. It's smeared with a pinkish tint. I didn't imagine it, or I'm still imagining it; I can't work out which.

My door crashes open and Mum stands there with her washing basket clutched to her chest like wicker armour.

Realising I'm naked, I pull up my bed sheet and wrap it around me, toga-style.

'How are you still in bed?' she asks.

'I was tired. And can you please knock?'

'I did knock. I knocked three times, even shouted for you. You never answered. I was worried.'

'I'm a grown up. I'd like a lock on my door,' I say.

'Jog on. If we were to put a lock on this door, it'd be on the outside. Now get dressed. Dad needs your help in the garden.' And with that, she storms off without taking any of my clothes to wash.

I shower and dress but skip breakfast. The anger vibes coming off Mum in the kitchen are almost choking.

Outside, Dad is wrestling with the hosepipe.

'What are you doing?' I ask.

Smiling he says, 'They're going to enforce that hosepipe ban soon, so thought I'd get rid of last night's little issue quick.'

I look down to see a red river flowing through the cracks of our decking. 'It did rain blood last night.'

'It's not blood. There's red dust in it, that's all. It happens from time to time. Probably caused by the wind picking up foreign debris on its journey here.'

In the light of the morning, I bend down and scoop up some of the running water. Now diluted, it's easier to see the red particles in it. Odd how that can happen. Something so scary at night can become mundane in the daylight.

'Mum said you needed help.'

'Hi-de-hi!' Mr Davidson appears at our gate. 'Awful business last night with the rain. Turns out we got a liberal shaking of Sahara sands.'

'Tell me about it, Davey Boy. Crazy weather.'

'Did you see that green lightening the other night?' he asks.

'I did,' I say.

'Oddest thing. And this heat!'

'I might as well give up on my garden all together,' Dad adds.

Mr Davidson moves further onto our property. 'Nah, you've got some good roots here. Let me help you clean up, then beers?'

'You got a deal.' Dad puts his thumbs up. Turning to me, he says, 'I'm good here. You go back inside in the cool.'

As I slip back into the house, my stomach growls so I linger by the kitchen. There are cakes in the cupboard. Mum is putting away dishes with her back to me. Quickly, I steal the sweet treats and head upstairs.

'Wait!' Mum's using her teacher voice.

I turn, putting the cakes behind my back out of sight.

Cocking her head, she says, 'I've been debating asking you out right. Part of me doesn't want to know the answer, but I've not seen him for a while, so I'm going to have to ask.'

'Ask what?'

'Did you do something to Lucifer?'

I'd laugh if her face wasn't such an angry shade of purple. 'Why would I do anything to next door's dog?'

'I didn't ask for a motive, I asked if you did something. Did you?'

'No. Apart from the night barking, I actually quite like the little guy.'

'Are you sure?'

'I'm sure.'

She tuts. 'I daren't ask about him next door,' Mum mutters. 'They're bound to accuse you of doing something.'

I should tell her about the man in the tree. He certainly didn't like Lucifer, but that would make me sound crazier. 'Can I go now?'

'Why not,' Mum sighs.

I spend the day in my room. It smells funky and, with the red dust still covering most of the neighbours' houses, the world outside my window gives off a familiar reddish hue. Ashley messages to ask about meeting at Andy's. It's now or never. Holding my breath, I text the Wraith,

> Andy, I'll meet you to talk. When is good for you?

Instantly, he replies.

> I'm out of town until tomorrow, but I do want to talk. I'll let you know.

As I'm updating Ashley, Andy pings me another message.

> I can't believe that crazy shit happened to you. We have more in common than you know.

Does Andy think he has a demon too?

Giving the police one last shot, I fire off an email to DCI Campbell pleading with her to check Andy's old rectory for evidence he was keeping girls there. Even just the hint of a police presence might stop them taking Megan, or any other 12th girl.

While waiting for a reply, I work on the documentary, then check Louisa's status on Facebook. She's gushing about how nice it was to see me yesterday, even refers to it as a *reunion*.

Mum and Dad creep up to my room a few times. Sometimes to offer me food and drink, other times to listen outside my door. If I knew what they wanted me to do, I'd just do it. I'm so tired and it's barely one in the afternoon. Oh, wait. There was something I had to do today. Scrambling through my backpack I find the yellow Post-it Mum gave me. Dr Taylor had booked me the flotation tank this afternoon. Best at least try the Buddhist concept; I need to keep my doctor on side. Afterwards, I can go straight to the pub for the Inspiration Cometh meeting. Stay out of Mum and Dad's way without being confined to my room.

The spa is nearer the house than I thought. It takes less than ten minutes to get there. The woman on the front desk eyes me strangely when I say who I am; I'm guessing they don't get many spa appointments booked by psychiatrists for patients.

After changing into an old swimsuit, I spend ten minutes trying to squash my backpack into one of their stylishly slim lockers. Eventually, I have to take everything out to fit it in like a game of Tetris.

The tank is smaller than I imagined. Rounded and white like a space shuttle. I'm helped into the salt water contained within, then told I'll be released in forty minutes.

'What if I want to get out sooner?' I ask the woman.

'You won't. Once you're in, you'll feel so stress-free you'll never want to leave.'

Slowly, I sink into the warm water, and before I can ask any other questions, the lid is pulled down over me.

Darkness extends, seemingly beyond the walls of the tank, as if reaching into forever. No smells. No sounds. Nothing.

In the absence of anything, I stare too long into the darkness. Red and blue spots dance before me; pinprick fairies of light gather and part as if in some unpredictable dance. For a moment, I see pictures in them, like when I close my eyes and flash on a lost object. Purposely, the lights then dash and undulate as if trying to tell me something. Phantom will-o'-the-wisps with a message just for me.

'What is it?' I ask. At the sound of my voice, the spell is broken and the dots fade.

I wave my arms through the water. The sound, dulled by the container, slips away from my ears, almost like I hadn't moved at all. I understand why Dr Taylor prescribed this. It's true calm, but only for as long as my thoughts allow it, as, without a watch, I've no clue how long I've been *relaxing* for, or how long I have to go; it's simultaneously freeing and annoying. How can I relax if I could be yanked from my solitude at any moment?

I close my eyes and my photo of Dara springs forth, with her bloody nose, mouth and ears. Her missing eyes... wait. The Wraiths are taking the girls' eyes, but they're stealing their tongues, and fingers too. They're also disabling their noses and ears. They're recreating a dark retreat! Dr Taylor must have told Andy about it too. The cruelty of putting all those unwilling victims into a permanent dark retreat chills me so far to the bone that I thrust out and bang on the lid. Again and again. Yelling and thrashing, like a baby desperate to be born.

My plastic cocoon is opened.

'I need to do something,' I mutter as I clamber out.

The woman snorts. 'You should have peed before you got in.'

Once I'm dressed and back in the heat of the day, I text Dr Taylor and ask if I can come by sooner. I need to check if she spoke to Andy about her Buddhist beliefs and the dark retreat. I then text my theory to Ashley. On the bus to the pub, he calls me.

'How did you come up with that?'

'It doesn't matter, but I think I'm right.'

'Lisa did look like she'd lost more than her eyes in that photo online.'

'Yeah, and…' *Don't mention Dara's body.* 'The police are covering up other injuries.'

'If there are three Wraiths, they probably have separate MOs. Maybe one doesn't do anything at all, but watches?'

Thinking of Betsy more as an onlooker to her husband and brother's crimes somehow makes her involvement more palatable – almost understandable, if she was scared of both of them. Maybe she was trying to reach out to me yesterday, but my red reaction scared her away.

'Can we talk more in person?' he asks.

'I'm going somewhere now.'

'Dee?'

'Yes?'

Ashley takes a deep breath. 'I think you're right about everything.'

-

Early for Inspiration Cometh, I meet Donald at the bar. Despite me quite literally saving his cat, it has done nothing to redeem me in his eyes. He looks over and instead of a pleasant greeting I get, 'How'd you know where I lived?' Clearly, this has been playing on his mind.

'I walk home too. I'm quite often a few steps behind you.' Damn, that sounded creepier than I intended. Quickly, I move away, and look around to find the rest of the group, which is so big tonight, we have to sit in the beer garden. The air is a muggy hangover of another hot day and the only seat I can slip into is near a brown bush that seems to be home to every wasp in the world.

Smiling at the other members, I feel all aglow. I figured out something important. I'm one step closer to catching the Wraiths, all three of them. Ashley is going to help me. I'm so busy marvelling at my Sherlock Holmes abilities that it takes me longer than it should to realise why tonight is so busy. Strutting through the pub car park towards me is Louisa.

Chapter Twenty-Eight

Janet invited her over Facebook. They now all know who I am. When I first came in, I was so wrapped up in my success that I hadn't noticed their faces had morphed from slight worry and disgust to significantly more worry and disgust.

I'd leave, but I've just bought a lime and soda. And truthfully, I don't want Louisa to chase me from this conveniently located group of creatives. The nearest other is three buses away.

Rising from her seat, Janet clinks a pen against her perspiring gin and tonic. 'I'd like to welcome a very special guest, Louisa Black. Writer, producer and director of *Possession is Nine Tenths*.'

Everyone claps but me.

'Thank you,' Louisa gushes. 'And let's not forget the little star.' She points at me.

A wasp suddenly buzzes by my ear and I bat it away.

'Did you guys stay in touch? Dee didn't mention it.' Donald asks.

'My success has taken me all over the world. And, well, it took Dee to a mental home. So no, we didn't keep in touch, but we're all caught up now.' She winks.

My hands are itchy. The salt from the floatation tank is causing a rash. I wrap both palms around my drink to feel the soothing coldness of the ice.

The meeting crawls by with Louisa making snide comments and the group practically kissing her feet, as if she were Jesus rather than Judas.

A normal person would seek advice from their friends. Slyly, I text Ashley and Father Jacob. Ashley comes straight back with, Play it cool. Father Jacob takes longer to reply with, turn the other cheek. He then sends a second text quoting a long passage from the Bible. It's supposed to make me calmer. It doesn't. How could it? She is infiltrating my life, yet again. Seeping through it like a rancid red stain. I half expect a team of have-a-go exorcists to crash the group and start chanting at me. I'm not sure I can take the bell ringing right now. I already have a headache.

A wasp crawls up my arm. I turn to look at it and realise it's the first living thing I've allowed to touch me in years. Its little legs tickle my skin, raising the fine hairs. So many people are sitting here and it has chosen me. The problem is, wasps can sting. Have I been so starved of real affection that I consider a predatory insect's interest a good thing? I bat it away.

'If you leave them alone, they leave you alone,' Trudy says in her saintly voice.

She's wrong. One particularly aggressive wasp keeps trying to dip into my drink. I wave my hand and it flies up and then down onto the table. Before I know what I'm doing, I smack the wasp hard with my exercise book. When I lift up the book, I see its crumpled, twitching body on the table. The thrashing legs are hypnotic. I can't take my eyes from it. Once it's still, I look up to see the whole group watching me. Louisa is smirking.

'I need to get home,' I say.

'You still working on that documentary?' Donald asks.

I shift my gaze to Louisa.

'Yes. Thanks. Bye.'

I gather my backpack and almost knock Trudy over as I hoist its massive bulk onto my shoulder. Quickly, I make my way out of the beer garden, past screaming kids on the swings and an already drunk teenage girl arguing with her boyfriend about the length of her skirt.

'Wait!'

I look back to see Louisa jogging up behind me. She's wearing a slim-fitting cheap white dress that, as the sun is behind her, is almost transparent. I keep walking.

'Dee, please.'

I quicken my pace. I could catch the bus at the top of the road, but it'll give her until the bus appears to hassle me, and I can't have Louisa following me all the way home, although it's not like she doesn't know where I live.

Suddenly, she's in front of me, palms out and empty. At least she isn't brandishing a camera.

'Look, I get you feel like I took advantage of you,' she says.

'*Feel like?* I *know* you took advantage. And you didn't even learn your lesson. You're doing the same to Megan now.'

'I'm really not. Let's bury the hatchet, okay?'

I should say, *in your head*. 'It's not okay.'

'You were ill, Dee. I was trying to help.'

'No, you weren't.'

'Can we be friends? I miss you. And you're better now, right? They let you out.' She smiles at me, all white teeth and flaking red lipstick.

'I have to go. Why don't you get back to *your* group?' I spit and continue walking.

'After my Wraith documentary, I want to do a sequel to *Possession*. It'll be better with your help.'

'Go to hell!'

'I'll do it either way. It'll just be easier on you if you help me,' she calls after me.

A whoosh of warm air whips through my hair, making me stop before crossing the road. I hadn't even looked. A car with its roof down honks, its ear-crushing pop music giving it a cheesy soundtrack as it careers up the road. Louisa's fault. I was almost hit, and I'm usually so careful. All her fault.

'Six, five, four, three, two, one,' I whisper, then ready myself to run. A screech and scream pulls my attention back to the road. In horror, I watch as the same car hits a man. His body rolls up the bonnet and, as the vehicle brakes, he falls motionless on top of the windscreen, twisted like washing in the wind.

I thrust my hand into my backpack and pull out my phone to call 999.

'I got it,' Louisa says from behind me, her mobile already to her ear. Of course, she would beat me to it. Rather than put my phone away, I take a quick photo of the number plate of the car, just in case.

I want to go over, to ask if everyone is okay, but my feet won't move in that direction. Blood is flowing freely from the victim, pooling by the front tyres like a red river. The driver and her passenger are slowly exiting their vehicle. At least they're not running.

'Yes, I'll wait for the ambulance,' Louisa says to the dispatcher.

I need to leave. Was the accident my fault? Did the driver not see the man because they were too busy honking at me?

'Bringing it all back, eh?' Louisa has managed to creep up beside me. 'That's okay. We all have relapses.'

She is pure evil. Did she arrange this horrific event, possibly killing an innocent man, so I would take a step back in my mental health journey? Or perhaps the drivers were aiming at me? No, this is just an accident. It has to be.

'Everything will be okay,' Louisa says as she tries to put a heavy arm across my shoulders. Turning to escape her touch, I accidently push her with my backpack, knocking her over.

'What are you doing to that woman?' the driver shouts at me, stumbling towards us. A potential murderer looking for a quick redemption.

'Sorry,' I mumble, then look left and right before bolting across the road.

–

At home, I grab a chocolate muffin, take a cold shower, then trap myself in my room with the night's events buzzing around my mind like lost wasps.

Tonight is, once again, unbearably hot and I can't sleep even with the fan turned up to the max and the blind pulled down. It's like I'm in an oven. The witch who tried to eat Hansel and Gretel must have felt like this, smelling herself cooking, feeling her skin crisp and curl as it burned. I think back to my short Dark Retreat and once again to the face of Lisa and the body of Dara. I know I'm right about the Wraith's MO but Dr Taylor hasn't returned my text, so it looks as if I'll have to wait until our usual appointment to prove it.

For the majority of my life, all my friends were people with diagnosed mental illnesses, but none of them were violent on purpose or evil by choice. They were simply damaged and complicated. What happened to Andy, Warren and Betsy to make them act like this? And how come no one has spotted these traits? Dr Taylor sees Andy regularly. It's her job to see things that are hidden. When we first met, she spotted me at ten paces; instinctively knew I was defective. But when I met the Wraiths, I didn't feel anything – well, apart from when I slammed my bag into Warren that day. His darkness was obvious. I know I'm right about them, but people think they're right about me when we meet. I'm dangerous. I'm weird. I'm not worth the time to see beyond my illness and what happened to me. Confusion is such a special torment for the mind. In St Alda's everything was obvious. There was no life subtext to have to dig out. I simply existed there, healing as best I could.

I can't take anything for granted. Assumptions are hurtful, and that's not just my truth. I need more evidence on the three Wraiths.

My palms are too sweaty to pray, so I decide to take matters into my own hands. I dress in a short T-shirt and leggings, grab my backpack and sneak out of the house. Remembering to leave the patio doors unlocked so I can get back in. I then jog down the path. As I do, I look over the neighbour's fence in the hope of seeing Lucifer, but he's not there. The trees are also free of men. There is too much strange shit going on to keep things straight. I catch the last bus to the edge of town and run, under cover of night, to Andy's house. With him out of town, it'll give me a chance to have a proper look around the property. The Wraiths may not have taken anyone new yet but I need evidence; something the police can't explain away.

Chapter Twenty-Nine

Reaching the old rectory, I peer into the windows. Nothing. Andy said he was going out of town, so no one should be home. I try the front door. It opens. Is that an invitation?

My backpack is heavy but I can't put it down, I might need it as a weapon. I steal inside the house and begin checking for signs of torture or death. There's none. All the bedrooms upstairs are empty with undisturbed bed sheets. I spend an hour going through the cupboards in the kitchen, the drawers in the bedroom, then the boxes in the room where I found Hayley's shorts: still nothing.

I expect the cellar to be locked, but even that's open. I switch on the torch app on my phone, then step down the creaking stairs. There's nothing here either. Just a few bottles of wine, a box full of old records that could probably be auctioned for small a fortune on Starsellers, and some jars of random fruit that appear to be older than me. There's only one other door. It's locked. Gently, I lay my ear against the damp wood.

'Hello?' I say.

Nothing.

I ask my question another two times, then realise it's probably just a cupboard and I'm talking to an old Hoover and a spider's nest.

The thought of DCI Campbell reading my last email and trusting me enough to search here herself, only to find nothing, irks me. Not enough to see red, but maybe a pinkish glare. I heard Hayley's voice, didn't I? But there's no evidence anyone was kept here against their will. Where else would the Wraiths take the girls? Andy's other place is a flat. Warren might have somewhere, but where?

I tidy up behind me and start the long walk back to town to catch the bus. It's now six in the morning and the sun is peeking over the horizon, ready to ambush the world.

When I get home, I'm so tired I fall straight into bed but can't sleep. After a restless few hours tangled in sweaty sheets, I get up and check the online news. No Wraith abductions. Megan is still safe.

–

Dad has already left for teacher training, leaving Mum at the breakfast table.

'Dee?' She pulls out the chair beside her and I sit down. 'Um, I really need to know what you did to that dog.'

'What?'

'It's okay. I understand your frustration. I heard him barking, too. But if you took matters into your own hands, it wasn't right.'

Rubbing my eyes, I say, 'I didn't hurt Lucifer.'

'Are you feeling…?'

Rising, I push my chair back across the kitchen tiles. 'Demonic?'.

Mum huffs. 'I can't help you if you don't tell me the truth.'

'I *am* telling the truth.'

'Look, I understand that things have been rough. You're not used to life on the outside, and you've lost that job now.'

If she knew half of the stress I was dealing with, Mum would have me in a straitjacket before I finished my cornflakes, which is why I can't ask her for help with this Wraith business.

'I'm really trying,' I mutter.

'You have to let me in. What did you do to Lucifer?'

My eyes widen. 'Nothing! I'd never hurt a dog! Why do you think I would?'

'Because nothing bad happened before you… came back here,' she says, then quickly clamps a hand over her mouth.

Before I can stop it, I say, 'There was a man in the garden the other night. He must have done it.'

'There was?'

'He was dressed in black Lycra and…' Damn, I sound insane, again.

'Um, okay. Perhaps we need to change your appointment with Dr Taylor. I'm sure she can get you in today.' Mum reaches for her phone.

'I know you don't believe me about, well, everything. But I'm telling the truth. I've never lied.' The pitch of my voice rises so high at the end of the sentence, only a dog could hear me – ironically.

'Okay, okay, but I'd be happier if we can get you an emergency appointment with Dr Taylor. She's the expert and all.'

That's the worst thing that can happen. The more emergency appointments I end up in, the more I look like I can't handle my life. I'm hanging on by the skin of my normal teeth. 'I'll see Dr Taylor for my regular appoint-ment tomorrow.' Before Mum can respond, I leave.

As I reach the hall, the letterbox creaks open and a white envelope is pushed through. I scoop it up and see it's addressed to me. I turn it around in my hands. It's probably from Louisa, trying to get me on board for her sequel. I won't trust her, not again. Opening the envelope, I read the contents aloud; imitating her whiny voice:

> *Hello Dee, I watched your documentary; not the one you're making about me, but… the one you starred in.*

Not from Louisa. I carry on reading.

> *You've got me all wrong. Looking forward to meeting you properly. Remember to bring your camera, so you can capture the best sides. You can shoot all the angels.*

Did they misspell angles?

> *I trust you to rip apart the frames. To slice the scenes. I feel like Possession is Nine Tenths gave me the chance to really get to know you. Best you don't tell the police, or media, about this little note. You know what they're like; probably wouldn't believe you, anyway. Don't want you to end up back at St Alda's, not when you're so close. You looked so sweet, hovering around Dara — just like another fly. Can't wait to meet your diabolic side.*
> *Meet me. Meet me. Meet me if you dare.*
> *Your friend in blood, the Righteous Wraith*

There's an email address at the bottom, waiting for me to ask for a time and place to meet:

WraithsRus@murdermail.com

I fling open the door, but there's no one on the step. Rushing out, I scan the perimeter of the house. Movement by the back gate. I spring forward and burst through in time to see Mr Davidson getting into his car. When he spots me, he climbs back out.

'What-ho, youngest Jones,' he says with a salute.

'Did you see anyone around the house?' I ask.

'I only just got here. Who were you expecting?'

There's an odd expression on his face.

'Someone just posted me a letter. Did you see a man?'

'You're socialising, that's good news. I know your dad was worried.' With that insulting statement, he then gets in the car and drives off.

Deflated, I go back inside.

The Wraiths are calling me out. They're so brazen they have given me the evidence I need to go to the police, but it's a different style of note addressing me directly and more inviting than taunting. And of course, the others are in the public domain, easy to fake. And like they said, who would believe me? The email doesn't help either. No doubt they'll know secret computery things to keep their identities hidden. Damn it.

Should I message them?

Stress can hit hard at any moment. A little red clouds my vision and I have to sit down. Unfurling my fists, I ask myself, can I do this? Father Jacob says God only gives you what you can handle. Should I pray? Ask for another sign? Or is that being needy? I've already seen at least three signs; I'm still sporting the stains from one. Mum and Dad won't help me. They think I'm relapsing, and maybe even a dog killer.

Did the Wraiths take Lucifer? No, that's ridiculous; he's not even my dog. But why send me this letter? Am I the 12th girl? No, there would be no public outcry at my death, just a collective sigh of relief. What if, in their own grubby grab for infamy, they want me to film what they do to the 12th girl for the documentary? There's no way in hell I'd do that. I'm weird and creepy, and I'll admit slightly deranged still, but they can't imagine I'd stand by and allow them to torture a young girl, just like Louisa did to me.

I can't help but think I'm missing something, so text Ashley about the note. After thirty minutes and still no reply, I remember my new documentary's mission state-ment – to hunt down the Wraiths. Just ensuring Megan's safety isn't enough. I need to do some real investigating. I re-read the letter. They know I found Dara, and the only way they could have seen me was if they were there too. I flip onto Wraith Finders and do a word search for Maple Industrial Estate – it comes up over a hundred times. That is where I need to go. It's where I found Dara and it was also the last place Fiona was seen alive.

I pile all my stuff into my backpack: books, laptop, and camera. A weapon would be great, but all I have access to is a plastic knife, which is not going to cut it, or anything else. I cup the fumsup in my hand and squeeze its wooden head for luck. Right now, I need as much as I can get.

'Dear Lord,' I say, sitting on the edge of my bed, hands clasped together. 'Me again. Should I go to Maple today?' I wait for an answer. There's none, of course. I'm not delusional, or at least I don't think I am, I'm just being polite to let God answer. He knows my past, and also my heart: that I want to catch the Wraiths just as much to stop their murderous rampages as to legitimise me. And I can't help but think if I was doing something terribly wrong and endangering myself, He'd stop me. 'Okay, I'm going to sniff around that industrial estate again. See what I can find. Thanks, God.'

The closer the bus gets to the industrial estate, the more stupid I feel. Although the sun is once again beating the world into an eye-wateringly bright vista, there are still shadows where bad things can happen. Maybe I should let the stop pass by? Carry on into town. Settle into a leather sofa at the Blue Sky Coffee Room and dig into the Wraith Finders website more, find other allies. But then, when the bus slows, without thinking, I get off at Maple. Award-winning documentarians don't shy away from confrontation. They don't avoid stories, they run towards them. Louisa would do this; I won't be outdone by her.

The estate's factories, warehouses and offices are all busy. I can't imagine someone thinking they could commit a crime here unseen, let alone two. Back in St Alda's, Craig and Tippy used to laugh at me for being naïve, but today I'm taking that trait to a whole new level, but even with this realisation sinking into my brain, like fruit in a trifle, I continue my vigil for something, anything to show me I can hunt down the three Wraiths and find the evidence I need to bring them to justice before they take the 12th girl…

Three hours later, and I've found diddly squat. I'm about to catch the next bus when I hear men yelling and laughing. I look over and stop dead. Warren is climbing into the back of a white van. Like a scared animal, I stand very still and watch him. He doesn't notice me, just goes about his business, loading stuff into the back of his vehicle. Lifting my camera, I film him. Zooming in, catching everything from his scratched-up hands to his shark eyes. It's not evidence, not by a long shot, but it does make the location more... obvious? No, damn, this doesn't prove anything. I could confront him? March up to Warren and tell him... what? To stop killing girls? He knows I know about him, so I've no cards left to play. Hell, Warren has a better hand than me right now. I could get arrested for accosting him in public, just like Andy is doing with suing the Wraith Finders. The site could still help me though. With them taking so many photos of Andy, maybe I can drop a hint on their forum about Warren and Maple. Perhaps one of the armchair detectives can make the connection to the police? But even with my limited capacity for the ways of normal life, I realise this plan is flawed, and I need to put more effort in. After all, this is *my* documentary. There's really only one thing I can do – something I should have done before now with someone who signed a waiver to be in my documentary. Confront Andy.

The Blue Sky Coffee Room. It's always just busy enough, and it's in town. I text Andy to say that, for the sake of our work together, we should meet there and clear

298

the air sooner rather than later. He comes straight back saying that he's willing to meet me now. To be safe, I then text Ashley and ask if he can be there too, just in the background in case he's needed. He's good at lurking unnoticed in the shadows.

Quickly, I change clothes, but rather than choosing one of my many black outfits, I slip on Hayley's shorts. They're a little big, so I have to put a belt around them to ensure they stay up. I then pull on a white and navy tank top and trainers.

As I bound downstairs, I find Mum waiting for me at the front door.

'What on earth are you wearing?' she asks, reaching for my arm. Recoiling, I almost lose my footing.

'Nothing,' I reply.

'They look familiar. Where did you get those shorts from?'

'It's My Look.'

'You've never shopped there in your life. And they don't even fit you. Seriously, Dee where did you get them from?'

'I'm going to be late,' I push past her and run down the stairs.

'Hayley had shorts just like them,' Mum calls after me.

–

Arriving at the Blue Sky Coffee Room twenty minutes early, I sit at a table, rather than on the leather couch; it would feel weird quizzing someone about terrible crimes sunken into a sofa like dried fruit in cake batter.

As I'm setting up my camera, Ashley arrives. He casually waves, buys a coffee and then sits behind me. I glance around and watch as he pulls out a copy of *Animal Farm*. Why are all his books from a GCSE literature exam?

Before I have time to think about it anymore, Andy strides in.

'Sorry, I'm late. I got caught up with my solicitor.'

A casual reminder he's suing the last people who accused him of being the Wraith. I rise to greet him. Clocking Hayley's shorts on me, he blushes.

'Do you like my outfit?' I ask with a smile.

His eye twitches, but he manages to nod and sit down.

'Don't you want to order a drink?' I ask.

'No, I don't think I'll be here that long.' As he looks around us, I hope Ashley has had the foresight to raise the book to cover his face.

'So, you wanted to explain everything,' I prompt, then point my camera at him.

'Yes,' he says. 'I know you think you heard something bad in the park the other day.'

I should point out that I've heard a lot of bad things, but instead say, 'Go on.'

'Warren is a little dark, I admit, but he's also a lot of fun when you get to know him.'

I use a hand gesture to tell him to continue, although it's not the hand gesture I want to use.

'I am not the Righteous Wraith. Yeah, the police spoke to me, but they let me go without charge. Warren is not a killer either; he's just really broken up over his divorce.'

'When was the divorce?' I ask.

'About six months ago.'

The Wraith killings started six months ago. Can anyone else say *trigger incident?* 'What a shame. And how's Betsy?'

'Better news there. We're back together.'

Nothing keeps a couple together like blood-soaked crimes. 'That's great. I noticed all three of you in the lecture hall at Louisa Black's talk.'

'Yes, we went to support you. We wanted there to be a few friendly faces in the crowd in case you came.'

Bullshit. They were there to scare me; probably to scare Louisa too.

'We watched *Possession is Nine Tenths*. I can't believe that happened to you.' He has the audacity to look ashamed.

'Lots of unbelievable things happen in this world, Andy.'

'So, are we good? Can we carry on filming the documentary? I'm really keen to get something out there, especially before the Black one hits. God knows what angle she'll take.'

God knows, indeed.

He continues, 'Dr Taylor says experimenting and getting out of your comfort zone can be cathartic. She encouraged me to work with you. She's not wrong, is she? About you?'

'About what?'

'That you tell the truth and want to help people. That you're not nutsy anymore.' He grins.

Nutsy? 'She's right about all that,' I say.

'And you don't think I'm really the Wraith now? You believe my text about what you overheard with Warren?'

Nope. 'Of course, totally makes sense. Sorry for the confusion.'

I must be getting good at insincere apologies, as he smiles at me. 'Can we continue with the documentary?'

'Try and stop me.' I get up.

Andy rises too. 'All settled then.'

I nod. 'Yes, back on track.'

Still smiling, he leaves and I fall back down onto my chair.

'That sounded oddly civil,' Ashley says, coming over and flopping down on Andy's empty seat.

'I guess.'

'Do you believe him? It would really help the narrative of the documentary if he were innocent.'

'No, I don't believe him,' I admit. 'But at least now he thinks I do, which might buy us some time.'

–

Not wanting to go home and face Mum's accusations of being a dog killer again, I stop off at St Godfrey's Church.

'Mum thinks I killed Lucifer,' I say by way of greeting to Father Jacob.

Instant worry-face. His mouth opens, but no words escape.

'Hello there,' comes another voice. Canon Matthew steps out from the confessional, a comical feather duster in his hand. 'Did you just say you killed the devil?' he laughs.

Screwing up my nose, I spit, 'No. It's next door's dog. He's missing.'

'Oh my,' Father Jacob says. 'That Scottie dog was such a pleasant little chap.'

Canon Matthew hands the duster to Father Jacob. 'Step into my confessional, Dee. It helps to get things off your chest.' He sweeps out an arm and opens the door for me. 'If we confess our trespasses, He is faithful and just and will forgive us our sins and purify us from all unrighteousness.'

'That's okay,' I tell him. 'I'm good just talking with Father Jacob.' Plucking the duster from my friend's hand,

I pass it back to Canon Matthew so he can continue his housework — or is it *church work*?

'Can't say I didn't try,' he mutters, then strides off towards the font.

Before Father Jacob can say anything further, I blurt, 'I think I'm... um... struggling.' I look down and away from my friend.

'What makes you think that?'

'Louisa has been hassling me, and I...'

Father Jacob sighs. 'It's okay. I'm aware of your encounters. She even contacted me, said you were out of control again.'

Barking a laugh at the absurdity, I throw my hands up. 'Out of control? She just wants her damn sequel!'

'I'm guessing that was why she wanted to meet with you before. I'm so sorry, Dee. I may have briefly thought better of her, but I have always believed in you.'

My lips twitch with a smile. 'Thank you,' I say. 'It would have been easier to think it was me flying off the handle and demoning out.'

My friend laughs. 'Demoning isn't a word, but I get your meaning.'

Thinking of Canon Matthew's speech, I realise I should get everything off my chest, just in case. 'I know now there's more than one killer. There are three Wraiths: Andy, Warren and Betsy.'

Father Jacob takes a breath. 'Tell me your evidence.'

'They sent me a letter, although I guess anyone could have faked that. I found the shorts, but that could be just a coincidence. I heard Andy and Warren talking, but it was out of context. You remember the voice on the recording, but Ashley said that could have been pipes or floorboards squeaking. The police really don't believe me, and they are trained in things like this.' Damn, I just explained away every piece of evidence I have.

'So, you did go to the police as we discussed?'

'Like I said, they didn't believe me.'

'I believe you,' he repeats.

'Thank you. And I promise I didn't do anything wrong at work, and I certainly didn't kill next door's dog.'

Father Jacob sits back in his chair. 'I'll speak with Teresa, tell her to look again at Andy and the others. Would that help?'

Teresa: the officer I asked for at the police station reception, who they couldn't find in the system. 'How do you know her?'

'DCI Worth? I've known her mum since I was a teenager. We sort of grew up together. Why do you ask?'

'Does she work at the new police station?'

Father Jacob cocks his head. 'She recently broke a big case and now works for the Cambridgeshire force, but her family are from Northamptonshire.'

Although this explains why I couldn't find her at the local constabulary, it makes me wonder how much influence she'd have over a neighbouring county.

'Dee? Can I speak to someone on your behalf?'

I want to say that it couldn't hurt, but having my priest fight my battles is worse than my parents wading in. And if Louisa gets a sniff of my story, there'll be a whole new angle to her follow-up documentary, one that drags Father Jacob into her sensationalised crap. I can see it now: Catholic Church encourages demon to accuse innocent people of crimes – or something catchier.

I'm quiet so long that he changes the subject. 'Has no one come forward about Cookie's death?'

Guilt for not thinking about my friend washes over me. 'No.' Then I say something that's been festering inside me since I puked at the bus stop. 'And that's not sitting right with me, either.'

'Of course, it'll take a while for you to come to terms with it.'

'Not that. Cookie knew some things, just not everything, and he tried to tell me. I don't think it was an accident.'

'You think someone at St Alda's is to blame?'

'No. The people there are wonderful. They would never hurt a patient. But something's not adding up, and I think it's to do with the Wraiths.'

'Pray with me, Dee?' He kneels down and puts his hands together.

I follow his lead, then listen as he asks God for guidance, for help, and for answers for me. All things I've been asking for, for weeks. Although I appreciate the sentiment, all it's done is hurt my knees.

-

Without a key, I can't sneak into the house. I knock and hope it's Dad rather than Mum who answers. This time my prayers are answered.

'Hi, love.' He ushers me inside. 'Mum's out with her friends, so it's just you and me for dinner.'

'Can I eat in my room? I have some work to do.'

'Work?'

'The documentary.'

'Oh, you're still doing that. Good for you.' He walks to the kitchen and hands me a plate of sandwiches and salad. 'Sure, you can eat upstairs.'

I tell him, 'Thanks.' Then take the plate.

Everything is falling apart. I don't know who and what to believe anymore. I email Megan's mum to check up on them. She replies almost immediately to say things are fine. Am I wrong? Are the Wraiths not going after Megan? Maybe I'm wrong about everything. Andy probably is innocent and will no doubt end up suing the pants off me too, although I didn't accuse him publicly like the Watsons. I take off the star shorts and turn on my laptop. I listen to the recording of Hayley's voice again. It could be pipes. I hear that now.

I don't remember falling asleep, but wake up at my desk. It's getting dark, so I pull down the blind, put the fan on and stand in front of it to dry my sweat. My phone beeps. It's a text message from Ashley: *Where are you?* I reply, *Home, why?* He comes straight back.

> Louisa Black has been abducted!

Chapter Thirty

I was wrong about Megan being the 12th girl.

I stare at the phone screen, not quite taking in his text. To think the Wraiths have answered my prayers by taking Louisa feels dirty and yet a soft, just, feeling settles over my soul, like the flutter of snow on a spring day.

I do a search online. Out of malice, I used to do this every day but now, as I punch in the familiar letters of her name, it feels like contacting an old friend. The first link is about the abduction. Louisa was at a pub interviewing a documentary subject. She left late and was seen by a witness climbing into a white van. Warren was driving a white van in Maple, but lots of people own them. It's only when I see the photo of the witness that everything crashes down on me. Dressed in a flimsy red sundress, her blonde hair tied in a messy bun, it's Betsy. Things like this don't just happen. God isn't a joker. I doubted myself, and that's when it all went wrong. The Watsons will see this too, and in case they've missed the photo, I email a link to them. They were right. Can you be sued for slander if it's the truth?

I email DCI Campbell. She'll probably not even read it, but at least I'm trying. *Betsy is your witness! Warren drives a white van. Check out where he works in Maple Industrial*, I tell her.

I try to get some sleep, but my mind is whirring. I write a plan of action in my journal. If I was willing to risk everything to save Megan, then surely, regardless of what she did to me, I should do the same for Louisa.

–

After a cold morning shower, I jog downstairs. Mum is at the kitchen table, deliberately not looking at me.

'Mum?'

'I don't have time for this. I've got a tonne of lesson plans to prep.'

Edging closer to her laptop, I spot she's doing an online crossword. 'I need your help.'

She closes the lid and sighs. 'What with?' She's looking at me like I'm the boy who cried wolf. Only this is my first cry, not my third. Wait, wasn't the boy eaten at the end of the fable? Lied three times and was punished with losing his life. How can you learn a lesson when you're dead?

I want to tell her everything – she'd make the police listen – but instead I say, 'Um, if you know someone is guilty of something, but you can't prove it. What would you do?'

'Everybody knows the wrong invoices were sent out at Lake.'

'They were, but...'

'It's good you're finally admitting *that* mistake. I must confess, I was starting to worry.'

This is one of those moral conundrums. A white lie pitted against a dark truth. The thing is, I know Corinne is an evil mastermind intent on destroying Lake so she can upgrade her job prospects. I might not be one hundred percent on everything going on now, but she confessed, albeit only to me. 'That's not what I'm talking about. I found out something damning about someone, just no one believes me.'

Considering my words, Mum sits back in her chair. 'You should talk to Dr Taylor about it – she's more qualified than me to give you advice. Also, you didn't mention your prescription. You must be running out. I picked it up for you.' She hands me a little white bag that crackles as it moves. I take it, then open my mouth to say thank you, although the words don't come out.

'I expect an empty packet by the end of the week.' And with that, she opens her laptop back up and stares at the screen until I go away.

Once I'm in my room, I put on my fan and draw the blind. It's a bright morning, but I need some sleep. I'm no good to anyone this tired, and Louisa has some time. I drop to my knees, squeeze my hands together and close my eyes. 'Dear Lord, I've done what Father Jacob advised and I'm turning the other cheek with Louisa. Please tell me where I should go to help her. Please sort out Mum. Bring back Lucifer – the dog, not the fallen Angel – and say hi to Cookie for me. Amen.'

When I wake again a few hours later, sweaty and with my head hurting, I spot the packet of pink pills precariously placed on the desk. Truthfully, I don't remember the last time I had one. They dull me, and I have to be alert. Like Ashley said, the red is my superpower. I need to trust in myself to short-circuit any potential hijacks to my amygdala before they take hold. Whether I believe my actions are born from a demon slithering about my soul, or from a blow to my brain shorting synapses, it doesn't matter. I've battled for decades to get better, but now I'm off the medication, I realise something: whatever it is, it is both enemy and friend. It could get me sent back to St Alda's or maybe, in a dangerous situation, could save my life. My condition is the ultimate frenemy.

–

Fortunately, the bus is on time for my regular appointment with Dr Taylor, and no one rings the bell. As I get off and walk down the street, I see St Alda's sprawling estate in the distance, all looming and lovely. I hate that I don't have a reason to visit anymore. I didn't lose just Cookie, but a free pass back home. I must remember it's still a possibility that I could go back there, just not until I put an end to the senseless murders.

Dr Taylor is late letting me in. Apologising, she hands me a drink. I'm not thirsty today, so I leave it in the waiting room.

'You can put your bag down there.' She motions to a corner of the room.

'I'm good, thanks.' I hoist my backpack further up my shoulder, then perch with it uncomfortably positioned between the chair and my back.

Smiling at me, she sits opposite. 'We're having a small service for Graham Cookson at the little chapel in St Alda's next week. It would be good for you to come, say goodbye.'

'What about the car that murdered my friend? Have they caught the driver? Do you even know how Cookie got out of the building to get through the hole in the fence?'

She sucks air through her teeth and flips through some notes on her desk. 'Not yet, but we're hopeful. I know this will feel particularly intense for you, Dee, what with your history, but it's important to have closure.' She then pulls out her *Words of Wisdom* book and flips to a page. She reads it silently, then lays the book open on her desk.

'What advice did it give?' I ask.

A smug smile spreads across her face. 'It said you need to be better with your medication. Your mum told me you're not taking it.' She opens a drawer and pulls out two pink pills. 'Here. Take them now.'

'They make me sleepy. I'll take them at home,' I say, scooping the tablets up from her palm.

Calmly, Dr Taylor stands and walks into the waiting room. She comes back with the glass of water. 'Take them now, please.'

'I'm telling the truth. One tablet makes me drowsy. Two would knock me out cold and I have to get a bus back home.'

The glass is shoved towards me so hard globules of water splash out.

'I can drive you home.'

'No.'

'Dee, please. You're not leaving me many options here.'

'I'll take them at home.' I snatch the glass and gulp down the contents. A silly tactic; she can always fetch more water.

Dr Taylor puts her hands up. 'All right. Take them at home. Promise?'

I nod. She's really close to me now; I prefer it when there's a desk between us. 'Look, I need to warn you there will be an investigation into Cookie's death. After all, he was killed outside the hospital. As a visitor, you'll be interviewed by the police. Would you like me there with you?'

Great, another police encounter. 'Yes,' I say, but instantly doubt my answer. It might make me look guilty having someone with me. 'Maybe, no.'

'Really, Dee? After all, it was me who let you see Cookie. Sometimes without the correct paperwork. I really thought that it was in both your interests; then this senseless thing happens. Don't think I haven't noticed you haven't agreed to go to his funeral yet.'

I want to say goodbye to Cookie, but if I go to St Alda's, will they let me out again? Is this the quiet way in which Mum and Dr Taylor get me back to where I belong, somewhere I can't act crazy, show them up, or do something worse. Has my new life's path narrowed to the width of a hospital bed? Though if it weren't for the Wraiths and my documentary, I wouldn't mind. To feel safe between the hospital's white walls once again, to have all my decisions made for me, could be just the thing I need. But then the Wraiths will kill Louisa, then the 13th girl, and on and on. They won't stop until someone stops them.

'I'll check my diary,' I say.

'Now you're not working, how are you filling your days? Are you still filming that thing about Andy?'

Her gaze is harder now, so solid I feel it weighing on me. I should tell her everything, but something stops me. 'No, it was too harrowing. And it looks like Andy has sorted everything out now.'

'How do you mean?' she asks.

'Oh, I shouldn't discuss documentary subjects, you know how it is.'

'Fair enough.' Dr Taylor writes something down. 'Let's look at getting you another job.'

I don't have the time to ride a desk all day, what with hunting serial killers and all, but I can't say that to her; instead I nod with little enthusiasm and break eye contact.

Sitting on Dr Taylor's desk is her giant vase of lavender. This time the stems seem old and wilted, the tiny purple petals drooping and discoloured. Only thorny stems remain of the roses. I wonder if she's still seeing her boyfriend. Why else would you hold on to something dead, unless it was a gift from someone you loved?

After an hour of discussing various topics, that I try to keep vague, Dr Taylor stands up and I follow suit. 'Do contact me if I can help you. You're not alone.'

'Thanks.'

'Oh, wait here, I want to give you something.' As she strides off into the waiting room, I scurry around her desk to see what the *Words of Wisdom* actually said. It reads: *Your lucky number is 13*. Not helpful. I sit back down on my chair just as Dr Taylor comes in.

'Here,' she says and hands me a plastic box.

Taking it, I can see it has seven compartments, each with a day of the week printed on.

'It's so you remember to take your pills. Fill it on Sunday after Mass, then you're all set for the week.' She smiles.

'Thank you,' I say and free the two pills stuck to my sweaty hand into today's little box. As I do, I can see the pink colouring has stained my palm; it looks as if I have stigmata. That's never happened before.

–

Mum and Dad are now both avoiding me. Leaving rooms when I enter, whispering when they think I can't hear. I'm surprised they haven't tackled the subject of Louisa. They must know about her abduction, it's all over the news.

Ashley texted a few times to discuss the Wraiths. He, at least, wants my thoughts. The thing is, they're getting muddier by the minute, rendering me incapable of making any meaningful decisions. Just in case, I should go to Andy's house and check for Louisa. No. I should go back to the police station and beg them to help. Definitely not. I should ask Ashley to help me. And risk the only friend I have left being targeted by serial killers? Maybe I should go back to Maple Industrial Estate? And look for what? No. I log onto Facebook and see Louisa's page is now covered in an ominous shadow. They are memorialising her already; the three days are not even up yet.

No barking. Lucifer is still absent.

Blind down. Fan on.

Tonight, my limbs are achy, and I've only realised I've been pacing for hours when, exhausted, I drop onto my knees.

'Dear Lord, what the hell? What am I supposed to do? Should I stay the course with the documentary? Is Andy guilty? He looks pretty guilty from where I'm kneeling. Is Louisa dead already? Am I really supposed to suck it up and try to save her? You better send me a bloody big sign, Lord. Amen.'

–

Morning. and I'm only just out of the shower when I hear Dad yell, 'Dee!'

Now what am I being accused of?

Still dripping, and covered only in a towelling robe, I follow his voice into the oppressive morning light of the garden. 'Dad?'

'Love, I just wanted to let you know Father Jacob came round last night.'

'Why didn't you wake me?'

'You went to bed so early, we thought we'd let you rest.'

'What did he want?'

'He spoke with Mrs Grant next door about Lucifer.'

'I didn't kill that dog!'

'We know. Look, Father Jacob found out Lucifer took a bite out of a prowler the other night. He was taken away by the police, but as he was protecting his family, they're letting him go at the end of the week. Everything is okay.'

I didn't kill anything. I'm innocent. And there was a prowler. The man in black is real!

'Was the guy dressed in head-to-toe black Lycra?'

'How do you know that?'

'I saw him too.'

'There's something else.' Dad glares at the ground, as he pushes a dusty lump of soil with his shoe. 'The prowler is someone you know.'

Chapter Thirty-One

Craig! The man in the tree was my friend.

My memory flicks back to St Alda's; he got better, he left with his brother last year to live a normal life free from his demons. 'Why did he do this?'

Dad rolls his eyes. 'You'd need to ask him. He was sent back to St Alda's. Anyway, your mum is doing a special dinner tonight. There's rumours of a nice big chocolate cake for dessert.'

'A special dinner to say sorry, or to celebrate I'm not a raving loony again?'

Ignoring my question, Dad says, 'Five o'clock for dinner. Don't be late.' With that, he starts to pick at the weeds growing between the boards of our decking. Ironic that only unwanted plants are surviving the heat. And anyway, who made the decision that only pretty plants were worth growing?

Partially vindicated, I grab a quick Pop-Tart breakfast, one to eat now and another in my bag for later, and then I'm out the door, my stuffed backpack weighing on my shoulder. I should be trying to find Louisa, but the news about Craig is weighing harder on me. What made him dress up like that and hang out in my tree? To find out, I catch the bus to St Alda's.

Brenda is on duty. She smiles at me. 'Sorry about Cookie,' she says. 'We all miss him terribly.'

Her words are so kind, I stifle a gasp.

'Bet you're here to see Craig,' she continues, tactfully ignoring my emotional outburst. 'You shouldn't, but he has been asking after you, so a few minutes won't hurt.' With a wave of a hand, I'm shuffled inside. Instead of letting me into his room, I'm given a chair to sit by the door, which is then opened. Through it, I spot Craig curled on the bed inside, a smile on his face.

'I knew you'd come to see me,' he says, craning his neck to meet my gaze.

Narrowing my eyes I ask, 'What the fuck?'

'Sorry I scared you. But I've been so lonely. My brother is always working, and I missed you and Cookie.'

'Why were you dressed like that?'

'Oh, I found the outfit online and thought it would camouflage me against the dark of the night, like a super-hero. Cool, eh?'

'Why didn't you just knock on my window?'

He sighs, 'I did knock. I kept knocking, you just never answered. Thought you didn't want to see me.'

The three knocks I kept hearing.

Craig adds, 'And then that man was always hanging about.'

'What man?'

'He kept parking on your drive. Is he your boyfriend?'

Mr Davidson! The thought of being romantically involved with our neighbour makes me cringe. 'No, he's Dad's friend.'

'Cool. Is he the father of the girl who was killed?'

'Hayley? No, he lives further down the street.'

'Good, I saw him spying on her. Although, she was pretty, so lots of men did that. I didn't of course. You believe me, don't you?'

Hang on. I rise from the chair and put my hands up. 'You saw men watching Hayley?'

'Yeah, there was this really hard-looking short guy, and…'

Rustling in my bag, I bring out my sketch book and flip to Warren's page. 'This guy?'

'Yeah, that's him. But there was a taller one with him. He wore a mask like me.'

I finally have a witness to place Warren and Andy stalking a victim, but he's an accidental weirdo now confined to a mental facility. Dear God, will anything go right?

'Sorry to freak you out, Dee. It's just I always slept so soundly next-door to you guys, and well, I couldn't get to Cookie. And your tree is strangely comfortable.'

To anyone else this would sound like madness, but I understand. Craig always had a routine at St Alda's and, with the unpredictability of real life, he was trying to scrape back some semblance of control.

'That's okay. Sorry the neighbour's dog bit you.'

I rise to leave, but Craig whispers, 'Wait.' To hear him better, I edge into the room. 'Cookie.'

'What about Cookie?' I ask.

'I had to know what happened so, when they brought me back, I got into his room.'

I narrow my eyes. 'What were you looking for?'

'Clues; and I found something.' He points to his drawers.

Opening the top drawer, I find a stack of neatly folded T-shirts with a piece of lined paper on top. Taking it, I open it up to see familiar childish handwriting. It's a letter.

Dear Dee,

I miss you. But I made new friends. They were mean. I tried to tell Dr T, but she didn't help. I'm sorry I told them about you. I don't want you to get hurt.

It's the last line that makes me gasp.

Warren has to die.

Cookie was going to kill Warren to protect me. His death wasn't an accident – Warren must have got to him first. But how did they even meet?

'Warren. Is that the guy in your picture?' Craig asks.

I nod.

'What are you going to do?'

Unsure how to answer his question, I put the letter back in the drawer and say, 'Keep this safe for me. I'll come back and see you.'

'Can't wait,' Craig replies. I can hear the happiness in his words. He's back home.

Running towards the bus stop, the fumsup on my bag jiggling by my side, as if he's running with me, I realise confronting Andy was a mistake; I need to confront Warren. Perhaps he'll break and tell me where they're holding Louisa. Never thought I'd ever admit this, but I do want to save her.

As I wait for the bus, my phone beeps. I pull out my mobile to find a text from Ashley: *Meet me behind the abandoned cake factory at Maple Industrial Estate. I've found something out.*

Chapter Thirty-Two

Thank God! Ashley must have seen Warren too. Maybe he's even discovered where Louisa is being kept. I let the Number 3 roll by, then catch the Number 8 that goes by Maple.

Deep down, I know I'm not alone. I miss Cookie and although Ashley cannot replace my dearest friend, it's nice to have someone here on the outside who can help. Together we can take down the Wraiths and produce an award-winning documentary. I can make it out in the world. There's no need for me to go back to living at St Alda's. I'm not Craig, and I'm certainly not Tippy.

The Number 8 slows to a crawl, and I'm too deep in thought to catch someone ahead of me ringing the bell. The sound slices through my brain and, dazed, I struggle up the aisle and off the bus, cursing myself for not paying attention.

Brain aching, I head towards the old factory, all the while watching for Ashley's car. Although the industrial estate is busy, this part is as eerily quiet as my first visit. The building itself, encased with wooden boards, looms over its chicken-wire gates, creating an unwelcoming shadow. With my backpack weighing on me, I jog to the far end of the factory. There's a scuffling sound and, behind the chicken wire, I see the Dobermann, Daegon. I put my hand through the gap and stroke the friendliest guard dog in existence. His tongue lolls over my wrist and I sit down with him to wait for Ashley. After I feed Daegon my pop tart, I text Ashley, *Where are you?* He comes straight back with, *Where are you?* I tell him I'm on the north side of the building. As he doesn't text back, I assume he's making his way to me.

'Got to go.' I pet my furry friend one more time, then rise to walk the length of the fence to grab a glimpse of Ashley's dark blue car. But he's still not here. Daegon trots along beside me, the wire fence between us.

'Where the hell is he?'

As my question hits the air, a white van pulls around the corner. Its windows black and paintwork dirty. It stops. The driver side door opens wide. In horror, I watch Warren leap out.

Without a word, he barrels towards me. Daegon barks and I realise that, if I'm fast enough, I can make it back to the gap in the fence. There'll be a security guard here at some point to pick up his dog, I can wait safely on the grounds till then. I run, Warren so close behind me I can hear his breath. Damn, I'll never get through the fence with him this close. Suddenly, I stop and swing my bag around, hitting him in the gut. Winded, he falls to his knees.

Turning, I run again. When I reach the gap, I look back to see Warren scrambling up.

Bending down, I squirm my shoulders into the hole. As I do, my bag catches on the wire fence and I feel Daegon snuffling my hair. But I've miscalculated the gap, or my body mass, maybe both, as I don't easily slide in, but have to wiggle through limb by limb.

Warren's fingers slip over my kicking feet. Reaching further, he puts an arm through the fence to grab a handful of my dress. Daegon lunges forward and bites him. With a bloody hand, Warren snatches both of my ankles and yanks me hard. I slip on the dusty ground as he pulls me out, like a baby forcibly expelled from the womb. I scream and flail. Someone must hear me... please.

I get in a few good smacks before he raises his fist and wallops me towards darkness. The last thing I see is my fumsup's blank face staring up from my backpack. The last thing I hear is Daegon's whines. And the last thing I feel is Warren's arms around my body.

Chapter Thirty-Three

Jerking awake, I have the sensation of tripping over. As I throw my arms out to break my fall, I find I'm restrained. I open my eyes. I'm lying on a bed. A plastic sheet beneath me is making an embarrassing squeaking sound as I move. My vision is blurry. Was the last month a dream? Did I not make it out of the halfway house or even St Alda's? Shaking my head, I blink a few times and my vision snaps into focus. I am back in the arts building, tied to an abandoned bed.

I'm wet. Have I peed myself? I don't smell urine. I smell something else though. A faint scent, dark with a coppery undertone. Blood. I move my body around as best I can to see if I'm injured. I don't feel as if I am. There's no pain but for the tension on my arms where I'm strapped to the bed, and a dull ache in my face.

Whispers. Straining, I scan for the door, but can barely see beyond the bed. I can still see, though. That's something. The relief doesn't stop me realising that I'm probably going to die here.

I am the 13th girl.

Red.

Sharp anger floods my body. The Wraiths broke the rules. Weirdos don't target other weirdos. But maybe that is where my advantage lies. With there being three Wraiths, they're used to outnumbering their victims, but they've made a terrible mistake in abducting me; there's something living inside me, a fearlessness that's allegedly not even human.

Also, unlike every other girl they brought here, I know my surroundings, especially the bonds meant to contain me. With little effort, I twist my small hands and clench my fists, allowing my thin wrists to slip through the restraints as if I were made of butter. I undo the other ties, then jump off the bed. My bare feet slap the cold concrete floor, so I jog on the spot for a moment to encourage warmth. The light around me is dim. It's night outside. I must have been unconscious for hours. Warren could have driven me around in his van, then dropped me off here after St Alda's routine lights out. Andy knew about this abandoned building; he could see it from Dr Taylor's house. With the secret hole in the fence for access and the asbestos warnings, it was the perfect place to keep the girls – a poisonous building no one would enter on the grounds of a gated hospital.

I need to fight. An image flashes across my mind's eye – the broken pipe above the stain in the corner. I run across to it and yank it away from the wall. There's a loud crack, but the building still hands me its weapon, as if I'm King Arthur pulling Excalibur from the stone. St Alda's itself is with me.

Voices. I bend down behind the door. Footsteps, someone is coming. As the door opens and a figure steps in, I spring up and use the momentum to thrust out the pipe, aiming it at his chest. As it hits my target, the force reverberates down my arm. The man is in a plain black mask, T-shirt and shorts; the sight of his thick hairy legs poking out takes away some of his menace. He doubles over and I use the pipe like a golf club, swinging up against his head. There's a wet thud and he falls forward. I ready myself for another Wraith, but no one else comes in. I close the door and kick the body at my feet. He groans. Not knowing whether this is Andy or Warren, I lean over and peel off the mask.

It's neither.

Ashley gurgles as he flops onto his back.

'I'm sorry,' he pushes out.

'What the hell? You're a Wraith?'

As if I'm about to strike again, he curls up. 'Sorry.'

'I trusted you,' I whisper.

'You were right, Dee. There are three Wraiths.'

Even used to betrayal, this thought hits me hard. 'You were my friend.'

'I am.'

'But you lured me into a trap to kill me.'

His answer is a half-shrug.

'Were you playing me from the start?' I ask.

He pulls himself to sit upright. 'I was there to ensure you didn't get too close to us with your documentary.' He smiles and I can see I've knocked out a few of his teeth. 'And…'

I nudge him. 'And what?'

'To recruit you.'

'You wanted me as a Wraith?'

Hiccupping blood, Ashley faces me. 'I told them you wouldn't go for it. But they never listen to me.'

Of course, the one group of people who want to invite me to spend time with them in the 'normal' world are sick serial killers! 'Why would the Wraiths want me?'

He shakes his head.

'As a scapegoat?' I offer.

'Nah, we had a plan for that. Then we would change MOs and start again. We'd have taken you with us.'

'I would never hurt people,' I mutter.

He looks hopeful. 'Maybe your demon would?'

'No.'

'I guessed as much when I left you my drawings to find.' He smiles and a tooth drips out of his mouth, taking a trail of blood with it in its wake. 'Unfortunately, you already knew too much, so it became join or die, and when you didn't email after the letter... Well, you know.'

'Yeah, it's all becoming clear,' I spit.

'It wasn't my decision. And I felt bad for you.'

'You felt bad for me?'

His lips tighten. 'I'm sorry,' he whispers. 'I didn't want to.'

My mind floods with possibilities, but what action could possibly contend with the evil he did to all those girls? 'What else did you do?'

Ashley closes his eyes. 'I killed Cookie.'

'What?' My hands grip the pipe so hard, rust flakes down my wrists.

'It was how my car got dented.'

Through gritted teeth, I ask, 'Why?'

'He stumbled into this place while we were finishing off Lisa. We were going to just kill him, but then he started acting like a little kid.'

'It was a symptom of his head injury,' I breathe. 'He was an innocent. How could you?'

'Warren got obsessed, wanted to recruit Cookie, but then he refused to touch Dara when we had her in the office here. I got him to promise he wouldn't say anything, but he couldn't keep his mouth shut; told a nurse about his *new friends*. Then he found out you were investigating, and well, Warren decided he had to go.'

My hand shoots up to my mouth. I was in this building when they had Dara. I could have saved her – if only I'd realised. I could have stopped all this before… Cookie, Hayley and Louisa. The pipe comes down and I smack the floor in frustration.

'I'm, sorry,' he gurgles, slumping onto his back. 'Call the police.' Ashley motions for me to look in his pocket.

Bending down, I pull out his mobile, which must have taken a hit when he went down, as the screen is dark and cracked.

Seeing it, Ashley groans. 'Just run, but be careful, someone…'

'…is not what they appear?' I finish his warning. 'Yeah, that's going around.'

'I can still be your sidekick.'

The thought makes me bark with laughter. 'How can I trust you now?'

'I'm sorry.'

I shouldn't take my eyes off him, but I have to close them. The hot, red familiar feeling is working its way through my bones like a lit fuse. To stop it from going off, I count, 'Six, five, four, three, two, one.' Then take three deep breaths. I can do this. Normal people are not violent. I am not a Wraith.

Grabbing the restraints, I tie Ashley to a radiator. He doesn't stop me, or yell out to his friends, only whispers *sorry* over and over. Gingerly, I then open the door to glance into the hall. No one is there. I slow my breathing and listen. There's someone talking in the room opposite, the meditation room. It used to contain only beanbags and inspirational pictures on the wall, so there's little to muffle the voices now, or the next thing I hear: a scream.

Louisa. I should run. If I reach the supply room, I can use the adjoining cupboards to steal into the kitchen, then ride down the laundry chute into the hospital grounds to get help. But that'll take time; she could be dead by then. Damn.

I edge out. The door to the meditation room is open. I peer in, just a peek. I want to see if Louisa will last. There's one spotlight lamp illuminating the scene. My own personal Judas is lying on a metal bed; straps holding her in place. She's whispering something to the Wraith standing over her. He's blocking my view, and when he turns, I see he's wearing a black ceramic mask and thick voluminous robe. He's about six feet tall, so it's not Warren; it has to be Andy. Three Wraiths. Three men. I owe Betsy an apology.

As he moves around the table, I notice a long thin rod in his gloved hand that glints in the light. Viscous liquid drips down it onto the floor; the floor where I used to pretend to be in a peaceful forest. Andy, almost comically, measures the rod against Louisa's head. Deciding it's too long, he scoops up a pen, then writes something down.

Louisa screams, visceral and wild. She's fighting. If she can keep that up, she'll live long enough for me to fetch help.

With Andy's back to me, I scurry past the open door towards the metal staircase. Quietly and quickly, I pad up the steps. Another scream. This one softer than the last. I know that sound; I was wrong. Louisa is giving up. She'll be dead soon, and although deep down it's what I've always wanted, it shouldn't be like this.

Demon or injury, whatever people call it, I can feel it banging in my head. Closing my eyes, I hold my skull. My vision clouds red again. Whatever is inside me, it wants to go. To leave Louisa to her fate. As I climb the next two steps, I swear I almost hear a bell-like giggle as the world glows red.

Another scream.

Damn it.

I run back down the stairs, burst through the meditation room door and charge Andy with my pipe held high. I catch him off-guard. As he falls down with a thud, his hands instinctively fly up to his face, dropping the scalpel. The sound of it hitting the floor is like a tuning fork. Raising the pipe, I strike him again, this time over his head. The mask cracks in two. He's breathing so hard, I smell the coffee on his breath. I lift the pipe to strike him again but, holding his mask together, he rolls over, scrambles up and runs out of the room.

Blood is everywhere and, with the commotion of my attack, Louisa has started to thrash about on the bed.

In the bright lamplight, I see two crusty black holes where her eyes used to be. Deep, empty sockets of pain and loss, that just like the abyss, when you stare into them, they stare back into you.

'It's all right,' I say. 'It's me, Dee.'

She doesn't greet me. Knowing what I'm looking at, she just whispers. 'It was the first thing they did.'

'They didn't want you to identify them, if you got away,' I offer.

She shakes her head. 'No, he told me it was so I could feel everything… more. Take one sense and the others make up for it.'

The horror of that thought shoots panic through my own senses. I take a deep breath and smell lavender, the ghost of a scent I'd long ago associated with this calming room. I need to take stock of the situation. I don't want to touch Louisa, but Andy could come back, and Warren is somewhere in the building. 'Stay still, I'm going to get you out.' Taking hold of the restraints, I slowly untie them.

'Dee?' she whispers, then the painful look on her face morphs to terror.

'I'm trying to help you.' I should tell her to trust me, but I doubt that would help; trust is a two-way street.

'Please, don't hurt me.'

I snap my hands back from the restraints. Am I going to be blamed for all this? Could she think it was me who did this to her? No. Andy is six feet, I'm five foot nothing; there's no way she could mistake me... but then again, she claimed I was possessed for her own devices, what would stop her from telling the police it was me to sell another shoddy documentary?

'Louisa,' I say next to her ear. Wait, that's creepy, I step back a bit. 'Louisa, they took me too. I just know this place better than them and, well, I'm not one to play the victim, apart from when someone else casts me that way—'

'I'm sorry,' she says, interrupting my speech.

'What?'

'Have they hurt you?'

'No. Well, I'll be sporting some interesting bruises tomorrow.'

She sighs and a dark tear dribbles from her empty socket. Or it could be something else. After experiencing trauma and fear so horrific, I'm surprised Louisa is still conscious. 'It'll be okay,' I tell her. 'I'm going to help you up. We need to get out before the other Wraiths come back.'

With nimble precision I untie my nemesis, then pull her around to the side of the bed. Wincing at my touch, she falls into my arms. Almost too heavy for my frame, I have to angle her so she leans on me as we walk. That way I can still brandish my pipe in one hand, just in case. There's still Warren to get past. Moving towards the door, I realise this is the first sustained touch I've allowed in a very long time. Wasps don't count.

When we make it to the stairs, I set her down to catch her breath. We can't go out the front door; Andy is bound to be waiting. I look around. If Warren's not downstairs, then he's upstairs where we need to be. I just hope he's not in the kitchen. Warren might not be as tall and broad as Andy, but I won't have the element of surprise with him. No matter what happens now, I have to get us both to safety. It will make a great addition to my documentary, *Surviving the Wraiths* – yes, that's an amazing title. I now have a better pitch than Louisa. Both my cameraman and subject were Wraiths, and I was also abducted by them, but I still have my eyes to do the editing. Saving my enemy will be the sweet icing on the redemption cake.

'We need to keep moving.' I pull Louisa up by her armpits and slump her against my shoulder.

'What's happening?' Louisa shrieks.

'Shh, we're trying to be stealthy.'

She slips a little, so I have to hoist her higher. The stairs are going to be tricky to climb quietly whilst holding her. We take a step up and the metal beneath Louisa's shoes ring like a dinner gong, giving me instant earache.

'Damn,' I whisper.

Louisa cries out, and I have to put my hand over her mouth. As she struggles beneath my fingers, I lean in and whisper, 'You have to be quiet.' There's a nip at my skin. She bit me! 'Really?' I say pulling my digits away from her fangs.

'I don't want to die.'

'Neither do I. Now, let's get up these steps as quickly as possible. At the top I'm going to lean you against the wall. If Warren is there, he'll come at me quickly. I need to be able to defend myself, and you.'

'You can't fight. You're tiny, Dee. He'll kill you.'

Even blinded and dependent, Louisa finds a way to insult me. 'I'll be fine. I'm possessed by a demon, remember?'

That thought flashes across her face and even without eyes the fear is obvious. She tries to get away. Weak hands paw at me as I hold her upright. I let go and she falls down to sit awkwardly on the step.

'Go on without me,' she mumbles.

Louisa needs me and the sooner she accepts that, the better. I say, 'Our options for survival here are limited. You can either stay here defenceless, or you come with me, and we can survive this shit show together.' Dramatically, I thrust out my hand to her, then remember she can't see, so clutch her under her armpits again. Together, we climb the stairs. One step at a time, it seems to take an eternity. Finally, at the top, I carefully place her next to a wall, and scan the corridor for Warren. Nothing. The supply room is immediately to our left, the door shut. I listen. Silence, apart from Louisa's laboured breathing. I open the door. At the sound, she flails her arms out to grab onto me. I step back and she almost topples over.

'Dee?' she whispers through a whimper.

I move forward and place my right hand on her shoulder. She slumps against it in defeat. Would she welcome death now?

Noise echoes from the old art room; a muffled voice.

Chapter Thirty-Four

Heaving Louisa up, I shuffle her as quietly as possible into the supply room. As I open the long cupboard that links to the kitchen, she cringes into me.

'This is how we get out,' I tell her.

Through the back of the magic cupboard, I can see the kitchen units. It's dark. There's only one window and it's covered in a black plastic bag. Louisa may be blind, but here, I might as well be too. I need to let in some light to find the laundry hatch.

'I'm just leaving you here for a minute. The cupboard is safe; no one knows it backs onto this room.'

'Don't leave me,' she whispers.

'I have to.'

Shuddering, Louisa edges back from me, hitting her body against the wooden sides.

'Christ's sake, just be still.' Just as I say this, the door to the kitchen opens and torchlight dissects the darkness of the room. Quickly, I pull the cupboard doors to, shielding us, but still leaving a crack to see through. Warren strides in, a mobile in one hand and a knife in the other, which he taps against his leg. He looks around, growls with annoyance, then leaves. There's the metal clang of feet on the staircase.

It's now or never.

I leap from the cupboard and sprint to the window. I pull down the black bag and moonlight hits my eyes. I blink, then open the laundry chute. It won't be pretty or comfortable, but it'll get us out of the building fast. Fetching Louisa, I pull her up. Having to use both hands, I prop my pipe up against a corner.

'This is going to feel weird. I'm going to push you down a slide. When you get to the bottom, roll aside so I don't hit you when I come down it. Once you feel fresh air, we're safe. Okay?' The chute latch is heavy and slowly creaks open as I manipulate Louisa's body to fit into the gap.

'I'm just going to give you a little nudge, then gravity will do the rest,' I say.

'No, no. You're pushing me out of a window!' Her leg thrusts out and hits the metal sides of the slide.

'Shh. He'll hear. Can't you feel it?' I place her hand on the sides of the chute. 'It's a long metal slide. They used it for aprons and blankets. You're going to have to trust me.' I give her a hefty push and she slides down out of sight, screaming as she goes.

If Warren was downstairs in the craft room, he'd have heard Louisa's cries as she shot down the side of the building. I need to get out now. Listening, I hear a thud as Louisa safely falls outside. My turn. I'm about to climb in when the kitchen door swings open. Warren rushes me. He yanks me from the chute opening and the hatch slams shut.

'There you are.' Lurching forward, he grabs my neck and pulls me towards him. Kicking and punching, I twist my body from his grasp and run for the cupboard.

'No, you don't.' Warren spins me round into an uppercut punch. The force jars my bones, propelling me backwards onto the floor. He tries to kick me, but I squirm out of the way just in time.

Twisting over, I belly crawl towards the slide, but am suddenly pinned to the ground. Warren's shoe is on my back. He bends down and pulls me up. Next thing I know, he's got me in a fireman's lift over his shoulder, my arms crushed to my sides. Effortlessly, he strides across the hall to the art studio. He flops me down onto another metal bed and then reaches for a strap. As he does, I roll over away from him, flailing my legs as I try to escape. But he is strong and determined, and unlike the many carers who held me down at St Alda's, he wants to hurt me, not keep me safe. Before I can wriggle free, I'm strapped down. As I scream out, my voice slaps against the walls I used to know.

A light flicks on; its greenish hue reminding me of the green lightening.

Warren steps back to admire his handiwork. 'That's better.' He then turns on a nearby metal-armed lamp.

Squinting, I shout, 'Go to hell!'

'You first.'

I spit at him and then feel the presence of someone else in the room. Quickly, I scan the space around me. Hunched in the far corner is a shape sprawled in a spray of blood.

'Oh, you've spotted him, that's great. There's no need for introductions though.' Warren gleefully skips over and grabs the man. As he drags him into the light, I see who it is...

Chapter Thirty-Five

Beaten, bloody and barely breathing, Andy slumps down onto the floor.

'What the hell? He's your fellow Wraith?'

'Andy was never one of us.'

'But I just saw him here.'

'No, you didn't.'

Confused, I push on. 'I found Hayley's shorts in his house.'

'Ashley left them there when you guys were filming. They were meant for the police, but then you nicked 'em.' He waggles his finger at me. 'You naughty thing.'

'How did Ashley know about the box room?'

Warren sniggers. 'You ask a lot of questions.'

'No more than anyone else in my position.' I flex my hands beneath my restraints.

'Nah, I shouldn't tell you everything.' Although saying this, Warren's eyes are alight with a sort of reverse curiosity; he wants to tell me his secrets.

'If you're killing me anyway, you might as well share.'

He doesn't need any more of an invitation; excitement dances in his eyes like violent flames.

'We used Andy's old rectory to hold the girls, before he ruined our fun by moving back in, so we had to find somewhere else to hide Lisa, then the other girls.'

'But I heard Hayley there?'

'We never kept her there. That was all in your crazy little mind. Do you often hear voices? Did you get that with the bump to the noggin too?'

On the tape, I heard what I wanted to hear. Damn. Without that misdirection, would I have figured any of this out? Would I have realised Andy isn't a Wraith? This question settles into my mind amongst the evidence I, and others, collected. 'But the Wraith Finder website? They have all those photos of Andy at body dump sites?'

Warren giggles. It's shrill and makes him sound like a wicked child. 'That was me!' He jumps up and down and claps his hands. 'I took all the photos. I'm Rabbits Foot on Wraith Finders! Get it, Warren, Rabbit? It's delicious, isn't it? I've been dying to tell someone. I followed him on his little de-stressing nature walks, then dropped the bodies after he'd left each location. Dumb fuck loves nature, so was always wandering into the perfect place to dispose of my dark dates. I'd then upload the photos to the Wraith Finders site. Clever, eh?'

All this time, the Watsons had actually found a Wraith, but instead of stopping him, they were enabling him to frame an innocent man – to whip up an online mob into a finger-pointing frenzy.

Warren's ghoulish glee grates on me, so, offhand, I say, 'You missed the possessive apostrophe in your handle. The foot belongs to the rabbit; you have plural rabbits.'

Warren snorts. 'I meant that.'

'If it were plural, it should have been feet.'

'Shut the fuck up. I don't need grammar tips from a weirdo.' His words are hard, but there's a soft blush on his cheeks. I'm getting to him.

'And what was with that silly Righteous Wraith name anyway?' I ask, rolling my eyes.

Cocking his head as if I've asked the stupidest question in the world, he replies, 'It sounds cool.'

I can't help it. I laugh. All this time, I tried to assign meaning to his ridiculous moniker, but forgot that not everything or everyone has meaning.

'Shut. The. Fuck. Up!' he yells. 'It's bad enough my plans have to change…' He looks thoughtful. 'I'll make it look like Andy kidnapped you, then you fought back with your demon strength. Then you killed one another.'

'That's an awful plan,' I say.

Warren purses his lips. 'Or you could just join us?'

Remembering what he did to all the girls, my first instinct is to cringe away from the beckoning monster who thinks I'm capable of such horror. But if I don't play along, he'll just kill me. Wait; that's a normal girl's reaction, and I'm not normal. It's high time I embraced it.

'Jog on,' I say.

'Shouldn't you be making the effort to accept invitations? What with you fresh out of the giggle factory.'

'I'm not taking social cues from a murderer.'

'You know, I could make it look like you killed him and then committed suicide. I hear that happens a lot to you people. Can't hack it in the real world.'

Biting back the red tingling thoughts, I remind myself I have to remain calm. Echoing his arrogance, I say, 'It'll look too staged.' Then whisper, 'Six, five, four, three, two, one.'

Warren jumps forward, pushing his face next to mine. 'Are you talking to yourself? That's a sign of madness you know.'

I turn my head. 'Why were you framing Andy?'

'Someone had to take the fall.'

'But he's your brother-in-law.'

'Yeah, and he's a shit. Constantly cheats on Betsy. He was fucking Erica Tomkins.'

Warren steps towards Andy and he rolls into the foetus position, preparing to take another blow.

'I'd never do that.' Warren merely looks down at Andy. 'Love is to be cherished. Romance is forever.'

'Your divorce did hit you hard. Did your wife cheat on you?' I say.

Warren shakes his head, as if I've asked the dumbest question in the world, then picks something up from a shadowy corner. As he moves into the lamp's light, I recognise my backpack dangling from his arm. Struggling against my ties, I try to reach for it.

'No, no. You've hit me way too many times with this little beauty; you're not getting your hands on it again.'

Grinning, Warren opens my bag. The sound of the zipper sends a wave of nausea rolling through me. Somehow the thought of his hands on my private belongings is too much. I close my eyes, but still hear it when he takes out my notebooks and laptop. Ripping. I open my eyes in time to watch him tearing out his portrait from my sketchbook.

'Can't be leaving evidence,' he says. 'Although, it looks nothing like me.'

'What the hell do you know about art?' I yell at him.

Dropping the book, Warren takes the two steps needed to loom over me. 'You saw *my* art, didn't you? I watched you find Dara.'

'Did you dump her for me to find?'

Warren snickers. 'Took time to set up, but fortunately I had Dara in the back of my van, ready and waiting. You know, I watched you at the church that day. Saw you get on the bus to Maple, and couldn't believe my luck when you went exactly where I wanted to dump Dara in the first place! Same wavelength, you and me. One quick call to Andy to come over and pick something up, then I stole away to pose Dara where I knew you'd spot her on the way back to the bus stop.'

What I thought had been a sign from God was a sign from Warren.

Leaning even closer, he continues, 'She wasn't my masterpiece, but she was still beautiful when I'd finished with her. Although, I must admit, I prefer my subjects younger.'

He smells of musk and disinfectant. 'The little girl in the park. What were you going to do with her?' I ask, unsure I want to know the answer.

'I'm not just a Wraith. There's another side to me too. But you know all about that, don't you? Having two sides.'

'You don't know anything about me,' I say, twisting my wrists around, testing my bonds.

Warren laughs. Not a real laugh people make when they find something funny, but a mocking laugh. He then yanks out another book from my bag. 'Oh, you write a journal too.' Warren flips through my personal words, skim-reading my innermost thoughts.

'You're gonna regret this,' I spit at him, along with a grunt of frustration.

'I regret a lot of things, but it's the stuff I don't do that really sticks in my craw.' He steps forward and sits at the edge of my bed. 'You know, Dee. I think we could have been friends. We have a lot in common.' Smiling, he throws my journal across the room. 'But I prefer friends I can have fun with, so I'm going to have to kill you. After that, I'll catch up with that simpering fool you shoved down the chute.'

He knows about the chute. 'Cookie told you about that,' I state.

'I liked him; told good stories. Let slip all about you.'

No, no, no, red crawls into my vision. My sight becomes a pinprick, then is completely gone. Thrashing is all I feel. Warren laughs at my efforts, and that's why he doesn't see me worm free my pinkie finger.

As the world drips back into place around me, a thought comes with it… I'm missing something. Three Wraiths, and the third isn't Andy…

'This other Wraith is using you. Tell me who they are,' I say.

Warren slips back into the shadows. I twist my head to see where he is, but can't spot him.

'Tell me!'

Silence. Has he left the room? No, I hear him breathing behind me, at the head of the bed.

'I'd never betray them. They're the reason I've had so much fun being a Wraith.' He steps back into view. The fumsup Mum gave me is in his hand. 'What's this piece of shit?'

'It's a good luck charm.' With the slack in my restraints, I next manage to wiggle my right-hand ring finger free.

Laughing, Warren throws the fumsup at me. It strikes my cheek and falls to my side.

He adds, 'Didn't bring you much luck, eh?'

I want to bite back, but I can't have him too close to me; he could catch me loosening my bonds.

'Well, guess I might as well get on with it.' He bends and drags a bag from a dark corner. Humming, he pulls out a knife, looks back at his injured brother-in-law, then shakes his head and picks out a second, larger knife.

'Andy,' I whisper. 'You need to get up.'

Blackened, swollen eyes look back at me. Slowly, Andy inches forward in a crawl.

'Can't be having that now,' Warren says, then kicks Andy over. No hesitation. He slams a knife through his stomach. As he pulls it out, blood sprays across the floor. Andy cries. Warren laughs. Damn. My only hope now rests with Louisa. That she can stumble her way to the hospital and alert St Alda's.

Suddenly, my right thumb slips past its bonds, my limp fingers sliding out after it. Hallelujah! I hold the tie; my captor can't know I'm partially free, not yet.

Warren grins at me, but drops the knife. 'Not your turn yet. Did you know, in mythology, wraiths kill everyone and everything? Even demons.' From out of his bag he reveals his next weapon, one just for me: a Bible. 'Those other exorcists, well, they weren't really willing to do what was necessary to yank out that demon, Dee. Me, on the other hand, I'm going old school. I saw a video on YouTube of a vicar down in Mexico. Emailed him for advice. Nice chap. He told me exactly what I need to do. Thought I'd give it a whirl, especially as I'm going to kill you now anyway, so it doesn't matter if things get out of hand. Oh, I have an idea.' He rummages in my bag again; it's as if his hand is in my guts. Freeing my camera, he jabs at the buttons then sets it on the end of the bed. 'We should record this. Our own sequel to *Possession is Nine Tenths*.'

The angle of the camera is all wrong, but I don't tell him.

With the flourish of a ham entertainer, Warren pulls across a wheelie table covered in a cloth, then reveals its contents. I can't see everything, but the lamplight glints off metal.

Andy groans. He's still alive. Warren hears it too.

'Maybe I should sort my mate out before we start. After all, he was first.' He turns his back on me and ponders the objects on the table.

I look above my head to see the straps holding me are only tied to the top rail of the bed; a rail that is broken. If I can topple over the frame, I can use my free hand to untie the other strap.

'Hey,' I yell at Warren. 'Demons don't like to wait.'

When he turns around, I can see he has an old-fashioned manual drill. 'Fancy a lobotomy after the exorcism?' he asks, rolling the crank around and around with an ominous squeal.

'Hey,' I yell again.

'Don't get your knickers in a twist.' Warren puts down the tool, then pulls out his mobile and props it up on the table. 'A bit of light music for our film.' He fiddles with his playlist.

'At least tell me why you stole their senses. What's your deal? Or was it Ashley that did that?'

'No, that was – oh, you almost had me there. Now, let's begin.' Warren taps his phone. Music plays: monks chanting in Latin. He then lights something on the table. A waft of smoke spirals out into the dark. Lit by the lamp, it looks like ghosts rising to freedom.

Warren stares at the drill, then, almost reluctantly, picks up the Bible. He reads a passage. Stumbling over some of the pronunciation, he continually breaks his speech with cheeky looks up at me. He's waiting for a reaction from *the demon*. I'm a terrible actress, so just stare back; it's not as if I can spew green filth or spin my head around on cue. I do roll my eyes though. After a couple of minutes, he throws down the Bible and turns off the chanting. 'I guess Señor Vicar was wrong. Let's try something else.' He fiddles about on the table. My free hand touches something: the fumsup. I move it around and its sharp edge nips at my skin. Quickly, I use my antique good luck charm on the restraints, sawing as fast and as hard as I can, without drawing attention.

Rustling under the table, Warren looks back at me. 'Sorry to keep you waiting, Dee. Oh, I just got that, Dee for Demon.'

'That's not what it stands for, arsehole.'

'Hmm, okay, how about this?' Warren lifts his arm up and I hear a jingle then a loud metallic crack, like a clap of thunder. It's a bell. He rings and rings it, dancing on the spot as he does. The vibration smashes through my brain, the pain wrapped in a memory. Suddenly I'm back in the living room, being held down on a smelly yoga mat, as Louisa looks on with her camera. I'm staring at my parents who both look away, but don't stop my pain. The world around me shrinks to just agonising sounds, choking smells and that one room that grows smaller by the second as it shrinks into a red dot.

I scream.

Warren doesn't stop ringing. 'Out demon, out I say. By the sound of this holy bell, I drive you out.' The words are the same as my original exorcists' and propel me further into the memory, into agony. As I writhe, I twist my head to spot a shadow cross the doorway. The third Wraith is watching. Shivering through cold memories, I buck harder at my restraints.

Red creeps in around me. This time, it's like the edges of a warm blanket. I don't bite it back, but instead welcome it. I'm not a little girl anymore. This curse that made me abnormal is my superpower. No more fighting. I let it in. Together we can survive.

Increasing the movement, I push and pull at my restraints with renewed strength. As I do, the bed rocks enough for me to push it over. I collapse in a heap, both floor and bed colliding with my body.

Warren stops ringing, then stoops forward to pick up the bed.

Beneath the edge of the fumsup, my restraints break to the point where I can slip my wrist free. Falling from the bed, I roll onto my side under the table, then jump up; I push it upwards, exploding its metal instruments and exorcism paraphernalia across the room. Turning, I see the shadow by the door has gone. Warren stomps towards me, but catches his leg on something and falls forward. Andy is gripping his ankle. My hands grope for a weapon. I find something metallic, scoot forward and plunge it into Warren's back. It's a scalpel and slices through his flesh as if it were Play-Doh. He screams; the sound as painful to my ears as the bell's clang. Stumbling forward, he flails, trying to release himself from the blade. One kick in just the right place and he falls forward, hitting his head off the side of the table, knocking himself unconscious.

As I move into the lamplight, I see my pale limbs splattered with blood, seeping into my pores, just like the blood rain. Wiping my hands down my sides, I approach Andy. 'It's okay. Warren can't hurt you anymore.'

'He was my friend,' Andy pushes out.

'Yeah, that Judas thing is going around.' I lift him slightly and see pooling blood. I rip the lace off my dress and tie it around Andy's waist, containing the wound as best I can. He doesn't make a peep when I do this, and it must hurt like hell – not a good sign.

Using the lamp, I scan the room for my bag. Once I find it, I pull out my mobile. If I were in a horror film, there'd be no signal. Fortunately, this is real life. I call 999. I explain that Louisa is somewhere outside the building by the laundry chute and Andy is in desperate need of medical care. The operator takes the details – help is on the way.

I should wait for the police. But there's a third Wraith still out there, and I have no idea who they are. I could spend the rest of my life looking over my shoulder thinking every six-foot man is a killer hunting me... But what do I know about them... the last Wraith knows the hospital, is interested in sensory experiments, and could easily manipulate the mental illness of both Warren and Ashley... I take a deep breath. Lavender.

I know who it is.

Part of me wants to use the laundry chute, but I no longer need to hide in the shadows. After gathering my backpack's contents, checking that Warren is still unconscious, and making Andy as comfortable as possible, I find my pipe, then race downstairs and out the door. With soft red glazing my vision, I run across the grounds to the hole in the fence, then crawl out into the night to face the final Wraith.

Chapter Thirty-Six

I knock on the door.

There's a light kerfuffle on the other side, then it opens. The first thing I notice is the look of sheer horror when she sees me; the other is the massive slash across her face. The mark I made when she was torturing Louisa.

'Got time for an appointment, Dr Taylor?' I ask, lifting the pipe.

She tries to close the door, but I push back, knocking her backwards.

'What? How?' she says stumbling back.

'Your killer boys weren't as good as you thought.' I slowly step forward.

'No. Um, let me explain.' She puts her hands up. 'Dee,' she says, then steps back, hitting her backside on the waiting couch, the one I've sat on so many times through the years, the one I'm betting Warren and Ashley both sat on too.

'Tell me why.'

'Have you been taking your medication? You seem out of sorts.'

'Of course I seem out of sorts. You and your crazy murder buddies abducted me. I then found out yet another person I trusted betrayed me!' I swing the pipe up high and she cowers, her previously imposing frame crumpling before me.

'Please, wait. I can help you, just like I did Cookie.'

I hesitate. 'What?'

'I was the one letting him out of the building. I knew he was never going to get better, not like you, so I gave him some freedom, as an experiment. He was so happy.'

Rolling this new fact around my mind, I cock my head. 'It was your fault he met Warren and Ashley?'

'No.' She quickly raises her hands higher. 'That was an accident. He shouldn't have gone into the arts building. No one was ever supposed to go in there.'

'Did you tell Ashley to run my friend over?'

Dr Taylor winces. 'That was Warren.' Quickly she adds, 'Everything was him.'

'At least admit it was you in the mask. How many girls have you sent into a permanent dark retreat before Warren slaughtered them?'

Slumping onto the floor, she looks up. 'Please, just let me explain.'

'I'm listening.'

'Warren was my patient. He was anxious about dating again after his divorce. But then, out of the blue, he calls me in tears saying he had accidentally killed Erica. He pleaded with me, said she had been having an affair with his brother-in-law and it was a crime of passion. That she deserved it for being the other woman. At first, I was scared of him; he'd already mutilated and dumped the body. But the more he opened up to me, the more I understood him. He's an old romantic at heart and was protecting his sister.'

I stifle a gasp. 'That's not an excuse! It's not even a real motive to kill… that many times. Andy didn't sleep with all those girls.'

'What would you know about motives?' she says, with a look in her eyes I've never seen before. Protective? Annoyed. I can't tell.

'The book you gave me. Dr Hawk says—'

'Dr fucking Hawk? We all know what she thinks, don't we? Well' – Dr Taylor starts to rise – 'she doesn't know everything. And I've now got something she'll never have.'

I wait for her to tell me.

Once she's on her feet, she spits, 'First-hand know-ledge.'

Every fibre of my being wants to smack her in the face. Dr Taylor was there for all the girls' deaths after Erica, and she is the reason the girls were taken without a fight. They saw another woman, a doctor no less, and trusted her; just like I did. 'How could you?'

Seeing my anger, she sobs, 'I'm sorry. Please under-stand... I had to.'

The change of tone jars me. Is she playing me? Has she done so all these years? Pretending to be a caring mental health professional looking out for her patients' best interests, but flip the switch and she's a manipulative crazy person, who has caused more damage than I ever could.

'Warren couldn't force you to hurt anyone.' I'm not great at emotion, having them or seeing them, but it's then I spot something in her eyes. Just a flash, but I catch it; a longing softness that I saw before when she spoke about the importance of love. 'You did it for him. You love Warren.'

Her lips twist into a sneer. 'I...' She tries to finish her next lie, but gives up with a shrug. She whispers, 'If you were normal, you'd understand.'

'If love makes you do horrible things, then I want no part of it.'

As if she'd drawn down another mask, her expression shifts back to psychiatrist. 'Maybe, we can sit down and discuss that. Part of being normal is having normal relationships.'

'Were you sleeping with Ashley too?' I ask.

'No,' she snaps. 'We… I mean, Warren…' She closes her eyes.

'At least lie quickly,' I say.

'You think I'm lying? After knowing me, trusting me, for all these years?'

'Then tell me something true. Why Ashley?'

Her stare slips away from me. 'I couldn't be there, all the time, with the girls.'

'You didn't trust your killer boyfriend with your victims?'

She blushes. Of course, there was a romance to how the girls' bodies were left, as if they were on dates. But unless she was willing to be murdered, Dr Taylor couldn't compete with his victims. To name the feelings as demons, mine is red rage, but hers was green envy.

'So, you rope in another person to keep watch on your boyfriend while he has his fun?'

'And he was there to be your friend too,' she says, as if his part in the crimes was my fault.

'Does he even go to university?'

'No. I gave you a false email address that went straight to Ashley. He doesn't go to university. He's still working on his English GCSE.'

The letters. Warren's handwriting didn't match and Ashley wasn't articulate enough to write them. That was my doctor, too. 'Why did you send those letters?'

'I wanted to see how…'

'What?'

'How infamous the Wraith could become, with social media and the news.'

Her envy drove her to make headlines. She wanted to eclipse other killers and maybe even draw the attention of Dr Hawk.

'How could three people come together like that?' I mutter.

'The Wraith wasn't three people per say, but a collection of the worst parts of all of us.' She looks away.

All three of them had exorcised their demons, rolled them into one persona, then let it loose into the world. 'And you thought I'd join you?'

'As a Wraith, you could have belonged.'

'Yeah, in prison!'

Looking me dead in the eyes, she states, 'I had a plan.'

'Andy was *your* plan?'

Dr Taylor fakes a smile. 'Look. Can we move past this?' She reaches out her hand. Without thinking, I take it. As I do, she grabs the pipe from me. 'Let's put this down. It's filthy and probably covered in asbestos. I wouldn't want my favourite patient to get ill.'

'I'm your favourite patient?'

Putting her arm around me, she says, 'Of course. We've worked together for so long. Been a team throughout your mental health journey.' The feel of her bicep across my back is firm and comforting as she guides me towards the chair. 'You know, we could even do a documentary together on this whole misunderstanding.'

It sounds like a wonderful idea, at first. As she chunters on about us beating Louisa to next year's Docu-Wow, I imagine my life going forward. A woman I've known for over a decade, who I trusted without question, by my side. Someone who trusts me with their sinister secrets… but then I remember all those dead girls, and how little I really know about what happened with them. It couldn't have all been Warren.

'…And we can work together now, through this whole incident, help each other.' She squeezes me. Pain shoots down my body, an echo of what I felt writhing on the bed through Warren's half-arsed exorcism.

'Oh, Dee. Are you all right? I bet you've not taken your pink pills today?' She drops her arm from me and walks into her office. Through the door, I watch as she scrambles in her drawers for pills. Every now and then, she looks up and smiles.

'Why put me through all this?' I ask.

Fetching a glass for water, Dr Taylor then walks towards me, pills piled in one hand, glass in the other. 'I knew I had to do something when you showed me Warren's sketch in your book.' She looks away. 'But none of this was your fault. I love being your doctor, maybe we could still work together. Although, my time in prison would be limited… so if we both just blame Andy like the original plan… The letters and the evidence at his house do all point to him now. We can just stay as we are. You'd like that?'

'The police cleared Andy,' I mutter.

'They have alibis from me and Warren. We were just going to say he threatened us, or we misjudged the timings. Andy is dead already, why ruin our lives?'

'And Warren?'

At his name she hesitates. 'Have you…'

'He's alive.'

'I'm a good doctor. I swear, I'll help him. He'll never kill again.'

I nod, everyone deserves a second chance. Without one, I wouldn't be free. And she is a good doctor... Wait. 'What happened to the lost pieces of the girls?' I ask. It's then I get a flash across my mind's eye – the cabinet in the corner of the office. As my gaze goes to it, I notice the glass shake a little in her hand.

I walk over.

'No, Dee. You can't do that, it's illegal.' I hear her move towards me.

As I open the door, I'm greeted by the sight of eleven jars, each with a matching pair of eyeballs, fingers, and a single tongue, and one jar with just Louisa's eyes. Bile boils in my belly. Eleven full jars. Erica is here too. She lied about the body being disposed of before she got involved. She's probably lied about everything.

Pushing back the cupboard door, Dr Taylor says, 'Okay.' She then raises her open palms. 'Remember, the girls were going to die with Warren. At least this way, their deaths meant something. I furthered my research. Research to help other patients. Just like lobotomies used to calm patients, a physical dark retreat could centre them within themselves.'

'But you took their senses, how could patients ever be normal again if they could never get them back?'

She points to her head. 'Ah, but that's why I exper-imented with the brain too. Once I knew it worked, I was going to create a sort of on and off switch where the senses are—'

'Stop!' I shout. She's madder than me! 'That's insane! And none of those girls deserved to be experimented on.' My eyes linger on the jars. They're not evidence of experiments, but trophies from kills.

Dr Taylor's expression softens. 'You really are better, Dee. I'm so proud of you.'

My head snaps towards her. 'Proud of me?'

'Now, be a good girl and take these. You'll feel so much better.' Her pill-laden hand pushes into my vision. Beneath the little pink capsules, a coloured stain leeches into her sweaty palm. Stigmata.

I can't trust my doctor. I'm the only one left who knows what she did. My doctor may have taken my pipe, but it was never the weapon that made me dangerous. No more counting backwards. No more suppressing what lives inside me.

RED.

My hands jerk forward to push her backwards. Pills fly everywhere. The glass drops and shatters. Dr Taylor, stunned by the strike, falls; hitting the floor hard enough to elicit a grunt. She's in shock, maybe even concussed. I scurry to her drawer and fetch the bottle of pink pills, then take the vase from her desk. Throwing out the dead lavender and roses, I kneel down by Dr Taylor's head, the vase in one hand, pills in the other.

'If I tell everyone about you, they won't believe me. You'll twist everything around.' I lift the bottle and shake the pinkish pills inside like a maraca. Now there are more of them, it's easy to see they are not my usual medication. My doctor was trying to poison me.

She sees the clarity fall across my face. 'If you had taken them before, you would have gently fallen asleep in my office. We could have taken you while you slept, rather than off the street.'

'Sorry I made my abduction so difficult.'

'That's okay,' she says with a sing-song voice. 'You weren't to know.' Dr Taylor then laughs like we're sharing a joke.

'It's not funny,' I tell her.

'But it's rude not to laugh when someone else is… Um, remember when we talked about social skills?'

Tired of her mind games, I shrug. 'If what you and Warren did was considered normal, then I don't want any of it. You need to admit your crimes. Give peace to the families you stole from.'

'Okay, okay.' She says, hands up, then mutters, 'I'll turn myself in. I promise.'

'No. You'll blame me for everything, just like Corinne did at work. I can't have that happen.'

'No, no,' she says with a whimper.

I place my feet either side of her body, then straddle her chest, allowing the full force of my strength to bear down on her. She struggles against me, but today I'm stronger than her. I feel the sensation of God's approval as I force open Dr Taylor's mouth and shovel down a few pills, then chase them with a glug of stale flower water.

After a few minutes she stops trying to reason with me, and calms to the point that she closes her eyes.

I wait a little longer just to be sure she's not consciousness enough to lie her way out of justice, then open the ornate cupboard door nice and wide. Once the police get a look at the eyeballs and tongues, they'll know for sure Dr Taylor was involved.

Exiting her house one final time, I leave her front door ajar.

Outside, I see police cars lined up at the gates of St Alda's. I hurry through the hole in the fence, then run towards where I'm assuming Louisa dropped out of the chute. As I near it, I hear her cry out.

'It's okay, it's me,' I tell her.

'Dee?'

Sitting in a sprawled heap on the ground, she lifts her arms out to me like a baby. I help her up.

'There are sirens,' she says.

'I called the police.'

Although she is blind, at least I stopped Dr Taylor before she stole Louisa's other senses. I help her towards the main hospital. Two carers run out when they see us. They take Louisa from me and rush her inside. As they do, police flood across the grounds. One jogs towards me.

'I'm Constable Miller. You all right, miss?' he asks.

'Not really, but there's a man in that building who needs help first. Top floor.'

'Emergency services already have him.'

'Is he okay?'

'Hard to know for sure, but he's alive.'

It's time to enact my plan. 'There's a doctor too. She lives a few doors down the street,' I say, then give him the address. 'We were all her patients. You should check on her as soon as you can. Make sure she's okay.'

Nodding, he radios it in. 'There's a unit outside the house now.'

Another police officer sprints over and, along with a paramedic, they take Louisa from me.

'Hey.' Miller nods in the direction Louisa was taken. 'That woman you were helping, is she a friend of yours?'

'No.'

'Oh, did you know that's Louisa Black? I loved *Possession is Nine Tenths...*' The rest of his words disappear as he recognises me.

Chapter Thirty-Seven

The police take me home. I'm so tired I willingly drive in their car. After all, police are almost like public transport. Mum's anger at me for not making dinner soon turns to freaked-out worry that I'd been abducted, then twists into guilt that she hadn't called the police to report my absence. Dad's eyes are red and, instead of saying anything, he rustles around in the kitchen and brings me a slab of chocolate cake and a cup of tea. The cake is creamy and smothers the inside of my mouth with sugar. It's just what I need as I recall the horrific series of events that led me to saving Louisa and Andy. Halfway through, Constable Miller takes a call; he then sheepishly explains Dr Taylor is the third Wraith. They followed my trail of breadcrumbs.

'My god, but she was so good with Dee,' Mum mutters.

I spend hours telling the truth, omitting the fact I helped with Dr Taylor's arrest. It's easier than I thought. This time all the evidence is on my side. They have to believe me, and even though my body has started to shake with delayed shock, I feel warm inside. Mum gives me a real pink pill – one she'd squirreled away in her bag – and sends me to bed so they can talk with the police. Still dressed, my mouth caked in chocolate, I fall into a deep asleep.

Morning, and there's a cool breeze coming from my window, the first I've felt on my skin for months. The sun, shrouded with clouds, hides from view as if ashamed of its previous brutish behaviour.

Getting out of bed, I fall to my knees.

'Dear Lord, I'm not sure if you had a hand in things. But thank you. Please look after Andy and, yes, keep an eye on Louisa.' I inappropriately giggle at my dark joke. 'Sorry, couldn't help it. Amen.'

–

The next few days are filled with so many new experiences I have to write them all down in my journal. There are only a few pages left now.

I visit Craig at St Alda's. It's sad that he couldn't cope in the normal world, but maybe I can help him next time. I still need a good cameraman, and Craig's attention to detail could be an asset.

Inspiration Cometh welcomes me back as if I'm a solider returning from war. They even clap and I get so many drinks bought for me that I have to cross my legs to stop from peeing. Donald half hugs me and asks if I don't mind telling him what it was like to be a potential victim. Not wanting to share my story with him, I smile and explain it's still a fresh wound.

The police interview me a few more times about my version of events. I'm so practised now, I have to concentrate on contorting my face to look timid rather than bored. I'm then invited to a press conference, just like the one I saw DCI Campbell do about the Wraith killings. Before it starts, Father Jacob invites me to a special sermon at St Godfrey's. Canon Matthew publicly declares me not possessed by a demon; after all, demons are evil and would have joined the killers, not brought them to justice. Afterwards, I linger in the back pews to talk to Father Jacob.

'My, what a time you've had,' he says.

I'd been sitting on some big news since the start of the sermon, and now almost explode in my rush to tell him. 'I got offered a deal for my documentary! I'm working with a studio and everything.' I'm so excited my teeth clash together as I push out the news.

'That's amazing. I'm so very proud of you. But…'

'But what?'

'Finding out about Dr Taylor's involvement in the murders. You must have felt very let down.'

'I did. But that's okay now.' I flash him a thin smile.

A question haunts his thoughts. I feel it. 'How did you escape from Warren?'

Lying is a sin, so I need to tell the truth here. 'I accepted who I am. What the accident made me. It gave me strength.'

'Are you referring to your brain injury? Or are you saying that you… you think you are possessed?'

Funny, he's never directly asked me that question. He always assumed we were on the same page. That it was all in my damaged head.

I should answer. Once and for all admit what I think has been wrong with me. But I can't. All this time, while I was dealing with my trauma, that invading redness has felt like an enemy – an obstacle to getting back to a normal life as a normal person. But when I needed it most, it became an ally. Why should I look a gift horse in the mouth? And in truth, I've been living with it longer now than before when I was just plain Dinah, the girl from the religious family whose amygdala was peaceful.

As I rise to leave the church, I spot her. Blonde hair curled to perfection, dressed in a white suit. Betsy.

Taking my acknowledgement of her presence as an invitation, she saunters over.

'Thank you so much for saving Andy,' she says.

'I'm Father Jacob.' My friend extends his hand to her. 'Sorry for your troubles.'

Flipping her hair across her back, she nods, but keeps her gaze on me.

'I'd like to take you to lunch, Dee. We can talk about... Warren. I feel somewhat... responsible. I grew up with him and never spotted his demons – Oh, sorry, that just slipped out.'

Did it? I'd always felt like she had been involved in the murders somehow; maybe she was the real author of those letters. Could I get her to admit it?

'Dee is very busy right now. But I'm sure we can all get together soon,' says Father Jacob.

Betsy smiles sweetly at him. 'Oh, better we have a girls' night, eh?'

'Sure,' I tell her. 'Can't wait.' Even if she is a Wraith, with the help of my reddish affliction, I bested three of them in one go. I can handle her.

-

TV cameras line up in front of me, all with matching journalists desperate for a sound bite. DCI Campbell stands with me. She apologises for not listening to me about Warren and I instantly forgive her, as she doesn't point out I was wrong about Andy.

'Hi,' I say into the microphone. 'My name is Dinah, Dee, Jones and I was the 13th girl of the Righteous

Wraiths. These horrible people have been formally identified as Warren Roland, Ashley Frampton and Dr Lara Taylor.'

A journalist leaps forward, microphone in hand. 'Dee, were you scared?'

Dumb question. 'Of course.'

'DCI Campbell?' says another. 'What's happening with the Wraiths?'

'All three have been formally charged.'

'Has there ever been a case of three serial killers working together before?'

'It's even rarer than partners,' DCI Campbell says.

'Cults kill people,' pipes up a journalist. 'Can you confirm this was a devil worship thing, Dee?'

'The devil had no hand in what those sick people did. God gave us free will. It's up to each of us to choose what we do,' I say, echoing something I'd heard Father Jacob say.

'Here!'

The DCI gracefully points at the owner of the voice. 'Yes?'

'How are the other victims doing?' the reporter asks.

'Andy Fryer is resting comfortably in hospital and is predicted to make a full recovery. Louisa Black lost her sight, but is adjusting.'

Louisa never officially thanked me for saving her life, but that's okay, I changed my narrative from crazy girl to hero. And my documentary deal is worth more than hers. It's bound to win a Docu-Wow.

'Dee!' a man shouts.

I point to him.

'Will your first documentary be on the Wraiths or a follow up to *Possession is Nine Tenths?*' The reporter's face is tense, ready to throw another question at me.

'My first documentary is called *Surviving the Wraiths*. I'd like to leave *Possession is Nine Tenths* in the past. It's haunted me long enough.'

Several hands shoot up to ask more questions. Smiling, I promise to answer each and every one of them.

After all that time I spent forgotten and ignored, I find myself growing in the spotlight like a plant plucked from the shadows. I swear my height has even increased.

I don't feel small at all now.

–

Home. I knock three times on the door. Dad answers and asks if everything is okay. Nodding, I grin at him. As I move through to the kitchen, he follows me.

'We've set you up with a new psychiatrist,' he says.

'You think I still need one?'

'More than ever. And this one comes highly recommended; she even suffered a similar trauma to yourself, so you have a lot in common.'

Rolling this information around in my head, I reply, 'Sure, maybe she'll help me with my documentaries.'

'Happy to hear you say that, love, because she's in the living room.'

I walk in and see a woman around my age on the sofa, talking with Mum.

'I'm Dr Fallon Hurley,' she says, rising to greet me.

'Dinah,' I reply.

'We'll leave you two to get acquainted.' Dad grabs Mum's arm and pulls her from the room.

'You survived a horrendous ordeal, Dinah. But believe me, you can work through it.'

Dr Hurley seems nice. She has a calming presence and reminds me a little of Father Jacob – she has a touch of resting worry-face.

'Dee, you can call me Dee.'

'Thank you.' She motions for me to sit next to her. I do. 'Just to let you know, I've not read Dr Taylor's notes on you. I want us to start fresh.'

Fresh? She's trying to send me back? Jumping up, I say, 'No, I won't go back to St Alda's. You can't do that, I'm doing well. I have a job again and I—'

'No, you misunderstand. I'm not saying that you need St Alda's. I just want to get to know the real Dee. Who you are now, what these past incidents have made you become.'

'I'm normal again,' I mutter.

Dr Hurley sighs. 'There really is no such thing as normal. You must understand that. No one is normal, believe me. We all have difficulties and traumas we need to work past. Triggers, like your aversion to cars. But they don't have to be part of us. Your...'

'Red,' I say to her.

She smiles. 'Your *red* doesn't have to define you. We all have *colours* to deal with.'

'Thank you. You seem nice.' And she hasn't wrinkled her nose at me once.

'I try to be. But for this to work, you need to be honest with me, and I will be with you.'

'You will?'

'I'm not Dr Taylor.'

'I hope not,' I whisper, but she hears me.

'I've spoken with her.'

'You have?'

'She held such promise. She was meant to help people – help you.'

Shrugging, I admit, 'She did help me, in a way.'

'Not like she should have. She put you in an awful position with her other patients.'

'Did she have Cookie killed?'

With her own shrug, Dr Hurley smiles. 'I'm not sure we'll ever truly know. None of the so-called Wraiths are talking now. Not even Ashley Frampton.'

'What do you think?' I ask.

'Hard to know for sure, but I suspect Taylor was more involved than she let on. Sociopathic tendencies, she hid them well. But I've cracked tougher people than her. We'll get to the bottom of it.'

'We?'

'Yes, we. We're in this together, Dee. I won't let you down,' she promises. 'No matter what you think you are.'

In truth, I still haven't decided what I am: the consequence of a traumatic brain injury, or a demon invited in by tragedy. As much as a plant can't decide which soil it grows in, I had no choice as to how I came into this world.

Defective or demon? People can make up their own minds.

Epilogue

I know you're there.

You've been reading my story; devouring it like a page-turner of a novel.

I've felt you along the way: a quiet and consistent presence. It was probably hard for you to stay silent all that time. I bet you were yelling at me a lot. How naïve I am. How trusting. How I missed the clues. More than once, I bet you cursed me with something like, 'Dee, you fool, you shouldn't trust anyone!' But that's okay; you did it out of concern. I'm sure, if you'd been physically here, you'd have stopped the Wraiths from taking me, but then I'd have lost what I'd gained from the experience. Dr Taylor always told me good can come from bad, although now I think about it, I shouldn't have listened to her at all. Part of me suspects she always had some darkness in her. I think she lied when she told me Warren had birthed it; he probably just coaxed it further across her soul, diluting her light until it was a pinprick of memory. But I had to believe in her; she was a doctor. How could I have known a person chosen to look after me would be... well, human, with all the flaws and sinister possibilities everyone has locked inside waiting to be free. Let's be honest here, you probably have them too. But don't worry, I still like you. To be honest, I've been glad of your company. It can get so lonely being me. Well, anyone like me is bound to get lonely. You've seen what I have to put up with. How often I'm judged and misjudged without even being given the chance to earn the opinion, let alone deserve it. Through a skewed view of the world, normal people think my so-called madness will bleed red into their shiny lives. A self-fulfilling prophecy, as I'm kept at arm's length from the things that would make me feel more normal. You didn't do that, though. No, throughout you listened to me, you were behind me, even probably tried to help figure out what was going on, who the Wraiths were. Thank you for that. People don't say that enough, how much they appreciate one another. I'll say it again.

Thank you.

I never chose to be this way – who would? It's how I was written, by life. You understand that though.

Through our time together, I've been good; never even addressed you once. Your secret, that you've been with me this whole time, will be mine to keep. I won't tell Dr Hurley, or Mum and Dad, not even Father Jacob. I mean, if I start talking about an imaginary friend who I tell my life story to, I'll be locked up back in St Alda's before you can say schizophrenia. And yes, people might think I'm worse than before, but really, I am doing much better. You must agree or you would have said something.

Now you know I know you're there. Now we are acquainted. Now you've travelled with me for so long, I think I can say we're friends, can't I? Or at least we are on the road to becoming friends. You and me. And I got the impression you like to read about the darker side of human nature. To be fair, most do. And, if you want to stick around, there are lots of unsolved crimes for me to get my teeth into and tear apart. I still suspect Betsy knew more than she let on – I mean, don't you?

Maybe we can go on another adventure together soon?

Bye for now, friend.

A letter from NV Peacock

You came back! So lovely to hear from you so soon. It's been six months or so from *The Brother*, what have you been doing? Anything exciting? We didn't exactly have much in the way of a sizzling summer in 2023, not like you found featured here, but I do hope you got out and about and ate some ice cream, read on the beach and found yourself on a picnic blanket or two – obviously not like the victims in this book though!

It's 2024, are you planning something fun this year? Fingers crossed, it's to buy lots of books to read! More fingers crossed you loved this one so much you are buying all of mine.☺

So, I've been writing – a lot! Some thrillers, some different genres. You'll have to wait and see nearer the time as to what they are. I've been working hard and can't wait to tell you about them all!

Now though, you want to hear about *The 13th Girl*. What inspired me to write it and how it got to sit before your eager eyeballs. Well, it was a number of ideas and random thoughts that came together into a perfect story storm...

Many people, who are close to me, work in mental health and I see the toll it takes on them on a daily basis. They all want the best for their patients, but as a society we are yet to fully understand the mind and how to open our hearts to those in pain we cannot see. More often than not, if a person seeks help, they are judged for getting help, or worse, they stay silent and suffer alone. That is why I wanted to have a protagonist who has serious mental health issues, yet is one of the most reliable narrators you'll find in any work of fiction – something of a rarity in psychological thrillers nowadays. Dee never lies to you; she just doesn't always understand what is going on, leaving the reader, more often than not, to read between the lines.

I wanted to write a book that didn't just vilify the usual suspects of religion and hospitals. In *The 13th Girl*, I ensured characters such as Father Jacob and even St Alda's itself were trying their best to help Dee without any sinister agendas. Bad things happen in this world all the time, but there can be many different culprits and causes.

As a horror writer at heart, I salivated at the thought of a serial killer biting off more than he could chew with a victim who had a supernatural ability. Although never truly admitted, Dee could very well be possessed by a demon. After all, the latest figures from the Catholic Church show that exorcisms have never been in such high demand as they are today. Not exactly hard proof of the supernatural, but it certainly makes you think – once your head stops spinning around and you spew up the last of your green vomit!

Although this book has themes of religion, superstition and mental health, along with my usual serial killings, it also features a character who took advantage of the protagonist; something that happens to everyone at some point in their lives, even me. Hopefully your interaction is not as dramatic as what happened to Dee, but these incidents can leave a mark. Don't worry though; I'm a strong believer in karma and redemption, so just ensure the person in question doesn't change who you are inside – if they do, then they won.

To write *The 13th Girl*, all these ingredients were carefully cooked up together in the bubbling pot of my imagination and then let loose onto the page just for you. I do hope you enjoyed it.

I'm sure we will speak again, so for now – see you real soon!

Acknowledgements

I have such a lovely, dedicated, and above all consistent group of family and friends that these parts of my books are going to end up looking a little samey! So, I'll keep this short and do it a little differently...

I'd like to thank my agent Maddalena Cavaciuti for her support, and above all for encouraging me to write the stories I love, explore my darkness and exercise my voice as an author. Big thank you to Keshini and Jennie at Hera for taking a chance on my books, and Canelo's PR team for promoting them to an unsuspecting public.

Now, I believe that the right acknowledgement here is to all those people in the world who have mental health issues – which, if we're being honest, is all of us at some time in our lives. The mind is a wondrous and unknown thing, which can be our best friend or worst enemy. We have no real control over it, and when it breaks, it's not like a limb in a cast that everyone can see and so will help you, it's hidden and oftentimes embarrassing to talk about. Each time you open your mouth you take a chance that the person in front of you will believe you are in pain and offer comfort rather than an eye roll.

Nowadays, there's more education and help available than ever before, but sometimes, for those brave enough to admit they have a problem, they can still be met by ignorance and scorn. Worse, lumbered into the category of useless to society, or even dangerous; unworthy of social interaction or support – two of the things desperately needed for anyone with mental health issues.

Struggles find us all at some time in our lives, and even when things seem bleak, we push through. As Winston Churchill famously said, 'If you're going through hell, keep going.' I often say these words to myself, and if you've never heard them before, then perhaps you could adopt them too for when you need them most.

Dee might not have been the most well-adjusted protagonist I've ever written, but she was the most interesting to date, and certainly the most selfless. She wanted to help. She was willing to give up everything she'd worked hard for to save the lives of others. I actually missed her when I stopped drafting this book. Her thoughts might have been fractured at times, but she was kind and had a dark sense of humour that always made me giggle as I typed. If she and I had ever met in real life, I think we would have been firm friends. If you've reached the end of the book you'll know that I left Dee in Fallon's capable hands (protagonist from *The Brother*). It just felt right to put these two characters together in the final chapter. I'm not sure what they'll get up to, but I suspect they will help one another. And you never know, you might see them again – keep your eyes peeled!

Thank you for buying this book, and remember to review it on places like Amazon, or wherever you bought it; you can't imagine how much a few words about enjoying a book can help the author ensure their work is in potential readers' eyelines. And not to be too blunt, but the more books we sell, the more books we can write for you in the future. And I love writing for you.